The Summerlands
A Mystical Tale of Angels, Elementals, the Afterlife, and Souls on Missions

Susan Butler Colwell

PAGE PUBLISHING, INC.
Conneaut Lake, PA

First originally published by Page Publishing 2021

Elemental logo by Helen Kruger
Cover graphics licensed by Dreamstime

ISBN 978-1-64544-098-7 (pbk)
ISBN 978-1-6624-1502-9 (hc)
ISBN 978-1-6624-1369-8 (digital)

Printed in the United States of America

The Summerlands

Angels & Elementals Book 1

Hardcover
Paperback
Audiobook
E-book

For more information on Susan Butler Colwell, visit www.
susanbutlercolwell.com or connect with the
author on Facebook and Instagram.

Contents

Contents

Contents

Contents

Contents

The Summerlands
A Mystical Tale of Angels, Elementals, the Afterlife, and Souls on Missions

Susan Butler Colwell

For Cerphe, thank you for finding me…again.

For Laurie, who returned to the Summerlands
much too soon for my liking.

And for my favorite elementals,
Kricket, Andrea, and Helen.

Your intent makes it possible.
Your belief makes it so.
Archangel Michael

CHAPTER

~ 1 ~

The Dream of Being Human

The Summerlands, Present Moment

The last time I died, it was a Tuesday. Don't ask me how I know that. It's just stuck in my brain as a cold, hard fact. Well…that and the slightly more troubling realization that I took the guy who's in charge of all evil as a mate. But I digress.

I don't recall the days leading up to my death, never mind the years. I remember arriving in the Underworld and Morgana's chaotic escort out of the place a short while later because of it. But then there's a big skip forward to the final minutes of my life. So I'll start at the end, and maybe that will help me piece it together myself.

Embarrassingly enough, I was asleep when it happened, so I was a goner before I'd fully registered what was going on. Not an honorable way for a warrior to die, but there you have it.

How Morgana even got close enough to do the deed is beyond me. There's an enchanted river to cross and an army of ill-tempered dark angels to navigate. So when the scent of sandalwood wormed its way into a rather good dream, I didn't think much of it. Why would I with all those hulking ex-celestials around for protection? And I'm sorry, but who wears perfume to a stealth mission?

The fragrance was enough for my subconscious to begin a reluctant climb to the surface. But it was the blinding pain that got me the rest of the way out—just in time to see the dagger buried in my chest. So mission accomplished, no matter how clumsily executed.

The dark witch stared into my face as I clod-hopped to the other side of the veil, her eyes wide and dancing with delight. Maybe because thirty years prior, my arrival got her booted out of Mortegol's bed…and tossed from a realm where she would never age. Nothing like three decades of pent-up anger as motivation to murder an enemy.

She did look older, and that's not just me being catty.

Okay, maybe a little catty.

Fun fact: you witness your own death. And here's an interesting aside, you also experience the emotions of those next to you. Like most, I hoped I would "go" peacefully. But that day, I tapped into the soul of an aging, angry witch intent on revenge. Not so peaceful in there.

Afterward (and by that, I mean once I'd croaked), two dark angels who should have been protecting me dragged my executioner away instead. The portal sucked me in soon after, so I couldn't tell you the extent of the fallout. But it's safe to say they didn't whisk Morgana Sorcha Balfour away for a champagne lunch. No matter her revered magical bloodline or witchy pedigree, she had just murdered the boss's girlfriend, and there was probably a steep price to pay for that.

So now you know as much as I do—except that I deserved to die that way, I guess. Mainly because I had broken just about every Universal Bylaw there is. For starters, light warriors aren't supposed to venture into the demonic realm. We lose our powers there…maybe as a sharp reminder not to go.

There are a bunch of other rules I won't bore you with, but I should tell you one minor detail. No one can force us into the Underworld, not even the king of the place. We must go *willingly*, and that means I happily plodded into the joint. And here's the real kicker. Somebody (and I'm guessing Mortegol) bulk-erased the memories of my previous life, so I have no idea why I would have done that.

After my less-than-heroic demise, I'd spent the equivalent of seventy years in Morningside—a human-back-to-soul settlement in the afterlife. They're called recovery villages, and we have ones that mimic every Earth-plane period and region here. All of them have veils that prevent all-knowing beings from *knowing* you're inside. And that's a huge plus when you're in hiding.

There *are* several drawbacks to using a recovery village as a hideout, though. They fall under the rule of stripped-down physics, so magic isn't even a possibility. You must do everything like a mortal on Earth. You also can't search the Akashic Records inside one, which I needed to do—badly.

Although I am a goddess, I do get to live as a human for the first twenty-one years of each incarnation. And when I die (or stupidly end up murdered), I come right back here ready to do it all again. I can stay in the Summerlands as long as I want between lives. (I don't need to be in any particular place to do my job.) But I was tired of hiding out in the simulated third-dimensional realm. I was eager to head back to the actual third dimension and just get on with it.

I am one of four gatekeepers of the Earth plane. Kricket, Andrea, and Helena are the other three. We're called elementals, and we are half-human half-celestial—mass infused with light code. It's our combined energy that makes up the ethereal superhighway connecting the Summerlands and Earth. That's only a small part of the gig, though. Preserving the balance of light and dark is the main reason we exist. Well, that and keeping aliens out of the third dimension.

Why the need for being half-human, you say? Why not skip the messy blood and tissue business and simply zoom around helping humans as heavenly beings? We tried that during the first incarnation of Earth with less than stellar results. Cosmic energy vibrates at a speed that works like an atom bomb on flesh and bone. Think of death metal blasting through the world's loudest speakers. Then stick your head between them, and that can give you a pretty good idea of the type of force I'm talking about. Got it? Now multiply that by a thousand.

On the other hand, our human mass vibrates slowly—like a funky slow groove with a low-thumping bass line. That makes it easier for souls to latch on and take the cosmic ride back home. It also keeps humans from blowing themselves sky-high when they tap into our power. Sort of like the governor inside a water valve prevents you from scalding yourself in the shower.

And that's where the first Earth went wrong. Horribly.

Souls got stuck in the void after slipping out of their mortal vessels. (Our astral energy vibrated too fast for them to recognize it as their ticket to ride.) The second (more gruesome) problem was that mortals who tried to engage divine power were exploding at an alarming rate.

But not to worry. By the seventh day of the seventh incarnation of Earth, we had witches, a cross between humans and elementals. We had the Underworld to provide balance, and we elementals got our mortal sleeves. Then there was light and dark upon the earth. People stopped exploding. Light beings got home just fine, and Goddess and every other soul saw that it was good.

Being half-mortal has another purpose too. It's a gift from Source. We call it *the dream of being human*, and I have always loved it. But it also means we can die just like straight-up humans. Archangels are the only ones among us who never push up proverbial daisies, never blink out, never have their memories wiped. They just *are* and have been since the beginning of time. I like my situation far better. I love believing I'm mortal, and I enjoy the intermittent breaks from knowing all the secrets of the universe.

So, all fifty-nine years of my previous life had gone AWOL. Slap out of my head. That meant I needed to piece some things together on my own. Like why I threw over Archangel Michael for the king of the blasted Underworld. Let's compare: The Prince of Angels versus the Prince of Darkness. That's quite the pivot even for me. Besides,

Michael has been my mate since the beginning of a little thing called *time*. And I knew Mortegol about as well as one might know their dentist. If that dentist were in charge of all evil on Earth, I guess.

I also couldn't fathom why I came back here again when I obviously belong on DarkStar now. That's the afterlife for low-energy beings, the place many people mistake for hell. It's not. It's more like a seedy nightclub that never closes, one that instills a constant need to rinse grime from your soul. There's no torture or lake of fire or some evil overlord punishing you for your sins. However, pride, envy, anger, sloth, greed, gluttony, and lust are available by the truckloads. Those might be known as the seven *deadly* sins on Earth, but DarkStar residents seem to live with them just fine.

Suffice it to say that waking up at home shocked me to the core. I was glad of it—like break-into-handsprings glad. None of it made any sense, though. I had no idea what would make me *want* to go to the Underworld, let alone *stay*. Had I grown tired of being a warrior of light? Had Goddess done something to anger me?

That's possible, you know, to be angry with one's creator. It's even possible to have full-blown shouting matches with her, although they *are* a bit one-sided. Goddess never shouts. She just observes, wearing a placid expression while you rant and rave red-faced and sputtering like a lunatic. Then she teaches you something that makes you feel foolish for doubting her Supreme Beingness. It can be downright annoying.

Anyway, my feet had barely touched the green grass of home when I flashed myself to the border of Morningside. I don't mind telling you I shot over that line like a deer escaping a hunter's bow. Archangels can read minds, and I knew Morningside would keep them from poking around in my head. Plus, the coffee is excellent there.

The universe has four such mind readers I'd been avoiding. Well, five if you count our sheriff, known around these parts as God, Goddess, Source, and I did count her—boy howdy. Veils don't work on her, and I'd spent a good deal of my time here waiting for *that* cosmic shoe to drop. It hadn't…and somehow that felt worse.

Now here I am on this lounger watching the countdown while my soul clan members get ready to play their roles in my next life.

I sighed and looked around the control room. A few minutes more and I'd forget again. Two decades of ignorant bliss. Two decades where none of them could ask questions about where I'd been or what I'd done. Talk about hallelujah.

I watched Alden saunter over, greeting everyone he passed.

Like everyone here, he is light code but often takes the form he's in now—human male, mid-thirties, slim build, chestnut hair, round tortoiseshell glasses. He's usually in this blue jumper, too, representing water, Alden's elemental sign.

"Okay, you ready?" he asked me, not a care in the world.

"You running for office? I think you missed some souls while glad-handing. Take your time. It's not like I'm dodging an archangel or anything."

"What? You said you wanted some time to think. But it looked to me like you were talking to yourself. Have you finally cracked? I wouldn't doubt it."

"I wasn't talking to myself. I was talking to my peeps."

"Your what?"

"The humans who share my fire energy. I want them to hold onto a few thoughts for me, so I can pull them up later."

"Aren't there rules against using mortals as your personal memory bank?"

"No...maybe... I don't know. Anyway, they don't mind. Here, let me have that." I snatched the tablet out of Alden's hands.

He rolled his storm-cloud-gray eyes. They were usually brown, but I like the new color. It gives him an air of mystery, which pairs well with his job. Alden is the lead coordinator for the launch site, the place souls go to get themselves to the third dimension. More importantly, he's my best friend, confidant, and co-conspirator in many a shenanigan. He says I enjoy tormenting him with my crazy ideas, but he always goes along...eventually.

My friend likes male energy, always has. He's also rather fond of his soul name and never changes it for Earth-plane visits. So far, I've had several thousand sons named Alden, all the same soul getting ready to launch me to the third rock from the sun. The very one who had his arms crossed and was frowning at me while I poked away at his handheld.

"What are you doing?"

I flicked my eyes at him. "Just making a few adjustments."

I found what I wanted and set it to thirty-three, the highest setting on this blasted thing. Souls bound for the Earth plane go with their *Intuition Level* set between one and seven. Elementals get a solid twenty, but I needed more this time—like full-throttle.

"You can't do that," Alden said. He grabbed the tablet and brought the setting back down.

"Says who?"

"You know very well *who*."

"If the highest settings were off-limits, they wouldn't be there, would they?"

I could see the wheels spinning behind his gray eyes. "But I'll get into trouble," he said, nudging the glasses he didn't need to his forehead. Where they added to his credibility before, now they looked more like goggles on a mad scientist.

I did some eye-rolling of my own. "That's an Earth concept."

"Uh... I'll get a stern talking to...at the very least."

"Oh, no," I said in mock horror. "In that case, bust that baby open and push my intuitive level to a hundred."

He didn't answer, just widened his stance and tucked the tablet under an arm—the side I couldn't reach.

"I wouldn't do it unless it was necessary. You of all souls know how much I love thinking I'm human."

"I do," he said, rubbing his face with both hands. That told me he already knew he would end up on the wrong side of this thing.

"And I usually take less than my allotted twenty because of it, don't I?"

He groaned, but I could tell I was wearing him down. I always do.

I dropped the tough warrior act and softened my voice. "This is a critical mission, Alden. When something's not right, I need to feel like I'm gonna barf. On the other hand, if something *is* right, I want to hear angels singing and get morphine-level high. Obvious signs. You know how the human mind tricks you into doubting yourself."

"Oh, yeah," Alden said. Then he shuddered, probably remembering one of his own human lives.

"Besides, if you don't let me do it, I'll turn off the boom filter, and when I hit the gate, everyone in the southern hemisphere will think the world is ending."

A look of genuine horror crossed his face. "That's blackmail. You wouldn't."

Probably not, but his doubt was working for me. I'd done crazier things in the past, uh, with Alden by my side doing them right along with me. "Just one of the tricks I learned on the Earth plane," I said, lacing my fingers behind my head.

He didn't seem to be budging, and Alden can be worse than an old mule at times, so I decided to bring the whip down. I propped myself on an elbow and set my jaw. "Who's in charge here?"

Alden gave me a blank stare.

"When *she's* not around."

"You are."

Well, me, four archangels and three other elementals, but they weren't here, were they. I waited for a beat to see if Goddess might pop in to give *me* a stern talking-to—she didn't.

"You're like a rock in the shoe. Anybody ever told you that?"

I fluttered my lashes. "You have…several times."

He sighed. "Okay, but hurry it up."

"Good boy."

I took the tablet and set my intuitive level back to thirty-three, wishing there really was a one hundred. While I was at it, I scrambled my wake triggers. Better not shake my noggin up too soon, I decided and passed the handheld back.

"Care to make any more adjustments, Fire Goddess? You know, to really help me lose my job?"

"Yeah. Let's make me a Sumo wrestler."

"Oh, you're hilarious," Alden said as he centered the atomizer over me. "Too bad I'm sending you to the twentieth. You'd kill in the eighth. Say…that's not a bad idea…do you know how to juggle?"

I stuck my tongue out at him, but he just smiled and went back to the task of blasting me into outer space.

All souls have their memories wiped clean before each incarnation, but we keep them for the journey. Traveling from here to the Earth plane is a heck of a ride, and we stay in full awareness until we integrate with the human body. That's just in case we panic and want to head back home—another gift from Source.

My memories are erased too, but I also get something called a *package*. It's like a time-release capsule that meters out bits of soul memory and measured doses of my powers once I turn twenty-one. This time, I was going with a second package embedded behind the first. That one was more like a pipe bomb, and if it went off too soon, I'd turn into a blathering idiot.

We call that *splitting*, and it means that every soul memory since the beginning of time rushes in on you at once. Think of a levy breaking, but the water it's holding back is the ocean, and you're standing at the base of the wall when it crumbles. Want to know the cherry on that cake? If I did have the misfortune of losing my mind in that terrifying way, I would live that way for a good long time. Basically, until my half-human body gave out from natural causes. Fun, right?

There were a million reasons to bury my trip to the Underworld in a deep, dark hole, and most of them screamed at me while I was embedding the thing. But because I needed to know more than I wanted to forget, in it went, and there it stayed, ticking like a time bomb in my head.

That second package was the one that had Alden's teeth on edge. I *had* to tell him about it. Otherwise, he'd discover it on his own during the final check and shut this whole business down. We'd argued…over several bottles of his favorite Earth-plane wine. He forgot a soul could get drunk in Morningside, and I forgot to mention it. (Whoops.) So he'd drunkenly agreed to let the explosive ride. Now the tension of our agreement was showing on his face. Well, that and a good old-fashioned human-style hangover.

"Nervous?" he asked.

"Do I look nervous?"

"No, I'm just nervous for you, I guess. Promise me you'll be careful." He met my eyes. "You know I believe in you, Seraphina, but having an extra package is dangerous, and I can't protect you from here."

Because of his job, Alden suffers from human emotional bleed-through more than any other soul here. And while I hadn't shared any of this *Prince of Darkness* business with him, he and I are close enough that he knew some kind of unsavory game was afoot.

I squeezed his hand. "Hey, Alden. I've got this. Besides, if I did blow my stack, you'd probably jump in as my Nurse Ratched, and I'm not giving you a sweet opportunity like that."

His nose reddened, and I could tell he was trying to put on a brave face. He nodded. "Want your song?"

"You know it." I glanced at the countdown—a minute thirty to go.

The Summerlands' launch site resembles mission control at NASA's Kennedy Space Center. (Well, Kennedy's mission control looks like our launch site.) And just like when human astronauts are about to blast off into space, souls filled our control room jostling to get an eyeful of me.

Elementals and archangels are the Summerlands' version of rock stars, I guess. Our job is to protect the dream of being human, and we've done it for several billion years. Just like souls, Earth has had many lives. And we warriors of light have stood guard over every reset, protecting the balance of light and dark in each of Earth's incarnations. Maybe that has something to do with it.

Alden busied himself entering the final coordinates, and I smiled at the soul who sings my travel song. He always comes for my launches, too, although he has the backstage pass. The song refers to the exhilaration I feel during every journey, my dream of being human, and the mysteries I rediscover. It's just shy of five minutes, the exact amount of time it takes to get from here to there. Clever boy, that one.

Speaking of rock stars, my travel song is only one of many that make my soul friend a famous human in the twentieth century. The period I would be entering the Earth plane this time.

To be clear, the years I would spend on the blue planet for this mission had already happened, hadn't happened yet, and were also happening right now. Time isn't linear. It's not even a loop. It's more like a big ball of yarn that keeps overlapping itself with no real beginning, middle, or end. In the Summerlands, there's no time at all. This 'time versus no time' business has always made my half-human brain hurt. More so when I'm not fully awake. Sometimes I'm convinced I've got a handle on it. Then poof. Off it goes again into the mist.

Alden rubbed his hands together. "Let's get this show on the road."

I glanced at the countdown—twenty seconds.

I uncrossed my ankles and placed my palms flat on the lounger, making full contact with the sub-generator.

Alden put a hand on my shoulder. "Okay. It's going to be a little choppy heading into the Milky Way. The interdimensional winds are heavy, but if it gets too weird, I can pull you back."

I blew out a breath and nodded.

The lounger vibrated, and a second later, I was inside a tiny ball of red light, about the size of the point on a needle. The familiar guitar licks of "Runnin' Down a Dream" kicked in, followed by a hard-driving beat that filled my brain, and I was off, zooming through space and time.

I played air guitar as I sailed by the Andromeda Galaxy. It was a super weird flight through the Milky Way—bumpier and louder than usual—and I was about two shakes from getting sucked into an alternate universe at one point.

Warp-speed navigation under control, I sang at the top of my lungs, roaring by constellations: Chamaeleon, Hydrus, Tucana, Phoenix. On approach to the South Gate—three-hundred-thirty-three miles above Australia—I laughed and flicked that boom filter right off. (Just keeping the boy on his toes.) He caught it like I knew he would, and I flew through the portal without a sound.

I entered Earth's atmosphere, and adrenaline coursed through my veins. My memories would be gone in under a minute. (That part always gets my blood pumping.) But I pushed it from my mind and slung my head from side to side, rockin' out as I shot through the blue skies of the Earth plane in the year 1998, Halloween day.

The song faded, and I wailed, having just taken the first breath of human life into my tiny half-mortal lungs. It stung like crazy.

Then...the lights went out.

CHAPTER

~ 2 ~

A Place to Call Home

Earth Plane 2019

It was only four-thirty in the afternoon, but I'd already had it. The economy bus I was on smelled like hamburgers and feet. Now and again, diesel exhaust assaulted my nose, courtesy of the farm trucks that blew by us whenever they got the chance.

I watched the super-cute toddler across the aisle waddle over, his blond ringlets bouncing as he purposefully navigated around my sleeping neighbor. That mission complete, he thrust a fistful of greasy fries at me. I politely declined, and he popped the whole wad into his mouth instead.

His mother snatched him up and frowned in apology. "Sorry about that. I just closed my eyes for a second."

I smiled and told her it was fine. I didn't tell her that her son was much more pleasant than the man in the seat behind me. That guy was a real piece of work, and he'd not once offered me a delicious snack.

I sighed and rested my head on the window—covered in fingerprints, and lord knows what else. For the better part of the trip, I'd done a decent job of avoiding direct contact with it. But I didn't care at this point. Hours spent in a metal tube with strangers had worn me down. The fast-food I'd inhaled at the last stop probably hadn't helped either.

Claudette let out a huff and pulled a travel blanket under her chin. We'd met when I changed buses in Baltimore, and within minutes, I'd learned more about my seatmate than I knew about people I'd grown up with. Claudette is from Fairfield, Alabama, and once she'd finished on that subject, I felt like I'd lived there myself. We covered her job, her boyfriend Ronnie, and her boss Gina who kept trying to steal Ronnie.

I also got the blow-by-blow on the decisions leading to Claudette's current hair color. It was a startling shade of red that she assured me would 'mellow' in a few days. My new friend also dropped "bless your heart" into every other sentence, and I'd only ever heard that on TV. You don't come across many southerners in New England.

Let me back up. My name is Sera Parker. Everything I own fits inside a handful of suitcases riding in the belly of this beast. I don't have a boyfriend or pets, or a job. I turned twenty-one last Thursday, and until yesterday I lived in Kents Hill, Maine. I'm on my own now, but I try not to overthink that last part, preferring to view my life in a glass-half-full kind of way.

Most people would call me upbeat, optimistic even. I'm open-minded, I guess. I believe in reincarnation. I like to think that people are intrinsically good, and I feel there's a better than average shot that God, ghosts, and UFOs are real. Although I don't heap them into the same category or think about them a whole lot.

As if reading my mind, Claudette turned to me and said, "Do you believe in angels, honey? I do. I talk to Archangel Michael all the time. He talks to everybody, you know. Not just me. Good lord, he loves humans."

My open-mindedness lurched forward. I'd never given angels much thought either, and now Claudette was claiming to communicate with them. While I was busy considering this, a familiar sensation kicked-off in my stomach—like a pilot light firing up. I teetered on the edge of euphoria; angels singing, optimism, awe, and love for well, everything, spread through me like a wildfire raging out of control.

Even though the heavenly chorus was new, I recognized the rest as my internal radar telling me her wild statement was true. Huh, so now I believe in angels too. And, I guess, that some people can talk to them. So, God, ghosts, UFOs, *and* angels. I experimentally shifted my focus to Big Foot. Nope. Nothing. I mentally struck him from the list.

In case I didn't mention it before, I have crazy-good intuition... like superpower good. I get goosebumps and fire in the belly when something's right, the need to vomit if something's wrong. And my intuition has *never* been wrong.

"I can be anywhere, and he'll come right through and talk and talk and talk," Claudette said. "You just have to know how to listen." She tapped the space between her eyes to demonstrate.

Admittedly I don't know anything about the conversational skills of heavenly beings. Still, Claudette had talked nonstop since we left Baltimore, and I wasn't sure how her angel got a word in edgewise. But instead of expressing that opinion, I said, "Wow. That's cool...um, I think I'm going to get some sleep."

"Well, bless your heart. You do that, honey. You get your rest. Oh, honey." Claudette fanned her hot pink bedazzled nails in my direction. "Archangel Michael wants me to tell you he loves you very much. I tell you what, that angel is something else. He works miracles, you know, and he's *real* good-lookin' too."

"Oh. Thanks," I said, feeling a flush of warmth near my heart. It faded soon after, and my intellect took the wheel. It's terrific when anyone loves you, and if it's a good-looking angel who's doing it, all the better. Now, if he could just do something about the guy behind me and the smell on this bus, that would be a real miracle.

Said *guy* snored and jostled my backrest for the umpteenth time. Between seat-kicker, Claudette's chatting, and my lack of sleep, I wondered why I hadn't flipped out by now. But I ignored him, *again,* and closed my eyes, remembering the tearful goodbye I'd shared with Celeste only hours before. She pressed an envelope into my hand, a little extra money to help me get settled. She also insisted I call her by her first name from now on, which feels a little strange.

Celeste Porter is the closest I've ever come to having a mother. She'd never married or had children of her own, and she'd raised me from infancy. Well…her, Pamela Paulson, and about twenty other staffers who came and went during my time at Sherman Hill. Moving here had been Celeste's idea. I had one of my positive physical reactions when she told me the town's name, and that's how I wound up on this bus next to the newly minted redhead who talks to angels.

After several minutes of pretending to sleep, I found myself inside a half-dream state where silly images floated around my mind. I was just about to fall asleep for real when the bus downshifted, jolting me upright. We made a sharp left and stopped in a large parking lot.

"Leesburg, Virginia," the driver sang out.

"Thank God," I said under my breath, reaching down to grab my handbag. Claudette had already vacated her seat, so I did a full stretch then glanced at my phone. Huh. An hour had slipped by just like that. Did I dream the part about the angels? I needed some mouthwash, that was for sure.

A smartly dressed senior gentleman in the next row was trying to reach a bag in the overhead bin. "Let me get that for you," I said. I guess I was happy to be getting off the bus, plus I wanted to annoy the guy behind me. I pulled the bag down and placed it on the seat, ensuring I thoroughly blocked the aisle as I did so. "Is this yours too?" I asked, holding up a gray wool fedora. The rude guy pulled several faces I caught from the corner of my eye. The snappy dresser took the hat and plopped it on his head.

"Thank you, young lady."

"Bye, honey," Claudette said as she made her way to the exit. "Archangel Michael says you're gonna love it here."

Not a dream, then. "Thanks, Claudette. Good luck with Ronnie. And don't take any more BS from Gina."

She blew me a kiss and headed off.

The man in the hat helped a frail woman sitting next to him to her feet, then hitched his trousers. "I'm Dr. Desmond, and this is my wife, Mabel."

"Sera Parker."

"Well, it's nice to meet you. Are you returning home?"

"No, I've just arrived, but I do plan to live here… I think."

"Excellent. You'll love this town. Mabel and I have lived in Leesburg all our lives; born and raised, weren't we, dear?"

"What?" Mabel yelled, cupping a hand to her ear and leaning in. The woman had to be several years—maybe decades—older than her husband.

"I told her you and I were born in Leesburg," Dr. Desmond said at high volume.

Mabel's face lit up. "Oh, yes. It's a wonderful place…you'll see."

I heard excessive throat-clearing and turned to see the red-faced seat kicker give me a get-on-with-it head toss toward the door. "Can you do your catching up somewhere else?" he said.

I ignored him, of course.

When I stepped off the bus, I noticed a handful of people had already crowded around the open baggage compartment. I said my goodbyes to the cute couple and walked over to my suitcases.

Seat kicker elbowed his way through the crowd and snatched a duffel out of the driver's hands. Wow. I crossed my arms and glared at the rude man, although at five-seven, he probably wouldn't see me as much of a threat. Most people don't…until I've got them pinned on the mat tapping out to get my foot off their throat.

I find that being underestimated works to my advantage.

"Have you found a place to live, young lady?"

Dr. Desmond's voice startled me, and I spun to face him. Mabel leaned closer with a hand cupped to her ear.

"I asked her—" The doctor pressed his lips together. "I'll tell you later, darling."

Mabel gave me a radiant smile, and I swear it felt like she was peering into my soul. (Not unnerving. Just noteworthy.) She had lovely cornflower blue eyes, and I couldn't help but smile back. These two were adorable. Wait. They were also lifelong residents and probably knew this town better than anyone. I dug into my bag and pulled several crumpled pages I'd printed from the Internet back at Sherman Hill. "Actually, I'm looking for a room to rent—"

"Baugh, you won't like any of those," the doctor said, dismissing my exhaustive research with a wave of his hand. "Our grandson needs a roommate."

"Really?"

"He sure does. Shall we give him a call?"

"If it's not too much trouble," I said, deciding I could swing by in the morning.

The doctor's face brightened. He pulled a cell phone from his satchel and poked out a number. "Braith? Yeah, we just got in. I have a young lady here who would like to see the room. Could we come by now?"

"Oh, I can't come tonight," I whispered.

Dr. Desmond nodded as he listened to the voice on the other end. "Sounds good. See you in a minute." He dropped the phone into his pocket and smiled at me.

Was he nuts? I'd only just met them…not that these two seemed up to no good. They looked more likely to stuff me full of cookies than into the back of an unmarked van.

While I entertained myself with the absurd idea of this sweet elderly couple hunting prey, a boat-like convertible pulled up to the curb.

"Our ride's here," the doctor happily announced.

I didn't respond, choosing instead to gawk at the dark-haired (incredibly hot) guy unfolding himself from the car. Boy, Uber drivers in Maine could sure take a lesson, I thought. With his slim-cut suit and chiseled jaw, this guy looked like he'd just stepped out of a stunt-driving film. He didn't do it for me like *that*, but he did deserve my appreciation for being so easy on the eyes. I wondered if anyone had ever told him he belonged in Hollywood, not in a small-town driving people around. Probably.

"Hello, Dr. Desmond. Mrs. Desmond."

Wow. The Irish accent only added to the appeal. Somebody needed to do an intervention, fast.

"Hey, Cormac. Thanks for collecting us," the doctor said.

"No problem. Happy to help."

Cormac flashed perfect teeth and set to work loading my suitcases into the trunk. I opened my mouth to protest, but Dr. Desmond piped in.

"My grandson lives in a great part of town. You can walk to everything, all the bars and restaurants in historic downtown. It has a huge backyard, plenty of light, several fireplaces, and the house is enormous, so you'll never bump into each other."

I smiled at his enthusiasm. "It sounds very nice. Your car is beautiful," I said to Hollywood, and it really was. I'd never seen one like it. The front and rear doors opened in the middle, away from each other, and although it was clearly an old model, it was pristine.

Cormac broke into a smile of such pure happiness; it rippled out into the street. "Sixty-five Lincoln Continental. Bought her brand new myself right off the showroom floor," he said, polishing the door with a sleeve to wipe his fingerprints away.

I did some quick math. Okay, so Cormac was mid-twenties, thirty if I had to stretch. No way he bought this car himself fifty-four years ago. Either he had a painting in his attic that prevented him from aging, or I'd misunderstood. I decided to go with the picture-in-the-attic theory.

The doctor adjusted his hat, tugging it lower on his forehead. "Where are my manners? This is Sera. She's coming with us to see Braith's room for rent, and Cormac is our dear friend. Our families have known one another forever."

"Oh, I can't come with you tonight." I shook Cormac's hand. "Nice to meet you."

The doctor shifted his weight from foot to foot, then creased his face into a look of…defeat maybe? "Uh, sure. You get some rest tonight and stop by tomorrow. I'll just jot down the information." He withdrew a pen and a small pad from his jacket pocket and began scribbling.

Cormac looked at the doctor, then me. He crossed his arms and leaned on a fender, enjoying the contest of wills playing out before him.

I hadn't had a bad feeling since meeting the Desmonds (quite the opposite, in fact), and the house sounded nice. So, I studied the three of them, deciding to check in with my super-strength intuition.

Then it came, a warm ooey-gooey feeling followed by elation. When the choir of angels struck the first chord, I knew I was about to get into a car with strangers to see a room inside a house where no one would hear me scream—nothing like putting intuition to the test.

"Your accent is lovely. Where are you from?" I asked Cormac.

"Átha Cliath," he said to the window as he made a left from the parking lot. Then he turned to meet my gaze. Cormac's eyes were light-gray and luminescent, and I had an odd feeling I'd seen them before, although I knew I hadn't. His face and mannerisms were strangely familiar, too, like one of those people you meet who immediately feels like an old friend.

"I don't think I've ever heard of that. Where is it?" I asked.

"Uh, well, technically Átha Cliath was a Gaelic encampment on the River Liffey in the ninth century. It means *ford of hurdles*. Most folks call where I'm from Baile Átha Cliath. Dublin, if you're American."

He gave me a dynamite smile that probably works like a panty dropper on Leesburg's female population.

"Guilty," I said.

As we drove through the narrow streets, Dr. Desmond played tour guide, pointing out various landmarks. "So that's Bob Nash's place. He's a good fella, and he's got a gold mine in there," he said as we rode past a diner in the middle of a triangle intersection. The plate-glass window read MOM'S APPLE PIE and had a giant turkey and several pies drawn out in grease pencil.

Lights were just coming on in the shops and restaurants housed in centuries-old buildings, and the streets glistened from rainfall earlier in the day. I'd spent the last month researching Leesburg, and we passed a few of the places I had on my list to check out—Eyetopia, Inc., DIG Records & Vintage, the Tally Ho Theater. I was delighted to see that all the buildings, boutiques, and eateries I'd viewed on my laptop were even prettier in person.

Cormac hung a right onto a narrow tree-lined street and rolled to a stop in front of a grand white colonial. Giant oaks stood sentry around a zealously manicured yard.

"Wow. This is your grandson's house?" I asked, gaping at the sprawling country estate in the center of town. A family of ten wouldn't bump into one another in this place. There was a massive wrap around porch, and the front yard was big enough for a professional football team to hold training camp.

"Sure is. Soon to be your house, so we'd better get a move on."

I got out to rubberneck while Cormac helped Mrs. Desmond to the sidewalk to join the doctor and me. Then he slid his hands in his pants pockets, body language that told me he didn't plan to accompany us inside. The car, the outfit, the hair, the smile, the hunk-factor times ten made him look like he was posing for an impromptu photo shoot.

As the three of us made our way along the brick walkway, Dr. Desmond explained that his daughter and son-in-law had just moved to Boston, leaving their son Braith behind. "My daughter said she wanted to let the boy spread his wings a little but to tell you the truth, I think she was tired of doing his laundry." He grinned as the red-lacquered door swung open.

"Nana. Pop-Pop."

The guy standing in the threshold was a shade under six feet, lean build, and maybe just a handful of years older than me. He was handsome, but his outfit was a little crazy: a blue-and-white flannel shirt, red long johns, neon-green Crocs. Strands of longish coppery brown hair escaped a gray beanie cap perched far back on his head like a deflated sock. I supposed he'd gotten dressed in the dark or had grabbed the only articles of clothing available as he fled a burning building.

He stuck out a fist to Mabel, who balled up her tiny hand and fist-bumped her grandson as she stumbled through the front door. I waited patiently as the two men completed an elaborate handshake ending in a shoulder bump.

"Braith, this is Sera."

"Hi," I said, flashing what I hoped was a thousand-watt smile. First impressions.

Braith made a sweeping bow and turned back to his grandfather. "Julia is in the kitchen, man. Why don't you like take Nana in for some tea while I show the place to Miss Sera? Looking good, Nana," Braith shouted as he motioned for me to follow him. Mabel waved her hand behind her and continued a slow totter down the hall.

"So, like...*this* is the living room." Braith bobbed his head, agreeing with himself. "I guess that's kind of obvious, though." He giggled at that.

The room was a tasteful mix of antique rugs in muted shades of blue and cream and plush white furniture.

"Oh, dude. Check this out." Braith jogged to an enormous wooden coffee table with thick iron legs, plucked a remote off the top, and triumphantly punched one of the buttons. Suddenly, the blinds closed, the lights dimmed, and a movie screen descended from the ceiling with a soft whirring sound. Okay, that's impressive, I thought, watching the thing glide to a smooth stop.

Braith giggled again. "Awesome, right? It's like magic." Then the giggling turned into a full out laugh. Braith bent at the waist, hands on his thighs as he snorted. "I'm sorry," he said, letting out several *whews* and rubbing his eyes. "I'm not sure what's so funny."

"It's okay," I said, my smile still fixed in place, only it was genuine now. This house was like a palace, and Braith's energy was beyond sweet.

My intuition told me he was kind, trustworthy, a kindred spirit, an old soul. On the other hand, my intellect told me this old soul was stoned out of his mind. I got a load of his eyes as he continued to giggle at nothing in particular.

Exactly how high is he? I wondered, studying him as he ran on about what the other buttons could do more to himself than to me.

I sniffed the air, and the faint smell of weed hit my nose. Remarkably high, I decided and smiled at him.

"She loves everything so far!" Braith shouted into the hallway, then laughed again.

"That's good," came his grandfather's voice from far off. The foyer and living room were enormous, so I guessed the kitchen could be in a different zip code.

My stoned tour guide pressed another button, and the whole sequence reversed. His eyes got huge, and he grabbed both sides of his face. "Oh, dude. Follow me. This will blow your mind."

Braith shot out of the room so fast, I had to scramble to keep up. He trotted across the entry hall—narrowly missing a vase on the table—and came to a screeching halt at a set of pocket doors. He slid them back, clicked on the lights, and invited me to step inside.

The smell of leather was comforting, and strangely, the room *felt* magical, alive somehow, almost as if it had a heartbeat. For a split second, I imagined I could hear it as I drank in my surroundings.

Bookshelves—mostly filled with ancient-looking leather-bound volumes—ran floor to ceiling around three walls, only breaking for a massive fireplace centered on one of them. A pair of wing-backed chairs sat angled toward the hearth. The French doors straight ahead led to a side porch with bench-style swings painted a soft white. Maybe I could just live in *this* room.

"So, my dad is like this well-known software dude."

"Wow," I said. Based on the house, he must be a *well-paid* software dude.

"Anyway, my dad's got this theory that we live in like this holographic universe, you know? Like everything we see is all one big computer simulation. Isn't that so right on?"

I nodded, thinking it *was* pretty right on, then read through the titles of the only modern books in the library. Their glossy spines promised expert opinions on quantum mechanics, the zero-point field, astrophysics, cosmology, and time travel. The leather books took up the rest of the space, and many seemed hundreds of years old. I reached up to touch one then hesitated, looking to my host for permission.

Braith gave me a nod of encouragement. "Go ahead."

I ran my fingers over an artfully tooled spine, feeling its thick raised bands and luxuriant gold embossing. The title, *Understanding Demons: A Complete Guide to Underworld Visitors,* sparked my curiosity. I pulled it down, cracked it open to page two hundred seventy-four, and read the first line that popped out at me.

"Bylaw Six Hundred Fifty-Nine: A demon's privacy is sacred. When a being from the Underworld interacts with a human or another supernatural, it prevents archangels from seeing that part of the timeline."

Huh. How odd, I thought and returned the book to the shelf.

I read down the line of titles, wondering if I would find anything that topped a guide on visitors from the Underworld. I wasn't disappointed. There were hundreds of beautifully bound volumes on angels, dragons, mythical creatures of every flavor, the afterlife, gods and goddesses, divination, more demons, more demons, wow, even more demons, and, oh…hello there, witchcraft.

Today was shaping into a real eye-opener—first, Claudette's open hotline to the angelic realm, and now this. I gaped in astonished delight at ancient tomes of the esoteric, the occult, and the magical, my blood humming. "These are amazing, Braith."

"Oh, yeah," he said, studying the shelves with a frown of concentration. "My mom has all these books on magic. Well, not like pulling rabbits out of hats and stuff. Like real magic. I've tried most of the spells, and they're all pretty good, I guess. I can't get the hang of crystal balls, though. Divination is tricky, cuz reality shifts like all the time. Man, that sucks."

I laughed. "Yeah, I know what you mean," I said—even though I didn't.

He pulled down a fat volume with leather straps and buckles, and I read the spine, *The Spellbinder's Guide to Ancient Charms and Enchantments.*

"This one's mine," Braith said. "Pop-Pop gave it to me on my twelfth birthday to like, strengthen my practice." He considered me a moment, and I swear his glassy eyes twinkled. "Don't worry, dude. We're good witches."

I smiled at his sincerity. "I had no doubt," I said, studying my new acquaintance who had returned his focus to the book. The more time I spent in his odd company, the more I liked him.

"We got most of these books from my grandfather."

"This grandfather?" I asked, hooking a thumb behind me.

"Yeah, dude. That grandfather. He's like super cool."

"But he's a doctor."

"Yeah, that's his side hustle. Pop-Pop and Nana are magical, just like my mom and me. My dad's regular and stuff, but he's super smart." Braith seemed to ponder that for an unusually long time, then his red eyes went wide. "Oh, hey—come see your new room!" He put a lot of energy behind the invitation like it was far more interesting than outing his family as a coven of witches.

I blinked at him a moment. I'd never met a real witch before—stoned or otherwise—and I was excited. I couldn't imagine how a gaggle of pot-smoking magical folks might go down in a small town, though.

We climbed the massive staircase and arrived at a set of double doors. Braith flung them open, and I had to focus on closing my mouth. Everything here was beyond the pale. But this room—I'd never seen anything so opulent, not even at Sherman Hill. Well, other than the library and the living room downstairs. I kept waiting for a butler to arrive with a tray of cocktails and finger sandwiches.

There was a sitting area centered on French doors leading to a private balcony. To my right was an airplane hangar disguised as a bathroom—the thing was big enough to put on a Vegas-style floor show.

Braith crossed the room and stood in front of another pair of doors. "Dude, you haven't seen the best part."

I didn't think that was remotely possible but followed him anyway.

"You've got a walk-in closet," he said.

Buttery lights clicked on as Braith threw the doors open to reveal glass-front cabinetry, drawers upon drawers, and shoe racks that had spotlights trained on them. Apparently, that was the last straw because my jaw finally dropped.

"This is the room you're renting?" I asked, knowing I could never afford to live here. Not even if I agreed to sleep on a cot in the garage, which probably had central air and a kitchenette and maybe a regular-sized bathroom with a wine fridge.

"Yup."

"And how much are you asking?" (What the heck, right?)

"Aw, I don't like money stuff, dude, but what about three hundred bucks a month?"

I almost did one of those cartoon head shakes followed by an *ahooga* with the big popping eyes. "Three hundred?" I said, trying to keep my voice from cracking.

"Yup."

"A month."

"Yup."

I gazed open-mouthed at the room resisting the urge to pinch myself or do somersaults across the vast sea of Berber carpeting. Then a familiar sensation blossomed in my chest—like someone filling my insides with hot cocoa—another one of my intuitive cues. It was almost as if the books and this house and these people had been calling to me. I know it sounds corny, but there's no other way to describe it. I also couldn't shake the overwhelming feeling of belonging here, in a house I'd never seen before but somehow felt like it had always been home...*my home.*

"Done," I said, sticking out my hand.

"Awesome. We just made, like, a business deal and stuff. Let's go tell Pop-Pop and Nana."

We found the Desmonds sitting at a marble-topped island, sipping hot tea. A lady was at the stove cooking something that smelled heavenly. I guessed this was the *Julia* Braith had mentioned early on—dark hair, skin the color of caramel, tiny waist, womanly hips. Her back was to me, but I could tell she was attractive; she was also incredibly focused on her bubbling pots.

The doctor dabbed the corner of his mouth with a cloth napkin and got up. "Well?" he asked brightly.

"It's unbelievable." I probably had a goofy smile on my face. I was still reeling from the crazy-low rent.

"Yeah, Sera's totally gonna live here," the stoned cutie-pie witch said.

"Excellent." The doctor hopped off his stool and helped Mabel down from hers, which ended up being a little touch-and-go. "We're off, son. Thank you for the delicious tea, Julia."

The woman clicked off a burner and turned around, giving me a full-on view. Okay, she was stunning. Maybe I landed in the sitcom version of a small town. These people were way too good-looking. Even the doctor and his wife were a casting director's idea of a handsome older couple, her being *much* older.

"You welcome, doctor," gorgeous Julia said. She placed several cookies inside a wax-paper bag, neatly folded the top, and handed the package to Mabel. "Will you and missus stay for dinner?" she asked with a formality that told me she wasn't Braith's mother. A chef, maybe? Okay, this just keeps getting better.

"We should get back to the house. Appreciate the invitation, though." The doctor turned my way. "I'll ask Cormac to bring your bags inside, young lady." He started to leave, then an odd expression passed over his kind face. "I'm so glad we found you, Seraphina."

Julia dropped a pot, and it clanged around on the floor as I rocked back on my heels slightly. It felt like a rubber band was unwinding itself in my head. Hearing the name surprised me. One, because it's not my name. I'm simply Sera with no neat flourish at the end. Two because it sounded like it *should* be my name. And three, what exactly did he mean by *finding me?*

The confusion must have shown on my face because Dr. Desmond took a big step back, the whites of his eyes prominent like a deer caught in headlights. Then his cheeks flushed red. "I have no idea why I said that. Must be tired from the journey."

Braith went rigid, his red eyes shooting between his grandfather and me.

Mabel rested a hand on my shoulder. "Are you all right, dear?"

I assured her I was even though I wasn't so sure of it myself. I didn't have a bad feeling. Just an odd one—like my brain was trying to take hold of something but couldn't land the plane.

CHAPTER
~ 3 ~
The Blue Orb

Earth Plane 2019

Cormac was on the front porch with Sera's bags when the Desmonds stepped out. The air had cooled, and he'd added a gray cashmere scarf to his chic ensemble. "And?"

The doctor nodded.

"Thank the good lord. You never know with that one. Clapping eyes on me works sometimes. Or the mention of Átha Cliath. She's spent a few lifetimes there. Always some trouble needs mendin'." He shrugged and deposited the bags in the foyer, then walked back out and lit a cigarette. "So, she recognized the house?"

The doctor rubbed his forehead. "I don't think so, and I hope I didn't shake her up."

Mabel patted his shoulder. "You didn't, Chet. Sera's begun the change. Hearing her eternal name will do nothing but help her remember who she is."

"Thank you, darling," the doctor said. He squeezed Mabel's hand and smiled into her eyes.

Cormac blew several smoke rings, watching the puffy circles get larger as they headed toward the porch light overhead. "It's this gap year business. Playin' it fast and loose if you ask me."

The doctor frowned. "You really should give those things up, you know."

"Aye, neither drink nor smoke can hurt a hair on this head. One of the benefits of being immortal, I suppose."

Cormac sighed, then studied his companions. "I think she's fine for what it's worth. Seraphina's a tough one, even when she's coming across like a young mortal. There's an ancient warrior in there behind all that gee-whiz."

He turned to address the deer standing at the edge of the porch. "What do you think?" he asked it.

The animal tossed its head up and down and ran off.

"See that, Dr. Chet?" Cormac said. "If we'd done her any harm, there wouldn't be a cute little deer in the front yard. It'd be an angry warrior angel wielding a great big sword."

A ball of shimmering blue light appeared. Although it had just popped out of thin air, none of them seemed the least bit surprised.

The doctor tugged the brim of his hat down. "Well, I've done it, Rachel, just as you asked."

Mabel blew a kiss to the mystical object. It shimmered in response and swooped down to hover only a few inches from Cormac's nose. He gave it a smile of pure affection as blue light bathed his handsome face.

"Aye, Rachel. You're as lovely as a field of forget-me-nots on a spring morn."

The blue orb shimmered once more and blinked out of sight.

CHAPTER

~ 4 ~

A New Life

Earth Plane 2019

After dinner, I showered, unpacked, and crawled into the enormous bed. A soft light slanted through the windows, and I gazed through the transom, craning my neck to see the waxing moon.

It was Elle who taught me about moon cycles. The best phase to cut your hair when you want it to grow faster (waxing). When to remove undesirable things (waning). The days to refrain from planning…anything (first quarter).

I've known Elle since we were both in diapers. Long ago, she'd taken to calling me *Valentine* because of the heart-shaped candies and corny little cards I loved so much when we were kids. You know, *Be Mine, I Heart U, Kiss Me*—all the classics. Truthfully, I still love them. They're just so darned happy.

When we were kids, and the other girls picked on me, Elle would appear as if by magic, coming to my defense. My friend has a thick mane of golden blond hair and was so fearless in those moments; she was like a lioness protecting a cub. After several bullying episodes,

Elle had insisted on teaching me to fight. Two bloody noses and a matching set of black eyes later, Ms. Porter enrolled us in karate classes at the local Y, and now we're both black belts.

I tried to convince Elle to come with me to Leesburg. But she'd insisted on going to Kentucky where she'd gotten a job as a stable hand's assistant—a fancy way of saying she'd be mucking the stalls. I told her there was plenty of horse poop to shovel in Virginia, but it hadn't worked.

The sting of sudden tears made my nose tingle. Until last week, I'd seen Elle every day of my life, and my feelings took a hard knock when she hadn't wanted to live closer together after we left Sherman Hill.

My phone chimed. I rubbed my eyes and picked it up to have a look.

Goodnight, Valentine. I Heart U.

I smiled at the screen. How does that girl always know when I'm thinking of her?

Goodnight, lioness. Heart U2.

Three question marks popped back in a moment later, and I laughed. Let her wonder about the lioness remark, I decided.

Phone charging on the nightstand, I settled into the cloud-soft bed and closed my eyes. A dove cooed outside my window, and I smiled, remembering doves mate for life.

"Goodnight, dove," I said and drifted off to sleep.

The next morning, I woke to the aroma of coffee and toast. I followed my nose to the kitchen and found Julia at the sink whisking eggs and humming to herself. Braith was at the table in a pair of bright red headphones, polishing off his breakfast.

"Hey, dude," he said, giving me an exaggerated head nod.

"Morning, Braith. Hey, Julia."

Julia smiled brightly and headed my way. "Good morning. You must have some breakfast. Come." She took me by the shoulders and gently pressed me into a chair. "I make eggs. You like eggs, Ms. Sera?"

"That would be wonderful. Thank you."

I learned at dinner last night that Julia has been with the Langmans for years. She's from Bolivia (the part that churns out Miss Universe contestants apparently), does the shopping, cooks the meals, and coordinates maintenance and cleaning. Even though she's only a few years older than Braith, I got the impression Julia was more like a mother to him than anything else. (Although I wasn't sure how Braith's teenaged self got past all those sexy curves and flowing hair without going into adolescent shock.)

I also learned you don't talk to Julia when there's a soccer match on TV. Not ever...unless the house is on fire and the flames are licking at her feet.

The dark-haired beauty set a plate of hot buttered toast and scrambled eggs in front of me. "You would like the coffee and the orange juice?" Julia asked, heading to the fridge, hips swaying.

I nodded. "Yes, please." I placed the napkin on my lap and tucked in.

Braith slid the headphones onto his neck, and I heard music thumping out, a soothing beat with a steady bass line. I guess I'd half expected it to be death metal, and the puzzlement must have shown on my face.

"It's trance, dude. It helps me get into my meditation space."

Julia spoke close to my ear as she set down my coffee and juice. "He is full of the surprises, yes?"

"Uh-huh," I said, thinking back on his *reality shifts all the time* comment. I took a sip of coffee. Delicious. Black as night and robust enough to curl your toes. It made every other cup of coffee seem like someone had passed a handful of beans over lukewarm water.

"Just you wait." Julia winked at me, then she straightened and smoothed her blouse. "Okay, I go now, Mr. Braith, Ms. Sera. Oh." She turned back to me and slipped a note onto the table. "Dr. Chet leave this for you."

I peered up from my breakfast.

Braith caught my face and chuckled. "That's my grandpa, dude. His first name is Chester, but everybody calls him Dr. Chet."

Today my roommate wore a black hoodie over blue scrubs with a black beanie and yellow Crocs. At least it matched. Well, with a little pop of color for added pizazz.

Julia nodded at the folded paper on the table. "Dr. Chet says you go see Mr. Bob at the diner this morning, and he gives you a job, okay?"

I smiled up at her. "Oh, great. Thank you."

"De nada. Bye-bye."

Julia collected her handbag, and power walked to the front door.

"Bye, Julia." Braith put his plate in the dishwasher and refilled his coffee. "Check you later, boss. I'm going to commune with the masters."

I wasn't sure what he meant, but I saluted my understanding, or lack of it, and picked up the note. Even though Julia told me what it said, I opened it anyway and smiled, wondering if she was the type to steam my letters.

I arrived at the diner a little before ten and stepped through the front door to find the whole town had managed to cram inside. My eyes wandered to the occupancy certificate hanging on the wall. We were well past that red-lettered number, but the fire chief was stuffed into one of the booths yucking it up with the sheriff, and they didn't seem to care.

A heavyset man with white hair, a close-kept white beard, and rosy cheeks crashed through the swinging doors from the kitchen. "Lookout," he said, balancing loaded-down plates in each hand. He wore a Hawaiian shirt, jeans, and sneakers, and I smiled, thinking he looked like Santa Claus on vacation.

The man deposited the plates at one of the tables and headed over to greet me. "Morning. Anyone joining you, or do you want to grab a place at the counter?" Despite being in the weeds (as I've heard servers say), this guy had a relaxed vibe and oozed kindness. He flicked a glance at the red vinyl stools—all of them filled—then widened his hazel eyes, pinching his lips together in apology.

"I'm Sera Parker. Dr. Chet asked me to come?"

Cool Santa checked his watch. "Punctual, we're off to a bang-up start. Bob Nash. Grab a seat. Uh, wherever you can find one. I've just got to take care of a couple of things."

I sat down in the only available booth, shrugged out of my jacket, and gave the place a good going over.

A blackboard spanned the wall behind the jam-packed counter with an unusual menu written in multicolored chalks, probably dishes named after Bob's regulars. There was a Mayor Burk's Breakfast Bonanza, a Cerphe's Up Veggie Sub, a Big Red's Bawdy BLT, an Umstattd Omelet, and a Todders Boxed Lunch Special. The *Savory Sides* included Juliana's Julienned Green Beans, Tammy Loves Bacon, and Roger Hates Brussels Sprouts.

I chuckled. I couldn't imagine those sprouts flying out the door with a name like that. At the far end of the diner, the interior racks of a lit pastry case slowly turned to display more pies than I had ever seen at once. Maybe free pie is an employee benefit, I thought hopefully.

Bob moved like lightning, offering refills, handing out menus, taking orders, and ringing the cash register. He walked over a few minutes later, carrying a pitcher of iced tea, and poured us both a glass before flopping himself down. "Whew," he said, slapping his forehead with a palm.

"Hey, Bob, could I get another donut?" a man sitting in the booth behind him called out.

Bob sighed and motioned to the counter without looking at the man. "Sure. Help yourself, Tony." Then his eyes met mine, and his face brightened. "So, Dr. Chet tells me I should give you a job. Have you ever worked in a diner before?"

"Not exactly. I did work the cafeteria line at the—"

I followed Bob's weary gaze to a cheerful-looking woman wiggling her fingers in our direction. "That's fantastic," he said, sliding out of the booth. "It's minimum wage plus tips, but those are decent." He froze, and I think he may have even held his breath a little.

"That's fine," I said.

Bob blew the air out of his puffed-up cheeks. "When can you start?"

"Uh, tomorrow?"

"Hot dang," Bob said, slapping his palms together. "I'll see you in the morning. Does six work for you?"

"Sure does."

"Fantastic."

Bob gave me a tired smile, the kind that says *I'm trying, but I'm not sure I'm making it work.* Then my new boss turned on his heel, ripped a check from his pad, and headed toward the woman who had just interrupted my first job interview.

It was a brilliant autumn day, and I left the diner, deciding to poke around town. The sun was shining, and there was a lovely hint of a breeze. People dressed in light layers moved along the wide brick sidewalks shopping, chatting, and going about their day. I shoved my hands in my jacket pockets, feeling pleased with myself. I had a home and friends, and now I had a job and delicious-smelling pies to go with it. Not bad, Parker, I thought.

I crossed the driveway that joined Bob's place with the furniture store next door and heard excited voices wafting up from the alley behind the buildings.

"Hey. Move back. Let me try it now," a high-pitched male voice said.

"You've already had a bunch of turns," another one said.

A chorus of laughter followed.

Hmm, the distinct sound of kids up to no good. I'm not exactly sure why, but I decided to check it out. Curiosity and cats, I guess, although the little idiom didn't turn out so well for the cat.

I walked along the edge of the building and turned the corner to see several boys throwing rocks at an actual cat who looked a lot more freaked out than curious. The size of the animal caught my full attention. Wow, kitty was a bruiser, and she was putting up a good fight, hissing and baring teeth as two stones hit the dumpster beside her.

Mammoth kitty tried to squeeze through a hole in the brick wall, but it wasn't working out.

"Stop this right now. You're going to hurt her."

"Why don't you make us?" one of the little snots said.

The dark-headed boy standing next to him served up a head-wobbling sneer to go with the verbal gauntlet his friend had just thrown down.

I moved toward the trapped animal, and a good-sized rock whizzed toward my head. I judged its speed and trajectory and dodged—a neat trick that—and one that kept many a roundhouse kick from landing in my face. But it made me angry. They didn't know I could do that. They'd planned on hitting me in the head... *with a sharp rock.*

Another boy grabbed a chunk of brick and drew back, ready to fire again. Oh, great. I'm the new target, I thought, getting ready to dodge more projectiles.

Without warning, a flash of heat hit my face, and my skin began to tingle. The sensation revved until it felt like fire coursing through my veins. Instinctively, I widened my stance and raised a palm, feeling raw power rise from deep within. The tingling raced down my arm, causing my fingertips to pulse. "Stop. Now," I said in a commanding voice. It sounded scary, even to me, like my brain was along on somebody else's ride. Trash cans rattled as my voice bounced off the brick walls and landed back in my ears.

Don't ask me how, but a blast of energy shot from my palm, moving the air in centrifugal circles. *Everything* stopped, and now there were no sounds at all—not even from the sidewalk and street beyond. No car doors, no people, no traffic, everything had gone quiet. A bird flying overhead appeared stuck in glue. The boys looked odd, too, like a stop-motion film, and several rocks hung in midair.

The cat wasn't frozen, and oddly enough, she seemed to be smiling at me. The weirdness stunned me for a moment, but common sense finally kicked in. I shot past the frozen boys, scooped up the smiling cat, and ran.

Kitty purred like an outboard motor, vibrating against my chest. The steady hum had a soothing effect—close to being hypnotic—and after a healthy dose of that, I had calmed down enough to get my breathing back to normal.

Then I tried to zero in on the strange current of power shooting from my hand, but the details of it were getting fuzzier by the second.

Wait. What happened? Something weird, I thought, trying to piece together the sequence of events. I'd shouted at them, and then *something*...happened with my hand. Had they just run? It's what I would have done at their age, but I couldn't remember anymore. I checked in with my intuition and felt fine. Whatever happened wasn't bad, I decided. Just odd, maybe.

Anyway, now I had a cat.

Mind cleared and wanting to inspect my damsel in distress, I lifted the feline to eye level. It took notable arm strength. "Wow. You are one massive hunk of fur. Why didn't you kick their little snot-nosed butts, girl? Oh, excuse me—boy," I corrected myself, having just taken a quick peek at the undercarriage.

Bruiser cat blinked at me with blue eyes the color of beach glass. He searched my face with a paw on my shoulder, his sweet little eraser-colored nose only inches from mine, purring even louder than before.

"You like me, kitty?"

The cat meowed, and I decided that was a resounding *yes*.

Back at the house, I deposited my furry friend on the floor and sucked in a breath, fumbling to find my courage. I had a landlord, and he probably wasn't going to let me keep a pet. The cat did figure eights through my feet, swished his tail across my ankles, and purred up at me with great big kitty eyes. He didn't seem to share my apprehension.

"Okay, mister, keep up the charm, and we just might have a shot."

The cat straightened, wrapped his tail around his body, and blinked at me. It *was* rather charming, so maybe he got the point.

"Let's find Braith and ask him about you, shall we?"

"Ask me what?" Braith said, trotting out of his study. "Oh, cool. Who's the big dude?" He dropped to his knees to pet the cat, who pranced and rubbed against his hands loving the attention.

Uh, huh, I thought, watching the world's most adorable animal act take place on the floor—purring, chirping, fuzzy head shakes. Oh. He rolled over, never taking those ethereal blue eyes off my roomie. Now that's a low blow. I folded my arms as I watched the exchange; way to work the crowd, smart kitty.

"Like holy cow. How much do you weigh, anyway?"

"Right?" I said in agreement.

"This is like a jumbo kitty. You could saddle this guy up and go for a ride." The cat gave his potential landlord the stink eye, but Braith didn't catch it and just plowed on. "Where did you get him?"

I noticed he said *him*, not *her*. Males recognize other males on sight, I guess, even across species.

"I rescued him in an alley. Some mean boys were pelting him with rocks."

"This dude doesn't need rescuing," Braith said, studying the cat while it focused on licking a paw. "This here is like a super cat. Does he have a home, or can we keep him?"

"I was about to ask you the same question."

Braith broke into a face-splitting smile and punched air. "Then it's a done deal. We have a cat, an attack cat."

Our feline friend yawned and licked his other paw, seeming unimpressed his living situation had just changed.

"Come on, boy, you hungry? I think I've got some tuna salad," Braith said, heading for the kitchen. Attack Cat trotted next to him, keeping pace—immediately at home—all bright eyes, upright tail, happy little chirps.

Way to bring it home, I thought, then did a double take when the cat winked at me.

A few minutes later, I scratched the kitty between the ears as he carefully separated chunks of onion from the rest of the salad.

"It's okay," I said. "Elle hates onions too, so you're in pretty good company, my friend."

The cat pushed several onion cubes onto the floor and gave them the feline version of a raspberry.

"Let's see. You need a name—"

"How about Cat Stevens or Cat Mandu? Oh, or Big Bad Kitty Kitty?" Braith said unhelpfully.

I studied the hungry guy. "I don't know. He looks like a Sebastian to me."

Braith shrugged. "That works."

"Do you like it?" I asked our new roommate.

The cat surveyed Braith's face. Then he turned his substantial head to me and blinked slowly.

I smiled. "Sebastian, it is then."

"Meow," the big kitty said, pressing his plus-size body into my leg. Then our onion-hating attack cat sneezed on my shoe.

CHAPTER

~ 5 ~

The Animal Years

Earth Plane 2019

Sebastian jumped from the counter and settled himself in front of the French doors to watch a softball-sized blue orb of light. It zipped around a while—up, down, side to side—and he followed the movement, his head keeping pace as if watching a crazily played tennis match.

It was Rachel, just saying hello. She felt sorry for him, and her visits did brighten his mood during what he called *the animal years*. It was sweet of her, really. What cat doesn't like a shiny ball of light?

Sebastian watched her fly over the trees, wishing he could follow. But he knew he couldn't and sighed at his entertainment prospects: bug chasing, sleeping, maybe a little TV if somebody turned one on. Watching one of the slow-moving ceiling fans might be fun, he decided.

Oh! Oh! Oh! A bird!

The cat double pawed the glass vigorously before remembering he could *flash* himself outside. He squeezed his eyes shut and focused.

No. Wait. He shouldn't do that…too many questions. Best to lie low until one of them opened a door.

Instead, he fantasized about how delicious that bird would be. He'd stalk it, hide in the bushes, wait until it was pecking the ground distracted by a worm. Then he'd pounce and gobble the thing up in one sitting. Afterward, he'd lay the carcass at Sera's feet as a trophy. She would be so proud.

Wait. *He* didn't want to eat a bird; his cat brain did. Horrified by the murderous thought, Sebastian dropped to the floor and groaned, resting his chin on his outstretched paws. The animal years were exhausting, and he had almost a year of this nonsense left.

When he was a cat, time always dragged out. The animal brain processed linear time slowly, and it was dull, bordering on mind-numbing. Being this way kept his feelings in check, though. Sure, he felt love for Sera when he was an animal, just not *that* kind of love.

The final year had always been challenging, but Sera had vanished for thirty years before this life began, which made waiting even harder this time. He'd searched every inch of the Earth plane repeatedly—like someone who's lost a set of keys and keeps going back to the same places hoping they will have magically appeared.

When his search efforts failed for the thousandth time, he'd asked Goddess, and she'd delivered one of her favorite lines, "All is as it should be, and all will be clear when the time is right." He almost stomped back to demand she tell him but thought better of it, remembering what happened to Lucifer after his failed rebellion.

Goddess has endless grace and boundless mercy. She's also unconditionally loving and benevolent beyond words; he knew that better than anyone. But when Goddess snapped… He shuddered and licked a paw.

The four of them had tried her patience on several occasions—to the breaking point at times. They always managed to reel her in just short of wrath no matter how egregious the error. But he thought it best not to test her on Sera's disappearance; that subject seemed a little too close to the bone.

When Sera's previous life ended, he felt it and immediately went home to be with her but had no luck finding her in the usual places.

Eventually, he tried her favorite recovery village and spotted her inside a café with Alden. Even though it broke his heart, he hadn't approached, and he hadn't questioned Alden afterward. Sera had done her best to avoid him, so he wasn't going to pry or spring himself on her—no matter how much he wanted to be with her. She would tell him when she was ready, just as Goddess said.

One doesn't live as long as he had without learning patience.

Sebastian stretched out on the carpet. Half of his body in the sun, half out—just the way he liked it. What he *didn't* like was the disgusting taste of onion in his mouth. He'd accidentally powered one down during the tuna-salad feast.

There weren't many things in any dimension he disliked, but onions, yech. He did not despise their essence and loved them, in fact. They were happy little atoms, charming in their way. No, what he hated was the slimy feel and taste they left behind on his tongue.

Sebastian got up, did a shimmying stretch, and padded off in search of water. But *not* from the toilet this time. He wouldn't let his cat brain trick him into *that* ever again.

CHAPTER

~ 6 ~

Angels and Demons and Me, Oh My!

Earth Plane 2020

My twenty-second birthday fell on a Saturday. More importantly, it was Halloween, my favorite holiday. Bob had given me the day off to celebrate, which was incredibly generous as he'd be manning the crazy-busy diner alone.

The morning was off to a great start; Elle called the moment my eyes opened, and we talked for nearly an hour. Lovely chat with best friend complete, I pulled on the world's fluffiest socks, tucked my phone into a back pocket, and headed to the kitchen for a scary-hot cup of coffee.

My perfect-day plan involved getting heavily caffeinated, going for a light jog, then snuggling in with Sebastian for a horror-movie marathon. I knew he wouldn't pay much attention to the clomping zombies and blood-sucking vampires. Still, startling him from sleep each time I jumped would get him into the Halloween spirit just fine, I decided.

My phone vibrated, and I slipped it out to have a look.

Celeste had sent a GIF of that cute British actor dancing across a hallway followed by *Happy Birthday.*

I laughed; she'd made me watch every one of his movies with her at least ten times. The one where he's prime minister is her favorite, the one where he's a regular guy in love with a movie-star is mine. Usually, we flipped a coin to decide which one to watch and then watched them both anyway.

I texted back: *Wish you were here to celebrate with me, or British cutie was dancing across your hallway.*

A bunch of hearts and exclamation marks popped back in a second later.

"Happy birthday," my roommate called from his study.

In the time I've known him, Braith has revealed himself to be much more than just a guy who smokes an insane amount of weed. Other than the fact he meditates more than a Buddhist monk, Braith is sweet, funny, loyal, and incredibly smart. He's everything I could want in a boyfriend, even though I don't think of him that way. He's never shown me any spells, though. Whenever I bring it up, he says he will someday, although someday never seems to come.

Besides being a self-proclaimed witch—who doesn't do magic—Braith is a lead designer for a well-known gaming company. He works from home inside a study decked out with more monitors, computer towers, laptops, and gadgetry than I've ever seen in one place. He also has *everything* delivered. I asked him once about the last time he'd stepped foot inside a grocery store, and he honestly couldn't remember. But I got the feeling he might have been inside a cart, fussing with the navigator over which cereal had the better prizes.

The diner is about the only place in town Braith deems worthy enough to venture from home. That and the Apple store, which he Ubers to and from. Probably so he can text with his designers and gaming buddies all the way there and back, or maybe because he has the good sense not to drive while high as a kite. I hope it's the latter.

The loveable shut-in trotted into the foyer where I had just arrived. "I have a surprise for you," Braith said, thrusting an envelope at me.

I shot him a smile as I opened it. It was a Halloween card with the word *Birthday* written in pen, so it now read HAPPY HALLOWEEN BIRTHDAY. The boy just gets me.

"Thank you. This is perfect."

"Wait, there's more. Come with me."

Braith took me by the shoulders and steered me into his study, inviting me to sit in his programming chair. He offered up a goofy smile, then tapped the keyboard, and DEMON STREET FIGHT: DEMO MODE appeared.

My mouth shot open as I watched an uncannily realistic woman with long honey-blond hair and green eyes swagger across the screen. It was me, a superhero version of me, but still.

Superhero me wore a skintight red outfit and high-heeled boots. She did a kind of vigilante-justice strut—all balled fists and smoldering intention—then roundhouse-kicked some of the words offscreen. After that bit of fancy footwork, she shot a steady stream of fire from her palms, burning the remaining letters into nothingness. The high heels were impractical for fighting, but they were stylish, so I suspended disbelief and went with it.

"Well, I could probably execute that kick in stilettos, but I can't shoot fire from my hands," I said, laughing at the thought.

"Or *can* you?"

I smiled at him, then watched as another sim figure sashayed into view. "Oh, wow. Is that—?"

"Yeah. It's Elle, dude. I watched a few of your karate championship videos to get your movements right. You guys are dangerous together. Um, I hope you don't mind?"

"Mind? I love it."

The two animated characters assumed fighting stances as the background materialized around them. Appropriately enough for any *demon street fight* worth its salt, an abandoned warehouse faced a dark alley. Light filtered through grime-streaked windows onto rusty fire escapes, and ominous music forewarned that something sinister was about to hit the fan.

"Okay, watch. This is lit," Braith said with a gleam in his eye.

Massive black creatures with enormous bat-like wings jumped from rooftops, swarmed through open windows, and swung down from the fire escapes. They attacked Elle and me from every angle. We were doing a great job mowing them down, though, and I wondered if we really could hold off a bunch of flesh-hungry demons. Probably, I decided, thinking more than a few of them might need tetanus shots from all that rusted metal.

Four good-looking angels landed on the street. They got down to the business of smiting, and as their swords connected, monster pieces shot around wildly. Trumpets blasted as the parts collected themselves, then funneled into the score at the top of the screen.

Braith smiled broadly. "A kill with your bonus angel is worth more skill points."

Now our screen selves were fighting alongside the good-looking angels, and I couldn't blame them. That was a fight club I'd happily sign up for any day of the week, demons or no.

My character pulled a sword from thin air and cut one of the creatures in two. While the poor guy was busy dragging his top half across the pavement, she shot a fireball from her palm, reducing him to a smoking pile of ash. He was really trying, and I felt sorry for him, then winced as warrior me punched another demon in the throat. He staggered backward toward one of the super-hot angels who lopped its head off with a broadsword—teamwork.

More demon appendages scattered, trumpets rang out again, and Braith's score climbed even higher.

I blinked at the screen as something danced at the corners of my mind—like a memory trying to fight through a murky haze. It felt like I was watching myself from a far-off place and floating farther away as each second passed.

Braith put a hand on my shoulder. "Hey. You okay?" he asked, searching my face. His touch grounded me, and I nodded. At least I felt like I was in my body again, sort of.

Sebastian came running into the room, and Braith scooped the cat onto his lap. "Do you want to make Sera and Elle kick the snot out of the demons, buddy?" he said, then inspected me as if he were waiting for something.

Sebastian wriggled in Braith's arms, his attention glued to my face. Then the cat whipped his head toward the door, and a couple of beats later, Julia entered the study.

"Hey, Ms. birthday lady. I just want to tell you I am making a special dinner for you. So, if you go out today, be home by six, okay?" She wagged a finger at me.

Thankfully, Julia's voice snapped me the rest of the way out of the fog, almost as if she'd reached out and yanked me back into the chair, hard.

CHAPTER

~ 7 ~

A Moment in Time

Earth Plane 2020

Braith's video game left me with one of those uneasy feelings that are hard to pin down, and I decided the light jog I'd planned should be amped up to a long and sweaty run to clear my head. So I stretched, filled my water bottle, and headed out to chew asphalt.

An hour and a half later, I was breathless and much improved.

I parked myself on a metal bench on the town green, enjoying the crinkle of leaves as people passed me by, the sun on my skin, the breeze on my face. There's nothing quite like the feeling you get from gazing at a cloudless blue sky on a crisp autumn morning.

Resting my elbows on the back of the bench, I smiled at the couple inspecting the marquee over the Tally Ho Theater. THE GIN BLOSSOMS it read, and they seemed excited about that.

It had been almost a year since I stepped off the bus to become a Leesburgian, and I adore this town and the people in it. Community pride runs deep here, and Leesburg residents go all out for holidays, another reason I love this place. I took a swig of water and surveyed the current version of *all out*.

Witches cackling over bubbling cauldrons, ghosts swinging from branches, black cats, zombies, and other nefarious creatures of the night filled the shop windows. A street-sweeper whirred several blocks away, and I smiled—the town was getting scrubbed up for the Kiwanis Club's annual Halloween parade.

After soaking up a bit more sun, I hauled myself up to begin the walk home and caught the faint smell of baking pies wafting up from the diner. They were probably the ones I'd made last night and put in the fridge. My boss is adamant about baking daily, and I don't blame him. Our pies are a big hit with the locals, and this scent brings them in droves. Sometimes our lines even wrap around the block.

Bob taught me to bake my second week at Mom's, and I immediately loved it. Unlike cooking—which is a little dash of this and a little splash of that—baking is precise, like chemistry, so my math skills give me an advantage.

I walked a few paces, then stopped short as a gaggle of four-foot monsters and a tiny princess wearing a baby-pink tutu rushed past. I sighed, feeling grateful for this town and my friends here, and wondered why I'd been so rattled before. Today was one of those perfect days, a day when you just feel lucky to be alive.

Out of the shower, I slipped into jeans, pulled on a light sweater, and sat on the love seat to lace up my sneakers. A book on the coffee table caught my eye, a field guide on trees Dr. Chet loaned me ages ago. I decided to return it before I forgot again.

"Sebastian. Hey, Cat Stevens, I'm heading out."

Yeah, that one stuck. Also, Big Bad Kitty Kitty, Bruiser Cat, Jumbo Kitty, and several other silly names Braith and I come up with almost daily. I waited for a beat to see if Cat Mandu might present himself. He didn't.

Sebastian follows me wherever I go, not because he enjoys my company, because the shop owners spoil him with treats and coo over his pretty blue eyes. That cat has a loyal fan base.

Jumbo Kitty waits for me outside the diner, too, and the whole town gets a bang out of that. Most days, I step out of Mom's to his entourage crowded around him in adulation, and it takes a while to pry him loose.

He's always up for parading himself through town, and usually, he's underfoot before I've made my way to the front door. But today, he'd done one of his disappearing acts. Probably off chasing a bird.

"Okay, no treats for you, I guess," I said to the empty foyer and grabbed my keys.

"Hey there, Sera," Caroline Walton called from the door of her real estate office. "Happy birthday. Where's the big fella?"

"Thank you," I said, then shrugged. "Dunno. He had other plans, I guess."

A few doors up, Mike Plummer was setting up a sandwich board in front of his bakery. Mike is tall with a pleasant face and used to have much more padding. He's upped his wardrobe game in recent months, and his hair looks suspiciously darker. I've noticed Caroline Walton with him a time or two, and I think they're doing more than discussing the community bake sale.

"Hi, Sera," he said. "Oh, wait right here." He disappeared into the shop and returned a few moments later with a pink cupcake box. The sticker read BLISS OUT AT CUPCAKE NIRVANA.

"Happy birthday."

I smiled at him. "Hey, thanks. How did you know?"

"Dr. Chet told all of us at the business owner's meeting last night."

"Well, I'm sure glad he told *you*. This cupcake won't live to see tomorrow. Thanks, Mike."

I popped the lid and sampled the buttercream frosting as I headed off.

A super-believable witch was entertaining the early lunch crowd on the next block. Most folks shy away from costumed people, but I adore witches and made my way over. The woman smiled broadly as I approached, revealing a mouthful of black teeth.

"Well, hello, dearie. Happy Halloween."

"Happy Halloween," I said, getting closer to inspect her face. Rude, I know, but I couldn't help it. The prosthetic nose was the best I'd ever seen, and her warts looked real too; one even had a hair sprouting from the center. "Your makeup is incredible."

"Thank you," the witch cooed. "May I read your palm, my dear?"

I love fortune-tellers and was about to say yes. Then I met the woman's coal-black eyes. My chest tightened, and I felt like I was about to throw up all over her pointy-toed boots. "I…really can't…"

She grabbed my hand before I could react. "It will only take a minute."

A chill ran up my spine, and I tried to pull away, but she locked those creepy eyes on mine, and I froze as if under an actual spell.

The woman dragged a long black nail (attached to a crooked finger) across my open palm. "Oh, you do have an interesting lifeline. See how it branches out in many directions? Highly unusual. Well, look at this… I see a handsome, ahem, man from your past. This man grows impatient and expects you to return, or you will pay a terrible price. You will lose those you love."

I found my strength and yanked my hand away, putting several streets between us before glancing back. When I did, the woman was gone.

I don't remember going the rest of the way to Dr. Chet's. I must have run because my shirt was soaked when I reached the office. I went inside, closed the door behind me, and leaned on it for support, noticing the book and cupcake were gone. I'd have to retrace my steps, or maybe not. I didn't want to risk running into the scary woman again.

Feeling a bit silly now I was in familiar surroundings, I moved through the front office and poked my head into the break room—no sign of Dr. Chet, Kricket, or Andrea.

"Hello?" I checked my phone for the time. It was noon.

I started to leave; then troubled voices caught my ear. I followed the sound down the back hallway and turned the corner to see green light streaming from an open door. My heart picked up speed again as I approached. So much for familiar surroundings.

I paused at the door and checked myself, putting my back flat against the wall. There was a good possibility this was some kind of medical procedure, and I'd see something I didn't want to, like the sheriff in his skivvies. But judging by the urgent tones, I couldn't leave without knowing my friends were all right. I sucked in a breath and peeked around the door frame.

Mabel was flat on an exam table, and Dr. Chet, Kricket, and Andrea held their hands above her motionless body. The green light emanating from the room was streaming from their palms, and Sebastian was on Mabel's chest, breathing green fire from his mouth into hers.

I stumbled backward, a whimper escaping my lips as Kricket rushed toward me. "Nobody locked the door?" she said, grabbing me under the arms a split second before my knees gave out.

"Oh, my Goddess... Sera. I... I didn't even have time to shift. I'm so sorry," my *cat* said.

"Sebastian?" I shook my head, trying to get a grip. It seemed as though reality were slipping away; the walls sucked inward then back out again like they were breathing. Kricket ushered me down the hall to the waiting room, and I slumped into a chair. Then several things happened rapid fire.

"She's splitting!" someone shouted. The voice sounded far off—like the person was at the end of a long tunnel.

Sebastian jumped onto my lap. At least I think he did. I was too busy keeping up with the images rushing into my mind at lightning speed, like a million people trying to cram into a phone booth at the same time. I'd lost complete control of my eyes—judging by the crazy-quick images of the wall, the ceiling, then the floor. And I needed to vomit.

My eyes fluttered, and I saw a man I didn't recognize. He was way too close to my face to make out details, but he seemed terrified.

I squeezed my eyes shut, shaking my head as more images sped by then shattered like glass exploding across the stars.

Now I was inside a rocket ship—red and translucent—and I was shooting through outer space at the speed of light. A Tom Petty song blared from somewhere, filling my head with a wall of sound, blotting out everything else. I saw Earth getting closer and closer, and it seemed as if I would crash into it.

The scene changed abruptly, and a tree filled my vision, then a man with dark hair and dark eyes, then a dark-eyed woman holding a knife over me while I slept. My heart hammered against my chest as I grabbed my throat and gasped for air.

"She has too many soul memories rushing in!" It was a male voice I recognized but couldn't place, and it was even farther away now, echoing in my head.

"Sera, open your eyes. Right now."

I felt a hard slap across my face and managed to pry my eyes open enough to see Dr. Chet rushing toward me with a brown vile in his hand. He drew out the cork with his teeth, spat it on the floor, and poured the contents into my mouth. I swallowed, and the images started slowing down like a carousel coming to a stop. Then my attention jerked to the sounds of the room, and six of Andrea's golden-brown eyes came into view. I closed my eyes again, allowing my head to slump to my chest. It was so heavy, and I was so tired.

"Sera? Sera," Andrea said. "Look at me, honey. Come on. You can do it. Hear my voice." She snapped her fingers next to my ears.

I raised my head and tried to focus on seeing fewer of her, and it was working a little. I was down to only one and a half Andreas.

"Did you slap me in the face?" I said, wiggling my jaw. Whoever hit me meant business. My cheek felt like it was on fire, and I reached up to rub it. "Ow," I think I said out loud.

"There you are, Sera. You're okay now." Kricket brushed the hair from my eyes and handed me a glass. I grabbed it with both hands, spilling water into my lap as I shook uncontrollably.

"What happened?" I said through chattering teeth.

Kricket helped steady my hands so I could take a drink. "You fainted, sweet girl."

I swallowed the water I managed to get into my mouth and peered into their anxious faces, the right number of them this time. I was still feeling queasy, but at least the room had stopped spinning, and I no longer needed to barf.

Wait. *Did* I barf?

I searched for evidence then got distracted by the soft glow emanating from Kricket and Andrea. For a moment, I thought I saw halos around them. Kricket's was yellow. Andrea's was green. "You look like angels," I said, then winced as my pounding head took center stage.

Andrea smiled. "Oh, we're much prettier than angels."

"And smarter," Kricket said, sweeping her cinnamon-colored hair over a shoulder.

"How did I get here?"

Kricket patted my hand. "You walked, silly goose."

"All right," Dr. Chet said, shining a small flashlight into my eyes. "I think you're back to the proper speed, young lady. You gave us a scare. Let's fix this up, shall we?"

Andrea squeezed my hand and mumbled something I couldn't make out. It had the words *protection* and *earth time* in it, but that's all I got. "Here we go, Sera. You'll feel better in a minute, promise." She nodded to Dr. Chet. "Do over in three, two, one."

Andrea tapped me on the forehead three times, and I saw the hands of the wall clock spin backward, then click into place at eleven fifty-nine a.m.

A moment later, a blinding flash of white light swallowed the room.

I walked through the empty reception area and poked my head into the break room—no sign of Dr. Chet, Kricket, or Andrea.

"Hello?" I checked my phone for the time. It was noon.

The creepy woman had shaken me up, so I decided to set the book on Kricket's desk and head home for a hot bath to wash it all away. Wait. The book and cupcake were gone. Oh, man. I wanted that cupcake and... Wow, my face hurt like somebody coldcocked me.

Kricket sauntered out of the side office. "Hi, Sera." She closed the file in her hands and gave me a homecoming-queen smile. "Happy birthday."

I wiggled my jaw. "Oh...thank you."

Andrea and Dr. Chet walked out of an exam room. They had even weirder smiles plastered on as they wished me a happy birthday too.

"Thanks, guys. I came to return your book, Dr. Chet, but I lost it somewhere between my house and here. I don't know what happened, I—does my face look okay to you?"

The doctor wrapped an arm around my shoulders. "Don't you worry about that old book. I've got too many. Glad to be rid of it."

I rubbed my cheek again, looking at him as he chattered away and quick-stepped me across the waiting room toward the front door.

"Yes, yes, your face looks fine," he said, darting his eyes at me. "A little red, probably allergies. It is the season, you know. Pollen and mold spores are just everywhere this time of year. Nasty business, allergies. I've got em' too." He coughed a couple of times, but it sounded fake.

The doctor opened the door and pressed me onto the porch by the shoulders. "Now, you go enjoy this lovely day while we get back to work."

The bell made a cheery little jingle as the door thunked shut in my face. "Okay...well...bye," I said to nobody. For a moment, I felt like going back in but headed home instead, taking an alternate route through the farmer's market.

I passed stalls of freshly baked bread, organic honey, and gigantic floral bouquets. The sights, sounds, and aromas did a lot to improve my mood. Still, all walk long, my head was buzzing. The bizarre things that woman said had a ring of truth to them. Something about her was oddly familiar, too, although my instincts told me she was ten kinds of bad news.

Then I had an idea and doubled back; I knew who would listen to my story, and I might even get a replacement cupcake out of the deal.

CHAPTER

~ 8 ~

A Stunning Transformation

Earth Plane 2020

Dr. Desmond closed the front door and whistled as he slumped against the wall. His skin was pale, his breath shallow.

"Hey, both your patients are doing fine," Andrea said. "You caught Mabel just as she was slipping away. And that memory-erase potion for Sera was quick thinking, even though your nerves were already rattled. You're good in a crisis, my friend."

Kricket nodded. "I'll say. You snatched Mabel from the jaws of death and Sera from the brink of madness without missing a beat. Make sure you're around the next time I split."

"You got it. Just don't do it today, or I'll be the one flat on a gurney," the doctor said. He mopped his brow with a sleeve and smiled faintly.

"Where did that cat go?" Andrea asked. She checked the front exam room then looked down the hall.

Kricket shrugged. "Once he knew Sera was okay, he took off. Probably doing a few laps around town to burn off the adrenaline."

Andrea ran a hand through her hair, her eyes on Kricket. "So, who's going to talk with the Fire Goddess about this gap-year business? It gets more dangerous each time."

The Goddess of Air blew out a breath, her eyes wide. "My money's on the one of us who doesn't mince words."

"Helena," they said in unison.

Kricket smiled brightly. "Besides, Helena can draw up the ocean to douse the flames if Sera doesn't react kindly to the suggestion."

All heads turned as Mabel sauntered out of the back.

"Mabel Desmond, you look thirty years younger," Kricket said. She drew the vial from her pocket and shot it into a nearby wastebasket.

"Well, I *am* thirty years younger. I had no idea you would all jump in to snatch me back like that. I was ready to head home." Mabel flicked her bright blue eyes at her husband. "What do you think, Chet? Quite an improvement, wouldn't you say?"

"I can't lose you, Mabel. We go home together, remember?" He smiled and stroked her cheek. "And you are always beautiful to me."

Mabel patted his hand and walked to the hall mirror. "I hope it's not too obvious," she said, running her fingers through shiny brown hair, then she leaned in to inspect her face. Peering back was the woman she remembered, not the stoop-shouldered crone that startled her each time she caught a glimpse of her reflection. The hooded lids had receded, and instead of deep lines around her eyes, she now had subtle crow's-feet. Her cheekbones were prominent. Her lips were full—her face had color and shape again.

"Uh, it's pretty obvious," Andrea said. "You're straight as a board, you can hear—and I have to say—your girls look amazing."

Mabel placed a hand on either side of her lifted *girls*. "Thank you, dear, although you might have overdone it a touch…not that I'm complaining." She smiled at her reflection then turned to the doctor.

"Chet, after you shaved a couple of decades from yourself, we almost had to move. I thought we agreed not to use any more age-reversal spells, you know, so we could stay in this town?"

"I know, sweetheart. I'm sorry." His cheeks flushed. "I was just trying to keep you here, but my magic was amped up with archangel energy, and Sera walking in on us…we all lost focus. I was only going for a few years. Just enough to keep you alive."

"It's all right, darling. At least you shut down the spell when I reached sixty. The way you all shot out of that room, I'm lucky I didn't end up a twelve-year-old."

There was a beat of silence, then they all burst out laughing.

CHAPTER
~ 9 ~
Sherman Hill

Earth Plane 1999

There was a mahogany desk in Celeste Porter's office. It was massive, ornate, and better suited to the Queen of England than the orphanage director. Behind this desk was where Celeste held court most days, and it was where she was sitting now, editing a presentation she would give later in the week.

The comparative quotes and budget numbers she was dutifully compiling were just a formality. The board never denied any of the children's requests. So, come spring, they'd be staking off the north field for new stables and a riding ring. The director did a final read-through, closed the document, and gazed out the window.

Unlike most of her colleagues, Celeste Porter loved winters in Maine. She sighed, taking in the glistening landscape outside. The trees, the cars, and the low stone walls donned a fresh blanket of snow—making it hard to tell where one ended and another began. It was beautiful and still, like a painting, she thought.

Snowfall had always been magical to Celeste; to her, it was something ancient and far more mystical than anyone ever dreamed. She tapped a pen on her lips. Today there was something else at work. Probably a snow pixie up to no good.

When Celeste was a girl, her grandmother told her stories of fantastical winter creatures while platting her thick brown hair. Celeste loved the tall tales but hated the tight braids and colorful beads Grandma Nell weaved into them. They made her look babyish, plus they gave her an awful headache. Besides, Celeste wanted to wear her hair in an afro style like Pam Greer in Coffy, a movie she wasn't allowed to see but had done anyway. She knew how to navigate Grammy. Well, for most things. She never did win the hair argument.

Celeste had been at the orphanage for a little more than a year. Although the facility looked and functioned more like a posh boarding school than a repository for abandoned children, the stories of these little souls haunted her. Some wards remained until their twenty-first birthday, the age at which the private California foundation would no longer pay to keep them on. Still, that was three years more than most, and Sherman Hill provided leaving young adults enough money to comfortably settle elsewhere.

The generosity, care, and respect Sherman Hill's board gave the children was unequaled in the field. It was the main reason Celeste had accepted the position when the mysterious offer came along.

An attorney had flown several thousand miles in his company's fancy Learjet—right into the little Augusta State Airport—just to interview her. At that strange meeting, Celeste learned it wasn't an interview at all. The job was hers; a man she didn't know wrote her name into a will. *Her name* specifically, although she couldn't fathom why. He had also purchased the derelict mansion and four hundred acres of surrounding land, restoring the buildings and grounds to their original splendor and far beyond. The rest of his fortune was left for the care of the place and the children.

To Celeste's amazement, a six-figure salary and three-bedroom cottage located on the stately grounds was part of her hire package. The home was more beautiful than any Celeste had ever seen, let alone lived in. At first, she thought someone might be pranking her, and judging by the expression on the lawyer's face, he probably felt like the prank was on him. But now Celeste had a life she loved dearly, all because of her shakily applied signature on a generous contract—one that never expired.

The foundation's continuing support was even more surprising. Funding came in a steady stream for upkeep, grounds maintenance, school supplies, staff salaries, the children's medical needs, you name it.

The snow stopped abruptly as if an unseen hand cut a giant switch, and the room went still, with no sounds piping in from the hallway either. Celeste shuddered against the odd sensation then slid a file from the drawer to review her notes. She blinked at the page. It was her handwriting, all right, but she didn't remember writing this. One Ms. Simone Stevens would be arriving shortly with Sera Parker, born on October 31, 1998.

Celeste's heart seized. The poor little dear was only three months old. She sighed, thinking about the baby who would make the orphanage her home.

Minutes later, Celeste made her way to the main entrance, and it was then that she became aware of the unease beginning to take root. Somehow everything was a bit off its axis. There were no administrators carrying files, no ringing phones, no chitchat coming from the offices. Celeste found herself wondering if everyone had gone without telling her. Even her new security guard was not at his station.

She walked to the empty desk to ring her assistant's phone, but at that precise moment, a woman with a baby stepped through the front door. Although it was below freezing outside, neither of them seemed the least bit cold. And the bitter blast of frigid air that should have accompanied their entrance—did not.

It struck Celeste that this might be the most beautiful person she had ever seen. The woman had long wavy blond hair held back on either side with two iridescent white combs. Her radiant skin shimmered, and she had lovely blue eyes shielded behind thick long lashes. Adding to the overall effect, the woman wore a blue coat, blue scarf, blue gloves, blue tights, and blue leather boots. Even the baby blanket was the same shade of blue.

Celeste realized she was staring and nervously ran a hand over her shoulder-length coif. Still not like Pam Greer's—more like Diana Ross, the non-disco years.

"Ms. Stevens?"

"Yes, I am Simone Stevens."

The woman said the name a bit too emphatically, making Celeste wonder if it was her real name at all. "Celeste Porter. I'm the director here at Sherman Hill. Thank you for coming in today. I know the roads must be a mess."

"It's a pleasure to meet you…and this," Ms. Stevens said, pulling the blanket away from the baby's face, "is Sera." As she tugged the fabric, little squares of glass fell to the floor. The woman quickly stepped on them, and when she lifted her boot, they were gone.

"You might want to check the bottom of your shoe," Celeste offered. "You just stepped in quite a lot of glass. We might want to shake out the blanket too."

Ms. Stevens only smiled. "It's fine."

Confused, Celeste turned her attention to the pink-faced baby girl who was fast asleep. "Well, hello, Sera."

The infant sucked away at her thumb, her button nose bobbing to the rhythm, her eyes moving behind closed lids as if watching a movie only she could see. She sighed, smacked her little pink lips, and repositioned herself in her caretaker's arms.

The sight of this serene baby girl—whose life was about to forever change—broke Celeste's heart. But she gathered herself and met Ms. Stevens' eyes. "Okay. Let's get Sera settled in. If you will follow me, please."

They walked through the empty corridors in silence, with Celeste stealing what she hoped were a few inconspicuous glances as they went. The woman seemed at peace with the terrible job, and Celeste couldn't imagine why.

Still, there was no movement in the hallways and no sound coming from the offices beyond. It was like they were walking through a snapshot of the orphanage with no other life forces for miles and miles.

Once they reached the office, Ms. Stevens settled the baby in the bassinet near the desk then removed her coat and gloves, making herself at home. Celeste invited the woman to take a seat, but she wasn't sure an invitation was necessary. Simone Stevens moved about the place as if it were her office instead. "Do you have any questions for me?" Celeste asked.

"No. Not at the moment." Ms. Stevens swept her long hair over a shoulder and sat down. "Thank you."

Celeste handed the woman the clipboard of documents she had prepared earlier. "If you could, please fill out these forms for me."

Ms. Stevens nodded and began writing in silence.

Rarely did anyone drop off a child in person. When they did, most broke down in great heaping sobs, and Celeste spent a good deal of her time comforting them. Not this one. This one was handling herself with robotic precision, making Celeste wonder if she even had a soul.

Ms. Stevens handed the paperwork back in record time.

Celeste stared at it blankly. There's no way to complete all those forms that fast, she thought. However, on close inspection, it was all there. Every page complete, every line was filled in, and written in tidy block letters. Under the *Relationship to Child* header, Ms. Stevens had checked the box next to *Guardian*.

Celeste set the paperwork aside and shot a puzzled look at the woman. "Would you like a tour of the grounds, Ms. Stevens?"

"No, thank you, Ms. Porter."

Oh, really. Got a hot date? Celeste thought angrily, then realized she was pursing her lips and focused on forcing a smile. She had to remain professional, no matter how much this heartless creature was getting to her. Celeste found herself wishing Ms. Stevens would show *some* remorse, discomfort at least. At this point, she'd take visible signs of indigestion.

No. What Celeste *really* wanted, she decided, was for the woman to sob, to admit she longed to keep the baby but couldn't because of…because of *what*, she wondered. Because Simone Stevens was the child's only living relative, and she was dying, and Sherman Hill was her only hope. But no explanation came, so Celeste went right back to her *hot date* theory.

"All right, Ms. Stevens. I'll make a copy of your driver's license, and you'll be all set."

The license was handed over before the words finished leaving the director's mouth.

Celeste snatched it, put it on the plate, and slammed the copier lid too hard. Copy and license in hand, she flicked her eyes at the woman and sat back down to check the information. Good lord. Simone Stevens even took a beautiful driver's license photo. Celeste resisted the temptation to fling the ID like a Frisbee. However, she *did* use her thumb and forefinger to pluck the plastic against the table to make an angry little *snap*.

"Do you have any questions for me?"

"No, thank you, Ms. Porter. Is that all?"

Okay. Now Celeste was furious. No, that is not all, little miss robot. You are leaving a child at an orphanage, one I believe you have the ability to keep. Do you care to take a stab at expressing the remorse a real person would feel when flinging an innocent baby into the great unknown?

All of that was what Celeste wanted to say, loudly, as she pounded her fist on the table. Well, that and several curse words that were flooding to mind. Ones Grandma Nell would surely wash her mouth out with soap for even thinking. (God rest her soul.)

Instead, she offered a tight-lipped smile and said, "Yes, Ms. Stevens, that's everything."

A cheerful-looking woman wearing purple scrubs entered the office. "I'm here to take baby Sera to the nursery."

Celeste got up, feeling more than a little confused. She hadn't called the nursery. Had she? The director cleared her throat. "Thank you, Pamela. Where is everyone?"

The nurse ignored the question and walked over to the bassinet to coo at the baby. "Well, hello, beautiful girl. I'm Nurse Paulson, and I'm going to get you some warm milk. Then I'm gonna sugar those cute wittle cheeks and tickle those toesies. Yes, I am. Yes, I am."

Awake now, the baby gurgled, kicked her chubby legs free of the blanket, and smiled broadly, exposing glossy, pink gums.

Celeste left the robot sitting at the table and walked to the bassinet. She swaddled the infant in a few deft moves. "It's cold today, little one," she said, giving the baby a tickle under the chin. "But we're going to keep you nice and warm. Nurse Paulson has a lovely bed ready for you. I'll bet she even has a fluffy bunny rabbit waiting."

The nurse nodded and smiled. "You have a teddy bear, too, darlin', and he's got a big red bow and soft ears to chew. Would you like that?"

In the next instant, Ms. Stevens was at their side, as if she had disappeared from the place she was sitting and popped in from thin air. Blue light emanated from the woman's pale skin casting an azure glow over the room.

She touched Celeste and Pamela on the forehead with glowing fingertips then gazed deeply into Pamela's eyes. "You are a member of Sera's soul clan, and you came to the Earth plane to help Celeste protect her. Remember that now, lovely soul."

The nurse staggered backward, touching a hand to her forehead as if fending off a headache. Then she took several quick steps forward—her orthopedic shoes squeaking across the hardwood floor as she struggled to regain balance.

Ms. Stevens turned to Celeste and cupped the director's startled face in her hands. "All is well. You are Sera's guardian on the Earth plane just as you planned before this life began. A second child is also on the way, Celeste, another baby girl. Keep Sera and the second child together until they are grown. This is your mission. Remember that now, lovely soul."

Celeste managed a slight nod.

"It's all right, dearest one," Ms. Stevens said, wiping Celeste's tears with her thumbs. "Your soul knows what to do. Follow your intuition from this day forward. It will be your guide."

The glowing woman waved her hand over the room then vanished in a swirling wisp of blue smoke.

The orphanage's typical sounds cranked up again: chitchat, footsteps in the hallway, Marcia answering the phone in the adjoining lobby. Strangely enough, Celeste now felt love for Ms. Stevens, for

Nurse Paulson, for this place, for the universe, and especially for baby Sera. It was as if a hidden doorway leading to a magical realm had been thrown open wide. She also felt—no, she knew with every fiber of her being—that she would guard this child with her life. It was her mission just as Ms. Stevens had said, but she could feel it now; it had taken root in her soul.

Wait a minute, Celeste thought. The woman disappeared into thin air. Startled, she ran from the office, adrenaline moving her feet faster and faster until she'd reached a full-out run. She hit the entrance hall at high speed, her pumps sliding across the tile as she rounded the corner.

Celeste grabbed the brass knob on the heavy-oak door, throwing it open wide. Looking out, she saw the snow on the walkway was spotless. There were no footprints, no car tracks, no trace of anyone having come or gone. She rushed to the front desk, where her new security guard watched her intently. The man's eyebrows were sky-high on his forehead, almost reaching his hairline.

"Steve, did you see a woman in a blue coat walk by?"

The guard shook his head quickly. "Uh…no, ma'am. There hasn't been anyone in or out since I got here this morning."

He pointed to the wall-mounted television. "There was a bad accident out on the state road. The sheriff's office has traffic in both directions blocked on either side of our entrance, uh, rerouting everyone to the main roads," he added distractedly. "No way anyone could get up here unless they walked, and that's a heck of a long way in this weather. They'd freeze to death."

Celeste stared at the screen. A battered sedan rested on its side at the bottom of an icy embankment, and mangled guardrail lay strewn across the forest floor. The car's windshield was smashed, the roof and hood crushed inward, the trunk open. The scene changed to a reporter standing before a snow-covered roadway flooded with emergency vehicles. EMTs and deputies moved about behind her as she pointed to skid marks and the broken railing beyond.

The reporter walked over to the sheriff. Although the TV was on mute, the closed captioning gave the details; the deceased were newlyweds according to documents found inside the glove compartment. A thorough search of the area left the sheriff to conclude there was no one else in the car at the time of the accident.

But Celeste knew differently and put a hand over her mouth. There *had* been someone else in the car, the baby that was in her office now. She couldn't explain it, but there was no doubt in her mind. The glass on the blanket. Simone Stevens not leaving tracks in the snow. The mysterious way she'd deposited the infant and vanished…literally.

Celeste turned back to the guard. "Didn't you see me talking to a woman in the lobby, a woman with a baby?"

"No, ma'am. I saw you go into the front vestibule about ten minutes ago, and you walked right back in with a baby, but no one else came in with you, ma'am. You were real focused on that baby, though. I got a quick peek, cute little thing. I walked right up to you and said your name, but it was like you couldn't see me."

"You did?… I couldn't?" Celeste babbled. Now she was shaking.

"Yep. I sure did. And you just kept right on walking down the hall with that baby. Cute as a bug's ear, that one. Hey, is something wrong, Ms. Porter? Here, sit down." The man steered Celeste into an armchair beside the fire. "You look like you've seen a ghost. Can I get you some water?"

"No, Steve, but you can get me some of that bourbon in your bottom drawer."

"Uh, yes, ma'am." Steve jogged to his desk, returning a short while later with the bottle and a small glass. Celeste unscrewed the cap and took a long pull, waving the glass away.

"Yes, ma'am," Steve said, studying the trembling woman. "Yes, ma'am."

CHAPTER
~ 10 ~
An Angel's Kiss

Earth Plane 2019

Two decades had passed since Sera Parker had come to the orphanage. Celeste and Nurse Paulson promised each other they'd never tell another soul of the strange events surrounding her arrival. They agreed that doing so might land them both in a vastly different kind of institution.

No one ever showed up to claim Sera like Celeste thought they would, and for the last twenty-one years, she and Pamela Paulson had watched over the sweet girl like two mother hens. The second child came just as the mysterious Ms. Stevens said she would. Her name was Elle, and she arrived at the orphanage as an infant a few days after Sera.

A smile deepened the lines around Celeste's eyes as she remembered Sera and Elle together. As babies, they cried whenever they were separated. She and Nurse Paulson had to enforce strict rules on keeping their bassinets—later their cribs, then their toddler beds—next to each other at all times.

Once the girls were old enough to move into bedrooms of their own, she got little rest until she granted them a shared room. Thinking back, Celeste wasn't sure if Sera and Elle had ever spent more than a few hours apart during their entire time at Sherman Hill.

Plenty of prospective parents showed interest in adopting both girls over the years. Celeste turned down several candidates on instinct combined with official reasons she could document for the records, of course. Of the applicants she did approve, some changed their minds. Others mysteriously vanished after a few rounds of home visits. None had ever reached the point of taking either girl home.

Although she hated to admit it, Celeste felt relieved whenever a placement fell apart then guilty afterward. She had promised to keep Sera and Elle together until they were grown. That would have been tricky had any of the adoptions gone through. Most people wanted only one child, not two.

But if *her girls* had to remain at an orphanage through adulthood, Celeste was glad it was here. She often felt Sherman Hill's children were better off than many, even those in traditional homes. Their funding included healthy budgets for nutritious home-cooked meals, medical and dental needs, tutors, field trips, birthday parties, and extracurricular activities.

Sherman Hill offered everything a young person could want, save for the obvious. They had stables, vegetable gardens, elaborate playgrounds, a football field, a regulation-size basketball court, tennis courts, swimming pools, and studios for music, dance, sculpture, and painting.

The board—comprised of the grandchildren of a man who had made a great fortune during the industrial age—never withheld funding, no matter the ask. One child was interested in beekeeping, so Sherman Hill even had a state-licensed apiary and plenty of fresh honey for morning toast.

As Celeste drifted off to sleep that night, her ears began to ring. She covered them and squeezed her eyes shut. The ringing stopped almost as suddenly as it started, and Celeste opened her eyes to see a glowing ball of blue light in the far corner of the room. It grew larger and larger, spreading out and changing shape until it became a recognizable form. Celeste rubbed her eyes. Floating at the foot of her bed was an angel with long blond hair, flowing blue robes, and white-feathered wings.

No. Wait, it was the woman who dropped Sera off all those years ago. It was Simone Stevens. Somehow Celeste wasn't afraid. In fact, she felt peaceful, almost as if she were under the influence of some lovely drug.

"Hello, Celeste," the angel said, but her lips weren't moving. "I am Rachel, Sera's guardian on Earth." The angel's bare feet were hovering several inches from the floor, flickering in and out of view. "Sera must join the rest of her soul clan. Look in her files to find the place she must go." The angel moved closer and kissed Celeste's forehead, flooding her entire body with warmth. "Thank you, Celeste. All is just as you and Sera planned. Complete this final task, dearest one, and your mission is realized."

A water glass fell off the nightstand, waking Celeste with a start. It was just a dream, she thought, blowing air through her lips. Unable to get back to sleep, she stared at the ceiling for a long while. Finally, she threw the covers back, dressed, and headed across the darkened grounds to her office.

Once there, she searched Sera's records, going back years and years until she found a copy of Ms. Stevens' driver's license. But the copier had smeared everything—the photo, the name, the street address. She dug through more pages until she got to the original intake forms. They were blank except for her signature on the final document. How is that possible? Celeste thought, rubbing her eyes in defeat.

Dawn had broken, and the first rays of sunlight spilled into the room. Something odd was happening, though, a trick of the early morning light, maybe. She drew the page closer. The city and state—which had been nothing but black smears a moment ago—were glowing. "Leesburg, Virginia," she read aloud.

Dream or no dream, and trick of the light or not, Celeste knew Sera must go to Leesburg, Virginia, and she would be the one to get her there.

CHAPTER
~ 11 ~
Tobey the Shapeshifting Fairy King

Earth Plane 2020

Sometimes you need a little tough-love, and I knew just where to get a healthy dose. I stopped by Helena's store on my way home from Dr. Chet's office, knowing if anyone could put weirdness into perspective, she could.

At twenty-six, Helena is prematurely gray with blue-green eyes that dance like sunlight glinting off waves in the ocean. She's sharp-tongued, witty, no-nonsense (okay, bossy), and she's one of my dearest friends.

Helena owns Crystal Clear, the only *woo-woo* shop in Loudoun County. It's a mystical warehouse of mysterious objects (stones, tarot cards, wands, spell books, dried herbs) and several items I'm not sure how to describe. But the place does seem to have everything a modern-day witch might need to change the weather or turn someone into a goat.

Helena trades with Mike Plumber—magic for sweets—and most days, his confections are on offer for her customers. So I did end up with that replacement cupcake—complete with a red candle—and Helena crooning an out-of-tune rendition of the birthday song.

I felt sure Helena would say I was blowing everything out of proportion—call me *little miss sunshine* and tell me to *put on my big girl pants*. Or any number of Helena-isms I'd come to rely on when feeling ill at ease—no such luck. Her eyes got huge when I told her about my out-of-body experience, the witch on the street, and the strange reception at the doctor's office. She pressed what she called a *grounding stone* into my hand, insisting I keep it on me no matter what.

At home, I hauled the thing out of my bra and ran my fingers over the smooth dark surface. Then I quickly tucked it back into place, worried what might happen next if I didn't. Whatever that rock was doing, uh, next to my boob, I wanted it to keep right on doing it.

I'd come to realize that Helena's magic was strong. I'd gone to her for toothaches, cramps, muscle strains, and to rid me of a creepy guy who kept hanging around the diner. She'd give me a stone or an herbal tea, burn a candle on her altar, lay a hand on me, or blow smoke in my face while mumbling, and within minutes, problem solved.

To give my mind a rest, I curled up in the chair by the window and thought about past birthdays.

At Sherman Hill, the staff organized special celebrations specific to each child. One kid got an insect-themed party; Celeste went as a cricket, Elle was a firefly, I was a ladybug. I still have the picture of the three of us in our costumes, beaming at the camera with Elle's tail lit up. To this day, I can't figure out how Elle got it to do that. I'd inspected the outfit and had found no batteries, wires, or light bulbs, for that matter.

I always had a Halloween party. No one else at Sherman Hill shared my birthday, though. And when I was younger, and October 31 rolled around, the other kids dug in, calling me a *witch* and asking where I kept my pointy hat and broom. Afterward, Elle would soothe my hurt feelings. She'd said being called a witch was a compliment. She knew lots of witches, and they were lovely magical beings who safeguarded the knowledge of the ages. They could also transform mean kids into toads.

I laughed, feeling relieved I wasn't a witch because some of those kids would be toads now.

There was a light knock on my door. "Come in."

"Ms. Sera?" Julia peeked inside. I noticed she wore a conspiratorial smile on her pretty face. "I am not supposed to tell you this, but I must...you know your special dinner? Well, it's a surprise party. I did not want to spoil the surprise, but if it were me, I'd want to know. So I could put on the party dress and fix my hair up real nice." She shrugged.

I crossed the room and hugged her. "Oh, I'm so glad you told me. Our secret," I said.

Julia put a finger to her lips and closed the door.

I showered and primped, as much as I could stand, then slipped into an above-the-knee red sheath with a gold zipper down the back. The dress had been heavily marked down at the outlet store, and at the time, I couldn't imagine where I'd even wear it. Now I was glad I'd made the purchase. I slid into matching red pumps, also on clearance, and added a dab of red lipstick. "You clean up pretty well for an orphan," I said to the mirror.

It was a little after seven, and I felt I could go down now—the shuffling, giggling, and *shushing* wafting up from downstairs having died into complete silence. "Surprise," the guests called out in unison before I'd reached the final few stairs.

I caught Julia's eye and winked at her, then felt genuinely surprised when I saw how many people were crammed into the foyer and beyond. Dr. Chet, Braith, Andrea, Kricket, and Helena stood at the bottom of the stairs beaming up at me. I searched the crowd for Mabel, but she was nowhere in sight. Probably taking a rest on the sofa, I decided, although I hoped she wasn't sick at home.

Julia handed me a flute and clinked with me as Cormac offered a hand to guide me off the staircase. At first, I thought Cormac worked for the Desmonds but quickly discovered he was a family friend who had an enormous crush on Julia. Cormac often showed up at the house to fix something, whether it needed fixing or not.

Julia pretended not to notice, but I could tell the attraction was mutual, and I wished they'd just date already.

Dr. Chet cleared his throat and tapped a fork on his glass. "Thank you for joining us to celebrate this lovely young woman who came to us nearly one year ago on the Cardinal Express. As we know, cardinals are the messengers of spirit..." Huh. I didn't know that, and judging by a few puzzled looks shooting around the room, I guessed I wasn't the only one.

"And I'm sure you'll agree," the doctor continued, "that since then, Sera has become like family to all of us."

"Here! Here!" Stilson said. He, Cerphe, Todd, and Bob all raised their bottles of tea. The four of them were obsessed with this particular brand of bottled tea, and I panicked every time we ran low at the diner.

"Happy birthday, Sera," Dr. Chet said, toasting me.

"Happy birthday," came the echo, all glasses and tea bottles held high.

"And Sera, we've cooked up a little surprise for you." Dr. Chet glanced over his shoulder. "A little bird told me—"

"He's not kidding, dudes. He talks to birds," Braith shouted, garnering several hearty laughs.

A broad smile played on Dr. Chet's mouth. "Thanks for outing me, son." He turned back to me. "A little bird told me there was a certain someone you might wish to see on your birthday."

My breath caught as the crowd parted, and Elle appeared from the living room. She looked like a goddess in a white fitted dress, her long golden hair spilling over bare shoulders. I was so surprised to see her, I wobbled in my heels, but Elle stepped up quickly and gathered me into her arms.

"Easy, Valentine, you don't want to go down in a heap in front of all these people."

The warmth of her skin, her fragrance, and the tone of her voice sent a jolt of electricity through me. Okay. That's crazy, I thought, trying to identify this new sensation. It felt like—Nah.

"Elle, I can't believe you're here," I said, nearly panting from our embrace.

"I haven't missed one yet," she said slyly.

Confused, I drew back to look into her eyes. Her face was only inches from mine, causing me to feel some electricity in a somewhat disconcerting spot.

I made the rounds thanking my guests and hunting for Mabel, wondering why I hadn't seen her since the party started. Then I took a gander at the brown-haired beauty talking with our neighbor, Paige. I hurried over, manners out the window, mouth open. Ready to catch some flies, as nurse Pamela would say while she poked under my chin.

"Mabel?"

"Happy birthday, dear," she said, then kissed my cheek. "Are you enjoying your party?"

I was speechless. "You look... Uh..."

Mabel gave me an actor's headshot smile and swept a hand over her body. "Turns out I'm allergic to gluten."

My mouth went slack. Mabel looked decades younger, and I doubted a diet change could have this much of an effect. "Gluten?" I said.

"Oh, and I got my hair colored at that new salon in town; they're miracle workers."

"I'll say," I said under my breath, then took a long pull of my drink.

Andrea appeared and refilled my flute, shooting a quick glance at Mabel, then back at me. "Slàinte," she said, clinking my glass before chugging her champagne, encouraging me to do the same with a nod. I had so much shock rippling through me, I didn't need more prompting.

Braith stepped in from the foyer. "Okay, like everyone?" he said, pulling my attention away. "Earlier today, I unveiled a special surprise for Sera, but I think you might like to see this too." He waved people into the room.

Once we were gathered, Braith brought the screen down and steered Mabel and Bob to sit in front of the game controllers arranged on the coffee table. Then with all the drama of a ringmaster opening the circus, he swept a hand toward Elle and me. "Ladies and gentlemen. We have two national karate champions in this very room. Sera, tell them how many titles you and Elle have won."

All heads turned my way. I smiled and waved off the compliment, still marveling at Mabel's new face, new body, new…everything.

"Nana, Bob, please pick up your controllers," Braith said. Mabel let out a giggle as she and Bob happily played along. "Okay, dudes. Here we go," he added, and a moment later, simulated Sera power strutted across the massive screen and kicked the letters out of view.

"Why, that's Sera," Bob said with a smile on his face.

"Yeah, dude, and here comes our other champion," Braith said, nodding as a look of surprised delight crossed Elle's face.

"Oh, wow, that's me," she said.

Helena lifted an eyebrow at Elle. "That's some pretty good acting, sister. You going for a Golden Globe?" I glanced at my friend, waiting for her response to Helena's strange comment, but she just shrugged and quickly turned her attention back to the screen.

"Nana, Bob. Hit it," Braith said as demons streamed from every possible nook and cranny of the alley.

Both of them immediately got down to business at their new monster-slaying jobs, and a moment later, the sim characters began landing solid blows. Given their lack of experience in fighting demons, Bob and Mabel were smiting the snot out of the bat-winged creatures coming at them from every direction.

Braith dropped to his knees beside the coffee table to work several joysticks, and three more action figures walked on-screen. They each wore similar skintight suits, only theirs were blue, yellow, and green. "Here's Helena, Kricket, and Andrea," Braith said, then stuck out his tongue to steer these new characters into knocking out demon brains too. Now that back alley was a blur of kicking, punching, grunting, sword-wielding mayhem.

Mabel, who was thoroughly enjoying herself as simulated Sera (in red), turned and gave sim Kricket (in yellow) a roundhouse kick to the throat.

"Oof! She's on your side, Nana. Get the demons," Braith said, then slurped champagne as Mabel's score dropped two hundred points.

Bob was expertly controlling sim Elle (in white) and wiped out several demons in a few quick moves. He was steering well clear of his team members, and his score was skyrocketing. He'd racked up three bonuses in the form of angels, and when Bob's smokin' hot celestial army swooped in, the room erupted in applause.

I said goodbye to my last guest a little after ten, then hugged Braith and Julia goodnight and grabbed Elle by the hand. "Come on. We have so much to talk about."

Sleepshirt (a Tom Petty and the Heartbreakers concert tee that had seen better days) and sweatpants on, I had just flopped onto the bed when Elle walked in. She had on flannel pajamas, sky blue with woolly sheep springing over little black fences. I smiled and playfully tugged a sleeve, thinking she was still gorgeous, even in this silly outfit. "Tell me everything," I said, patting the bed next to me. "I want to hear all about the horses and your friends at the farm."

Elle laughed. "We just spoke this morning, Sera. There's not much left to tell."

"Okay, then. Tell me how long you and Dr. Chet have been planning this?" I tucked my hair behind an ear and looked expectantly at my dearest friend in the world.

"Well, let's see…"

"Weeks? Months?" I blurted.

Elle picked at a thread on her sheep-pajama pants. "Oh, a little longer than that…"

"How long?"

My friend cut her eyes at me. "Um, since before you were born?"

"No, really. How long?"

"So, you know those shapeshifter books we loved as kids?" she said, ignoring my prodding.

"The one where the little girl, Clara, is friends with all the woodland creatures? I adored those books."

"Yes, and Clara's best friend was?"

"A fox named Tobey, who was really the fairy king," I accidentally shouted, then covered my mouth and adjusted my volume. "Oh my gosh. I haven't thought about that in years."

"Right, Tobey, the shapeshifting fairy king." Elle searched my face. *"Tobey, the shapeshifting fairy king,"* she repeated with even more emphasis.

"Yep. You said that."

Elle studied my eyes. "Nothing?" She sighed deeply and rubbed the back of her neck. "That should have worked."

"What should have worked?"

"The mention of the books. It's a trigger." Elle's expression couldn't have been more troubled. She held my gaze as if waiting for something.

"A trigger for what? You're not making any sense. I think you've had too much champagne."

"Sera... You should recognize me by now."

"Uh, I've known you all my life," I said, thinking she might have lost her marbles. "Of course, I recognize you."

Elle puffed out some air. "I'm not sure what's going on, but I'm going to try something else. Try not to freak out, okay?"

"Okay...you're acting kinda weird, though."

She took my hand and lightly brushed my fingertips over her mouth. Her lips were warm and soft, and I felt butterflies in my stomach as I imagined what it would be like to kiss her. She moved closer, softly running her hands along my neck until her fingers rested in my hair. Without a word, Elle gently pulled me to her. My heart did a few somersaults, my face grew warm, and pleasure shot down my spine. Was this passion? Whatever it was, I desperately wanted to give in, let it wash over me like water.

"Sera, just kiss me. Then this will make sense, I promise," Elle whispered, but her voice had grown deep, and she was flickering, shifting in and out of focus.

Without thinking, I parted my lips and moved closer to her waiting mouth, her breath was soft and sweet, and now the sensation ripping through me was almost too much to bear. A moment before our lips met, I jerked back and ran my fingers through my hair.

"Wait," I said. "Let's just hold on a minute and think this through." About a million thoughts were ramming around my head, mainly having to do with risk and reward. I'd almost kissed my best friend, and if we went down this road, there was no turning back. Was there? I blinked at Elle, still wanting to kiss her, but a voice inside my head was clearly saying *no, no, no*. I knew it wasn't my intuition talking—that was telling me to go for it, loudly.

I'd never felt this way about Elle, or anyone for that matter. Oh, wow. Am I gay? I hadn't realized it until this moment. It *did* make sense, I guess. I'd never had posters of hot guys. I couldn't have cared less about boys or kissing or sex.

My head was swimming, and strangely, I felt relieved. This explained a lot. Even Cormac, with his movie-star good looks, had never done anything for me. I'd seen him without a shirt while working on our driveway, all sweaty and powerful with sculpted muscles that glistened in the sun. Even though I tried, I'd felt nothing and wound up thinking something must be wrong with me. Any other woman would have offered to bear him children on the spot.

So I'm gay and in love with my best friend—hot diggity dog. Now the deep ache and constant longing to be with Elle made perfect sense. I felt giddy, ready to shout my feelings to the world.

"Elle, I think I'm—"

"Wait, Sera. I don't want to confuse you."

"Well, it's a little late for that," I said, eager to declare my love.

"You haven't seen Sebastian tonight, have you?"

Now I was baffled. "Uh, no…but Sebastian always wanders off. Why? Do you know where he is?"

Elle put her hand on my breast. "I do…"

It seemed more tactical than sexual, but still. I smiled. "Wow. Way to go for second base without a warm-up."

She felt around the sides and top of my bra with her fingertips and stopped when she reached the stone Helena had given me. She patted it. "Good. You've got it on you. I need you to focus on that rock. It will ground your energy. Draw strength from it, okay?"

I wanted her to keep going and felt disappointed when she pulled her hand away. "What does *that* mean?"

"Trust me, Sera. Focus on the stone."

I mentally poured a bucket of ice water over my head and concentrated on the stupid rock in my bra. "Okay, done."

"You haven't seen Sebastian tonight—"

There was a flash of light as the person I trusted more than anyone on the entire planet transformed before my eyes.

"Because *I am* Sebastian," my *cat* said, blinking up at me.

My ears buzzed, my vision blurred, my lips went numb, then everything collapsed into darkness.

CHAPTER

~ 12 ~

Awakening

Earth Plane 2020

The early morning sun streaming into the room was intense. So I stretched with my eyes shut, noticing my shiny new feelings for Elle were still there. I cuddled the pillow, replaying every delicious moment of our almost kiss. Then I remembered her turning into my cat and laughed. That part was a dream.

"Good morning, sunshine." Elle's voice was like music in my ears.

"My head feels like somebody jammed a bunch of cotton into it," I said. "I had too much champagne, I guess."

"Not as much as you think. And you may need a slug of whiskey in a few minutes."

"At seven-thirty?" I asked, glancing at my phone.

Salacious thoughts had me hoping Elle would crawl into bed with me, and I rolled over to say so, then stopped cold. Dr. Chet, Kricket, Andrea, and Helena peered down at me from the foot of the bed. "What the—?"

Elle squeezed my hand, and it sent a flash of heat through me, but I quickly shirked it off. "What? You guys didn't invite the whole town?"

"Get dressed, Valentine, and meet us in the kitchen. We have something to tell you."

The gaggle of bedside tourists left, and I peeked under the sheets to make sure I was still wearing the clothes from the night before. That confirmed I whipped the covers back and marched downstairs in my bare feet, following them to the kitchen.

I arrived to find Braith and newly minted Mabel at the table wearing troubled expressions. Julia stood behind the island, an open bottle of Jim Beam in front of her. She looked more like she'd hung a hard left at *troubled* and kept right on going until arriving at full-out panic.

My alarm bells started clanging. "What's going on?" Even someone without my super-strength intuition could read this room.

"Have a seat, Ms. Sera." Julia nodded at the brewer on the counter. "You want some coffee?"

"Uh, no, thank you," I said, studying each face as I eased myself into the chair opposite Braith.

Before I had a chance to blast through the million questions swimming through my head, Julia thunked down a shot glass overflowing with whiskey. "You going to need that," she said, wiping her hands on a dishtowel and making the sign of the cross before retreating to the stove. Then she kissed the actual cross that hung around her neck and busied herself by aimlessly shuffling pots around non-lit burners.

Everyone except Elle took seats around the table. If they were about to deliver bad news—*horrible news* judging by the ominous feeling hanging over the room—I wished she would hold my hand.

"Sera," Mabel said in a clear, calm voice. "We are your soul clan."

"My what?" I asked. I'm not sure what I was expecting them to say, but it wasn't *that*.

"Your soul clan," Dr. Chet said. "We came to Earth with you… to help with your mission."

I sputtered and did a *you-people-are-crazy* laugh.

Nobody blinked. They just sat there with their eyes clapped on me. There was a long stretch of silence underscored by the faint sound of a lawnmower outside. "Is this a joke?" I finally said.

Wait. This was a birthday thing—probably a treasure hunt where they'd hidden little presents, and I'd have to solve clues to find them. "Okay, and what is this *mission?*" I asked, holding out my palm to receive the first clue.

After exchanging a few troubled glances with Braith and Mabel, Dr. Chet said, "Helena, Andrea, and Kricket are elementals...you are an elemental too, Seraphina."

There was that name again. "A what?"

The doctor *looked* serious, they all did, and I knew (from watching the train wreck of a community play he'd done last spring) he wasn't this good of an actor. People paid twenty bucks a pop to see him, and other pillars of our community embarrass themselves on stage. The director (Leesburg's top orthodontist) shouldn't have tried Othello with such a limited pool of talent. Still, they had raised a respectable amount for the local food bank. So, all's well that ends well, I guess.

I studied their expressions, waiting for the laughter and rounds of *we got you* to kick in.

Braith scrunched his face. "It's not a joke, dude. It's real. We thought you'd remember when I like showed you the game and stuff."

"You're an elemental like us," Kricket said. "I'm Air. Andrea is Earth. Helena is Water."

Andrea placed a palm on my shoulder. "You...are Fire."

It took a full minute to respond to that.

"Let me see if I've got this straight. My three friends are really Earth, Air, and Water, and I'm Fire? No offense Helena, but if we kicked you out of the group, we'd be a kick-butt band with cool, glittering capes and platform shoes."

My joke landed on deaf ears.

"Come on," I said. "Earth Wind & Fire? You know "Boogie Wonderland"..."September"...nothing?"

I laughed, still waiting for one of them to crack, but they didn't. Suddenly, my gut told me this wasn't a game. I opened and closed my mouth several times, then picked up the glass and downed the whiskey in one gulp. It made my eyes water.

Julia wagged a finger at Dr. Chet. "I told you it was too soon." She refilled my glass and eyeballed the ceiling.

"And I suppose Elle is the fairy king?" I said, shifting focus to my best friend.

She shrugged. "No. I'm Archangel Michael."

I blanched. "All righty. I'm still dreaming, and that means I can have another shot of whiskey." I knocked it back, extending a finger as I waited for the liquid—which tasted and felt pretty real—to burn its way down my esophagus. Then I slapped my cheeks. "Wake up."

"Not a dream," Elle said. "I am Archangel Michael, and somewhere deep inside, you know that Seraphina."

"Well, sure, and I guess you're my cat too. Everybody meet my best friend Elle, who is also Archangel Michael, and a cute little fluffer-butt named Sebastian." I felt a little drunk, but I didn't care. If this wasn't a dream, these people were nuts.

Julia placed a cup of coffee in front of me and crossed herself again. "You drink this now."

"So how does this work? This mission?" I asked, laughing oddly. "Oh, wait. I know. We turn into superheroes and save the world from zombies, right?"

"Kind of," Braith said.

"Demons," Mabel said.

"Oh, right. We save the world from demons. I knew that. Zombies are so last week." I placed my palms over my face and breathed into them, feeling a little crazy.

Elle put a hand on my shoulder, and it felt good. Not *last night* good. Good as in soothing. "It's the reason Ms. Porter signed us up for those karate classes. I needed to start your training."

"My training? For what? Oh, right. Fighting zombies."

"Demons," Braith said.

"Yep, that's what I meant." This was getting weirder by the second. "Wait. Celeste is in on this?"

Elle smiled at me. "Not exactly. You and Celeste agreed to it before you came to Earth. Her mission was to keep you and me together so I could protect you until you regained your memories."

"Okay… Celeste agreed to this. Uh, before we came to Earth. Right."

Andrea's eyes welled with tears as she touched Elle's arm. "Something's wrong. She's never been this far in, and now I'm scared. It's time for Rachel."

Kricket and Helena nodded their agreement.

"And who is Rachel, my fairy godmother?" I asked.

Braith perked up. "Oh, hey. She's getting it, man."

Andrea gave him a worried smile then turned back to me. "Rachel is your guardian angel, Sera. Would you like to meet her?"

"Well, why not? Bring on the angel, and what about a flying monkey and a talking car? Do we have those too? I think we're gonna need them to fight demons." At this point, I didn't know whether to laugh or cry. I should probably do both, I decided. It *is* the same release. Then I did just that as a blue ball of light flew into the kitchen and hovered beside Elle.

"Thank Goddess," Helena said, worrying her lip. "My nerves can't take this anymore."

The light grew larger and brighter, and I watched with my mouth hanging open as it transformed into a beautiful woman with long blond hair. She had piercing blue eyes, and celestial blue and white robes flowed around her in a swirl of air I couldn't feel. My skin tingled as the angel leaned in and kissed my forehead. "It's time to wake up, cherished one."

At once, everything in my field of vision collapsed into darkness. I saw the birth of stars and entire universes in my mind's eye—the creation, destruction, and reincarnation of Earth several times. I saw humans in their various forms throughout the ages, the rise and fall of civilizations, and through it all, these same people were with me. Their faces, skin color, and bodies changed with each incarnation, but I knew they were the same souls who were in this room with me now. They had always been with me, Michael too.

My vision returned, and intense love washed through me. All fear, confusion, and doubt drained away. I closed my eyes as Rachel placed both hands on my head, allowing me to feel her energy. She and I had always been one. I knew that now, too, as she spoke to me in low, soft tones.

"Awake from your dream of being human and know thy true self. You are Seraphina, Gatekeeper of the South Quadrant. The Fire Goddess, revered throughout the ages and across galaxies as a fearless warrior, one of eight sworn protectors of the Earth plane."

I felt her energy gently separate from mine and opened my eyes to speak to her, but she was gone. Slowly, I turned toward the place Elle had been standing. Even though I knew I would see the man I love there instead, I still sucked in a breath at the sight of him. "Mick-Eye-Elle," I said, pronouncing each syllable of his true name, written at the beginning of time itself.

I took in the six-foot-four Adonis with golden hair and the muscular build of an insanely hot twenty-five-year-old red-blooded male. I moved closer and cradled Michael's face in my hands as tears streamed down my cheeks. It had been too long to be away from him, and I felt relieved to be free of my mortal confines, like slipping off a tight shoe.

"Hello, Seraphina. I've missed you."

Looking into Michael's sapphire blue eyes was like gazing into the soul of the universe. Now my human life seemed like a dream, and I smiled. That's what we call it—*the dream of being human.* I turned back to face the rest of the group. "You *are* my soul clan," I said, laughing through my tears. "But how can you stand doing this over and over? You must want to slap me."

"Hug you is more like it," Mabel said. Then, she took me in her arms and gave me a bracing grip, one you might get from a three-hundred-pound strong man. Whatever she was on should be bottled and sold at the local drugstore, I thought, trying not to pant as air escaped my lungs.

When Mabel and I had finished our python-death-squeeze, Michael gathered me to him. His hug was soft and warm and filled with firm-muscled goodness. "This was the hardest one yet," he said, placing his forehead on mine. "You liked being this particular human."

Suddenly, I remembered we did this forehead *thing*.

Wait. It's called an *exchange*. The moment I remembered the name of it, more information flooded in, crashing through my brain in words and pictures:

> THE EXCHANGE IS A SOCIAL GESTURE IN THE SUMMERLANDS, OUR ETERNAL HOME; IT REPRESENTS UNCONDITIONAL LOVE BETWEEN SOULS. THE EXCHANGE IS ALSO USED AS AN ENERGY AND INFORMATION TRANSFER MECHANISM BETWEEN LIGHT BEINGS. THE EXCEPTION IS GODDESS, WHO CAN FACILITATE AN EXCHANGE WITH DARK BEINGS AS WELL.

Whoa, that was intense.

My face grew hot, and every nerve in my body tingled from being in Michael's arms. Okay, not gay then. I drew back from my forever love, which was hard to do. I just wanted to stay wrapped up with him in our human forms for the next hundred years. But something was nagging at me, so I reluctantly pulled myself away and asked Mabel. "I know how Michael and the elementals find me, but how do you, Braith, and Dr. Chet know who I am and what to do? In different lifetimes, I mean?"

Mabel patted my hand. "We're witches, dear. Always witches." She raised an eyebrow, and a mischievous smile formed on her lips. "We know everything." I felt a little jolt as more information rushed in:

> WITCHES ARE HALF-HUMAN, HALF-ELEMENTAL, A SPECIES CREATED TO BRIDGE THE ENERGETIC GAP BETWEEN MORTALS AND THE DIVINE.

Wow. That built-in encyclopedia was a kick in the head. If I'd had this in school, I might be president of the planet now. Mind-bank settled for the moment, I rested a hand on Michael's arm. "Oh, I'm going to miss Elle," I said, surprised by how good his skin felt. His eyes fixed on mine, giving me a zap to the nether regions.

My heart thumped wildly as several forgotten sensations fought their way to the surface, all of them punctuated by a desire to sweep those dishes off the table and devour the boy. It was probably the same restlessness one felt when a lover returned from a six-month sabbatical in some faraway land.

"Or when an elemental wakes," Michael said.

"Huh?"

He didn't answer, just smiled broadly. "Your memories started to bleed through a little last night; that's why you wanted to kiss Elle. You were trying to remember me, but the human part of your brain was fighting to keep control. We stood guard throughout the night."

"Thank you," I said, remembering things could go horribly wrong if the human brain hung on too long during the transformation. So, that's why they had been in my room. My friends were watching over me, ready to help.

Then another thought hit me, and I threw my head back and laughed. "An archangel in jammies…with sheep," I howled and held my sides. "And…and…you ate all that cat food." This brought a fresh roar, and I wiped my eyes, struggling to catch my breath.

Michael shrugged his brawny shoulders. "Hey, when I'm a girl, I'm a girl. When I'm a cat, I'm a cat."

Now everyone in the room was laughing and hugging and crying all at once.

CHAPTER
~ 13 ~
Faulty Triggers

Earth Plane 2020

The awakening or the champagne last night, or the two shots of whiskey I downed for breakfast, left me with a nice little hangover. Or perhaps it was the soul memories that had been streaming in over the last two hours. In any event, my head was full of universal knowledge and was throbbing slightly.

Andrea, Kricket, and the Desmonds had just headed to the doctor's office. Helena was back at her shop, and Braith was in his study working on a deadline for his boss. Michael had found his way to the front porch swing, Sebastian's go-to spot to lounge in the sun. Old habits, I thought.

When Michael appeared this morning, he was wearing a white above-the-knee tunic. Most artists paint ankle-length garments onto heavenly beings—to portray piety, maybe—but that's far from the mark. While painters and sculptors have never captured an archangel's physical features, they do get the swords, the battles, the demonic beasts, and the tunics. Well, with a lot more fabric added for piety's sake.

By the way, Archangel Gabriel is not female—as depicted in countless works of art for hundreds of years—at least he hasn't been for the time I've known him, which is a few billion. I've never understood where that came from, either. Maybe he throws off a metrosexual vibe because of his snappy wardrobe and impeccable grooming. Who knows? But if my buddy Gabe were female, Helena and the countless children they've had throughout the millennia would probably know by now.

I sauntered over to my mate, who needn't be shirtless and sweaty and doing manual labor to catch my attention. He could wear a potato sack with a bucket on his head, and he'd still be the sexiest being in the entire universe. For hanging out mortal-style, Michael had selected jeans, a blue T-shirt, and a hip pair of black runners. An outfit he'd pulled from thin air to blend in.

Michael isn't the type of guy who puts his pants on one leg at a time, as the Earth saying goes. He's not even a guy. Michael is light code, pure energy that can take any form on a whim. Now, he was in the vessel of the *man* I have loved for a long, long time. I sized him up, trying on a sexy walk as I got closer, but I'm out of practice, so it probably just came off like I needed to pee.

"I adore men's clothes from this era," Michael said. "No armor or chain mail or codpieces. No itchy wool three-piece suits either."

I tried flipping my hair over a shoulder, you know, like in a come-hither way, and nearly spilled hot tea into his lap. "Oops," I said, managing to slip the liquid back into the cup…with my mind. I'd forgotten I could do that. "Here you go. Codpieces, huh?"

"Yep."

"Sheesh, I'm glad I always come back as a woman."

"I'll second that." Michael held my gaze, his mouth curving into a swashbuckling grin.

Good lord. Why couldn't I have awoken on my day off? I sighed, drinking in the features of my smokin' hot mate. I would need several days of uninterrupted, ahem, *catching up* to take care of what I was feeling now. "You still like Earl Grey, right?"

"I sure do." Michael held the cup in both hands, breathing in the steam. "My favorite. You remembered."

91

"It's one of the few things I do remember."

Michael took a long sip while he pondered that. "Yeah, it takes a while. You'll latch onto little things like this at first. The bigger stuff will come. We have time."

"Time? Before what?"

"You always ask that. We'll get to it." He gave me a smoldering look that ignited feelings of, well, lover, sabbatical—gulp.

I sat down beside him and sipped my coffee, imagining myself ripping his clothes off right here on the porch in front of God and the world.

"Don't you mean *Goddess* and the world?" he asked.

My head snapped. "Oh, right. You can read minds. That's so unfair."

Michael chuckled. "Agreed, but I don't do it on purpose, you know. Hazzard of the job." He paused. "I like this shirt, so I'm glad you didn't rip it off me. These pants are mighty fine, come to think of it. And you'd have to answer to mama Langman if you'd swept those dishes off the table like you wanted to earlier." Now he was laughing.

I smiled at him, wishing I could stay and *catch up*. "I need to shower before work. Bob's expecting me at the diner—" I glanced at my phone. "Ooh, in thirty-eight minutes." I reluctantly tore myself away and headed for the door.

"You do that. I'll be here with my clothes intact, enjoying the look on your face when you realized I could read your mind."

I stopped and turned back. "And you have always been able to do that, right?"

"Oh, yes, but the real racy stuff came on the heels of last night's encounter. I like where your mind goes, Valentine."

I laughed, then studied him with my hand resting on the knob. He was even more handsome in his twenty-first-century clothes than his sexy tunic. The T-shirt showed off his muscled arms rather nicely, and I could see the outline of his abs, or maybe I just imagined that part.

Michael's face brightened, and he flashed a grin that was way too-sexy-for-his-own-good. Well, for Bob's own good. As tempting as it was, I couldn't leave my boss to fend for himself on our busiest day of the week.

"Thanks," Michael said. "I do try to stay in shape."

I let hot water run down my back as I thought about the preceding year. Celeste insisting I move to Leesburg, the Desmonds on that bus, the books in the library, this house, all an elaborate plan I made before coming to Earth.

Michael gets a download of all the triggers I choose. This time, *Tobey, the shape-shifting fairy king*, had been one of them, the entire phrase. (Because I love hearing my fearless warrior say bizarre things.) I'm kind of goofy that way and detailed in my planning. No wonder Michael had been so surprised when it hadn't worked.

Demons was another trigger word Braith and the others had tried without success, and I was a little baffled. One is usually enough to do the job. Two and I'm wide awake, like sixteen-cups-of-coffee awake. Michael's kiss is the barn burner, designed to reach me when word triggers would not, and I've never pulled away like that. Elle's form shouldn't have mattered.

I chewed my lip. None of the usual systems had worked, leaving Michael with no choice but to call in my guardian angel. Having Rachel wake me is the equivalent of pulling the emergency ripcord on a parachute. If that hadn't worked—well, let's just say it's like hitting the ground because your shoot doesn't open. But no sense dwelling, I suppose. My eternal memories were activated, and I hadn't gone insane in the process, so I decided to take the win.

Unlike the other elementals, I miss believing I'm mortal, and my heart aches a little after each awakening. I thought about my job at the diner, the one I was dutifully getting ready for now. Although I couldn't remember all my lifetimes yet, I knew I'd kept working in almost every one of them. Human employment is part of a system I set up to stay grounded long ago. I've had fancy jobs and not-so-fancy jobs; it really just depends on the mission and my mood.

Kricket, Andrea, Helena, and I were healers during the witch trials and slipped through without roasting or drowning. Because I did a spell to hide our village from the law, which was a teensy bit against the rules because I also hid the other practitioners. I couldn't stand the thought of them getting dragged from their cottages and burned at the stake. Or being drowned in a rousing game of bobbing for witches. I shuddered at the memory. The Puritans were an angry, scary lot.

The four of us got a little *Goddess talk* once we'd arrived home. It had been my idea, so I took the blame, reasoning we were simply protecting the balance of light and dark, but Goddess didn't buy it. "Those souls wanted to experience persecution, and you took that away from them," she'd said…sternly.

It made our magic-practicing neighbors happy, though. (All Grade-A human beings, by the way, not a true witch among them.) They weren't mad at us until they returned home. And mad isn't really the right word. Maybe disappointed because they had to repeat the exercise when they wanted to check that *persecution* box and move on to something else—like dying from some horrible disease.

I typically feel uneasy about the universal knowledge stored inside my brain. It's a little odd, knowing there is an invisible force that will keep unlocking information in my head until I am like Michael. Well, almost. I can't read minds as he can. I have a third-dimensional body and brain that prevents it.

I do know just about everything else in my full elemental state. Those memories come with me to the Earth plane, inside a microchip that fires up, well, now. And usually, when I'm on this side of the fence, inside what we call the half-life, I try to roll with it, suspending disbelief as each new memory comes through.

This time, though, there was something else, a dread clawing its way through my subconscious. I could sense a critical memory locked deep inside my mind-vault, and I wasn't sure I had the keys. I shut the water off and shifted focus to my soul clan, thinking I should probably make it easier for them to wake me next time.

Nah, I decided. What's the fun in that?

CHAPTER

~ 14 ~

Phoenix Rising

Earth Plane 2020

My transformation ceremony was to take place this evening at Dr. Chet's, and I'd been distracted all day. I guess I was expecting to see Sebastian waiting for me in his usual spot on the low stone wall. But when I stepped out of the diner and into the brisk autumn air, I found Michael there instead.

He was in mirrored aviator shades, a stylish brown leather jacket over a fitted gray T-shirt, dark skinny jeans, and brown triple welt boots. He had his powerful arms folded over his muscled chest, his ankles crossed in front of him, and he was smiling at me.

Yowza. That boy is all kinds of beautiful.

I took in his chiseled jaw, tousled golden hair, and his beautiful white teeth as twilight enveloped him in a surreal glow. Then I gulped down the delicious thoughts thronging around my head, and a clump of something suspended by a strand of hair swung into my chin. Oh, great. Pie dough. I plucked it out and tossed it into a nearby bush.

Wait a minute, is he doing that glow thing? I checked the location of the setting sun. Sure enough, that heavenly light was angel-made. I crossed my arms and scowled. "Hey, you're not my cat," I said to my angelic boy in bad-boy clothes. "Well, that's just disappointing."

"I can shift now if you don't mind wiping the memories of everyone on this block." Michael nodded toward the diner. "Including him."

I turned in time to catch Bob spying on us from the furthest edge of the plate glass window, hiding most of his body behind the wall. I wiggled my fingers at him, and he returned an embarrassed wave then pretended to adjust the blinds.

I thought about it a moment. "Wiping memories isn't allowed, right?"

"Not allowed. It's that pesky *free-will* clause. That's in your wheelhouse."

"Huh?"

"You know, the element of fire is *will*. As in *free-will.*"

"Oh, right. I can't break one of my tenets."

Michael chuckled. "Nor can I."

We held hands as we walked, and I found myself thinking that to the rest of the world, we looked like an ordinary couple. Not the Fire Goddess and Archangel Michael, celestial warriors assigned to protect the entire human race. I smiled at the thought.

"It was tough to concentrate today," I said. "I served everybody the wrong thing and spilled coffee every five minutes. Bob finally asked if I wanted to go home, and I almost took him up on it but decided that would be worse. Oh, he said I seemed *different* too."

"Did you tell him that's because you're the Fire Goddess newly awakened from your dream of being human?"

"You know it. And once Bob hung up with the asylum, we chatted about how the universe really works over coffee and pie." I paused. "Now he's seen you, he'll just think I'm acting strange because I have a new boyfriend."

Michael laughed. "If fourteen billion years is *new*, then sure."

I knew he was right; we had been together that long, although I blink out for big chunks of it. Then after each awakening, I begin to remember things just as I was doing now. Not Michael, though. He never dies, never blinks out, never forgets. He just keeps on keepin' on. I gasped, deciding to go for a joke. "That's all? It feels like so much longer."

"Ha-ha. Very funny."

I stopped, turning to meet my beloved's eyes. "How do I typically do it? Remain engaged in ordinary life...after I'm awake, I mean?"

"Sera. Do you remember your life before this one?"

I shook my head. "I know I have lived many times. I'm just fuzzy on the details. Why?"

"Just wondering." He tossed it out without any real emotion behind it, but I heard a tinge of sorrow in his voice.

"Hey, why haven't you kissed me yet?"

Michael rubbed his chin. "It's the way you woke up this time. In every lifetime, you kiss me whenever I try. You can't help yourself."

"Oh, so you're all that, huh?" I fluttered my lashes to tease him, although I was worried about that too. I still couldn't lock onto the reason it had taken me so many tries to wake either, but there it was, hanging over us like a dark cloud.

"I don't mean it like that," he said, not responding to the playfulness in my voice. "The fact you stopped yourself...well, you've never done that, and I don't want to risk hurting you." He cupped a hand to my cheek. "We should figure out what's going on before we do, that's all."

I knew he didn't just mean kissing.

In every lifetime until this one, Michael had fully awakened me with his kiss. He could do it any time after the celestial hands of the Earth-plane clock snicked into place on my twenty-first birthday. Usually, the reunion didn't stop there. Unlike me, the other elementals elect to wake as soon as they turn twenty-one—with their own triggers and a kiss from their own archangel mates, not mine.

"Thirty-one lives ago, you decided on having an extra year of believing you are mortal," Michael said, plucking the thought from my head. "Your *gap year*, you called it." He fell silent, and I thought about Sebastian and all the other nonhuman forms he had taken over the years to make the waiting easier.

In sharp contrast, I have a factory-installed libido blocker fixed in place until I reach my half-life. (My idea because who needs the angst?) But once it was off—baby, it was off—like boosters jettisoning away from a rocket ship on its way to outer space. Unfortunately, Michael doesn't have that option.

When Michael takes a child's form, his brain and emotions follow unless he steps out to catch a breath. The roughest vessel to inhabit is that of an adolescent male, so Michael sticks with being female then takes animal form for the gap year. Living as long as we have, you learn to navigate earthly desires.

Speaking of those, I had remembered something else while fumbling into my clothes for work. Something I was eager to act on. So I pulled my handsome archangel into a grove of lush evergreens and laced my fingers through his.

Reading my thoughts, Michael smiled and placed his forehead on mine.

Firing up a sexy *exchange*, I gathered the strings from my crown and root chakras, feeling the current making its way through my body. I allowed it to build to a steady hum, then pulsed my love into Michael. It flowed from me in gentle waves, and I breathed him in as he drank from me, the sweet scent of his leather jacket blending with his intoxicating pheromones.

Michael drew in a deep breath and his muscles tensed. I watched the vein in his neck pulse lightly as the essence of my being coursed through his body.

In the spirit of being an attentive lover, he reversed direction, flooding the current back into me. Michael's celestial energy made its way through my chakras like a sensuous massage. Weak in the knees, I found myself struggling against a deep desire to kiss him. We couldn't risk it, though, and I knew that.

Neither of us had any idea what might happen if we pushed my subconscious too far. Maybe nothing. Then again, maybe my memories would shoot out like a tightly coiled spring from a pocket watch and shred us to bits. I wasn't up for finding out, and I'm sure Michael wasn't either, given I could lose my mind if we misjudged.

After several immensely satisfying minutes, I collected myself, running my fingers through my hair. Then I shuddered as the last burst of energy reached its intended target.

What we had just done is the cosmic version of getting busy. It feels incredible, almost as good as physical contact, but not quite. (Another reason third-dimensional mass is so popular with the light-being set.)

I cleared my throat. "Hey. We'll figure this out. I promise."

Michael let out a deep sigh, a faint smile playing across his mouth, and he nodded, causing my head to move up and down with his. But I could see something else behind those beautiful blue eyes, still half-closed from the moment we'd shared. Was it sadness? Worry? Did Michael even feel lower-vibrational emotions? I couldn't remember, and he didn't seem to be reading my thoughts now. At least he didn't respond to my silent query.

Another memory came roaring in—words, pictures, sound, and vibration.

"Wait a minute," I said, focusing on building a wall around my cerebral cortex. I made it out of brick and mortar and watched in my mind's eye as it stacked itself at high speed, encircling the part of my brain responsible for producing thought.

Michael twisted his mouth in feigned disappointment as he traced my bottom lip with his thumb. "Well, that didn't take long."

I had just remembered how to block my hunky archangel from reading my mind.

We found the rest of the group gathered in the back of the doctor's office, inside a room I'd never seen before. I peeled off my jacket and had a look around. There was a glass dome instead of a ceiling, and the last rays of sunlight cast a magical glow around the windowless room.

The shelves lining the walls were filled with spell books, jars of dried herbs, and small bottles of essential oil. A fat candle sat on a wooden pedestal inside a circle made of pillows. I wondered what would happen if a patient wandered in here by mistake. This room was a dead giveaway Dr. Chet was a straight-up witch.

Helena laid stones and crystals in a grid pattern in front of each pillow. "To help you lock onto your elemental form," she said when she saw me watching her.

Andrea lit a bundle of white sage, bathing each of us in turn in sweet-smelling smoke. When it was my turn, she smiled at me while she worked. The Earth Goddess has a beautiful smile. Her teeth are super white but not blindingly so. And she always seems to know the right shade of lipstick to match her orange-red hair and topaz eyes. Today it was a cheerful hot-pink.

Braith burst through the door. "Sorry, dudes. Hey, everyone."

Andrea gave him a smudge bath too.

"Hi, son," the doctor said.

Braith's eyes were clear and bright, and he wore an outfit that made him look like a young professional on a job interview. I smiled, thinking this might be the first time I'd ever seen him not baked and looking so well put together. He noticed my inspection.

"I'm not really a stoner. Well, not before you came, anyway. The first joint I ever had was when Pop-Pop called me from the bus station. I got nervous and smoked the whole thing. When we met that day, I was so high I thought I might die." He laughed and grabbed his face with both hands. "I've been smoked-up for a year straight, and I'm exhausted."

I laughed along with him. "Why would you do that?"

"Weed blocks my magic. I was afraid you'd feel it before you were ready and do that brain-split thing, so I smoked the magic right out of me...every freakin' day." Braith's expression shifted to one of pure relief. "I'm glad that's over. I created a bunch of kooky video games stoned out of my mind." He thought a moment. "Well, the one where the zombie's only goal is eating a huge bowl of cereal is a big hit...in Japan, anyway."

I hugged him. "Thank you for taking one for the team."

All of us laughed.

"Braith's one of your anchors," Dr. Chet said. "He's going to help Mabel keep you from spinning off the planet."

"Spinning off the planet?" I asked in alarm.

"Figure of speech," Andrea said. It was her nurse's tone, probably the same one she used to tell someone they were suffering from an irreversible case of erectile dysfunction…or worse. "You'll be fine. We're here for you."

Helena snorted. "Huh…figure of speech, my tuchus." She turned to me with a witty grin. "Sera, why don't you light that candle?"

I nodded, walked to the sideboard, and grabbed a book of matches.

Michael chuckled. "Not that way." He tossed the pack back on the table. "Like this." He took my hand in his, directing my index finger toward the candle in the center of our circle.

I stood motionless for a moment, blinking at their expectant faces. Wait. I am fire, I thought, focusing on the wick. A moment later, heat traveled down my arm, tingling my skin. Then a spark escaped my fingertip, and the wick ignited with a satisfying *whoosh*.

"That's it, Fire Goddess," Michael said, and I noticed a hint of pride in his voice.

I aimed all my fingers at the candle.

"Careful!" everyone shouted in unison, but I'd already sent a fireball shooting across the room. It blew the candle, the wooden pedestal, and a chunk of fire-engulfed carpeting through the back wall. All of it narrowly missing Helena as it went.

"Sorry!"

"Oy vey," Helena said, smelling the ends of her singed hair.

Michael waved his hand over the room, resetting the candle and pedestal, and carpeting, and Helena's hair to their original state. Not wanting to set off another explosion, I gently lit the wick with just my fingertip and gingerly lowered my newly loaded weapon.

Smiles followed all around, and Kricket's eyebrows climbed. "How did *that* feel, Goddess of Fire?"

"Amazing."

I glanced up at the glass dome to see darkness beginning to swallow the orange and red hues of twilight. Although I could not yet see it, I knew it was a waxing moon, and the ceremony could not start until it rose higher into the sky. I also recalled (from Elle's endless lectures on the subject) this was the phase best suited to new beginnings, which I was undoubtedly about to embark on.

I thought of all the ways Elle had prepared me for this life. Moon phases, fight training, the way she lovingly spoke of witches and other magical beings. Michael (as Elle) had been training me since childhood. I smiled at him, and the archangel caught my eye and winked as he helped Dr. Chet wrestle a rather large book from the upper shelf.

The eight of us talked until nighttime fell, the three other elementals filling me in on details of our previous lives together and me piping in whenever something came to me. "Helena, you come to the Earth plane first, then Andrea, Kricket, then me," I said.

The statement got nods all around.

"That's right," Andrea said. "Gabriel woke Helena this time in 2016. Uriel woke me the following year. Raphael woke Kricket in 2018." She paused. "We're usually a year apart, but with your gap year, you're now four years behind Helena."

The three elementals glanced at one another, and I suddenly remembered the reason for the discomfort beginning to crop up in their faces. My *gap year* had been a sore subject for quite some time—but to their credit—they didn't express their opinions on the matter. Instead, the Goddesses of Earth, Air, and Water told fantastic stories of our battling demons, aliens, dark forces, and the King of the Underworld himself. Some I remembered vividly as they spoke; others were distant.

I didn't recall fighting the King of the Underworld and his Army of Darkness, for example. And the thought of that made me feel like a child in a superhero costume on All Hallows Eve; I might look like the warrior they knew so well, but there wasn't anything behind the mask to back it up. Not yet, anyway.

Thankfully, my friends told me we wouldn't be doing that in this lifetime; there was still a century left on the current light-reigning years. But my great sense of relief was short-lived as they added the need to stay in fighting shape because battles to control the Earth plane could spring up over unexpected events. I don't think they meant to share that at this point in my awakening because everyone seemed a lot less talkative after that horse escaped the barn.

"Oh, look," Kricket said, pointing up. "The moon has risen." She seemed relieved to be off the topic, and truthfully, so was I.

At Mabel's direction, we circled Dr. Chet to begin the ceremony.

After a few deep breaths, the doctor placed his palms together, moving his hands slowly. Up, back to center, out to the sides, center, down at an angle, and back again, palms together. His movements formed a pentagram of light that hung in the air around him. Once complete, the glowing star floated upward, casting a faint glow down into the circle. I suddenly recognized it as a symbol of white magic, designed to shield us from dark forces while we worked.

Dr. Chet took a seat on his pillow, and the rest of us did the same.

"We extend our root chakras down, down, down, into Mother Earth, anchoring ourselves to her in grounding and protection," the doctor said. "We call upon Earth Energy to work with us, through us, and for us." He raised his arms overhead and gazed through the glass ceiling. "We lift our spirits and call upon Source Energy to work with us, through us, and for us."

The doctor sketched an elaborate shape in the air with his finger, leaving a trail of shimmering pink and purple light. He pointed one end toward Kricket, the other to Helena, then drew the same thing again and used the two glittering shapes to connect the four elementals. He snapped his fingers, and the symbols began to spin. Slowly at first, then faster and faster—like a propeller—with each end growing longer until whirring light extended through our chests, reaching the walls. The room buzzed wildly as electrified air whipped up around us.

"Together, we build an energetic bridge connecting space and time, past, present, future. So mote it be," Dr. Chet shouted over the growing din.

The symbols spun faster, the whirling light making me dizzy.

Michael took my hand as the glass dome above us vanished, and the night air whooshed in, cooling my skin. I smiled at him then gulped down hard, feeling a shift inside my body as Andrea began to transition before my eyes.

A few surreal moments later, my friend was a fairy with hunter green eyes and ears sculpted into points at the top. She wore a golden crown of branches and leaves, and hair the color of emeralds swirled around her pixie-like face. A pair of shimmering green and gold wings unfolded from Andrea's back. Then the sparkling light swirling around her body shot upward and rocketed across the heavens like a comet.

Flashes of white light caught my attention, and I turned to see Kricket transforming into a snow-white horse with a soft pink muzzle. Her gray eyes were growing larger, emitting pure-white light that filled the room. The animal pawed the floor, her gray hooves shooting sparks.

By the time I looked at Helena, she was in her elemental form. Her shoulder-length gray hair now long and blue and moving as if caught in a gentle current. Helena's eyes—already an ethereal shade of aquamarine—had grown even more luminous. A light shined from them that cast a blue-green hue over the room. What looked like a bodysuit made of shimmering scales covered her skin in magnificent shades of purple, teal, and blue, and golden bracelets encircled her upper arms.

My heart pounded hard against my chest. It felt as if my rib cage was breaking open, and my insides were ripping apart.

"Hold the space," the doctor said.

Mabel and Braith placed their palms to face each other. As they chanted, white light shot from Braith's hands into Mabel's. A translucent bubble formed around us, extending through the walls above our heads into the night sky and disappearing through the floor.

A loud screech pierced the room. I was so disoriented; it took a moment before I realized it had come from my mouth. Suddenly, the skin on my back started to burn like it was splitting open. I looked over a shoulder and caught a glimpse of enormous red and golden wings unfurling behind me, crashing into the bookshelves, spilling their contents onto the floor. I struggled to control them, but they were going crazy, forcing Michael and the others to the farthest corners of the room. My feet burned, and I looked down, stunned to see they had transformed into red claws with sharp talons that shredded the pillow beneath.

"Hold the Space!" Dr. Chet said again, his hair and clothes whipping around him. "The phoenix will try to break free of the room. Keep—her—in!" he shouted into what had grown into a gale-force wind.

Braith and Mabel chanted louder still, yelling what I recognized as a binding spell, although it was hard to hear them against the steady roar in my ears.

Muscle and bone shifted beneath my skin, and feathers formed over my newly shaped body. My mind reeled as my eternal being broke all the way through. Suddenly my fear and pain vanished, replaced by raw power that washed through me like a hard-rushing river. I crouched and flew upward, breaking through the magical bubble that encased us.

Higher and higher and higher still, I soared through the inky black sky, flapping my broad wings against the backdrop of the crescent moon until the town was merely a spec below. I opened my mouth to howl, but instead of sound, flames roared out. I did it again, making the fire stretch farther as the night air streamed against my face and body.

A flash of white light streaked toward me, and adrenaline hit my bloodstream with the force of a bullet fired from a gun. I kicked off hard against the air to stay ahead of it. But I was slowing, and it didn't make sense; I was giving everything I had. My bones felt like they were snapping beneath my skin. My head was on fire, I couldn't breathe, and I was falling. Back in human form, my arms and legs swam through the air as I plummeted downward. I stopped flailing and closed my eyes, allowing the doom to wash over me. At that moment, I knew I was going to die, but I wasn't afraid. Even with limited memories restored, I knew surrendering to death would bring a swift exit.

I felt Michael's arms around me before I saw his face. The archangel's white wings moved effortlessly, commanding the wind as he held me close to his body. Overcome with emotion, I began to cry.

"Shh. It's okay, Sera. I've got you, my love. I've got you."

CHAPTER
~ 15 ~
William & Elizabeth

Earth Plane 2021

It was January, and the wintry mix that clung to our little town was keeping me indoors. Icicles hung from the eves, and road crews had cleared and salted the streets several times over the past week. I've never been a fan of cold weather, and now I understood the reason. Fire Goddess. Right.

I'd spent the months following my impromptu flight over Leesburg in the living room (next to the fire) in marathon meditation sessions with Braith. Today he'd brought me upstairs to work inside a space I didn't even realize was in our house. Braith explained he'd cast a spell on the door to keep me from wandering inside before I was ready. Mission accomplished because all I could see was drywall between his room and the hall bath.

Braith placed his hand in the center of the wall, and a door materialized before my eyes. Well done you, I thought as we stepped inside.

Four silk tapestries hung floor to ceiling, each one depicting a different elemental. Mesmerized, I walked around the room, mouth open, blood humming, and the hair on the back of my neck at sharp attention.

"These are us," I said, touching the finely stitched embroidery. I recognized Kricket, Andrea, and Helena in their elemental forms; they looked exactly the way they did that night at Dr. Chet's. "Is this really what I look like?" I asked, standing before the phoenix, a majestic red, yellow, and golden bird—slightly larger than I am in my human form. The image of, well, *me* was beautiful and terrifying at the same time.

"Oh, right. You've not seen your elemental form. Next time you're the phoenix, fly over some water and check yourself out. You're awesome."

A not-stoned Braith was a very different Braith. He'd stopped trotting everywhere, and his sentences were less question-like, more direct. Turns out, my roommate is intensely focused, more than a little punctilious, and surprisingly well organized. Apparently, his munchies had packed their bags and moved on, too, leaving me wondering what to do with the ten boxes of Fruity Flakes taking up space in the pantry.

"Is it always us who are the elementals?" I felt a little silly asking, but I honestly couldn't remember.

"Uh, yeah," Braith said, chuckling as he lit a candle. Then he smiled at me and rubbed his hands together. "Okay, let's work on conjuring objects."

A few deep breaths later, I had dropped into my higher consciousness.

It was getting easier to clear my mind and tap into universal energy. Holding on to it was the tricky part. But keeping a steady hum of divine power coursing through your body is the only way to pull objects from thin air or flash yourself around the Earth plane.

Flashing works like the cut-and-paste feature on a computer. You simply cut yourself from wherever you are and paste yourself into the place you want to be. You can also *flash* something up— meaning you've used magic to acquire it. These skills come in handy, like when you're desperate for lasagna at midnight, and all the good restaurants in town were closed.

Braith ran drills, gave me time limits, and challenged my conjuring abilities for hours. After failing miserably for what seemed like days on end, I finally managed to cobble together a water glass with my mind. (Yes, it was lopsided and filled to the top with more glass, but still.) The trick, it turns out, is combining your will with Source and Earth Energy to reorder molecules and dark matter into whatever object you're focused on. Oh, and I guess you need to be an elemental, a witch, or an archangel to do it.

A quick peek through the blinds told me the sun was setting. We'd entered Braith's magically hidden room at nine this morning. No wonder I was so beat.

Michael poked his head inside the door. "Hey, if you're up to it, I'd like to show you something," he said to me.

I smiled up at my mate, happy for the distraction. After several hours of streaming cosmic energy through every cell of my body, I was tapped out. "That would be great…if it's okay with you?" I said to Braith.

"Yeah, dude. I need a break anyway, but we have a lot more work to do on these." He wagged one of the pitiful water glasses at me. "Call me when you're done."

Disciplinarian, indeed. I saluted him. "You got it."

My drill sergeant left the room, and Michael joined me on the floor. He placed his palms near my head, then paused and smiled at me reassuringly. "It's a surprise, but I'm not sure you'll remember right away, so try not to freak out."

"Last time you said that, you turned into my cat."

Michael's flirty smile broadened, and he raised a brow. Even his teeth are sexy. "You'll like this, I promise."

I nodded and closed my eyes.

"Okay, here we go," Michael said and lightly placed his hands on my head.

A second later, I was traveling through what I immediately recognized as a wormhole. "I adore these," I said, knowing my archangel mate could hear me. My skin prickled with goosebumps as a shiver of pure delight raced down my spine.

"I know. Good surprise?" Michael's voice sounded far away.

"Great surprise," I said, doing a breaststroke through the brightly colored rings of time, snaking left and right in front of me. I didn't have to do anything to keep going. Michael's energy would carry me to the intended destination. It was just fun to play with the weightlessness.

"Please keep your arms and legs inside the wormhole at all times and enjoy the ride."

I laughed at his joke doing a couple of slow-moving somersaults as I moved through the tunnel.

A few moments later, my feet landed on soft earth, and looking down, I watched clouds of dust fly up around dainty ankle boots. They were soft leather the color of butter, with cream laces that ended in a bow at the top. My eyes slid past the shoes to the rest of my new outfit—an ankle-length blue linen skirt with yellow bands near the bottom, a white linen blouse, and white cotton gloves. I patted the large straw hat on my head and chuckled, thinking I must look like a character from one of those period pieces on the BBC.

It was a dazzling summer day, the kind that makes you forget your worries. The sun was bright with puffy white clouds lazily making their way across an azure blue sky, and a fresh breeze swept the heat away in little wafts now and again. I inhaled, breathing in the fragrance of the blooms and rich-smelling soil filling the warm summer air. Then I noticed a basket of cut roses and a pair of shears on the ground a few feet away.

The setting was gorgeous, a garden with an ivy-covered brick wall surrounding a half-acre spread. There were red, pink, and yellow roses in full bloom all around me, and a lion's head fountain on the far end gurgled water from its half-open mouth into a stone vessel below.

I heard whistling and spun toward the palatial brick home to see a man in a tan linen suit walking up the pea-gravel drive. He had a hand in a pocket, and the tune he was whistling was one I knew. Not now, but then. He regarded me with a breath-stealing smile, skipped sideways, and headed my way. His eyes fixed on me as he approached.

The realization smacked me in the face like a spray of icy rain. I had traveled to 1910, and I knew this place; I used to live here. I didn't recognize the man, although he acted as if he knew me well. He waltzed up and swept me into his arms, whirling us around the rosebushes until we collapsed in a heap of laughter.

"How are you, my darling?" he said, brushing a strand of hair from my eyes. His Irish accent surprised me, and it didn't make sense at first. I knew this house was in Northern California. But before I had time to ponder that further, he drew me to him and kissed me passionately, knocking the hat from my head.

While I was enjoying that incredible kiss, four children poured out of the house, shrieking and throwing their arms around us both. "Papa! Papa!" they cried in rounds. All four had reddish-blond hair, fair skin, more than a smattering of freckles, and Irish accents. Okay, so we were an Irish family living in California in 1910 and a successful one judging by the lavish surroundings.

"Well, look at you lot, all gussied up in your finery," the man said. "But where are *my* children?" He made a big show of looking past them as they crowded around his legs in a squirming mass of unbridled joy. "You fine-looking little ones can't be mine. My children are disheveled urchins who spend their days romping through the mud and pucker brush. Let me get a look at this stranger in the fancy dress," he added, scooping up the littlest one for closer inspection.

"It is us, Papa. We're just all cleaned up. Mrs. Newton made us take baths and sit in the parlor until you got home. It was awful." A pout formed on her lips, and she dropped her chin, causing her hair bow to flop forward. She pushed it back, and her face brightened. "We had to stay put a long time, but Mr. Cormac felt sorry for us and sneaked us some candy."

I looked past them toward the house and saw a dark-haired man in the doorway. It *was* Cormac. Well, imagine that.

I waved, and he returned the greeting, giving me that thousand-watt smile of his. His hair was shorter, and his clothes were different.

However, they were still impeccable, probably the latest fashion of the day.

Wait. This was one of my more recent lifetimes, and the man beside me was my husband, William. No, I called him Will, and these were our children—George, Mary, Ruby, and Alden.

"We'll just see about that," my incredibly handsome husband said to the overjoyed little girl in his arms. He inspected her hands and ears, then scrutinized her emerald eyes. "Oh, my goodness. It *is* you, Ruby. Well, isn't that just swell."

He placed her on the ground, where she hopped up and down, her ringlets bouncing with the movement. "Let's get some lemonade, and I'll tell you about my trip," he said, snatching his hat from the bush. "Alden, pick up Mother's bonnet, would you, dear boy?"

"Here you go, mama," the sweet-faced child said.

I was still me, but I was also her—Elizabeth—both of us occupying the same body. I knelt to kiss Alden's rosy cheeks and blinked back tears as I lingered on his eyes. There was something special about him I couldn't place—like he and I had been mother and child many times. I also had the feeling we shared a deep bond that went far beyond our earthly lives.

"And do you know what's in those?" Will asked, pointing at two hard-sided suitcases near the steps.

"What is it, Papa?" Alden squirmed out of my arms, sheer delight on his adorable face.

"Presents for you," he said, tossing the boy's hair.

"For me, too, Papa?" Mary asked.

"Yes, my darling girl," he said, touching her nose with his fingertip. "For all of you." Will turned to our oldest, fighting back a grin. "George, somebody told me you wanted a microscope. Could that possibly be true?"

George's bright blue eyes went wide. "Oh, yes, father. I want one, so I can see little do-hickeys real big." The boy looked excited enough to somersault in midair.

"All right then, let's go take a look at some little do-hickeys real big."

George yelped and took off toward the house.

"I also have something for you, Madame," Will said, a sexy grin lighting up his handsome face.

"That sounds ominous," I teased. Hey, I had an Irish accent too. It sounded odd in my ears, and I paused. Then Elizabeth took the wheel of our shared vocal cords to finish saying what she'd started. "Our little urchins clean up well, don't they?"

Will took me in his arms and kissed me tenderly. "I love you, Bets."

Minutes later, we gathered in the parlor, and Will and I sipped lemonade with Cormac and Mrs. Newton while the children opened their gifts. Mrs. Newton scowled whenever our brood got too loud but soon joined in the fun, seeming unable to help herself. Before long, Will and George had the no-nonsense woman shrieking in delight as she looked at little do-hickeys real big—including her gift—a lace shawl she'd talked about for months.

While the rest of them took turns with their treasures, Will and I went to the bedroom. Our bodies ached to connect, hungry for every touch, and I found myself wanting to stay forever. But just as we decided to dress and rejoin the household, I was pulled back through the wormhole, softly landing on the floor pillow in Braith's meditation room.

Michael leaned forward, touching his forehead to mine. I noticed his cheeks were flushed. "Good surprise?"

I exhaled deeply. "Great surprise."

CHAPTER

~ 16 ~

Archangel, Baby

Earth Plane 2021

There hadn't been time to ask the questions zipping around my head. Braith entered the room immediately after my sexy time-travel vacation ended, insisting we get back to it. After several more failed experiments, he finally gave up for the evening and released me from duty.

I flopped down on the love seat in my bedroom and called Michael's name in my mind. In the next instant, he was sitting beside me.

"Hey, Valentine. How did it go?"

"Not as well as one might hope," I said.

Michael gave me an empathetic frown, wrapping an arm around my shoulders. I folded myself into him, breathing in his scent. Michael smells fantastic, a combination of pheromones that drive me wild mixed with lavender and sugar cookies, maybe.

"Michael?" I said, lacing my fingers through his. "Why did we have those names—William and Elizabeth—and why didn't I recognize you? Don't get me wrong…it was a nice package and all, just not *you*, you."

"Right. You probably don't remember that yet. Not that I would know anymore."

I poked his ribs. "Hey, mister. My head is not your playground. I need to keep an air of mystery if we have any chance of making this relationship work long term."

Michael laughed. "Good point," he said, rolling his eyes. "So, mystery lady, when you time travel, you see our holographic overlays, not the being inside. It's like viewing a snapshot from that slice of time. You can only penetrate an overlay if you're *you*, and you're currently inside the timeline or if you're in the Summerlands."

"Not to sound thick, but why?"

"For our protection. So other supernaturals can't come after us while we're busy enjoying family life."

"Hmm," I said, letting that sink in. "Pretty slick, like a witness protection program for celestials."

"Precisely. We'd completed our mission and decided to live as a human couple for your remaining years—Elizabeth and William T. McKenna. We had a marriage license and everything." Michael chuckled, seeming lost in thought. "We got a real charge out of calling each other Will and Bets. We had those lovely children, and you had your rose garden. I even had a job."

"What kind of *job* did you have?" I asked incredulously.

"I owned a mining company with operations all over the west coast…metallic minerals, gold, copper, and zinc, mainly."

My brow furrowed. "That's not exactly a job… Wait," I said, horrified by the thought. "Mining is bad for the Earth."

Michael smiled. "Sera, I didn't bore and blast. I asked."

It took a moment to realize what he meant. Michael had asked Mother Earth for the ore, and she had given it to him willingly. "Oh," I said and relaxed my shoulders. "And what did *you* do…at this pretend mining company?"

"Not much. Just protected a large part of the west coast from real miners. Oh, and made a shocking amount of money and gave it to our kids. You know, like a real human father."

114

I laughed. Then my mood shifted as a dark cloud crossed my thoughts. "I wish I could remember more. I think it's taking too long this time, and I feel ridiculous my magic hasn't come back fully. I nearly killed Helena with that fireball."

"Helena's a lot tougher than she looks."

"No kidding," I said. "But really, why is it taking so long?"

"I'm not sure, babe."

I noticed a tinge of angst in his voice and pressed further. "How long does it usually take?"

Michael remained silent, and I shifted my body to meet his eyes. "Michael?"

"About three weeks," he finally said.

Fear plucked at me. It had been nearly three months. "Oh God, am I doing this? Am I intentionally blocking my memories? What if my human brain hangs on too long, and I——?"

"Hey, Valentine, don't do this to yourself. You *always* know what you're doing even when you don't think so."

We sat in silence for a while. Finally, I said, "Okay, since I don't remember that much *of anything,* why don't you tell me some things that will blow my half-human mind."

Michael laughed. "Like what?"

I thought about that a moment. "Secrets of the universe," I said, blowing out a breath. "Like what happens when you're sleeping, or you're with me, and someone else needs you?"

"Well, I can be in all places at once. I am, in fact, in many places now just as you are in your energetic form."

The moment he said it, something clicked, and I remembered. In energetic form, we are infinite. Archangels and elementals can split their souls into countless pieces. "We do something called soul parsing," I said. "And of the 7.9 billion people on Earth, some are humans piloted by souls, and others are extras piloted by Source until we need to jump in to complete a task."

"See? You remember a lot," Michael said, snuggling into me.

I'd recently remembered that archangels are physically incapable of lying, so I knew everything Elle told me was true. "So, is Elle still at the farm?"

"She is, although another soul is occupying her body now," Michael said.

My head snapped toward him. "What?"

"I shared Elle's body with a soul named Adisa. He went through Elle's birth. I stepped in the day Elle came to the orphanage. And before you ask, each time Elle was with you, or spoke to you on the phone, or even texted you, it was only me. Now, Adisa has taken over fully to help his soulmate through a dark time."

"Hmm," I said, worrying my lip. I sort of remembered the whole body-sharing thing, but it was a little jarring to think of light beings popping in and out of my best friend. "They're together now?" I asked.

Michael nodded. "The moment you woke, Adisa stepped in again, and I sent Elle back to Kentucky. To her, she left the day after your birthday and took a flight home."

I wasn't entirely sure how I felt about that but didn't say. What I did say was, "And what is the dark time?"

"The young man she's with is considering suicide, and Elle is there to prevent that from happening."

I felt glad the soulmates were together, but a troubling thought wormed its way into my brain. "Are suicides really punished?" I asked.

"You mean by Goddess?" Michael chuckled. "Nope. A grim fairytale made up by the muckety-mucks. Too many people leading oppressive lives were happily swan diving into the afterlife. Once it started affecting the coffers, it became a sin punishable by damnation. It worked too. Suddenly those poor people didn't think they had it so bad compared to spending an eternity in a lake of fire. So they kept plodding along, handing over their grain and livestock to church and state."

My mouth flew open in surprise, and Michael shrugged in response. "Desperate times. Desperate measures," he said. "Some souls choose to punish themselves while they are still experiencing human energy. The confused and angry ones hang around as poltergeists. Some get into a loop of their own making, reliving the last moments of their earthly lives."

"Wow," I said, thinking souls had the market cornered on beating themselves up when in human form and even afterward, I guess. Then I thought of Claudette and decided to query my all-knowing mate. "There was a woman on the bus with me—did you ask her to say—?"

"That I love you? Yes, I did ask Claudette to tell you that." Michael raised a brow. "I was there with you too."

"You were not," I said foolishly. If it came out of an archangel's mouth, it had to be true.

"Sure was. I've always been with you in this lifetime."

"You might have been inside Claudette's head on the bus, but you weren't physically there with me."

"Oh, yes, I was."

"Where?"

"You looked right at me. I offered you a snack."

My eyes felt like they were bugging out of my head. "The toddler?"

Michael laughed. "We prefer the term young human if you please."

"I thought maybe you were the super-annoying guy sitting behind me."

"Well, thanks a lot. Anyway, that's Rick. His wife left him and moved the kids to Leesburg, so he's gotta ride that bus every week to spend time with them. He's usually an okay guy. He's just mad at the world."

I screwed up my face. "If you say so."

"I do," Michael said, tapping his head. "Archangel, baby."

I laughed, then chewed my lip, thinking. "*Always*, huh?" I said, challenging him to a mental duel. "What about when Elle left for Kentucky the week before I came here?"

"New proctor at Sherman Hill. Mrs. Chapin."

"I wondered why she was always popping up. It freaked me out a little."

Michael shrugged and shot me a gregarious smile. "Sorry."

"Okay, mister," I said, jumping up and pointing my finger at him. "When I got off the bus and came to this house that first night before I found Sebastian. You weren't with me then," I announced, then added a saucy little shimmy to drive the point home.

"Hawk, deer, dove," Michael said.

"Huh?"

"Hawk flying above Cormac's car. Deer outside the house. Dove on your balcony. I win." He polished his nails on his shirt.

"Oh." I did remember the dove outside my window and sat back down. Michael wrapped his arm around me again, and I put my head on his shoulder. "Thank you," I said. "Thank you for always being with me."

"Just doin' my archangel duty, ma'am," he drawled.

The air shifted, and I tilted my head back. Michael had flashed a ten-gallon hat on his head and a piece of straw into his mouth. They both vanished once I saw them, and Michael shot me a devilish grin. I suddenly remembered something else. "There's no devil or hell," I said, feeling relieved for the entire human race. The way they told it, just about everyone was going to this made-up lake of fire on a greased pole, relegated there by God Almighty himself. "That causes a lot of unnecessary fear."

Michael blew out a breath. "Well, souls do like their drama."

I did sort of remember that too.

I climbed into Michael's lap, face forward, and laced my fingers behind his neck. It felt so good to be this close, and I found myself longing to reconnect fully in this life, in this body. I rested my forehead on his. "Let's just try," I said, not caring what might happen anymore. Michael put his hands on my hips. He scooted me forward until I felt his growing desire beneath me, causing both of us to suck in a breath.

"I want it too, Sera," he said, looking deeply into my eyes, "but we need to figure out what's going on first, babe. We shouldn't risk it. Not until your powers come back fully." He paused, and in his silence, I felt the weight of the universe on his shoulders. "Something's going on with me. Something unexplainable. I don't know why, but I just feel...like if I lose you now, it will end me."

I stroked his hair. "Oh, Michael, no. Nothing is going to happen to me. We'll be careful." He nodded and squeezed my hand. I'm not sure how long we sat there in silence, but the sun was coming up by the time I went to bed alone.

CHAPTER
~ 17 ~
Yggdrasil

Earth Plane 2021

Turns out knowing you've fought demons and fighting them for what *feels* like the first time are two vastly different things. That bit of unpleasantness was something I was figuring out now in an empty rock quarry on the outskirts of town.

"Sera, behind you!" Andrea's voice was barely audible above the shouting, grunting, roaring, and metal against bone.

I wheeled around to see a whole lot of angry teeth and claws barreling down on me. The demon lunged, and I jumped back. Not far enough because his talon caught my shirt, shredding the fabric and carving a line down my arm. Blood welled to the surface, the sting growing as the air hit the open wound.

Ignoring the human part of my brain (as it shouted at me to run away from the enormous demon), I swung at his torso. My blade connected, and a second later, the creature lay in halves at my feet before vanishing.

Okay, so these weren't actual demons but close enough. Michael had conjured solidified holograms for my benefit, like a live-action video game with sharp teeth. I doubted he'd let them kill us. They could, though, and that was all the motivation I needed to keep on fighting through the pain.

Sure, I'd seen these guys in Braith's video game. But there's no way to impart the feeling you get when seven feet of demonic energy in the flesh trains its enormous red eyes on you. It's as if your soul is being devoured by the hellish beast staring you down.

The three other elementals and I had spent hours wielding swords to liberate wretched heads from miserable bodies, and I was exhausted. But you don't get to take breaks during real battles, so I had to find other ways to keep my energy up. The threat of death was at the top of my list at the moment.

I turned on my heel to cut down three at Kricket's back. Got two, missed one, and the survivor bulldozed me to the ground, pinning me with his body weight. I struggled to breathe as he opened his jaws and headed for my jugular. Thick saliva oozed from a fang and dripped onto my face as he growled. Disgusting. Did they have to be *this* real?

Grunting with effort, I wrenched the dagger from my side belt, armed him away, and finished him off with a slash across the throat. A sigh of relief escaped my lips as he slumped against me a moment later.

"You'd better get up. Nap time's not for at least another hour," Andrea said as she battled her way past my head. The dust kicking up from her boots caught in my throat, and I coughed.

"Hilarious," I said as I pushed him off and sprang up to give a roundhouse kick to a beast stalking up on Helena. Unfortunately, all that did was make the thing angry. He wheeled around and launched himself at me, spreading those enormous bat-like wings. They were veiny, deeply unsettling things, spanning a good six feet on either side when fully extended.

Before I could grasp the extreme discomfort seeping into my bones, my gigantic opponent rammed into me with the force of a runaway train. I dropped my weapon on impact and let out an "oof," hitting the hard-packed dirt—fanny first.

While I was busy seeing stars, demon boy snatched me up by the ankle, raking my back ever so thoroughly over the sharp gravel as he did so. He took to the sky—with me in his claws—flying me swiftly away from my weapon. Uh, upside down with my shirt over my head.

Great.

I wrenched my shirt down, tucked it into my pants, and squinted at his enormous head, trying to figure out what might be going through his demonic pea brain. All he'd managed to do with this neat trick was give me the advantage. If he dropped me, I'd just transform and fly away. Was he planning to throw me into the engine of a passing jet?

Unlike fallen angels, this kind of demon is incredibly stupid.

I shifted into the phoenix, slipping his grasp as I transformed into an ancient flame-throwing bird. Dropping back, I blew fire over my opponent, barbequing him into a black powder that drifted away on the wind. Then I flew in circles, studying, calculating. Once I knew I had a lock on my targets, I breathed a steady stream of fire over them, careful not to harm my friends. Turns out, my aim is outstanding.

Minutes later, I slipped back into human form, grabbed my blade, and the four of us limped away from the simulated exercise with an array of genuine injuries. But we'd all kept our heads attached, so I chalked that up as a huge win.

Safely back at the house, I wiped the steam from the mirror, inspecting the gaping hole in my forearm where a chunk of flesh should have been. Helena, Kricket, and Andrea healed themselves before they left the quarry gates and encouraged me to do the same. I made some excuse about wanting to wait, but I'm sure they knew I was stalling, Michael too. Truth is, I wasn't sure I could do it yet, and I didn't want them to know. I sighed, pride goeth before the fall.

I had just finished picking up the bloody gauze and tape littering the counter when I decided to give it a whirl. Removing the latest round of hard-packed dressing, I focused on the wound. Flesh began rebuilding before my eyes, and a layer of skin knitted itself over the newly formed tissue, casting off a shimmering red light as the final stage of healing.

I inspected my lesser cuts and bruises and worked on those next. Moments later, I was good as new. I even took care of a few old scars like the one I'd gotten under my chin falling out of a tree at Sherman Hill. That's the beauty of returning powers. One minute you can't imagine how you're going to do something, and the next, it's automatic, like breathing—mindless and mechanical.

To prepare for pop-up battles to defend the entire human race (a prospect that still had my teeth on edge), Michael had spent the last several months training me. Thankfully, most of my skills had returned. I had sword fighting down again, and I could conjure and hold my elemental form as long as I wanted. I could also throw fireballs at will—without blowing anything up that I hadn't intended. And I'd flashed together some attractive and straight glasses, this time filled with water.

I laughed, thinking the only magic I could pull off at this point was to hurl a glass of water into someone's face. I doubted that would stop anyone intent on doing me harm, a socialite, maybe, if it ruined her fancy party dress. I needed a lot more elemental memory to come back before I could flash up a lasagna at midnight, or more importantly, pull a weapon from thin air.

Hang on. If I could heal myself, maybe other skills had come back as part of a package deal. I trained my mind on conjuring an object, and a moment later, it was in my hand; my broadsword forged in the heat of the sun at the beginning of time. I ran my fingers over the salamander engraved on the hilt—the emblem of the Fire Goddess. I laughed at the sight of it, feeling exhilarated. I was back in full form.

I spent several minutes sending my sword to the aethers and conjuring it again. After marveling at my new skill for a while, I had a far better idea and focused my mind on a different object, something a little softer. In an instant, it appeared; a short, blue silk robe. I slipped it on and headed to the bedroom, ready for the argument I was about to start.

Since my awakening, Michael had spent the days with me, but the nights somewhere else—a cloud, Mount Vesuvius, a youth hostel in Spain—I hadn't a clue. Although he'd left his energy with me, tonight, his physical body was staying with me, too, whether he knew it or not.

Michael was in a chair in my bedroom, flipping through a book. He was shirtless, his muscled chest, arms, and abs on full display. I took an audible gulp.

"I just love Einstein," he said, keeping his focus on the book and shaking his head. "He is such a funny guy. Hey. Oh, *hey,*" he said, catching sight of me.

I planted my feet and squared my shoulders. "Mick-Eye-Elle."

Michael's eyebrows shot up. "Uh, oh. This feels big." He put the book down, keeping eye contact. "You only call me by my eternal name when you're insanely mad at me. Or when you've just accidentally blown something up. Or when you're plummeting to earth from six thousand feet." He ticked each item off on his fingers.

"That happened once," I said huskily, addressing only the last one. "Okay, twice," I conceded in my non-sexy voice.

"What is it?" he asked, but something in his expression told me he already knew.

"My memories are back, I've fully regained my powers, and I am in control of my elemental being," I said, walking toward him slowly. This time I *did* look sexy. I was sure of it.

A besotted smile formed on Michael's lips, and he narrowed his eyes at me. "What exactly are you getting at here, Valentine?" I reached him and ran my fingers through his hair. Without another word, Michael placed his hands on my hips and gently eased me onto his lap. "I love you," he said, kissing me hungrily.

Relief and desire washed through me as our lips met, and a loud hum filled my ears as the elemental part of my being took control. I saw the birth of the Milky Way, and at the center of it, a seed that transformed into a tree with roots that extended downward through space and time. The roots twined and tangled, reshaping themselves until they had formed the earth, and I saw myself as part of that awe-inspiring mass. I was one with the cosmos—an eternal being made of stardust and light and the unwavering love of the Goddess.

I looked into Michael's eyes as he picked me up and carried me to bed. Our clothes vanished as he laid me down, pulling me tightly against him, and I shuddered at the warmth of his body pressed against mine.

"Are you cold, my love?" he said, suddenly aware of something other than the passion we shared.

"I'm fine…more than fine, I'm wonderful…don't stop," I breathed as Michael kissed my chin, making his way back to my mouth a moment later. He took his time with me, running his lips over my neck and shoulders, and whispering words of love and longing in my ear as he stroked me tenderly.

Unable to wait a moment longer, I grabbed Michael's hair and kissed his mouth, lightly at first, then with fevered intensity as we joined. Lost in the moment, I'd forgotten…in this body, I was still a virgin, and my eyes flew open at the sudden burst.

Michael spread his wings over us, quenching my pain by engulfing me in the warmth and purity of his unconditional love. At that moment, I saw the universe as it truly is—vast, infinite, and filled with a love so complete, it took my breath. Now I understood everything from the perspective of my soul body. I am eternal, mighty, a fearless warrior.

I made love to my angelic mate as the Fire Goddess, Gatekeeper of the South Quadrant. Sera Parker, the human, had become a distant memory. Like a dream, she had vanished in a wisp of smoke.

A few blocks away, the three other elementals sat in Helena's shop, drinking 'tea' and excitedly recalling the day's battle. All three had magically added a *little tipple*—without telling the others—and took long, appreciative sips while they chatted. After several hours of *just a splash more*, the three elementals were three sheets to the wind.

Andrea was about to slur something witty when the room began to vibrate. She opened and closed her mouth several times, staring at the rattling china. "Are you guys doing this?" she finally said.

The two other elementals shook their heads vigorously.

The cups and saucers began to buck wildly, splashing out a hundred-proof hot liquid onto the table and floor. The elementals shot one another worried, if not slightly drunken, glances as the vibration increased. Lights swayed overhead as a small table shimmied across the floor, kicking its legs from side to side in a magically induced cha-cha.

Kricket covered her mouth and pointed at vines growing up the walls, weaving their tendrils together as water poured down onto the floor. The hum grew louder until it rattled the windows with waves of invisible energy. Papers took flight, swirling around their heads in a torrent of parchment, and a spell page for Matrimony Cookies plastered itself squarely on Andrea's startled face.

"What's happening?" Helena's blue-green eyes were the size of beach balls and growing increasingly troubled as inanimate objects shot around the room.

A thick rope of raw electricity popped out of nowhere and whipped side to side like a downed power line, causing the elementals to shift in and out of their eternal forms with each pass. As Kricket turned, she kicked a wooden book pedestal to splinters with her back hooves. Helena's shoulder-length gray hair grew long and blue and wrapped around the horse's head, creating magical blinders.

Half in fairy form, Andrea spat paper from her mouth as she fought to control her wings, which were now smacking Helena in the face. "Hold on, ladies!" she shouted, putting hands on her friends to ground them all in Earth magic. In the next instant, the three of them settled back into human form. They locked arms, and as they did, the roof flew away, exposing millions of stars in the clear black night.

A sonic boom thundered across the heavens as a giant red comet ripped through an impromptu portal in the southern sky and streaked toward them.

"Incoming!" Kricket shouted, swatting spell pages out of her face as the comet grew closer. Andrea shut her eyes tightly against the blinding glare as red light crashed down around them, shuddering the walls of the shop.

Moments later, the cacophony stopped, and ethereal purple light oozed through the cracks of the backroom door. The three elementals sloshed through a foot of water toward it, and Helena yanked the knob, nearly ripping the door from its hinges. The pool at their feet shaped into a channel of water that sauntered down the glittering silver walkway to spill into a dry riverbed.

And there it was. What the three elementals had eagerly awaited since their respective awakenings. The mighty magical ash, hidden in the aethers for more than fifty years, was once again on the Earth plane.

The Goddesses of Earth, Air, and Water peered through the open doorway in wonder. The storeroom was gone, and a landscape was building around the gigantic tree before their eyes. Her branches grew longer, stretching up into the newly created sky. Her roots undulated, driving themselves down into the soft earthen bed she had just manifested all around her.

Blue light emanated from the center of her ancient trunk, swirling around and around until it was a doorway big enough to step through. Beyond the opening stood a beautiful meadow bathed in the light of three glowing suns.

"Girls?" Andrea said. "Yggdrasil's back."

Without another word, they ran down the glittering walkway, took the translucent bridge in a single bound, and sprang through the portal into the world beyond.

CHAPTER
~ 18 ~
The Womb of Creation

Earth Plane 2021

Archangels don't need any sleep, and awakened elementals need little. Maybe a quick nap every few days, and that's about it. I guess I was in the habit, though, because I had slept like the dead for—I glanced at my phone—ten hours? I yawned and peeked over Michael's shoulder. He was still out cold, and I smiled at him, remembering we had always done this. Sleep is a beautiful invention. Hats off to the Goddess.

Michael and I were planning to head to Helena's shop later this morning, answering a text I'd received from her in the night. *Come first thing tomorrow*, she'd typed, and she'd included a lot of exclamation marks and surprise emojis behind the command.

The Water Goddess could have sent a pterodactyl with a calligraphed invitation in its mouth if she wanted. But Helena adores texting; it's one of her favorite things about this period. *Magic for Humans*, she'd called it during our last visit to the twenty-first. Excessive punctuation aside, I needed java before venturing out. So she would just have to wait until I'd had enough caffeine to form complete sentences. I quietly slipped into jeans and a T-shirt and padded downstairs to the kitchen.

When I arrived, Braith was sitting at the island with his nose pressed in the newspaper, and he was wearing glasses. Funny, I'd never noticed him in those before.

"Morning, Ms. Sera," Julia said. "You would like the coffee?"

"Oh, yes, but I'll get it."

"You sit. I'll get it for you."

"Thank you," I said, tapping two fingers on my inner arm as I had a seat, making her laugh. I could have flashed coffee, a full breakfast, or an elephant to my room, but this was better. Elemental or not, this was my family, and I loved being with them in this way.

Julia gave me a knowing grin. "You're different," she said before heading off.

Braith lowered his paper. "Dude," he said, peering at me from behind thick, black frames. (They made him look older and much less dude-like.) "While you were sleeping, one heck of a storm ripped through town. A crazy-big red comet streaked across the sky too."

Julia raised her eyebrows as she placed a steaming cup of coffee in front of me. It smelled delicious, and I immediately took a sip.

"For the witch with all the hocus-pocus, you are not too bright about the romance," she said. Then she caught my eye and winked. I giggled. (I'm not trying to be cute here. I actually giggled.)

Michael entered the room whistling. "Good morning, people I love with all my heart."

I knew he meant that in the literal sense.

Michael loves everyone with a passion and intensity you wouldn't think possible. His love never turns off, never goes into screen-saver mode. It is constant, unconditional, and flows from every pore of his celestial body. Humans can feel it, even though they don't know what it is. Typically, they just stare at him with a dazed grin until somebody breaks the ice or throws a bucket of cold water.

Julia beamed at Michael in this way as he waltzed her around the kitchen. Although she's used to Michael's love energy, he was *really* pumped, and Julia had surrendered herself to that silly-happy feeling others get when he's around.

The arc shot a sexy grin my way. "Hey, Valentine, you're looking particularly beautiful today," he said as they took another turn around the room. I went a little weak in the knees as I watched his muscles flex underneath his thin T-shirt. Perhaps he needs to be dragged back to bed, I thought, then swallowed the coffee I'd been holding in my mouth.

"Dude. I don't think I've ever seen you this happy," Braith said to the archangel. "Good for you, man."

Michael stopped the dance and bowed to Julia as he gently deposited her into a chair. (She had devolved into a puddle of girlish mush, and that's saying something for the Bolivian beauty who is not easily wowed.) Then he went down on a knee to gaze into my eyes. "And what about you, my love? You slipped out of bed before I had a chance to say *good morning*." He arched a brow. "In fact, I think you need to greet the day properly."

"I do, huh?"

"Yep. I'm pretty sure you do. You know, start the day off on the right foot as they say."

Before he had time to utter another cheerful word, I'd flashed us back to the bedroom.

It was noon when Michael and I got to Helena's shop. We stepped through the door to find her, Andrea, and Kricket lined up near the front, grinning like circus monkeys.

"Well, hello, kids. How'd ya sleep?" Helena asked. "Wanna see what I got?" Without waiting for a response, the water elemental turned and nearly skipped down the hallway. We followed on her heels, and I almost ran my friend down as she stopped short in front of the storage room.

Helena grinned triumphantly as Kricket and Andrea bounced around a bit. I laughed, thinking all three of them were about two shakes from doing cartwheels across the floor, then Helena swung the door open with a "Ta-da!"

One glance was all it took to see the reason for their high spirits. The small room, typically crammed with metal shelves and inventory, had vanished, and in its place was—well—the great outdoors, sort of. What I was looking at was not on Earth.

A pink and purple sky streaked with grayish-white clouds loomed overhead, and thousands of fireflies blinked out a magical light show. grass, wildflowers, and moss-covered rocks made up the landscape below. Two hillocks sloped toward each other, and in front of them, inside a rounded bed of twinkling soil, stood the mighty ash with her gigantic trunk and massive, green-leafed canopy.

"Yggdrasil," I said, already moving along the glittering silver walkway that led to my ancient friend.

I crossed the translucent bridge, peering over the sides at the turquoise stream. An otherworldly glow emanated from the water flowing over thick and tangled roots like a magically lit swimming pool at night. I stepped onto the sparkling soil near the base of her trunk, my heart pounding in my ears.

"When did she arrive?" I heard Michael ask them, and the question struck me as a bit odd. He didn't know, and that should have been my first clue.

Helena snorted. "You mean riding in on Sera's comet like a bat out of hell. Nearly shook this place to the ground."

And there was the second one.

"Hello, old friend," I said, laying a hand on Yggdrasil's massive trunk as the happy chatter continued behind me. The moment we touched, a new memory came crashing in, this one about as appealing as the stench of rotting meat. I stumbled forward and clapped a hand to my mouth as tears sprang to my eyes. I'd spent thirty years in the Underworld...with Mortegol...as his mate?

Touching Yggdrasil was a tactile trigger, the celestial key that unlocked the secret package Michael and I had been so afraid of turning loose. Now I knew the reason I stopped myself from kissing Elle that night in my room. I was a traitor to my realm, a light-being turned dark. This version of me didn't want to remember, but I had installed that second memory package to make sure I did.

130

"Hey," Helena said. "What are you saying to that tree? Did you ask where she's been the last fifty-four years? Inquiring minds, you know."

I didn't respond even though I knew where Yggdrasil had been, I had hidden her, and we weren't allowed to do that. I had also programmed my comet to bring her to the Earth plane only after Michael kissed me in this lifetime. I hadn't wanted any of them following me to the Underworld using Yggdrasil's memory as a heat map.

Helena huffed. "Oh, never mind. I'll put the pot on."

I stayed a few minutes more, long enough to collect myself and slap on a happy face. Eventually, I found my courage and walked back down the path, joining the others as Helena's magical tea arrived. I'd forgotten until this moment that *putting the pot on* for Helena means flashing up a feast. Cakes, pies, cookies, fine china, and sterling silver on a linen-draped table. It also means transforming her surroundings into an English garden, Helena's sacred space.

Now we were under a trellis draped in climbing roses that shaded us from the magically created sun. Soft-pink peonies, yellow primrose, and purple phlox had filled in around us, and bees lazily made their way from petal to petal. None of it was real, of course. If you didn't remember where the walls were, you'd walk right into them.

Helena sighed deeply. "It's so much more fun when we're all awake. This is nice," she said as her conjured bluebird chirped out a cheerful little tune. We took seats, and I smiled at my friends, hoping they couldn't see through it.

"Have any of you stepped through?" Michael asked.

"We did," Kricket said, tossing her head toward Andrea and Helena. "We went home and spent three glorious months."

Andrea turned to me, mistaking my silence as a lapse in memory. "We don't remember the details of home because of our Earth-Plane forms. It's wonderful, rediscovering everything like it's the first time."

"It's these meat brains," Helena said, pointing to her head, reminding me she has never enjoyed being human as much as I do. "They've got governors on them. I'd like to rip mine out and send it to the bottom of the ocean." She paused and screwed up her face. "And let a shark eat it."

Kricket grimaced. "Oh, thanks for the image."

"I find the human brain miraculous," Andrea said.

Michael nodded his agreement. "I love everything about mortals, their brains, their emotions, their drive. They are magical beings, magnificent in their complexity."

"We know. We know," Helena said. She lightly pushed his head.

Helena enjoys ribbing Michael about his love of humans, but truthfully, she loves them just as much. She's given her life for them countless times and will do it again without hesitation.

I felt another wave of tears struggling to the surface and forced them back down. I wanted nothing more than to be awake and happy about it, just one of the gang. But I had betrayed Michael, then reconnected with him as if I hadn't. Why didn't I craft that spell so the memory would come back before we—?

My heart clogged with guilt. I know how *specific* magic needs to be. You must put every ingredient into a spell with precise measurement, laser-sharp intent, ironclad belief, and perfect tone. Otherwise, the results can slide in dirty or sideways. This was both.

Helena and Michael continued their playful banter, then Helena stopped abruptly and turned to me. "Honey, are you okay?"

I nodded. "I'm fine," I said. "Just a few memories coming in, gumming up the stem cells." I laughed, but it sounded hollow in my ears.

I caught the water elemental's raised eyebrows. "Sera, do you remember the life before this one?" she asked, blowing on her tea. My skin prickled as Helena's bluebird landed on her shoulder, cocked his head, and chirped at me accusingly. Or maybe that was my imagination at work. Either way, it made me suck in a breath.

"No, not yet," I said (lying through my teeth), then sipped my drink, thinking of the right thing to say next. These three knew me, but more importantly, I knew *them*. Something in the way she asked, at this precise moment, in that carefree way of hers told me I was on the edge of a steep cliff with my toes hanging over the side. "Why do you ask?"

Helena studied me. "Well, during our last lifetimes, you vanished for thirty years, and none of us know where you went. You left the Earth plane in 1967, and when you didn't show up in the Summerlands right away, we searched everywhere. The three of us didn't see you again until you arrived in Leesburg last year. That's never happened."

I did my best to look confused. "I don't have any idea. I wish I did." I paused, thinking a change in subject was in order, and decided to go for the big guns. "The Summerlands?"

Kricket leaned in and placed a hand on mine. "That's our home, the place humans call heaven," she said. "When elementals die, we go straight to the Summerlands to plan our next incarnation, but you didn't last time."

Well, *that* didn't work.

"This one went berserk," Helena said, hooking a thumb at Michael. "He nearly destroyed the Earth plane searching for you."

"Michael, do you know where I went during that lifetime?" Since we were still doggedly on the painful subject, I needed to know if he suspected anything.

Michael shook his head and shrugged. "No, Sera. I don't have any idea."

My heart ached, but I couldn't tell him without learning the reason I'd done it. Instead, I kept going, stretching the lie further. "I want to remember."

"You will, honey," Andrea said, patting my hand and smiling sweetly. "Give it some time."

Helena peered at me over her cup. "And maybe you'll remember why that tree came roaring in on your fire comet."

She smelled a rat—a big, fat, juicy one. I tried hard to keep my face neutral, but I'm not sure I pulled it off.

We sat in silence for several painful moments. Then I heard someone calling my name from far away, but the sound was in my head, not my ears, and I recognized the voice.

"Gabe needs you," Michael said. He'd heard the call too. His radiant smile widened, and his eyes were filled with such undying love, I almost cried. "Go on. I'll keep your tea hot," he said with a wink.

Getting up from the table, I nodded. "Okay, be right back," I said, then headed down the glittering path—which now looked like it cut through a lavender field. Yggdrasil's portal shimmered open, and I stepped through into the darkness, into the Womb of Creation, blacker than the blackest starless night. The door closed behind me, and I let out the breath I'd been holding, grateful for the solitude.

No time passes here, so to my friends, it would seem as though I stepped in and right back out again, no matter how long I stayed. I had no idea what I would say to the others when I finally did come out. But I wasn't about to tell them Yggdrasil had been hiding in the aethers for five decades at my request. Or the reason I'd asked her to do it.

CHAPTER
~ 19 ~
Lieutenant Sam Rodgers

Womb of Creation, Present Moment

The horrible memories had slicked their way in like an oil spill, covering my happy thoughts of last night, and twice this morning, in a greasy black ooze. I had installed a second memory package to force myself to search for answers in this life. But now, I was confused, ashamed, and sickened by the prospect of learning what else might be lurking inside the truth.

Adding to my anxiety were huge chunks of time still missing from those three decades spent in the Underworld. A trip to the Summerlands was the only way to learn what they were. Figuring out my reason for going there in the first place was also a priority, even though I wasn't sure I really wanted to know. My stomach heaved at the thought, and I flashed a bucket into my hands, afraid I might need to throw up. I cradled it, blinking into the darkness for a long while.

Eventually, my nausea subsided, replaced by a sinking feeling that draped itself over me like a smothering coat. But the major freak-out would have to wait. Right now, I had a job to do, so I locked the upsetting thoughts into a mental vault and turned my attention to the present moment. Be here now, as Michael would say. Easier said than done, but I gave it my best shot.

"Hello? Just follow the sound of my voice. I won't hurt you. I'm here to help."

There was a trapped soul in this void, stuck in a loop, hovering between space and time. Any of the other elementals, or even a skilled human medium, could have tackled this job. But Yggdrasil had patched Gabriel's call through to me as an escape, and I was genuinely grateful.

"Thank you," I said into the darkness, careful to keep the shield around my cerebral cortex in place, another arc roving about and all.

Archangels are telepathically linked. The second Gabriel learned of my betrayal, Michael, Uriel, and Raphael would, too, unless Gabe blocked the thought. But the arcs don't do that often, and Gabriel would never hold onto something this big. So my world could shatter into a million pieces if I brought that wall down, even for a second.

Shuddering, I switched focus to the total darkness surrounding me, trying to make my mind as blank as the Womb of Creation. A few minutes into that mental exercise, my internal radar pinged; the soul was getting closer. Sensing male energy, I thought for a moment, pondering what I should conjure. Something soothing, I decided, something a man would like. I waved my hand, and the image in my mind built itself around me.

One minute, I was in the void surrounded by darkness. The next, I was standing on a bearskin rug inside a one-room log cabin. There was a fire in the hearth, leather chairs around it, and a bed in the corner partly hidden behind red and black plaid curtains. I conjured a cup of tea and had a seat. On second thought, I snapped my fingers, transforming my cuppa into a glass of scotch; Macallan 25 because I'd just seen an ad for the stuff.

For what seemed like hours, I kept myself busy. I stoked the fire, gazed out at the pretty stream I'd created, flashed up a cupcake, ate it, and had another healthy pour of single malt. Then I went outside to split some wood with my mind. When none of that stopped the internal chatter, I went back in, had even more Macallan, not the best of ideas in my mental state, and juggled fireballs. Finally, and only once I'd reached the point of giving up, a young man appeared in the room. I drained my drink and stood up to have a look. My visitor wore combat gear and an olive-green helmet with the chin straps dangling. Fresh blood covered a good portion of his fatigues; his energy was so raw, his spirit broken.

This bit of unpleasant soul reality was not one of my better memories, and I'd spent the last few months feeling heartsick for the ones who stayed trapped in a hell of their own making. Fortunately, the moment they consider the possibility of something other than the loop, help arrives. In this case, a tipsy worried-out-of-her-mind elemental.

The man staggered forward; a hand clamped to a substantial leg wound. To my great surprise, the homey man cave I'd conjured to attract him vanished, and now we were in a jungle, the air suddenly wet and hot in my lungs.

"Whoa, you're strong," I said, knowing it had taken significant energy to override my log-cabin creation.

While I was marveling at that, an old military jeep popped into view. The soul lumbered over to it, writhing in agony with every step. He half-leaned, half-fell into the back, and pulled a black phone receiver from the console. Then he dropped it and collapsed against the vehicle, sliding to the ground. A tortured cry escaped his lips, followed by anguished sobs. I wished he would acknowledge me. I couldn't do anything to help him until he did.

Wait. If this soul brought me here, he wasn't finished experiencing this place. While I can't read a human's mind, souls are another matter. I ticked through his memories until I landed on the right one and transformed.

"Name and rank, soldier." My stance was wide, hands firmly on my hips. The poor soul grimaced. His face was covered in a mixture of blood, sweat, and grime. At first glance, his features were delicate, boyish even. A closer look revealed trenches carved by pain and the horrors of war.

"Colonel?" he asked, confused because this wasn't part of the original loop. It probably didn't make sense that a high-ranking officer would be here at this moment, either, but it was enough to grab his attention. "Lieutenant Samuel Jeffrey Rodgers, Sir." His voice was weak, but I could hear the hint of a southern accent. He tried saluting me, but his hand flopped to his chest, and his head slipped off the fender, landing on a tire.

"At ease, soldier," I said gruffly. To him, I looked and sounded like Colonel Maxwell Frank, commander of Sam's battalion during the Vietnam War in 1968. I crouched down and pushed the helmet out of his eyes.

"Get the men out of here," he said, grabbing the lapels of my jacket, pleading the same phrase repeatedly.

Explosions fired off around us, and his eyes went wide as they darted from my face to our surroundings. Sam Rodgers was looping the last moments of his life, and his energy was significant. A quick peek into his psyche told me he was driven by shame, remorse, and guilt—ah, the trifecta. This was going to be a lot tougher than I'd bargained for—especially since I wasn't firing on all pistons.

Human mediums can take an emotional beating from a soul's madness. Although it takes a lot more to penetrate an elemental's energetic wall, he could still imprint his fear onto me if I wasn't careful. I'm fortified, not bullet-proof, and I would have to take extra care with this one.

I inspected his human-looking face; his pupils were huge and dark, enveloping most of his brown eyes, his lips had gone blue, caused by the shock he felt in the last moments of his life on Earth. He closed his eyes, his head slumping to his chest, and I jostled him lightly. "Wake up."

He opened his eyes and searched my face, but his mind was somewhere else. Still, he had acknowledged me. Step one complete, I went on to step two and dropped the hologram, hoping to bring his attention to the present moment. "Lieutenant Rodgers. Look at me."

"My men are dead, and it's my fault." His face twisted in anguish, then went slack as he contemplated my presence. "Are you an angel?"

"Sam, you're safe now. You're going home."

He studied me, then his head jerked skyward, but it took several moments before the whine of the B-52 engine reached my ears. Usually, those boys flew so high, you couldn't detect them from the ground, but my senses were heightened by need, so I could hear a gnat flapping its wings over in the next province.

I looked at Sam's face, my sorrow deepening. This poor soul had repeated this scenario so often he'd started reacting before each event took place. Good thing because I needed the heads up if I was going to stop his madness.

"Get down!" Sam said, throwing me to the ground prematurely, using his body as a shield. Mud seeped into my clothes as I lay there pinned beneath his weight, breathing hard, my eyes fastened on blue sky.

Sam's terror slammed in like a punch to the gut, his emotions ripping through me as if they were my own. I knew I needed to disconnect, but the longer it went on, the harder it was to find the off switch. My heart raced, my mind reeling along with his. My sorrow for him was almost enough to cut through the fear. This is how he'd felt for the duration of being stuck in this loop, Goddess help him.

Finally, the bomber came into view. It looked like a pin-dot in the sky, but I zoomed in, watching the bay doors open a moment later, raining death over the jungle to the west.

The foliage three hundred yards to our left exploded into flames, with more bombs whistling toward the ground. I wrenched a hand free, planted a palm up, and now the remaining explosives hung in mid-air, sixty feet above the tree line. This was the strike that killed Sam and his men, and had I not stopped it, we would have gone back to the beginning of his loop. I wasn't about to let that happen. Once around this crazy dance floor was plenty, thank you very much.

I used my knee to flip us and rolled him onto his back, grabbing him by the shoulders. "Lieutenant, stay with me. This *isn't* real."

Sam Rodgers struggled to focus. He gaped at the bombs suspended from their freefall, and seeing them that way, like a video on pause, was enough to break the spell. His eyes slid from the strange sight to the light-filled doorway that had just appeared behind me.

I couldn't see it, but I sensed its arrival, and my energy kicked up a beat. "I *am* an angel, and I'm here to take you home."

Okay, so I lied. Not exactly my finest moment, but I wasn't about to let Sam slip back into his self-made prison. Unfortunately, my fib backfired, and horror washed over the soul's face as he scrambled backward out of my reach.

"You're the devil, and you're trying to trick me. I'm going to hell, and you're here to send me there." He grabbed his leg again, grimacing against the pain, and I uttered a curse word. He was slipping back into the loop.

I squeezed my eyes shut and focused on cutting his emotions away from my energetic field. And a few terrifying moments later, I felt Sam's fear slowly draining from my body. I went to his side, removed his helmet, and brushed sweat-slicked hair from his face, deciding to give it to him straight. That doesn't always work, but it was worth a shot, so I went for it.

"Listen to me. You died in that airstrike, and now you're reliving the last moments of your earthly life. But you're not human. You are an eternal being, and you have a soul name. It will come to you if you focus."

"I've killed people. God is going to judge me, and I will be condemned for all eternity. I won't go with you. I'm not going to burn."

Anger was the next emotion I struggled to control. The hell and damnation story believers tell themselves is just a flat-out lie; everyone cowering under the threat of hellfire, praying to a vengeful creator for redemption and mercy. Dear Goddess.

Pushing my temper down, I slipped into Andrea's soothing nurse voice. "Sam. There is no hell. It's all made up, a dark fairy tale to scare you into submission." (I left out the part about that fairy tale being used for economic advantage because I didn't think that would help just now.) "Hey, I'm from the place you're headed. It's a paradise filled with love and joy. You'll see the moment you step through that door."

While I couldn't lock onto specifics, I did know that what I was telling him was the truth. On the tail of that thought, I found myself wanting to go back in time, find the greedy bozo who started the damnation lie and give him a good punch in the nose. But I shook that satisfying image loose and said, "You went to Earth for a reason. Try to remember what that was."

He was drifting away again, and I felt him pulling us back to the start of his loop. The old military jeep flickered in and out of view. "No, no, no," I said, feeling him slip my grasp. I pulled Sam's head into my lap, tapping into his memories to find anything that would keep him with me. I knew I needed to work fast and flipped through his mental vault like one would flip through a card catalog. Not that one, or that one, definitely not that one, then... *Gotcha!* "Tell me about your sister," I said so quickly the words all but train wrecked into each other.

He opened his eyes, and I breathed a sigh of relief.

"Oh, God," he said. "Peggy, I'm so sorry."

The air shifted as our surroundings changed. Now we were back inside my log cabin on the bearskin rug in front of the fire. Okay, we were on track and chugging toward success. Now I just had to pull this baby into the station.

"What happened to her?" I asked, but I already knew the answer, having taken it out of his thoughts. Sam had always blamed himself for his only sibling drowning in the pond behind their house. It wasn't his fault. She simply wandered off while he was busy working on a car.

Tears streamed down the tormented soul's face, and I could tell from his expression that I'd made the connection. Now all I had to do was get Sam into my energy field to take the cosmic ride back home.

The portal behind me disappeared, the front door blew open, and I glanced up to see Gabriel standing there in a haze of brilliant white light. He only shows up when a soul is ready to cross over, and his presence meant I was getting close.

Gabe has been at this soul-crossing business a while. He closed the portal and gave the confused spirit, who still believed himself to be human, an actual door. Easy as pie to walk through; it was just another door, after all. I nodded hello to my friend, did a quick check of my mental blockade, and returned my focus. "Your sister is fine, and she's waiting for you at home."

A being appeared next to Gabriel—right on cue. It had the general shape of a woman, but it was light, not flesh and bone making up her form. "Look," I said, taking Sam by the chin and turning his face toward them.

"You're almost there, Sera," Gabriel said. "See if you can get him on his feet."

I wrapped Sam's arm around my neck and helped him up. He stumbled forward, and as he made his way toward the door, his wound disappeared, and his clothes transformed. In the next moment, Sam Rodgers stepped from the cabin into the Arrivals Meadow of the Summerlands looking crisp and clean in khakis and a blue shirt.

The being reached out to him, and when Sam took her hand, the form shrank in height, human features taking shape until a little girl with hair the color of chocolate and big brown eyes beamed up at him. The two embraced, then Peggy led Sam further into the meadow.

Gabriel saluted me, and I returned the best smile I could manage. Then he started off after them, and the cabin door swung shut on its own.

Alone again, I slumped onto the sofa and poured another scotch, turning my attention to the next problem. I sighed deeply and rubbed my face with both hands. I knew I would have to tell Michael what I had done.

Just not yet.

CHAPTER
~ 20 ~
Glara & Udar

The Summerlands, Present Moment

The light of the three suns sparkled across the Lake of Reflection. Glara sat on a moss-covered rock near the edge, shielding her eyes to watch Hira glide on the wind. The dragon dipped low before soaring off again, and soon, Halbom, Hita, and Heron swooped in from the trees to join her at play. The elemental dragons were never far from one another, like the four elementals themselves.

A glowing figure hovered a few feet away, changing form until it became a man dressed in blue and white ankle-length robes. He made a small step from the air to the ground. "Love and light, dearest one." It was Udar, holding a hand over his heart.

Glara returned the greeting, keeping her eyes on the sky. "Are they not magnificent?"

Udar settled in beside her, then laced his newly manifested fingers through hers. "They most certainly are," he said, noticing the strange feel. It had been a while since he'd taken this shape to teach a class, and even though he knew he was still light code, mortal form always seemed heavier somehow.

"In human stories, dragons are fire-breathing tyrants," Glara said as she watched one take a playful nip at the other. "The truth is far more magical than they could ever dream."

"You are thinking of humans, my love?"

"One in particular."

Glara looked so much like their daughter in this form; Udar's heart almost gave in to the earthly emotion overtaking his mate. "Ah, yes," he said, patting her hand. "I thought so. Come, take a walk with me."

The two souls made their way along the shoreline and paused once they reached a path cutting through majestic oaks. "Love and light," they each said.

The trees bowed in response.

He wants to surprise me, Glara thought but decided to ask anyway. "Where are we going?"

Udar wrapped an arm around her shoulders. "Wait for several Earth-plane moments, and you will see."

They followed the winding forest path, enjoying the company of the trees, the sweet fragrance of oak and pine blending with jasmine and honeysuckle, and the lovely birdsong that filled the air. After meandering a while, the couple arrived at a clearing. Smiling at each other, they took a step forward from the path to the pavement. Suddenly, flowing robes and buckle sandals transformed into twenty-first-century Earth-plane attire.

Glara broke into a pixie-like grin. "You know me so well," she said, inspecting Udar's gray pullover, dark jeans, and slip-on sneakers. Then she regarded her own clothes—a black cable knit sweater in soft wool, black leggings, and black biker boots. Oh, how she adored these clothes and this place.

The soulmates strolled hand-in-hand, passing quaint cottages with deep front porches. Along the way, they greeted other human-looking souls, all enjoying what they believed to be the fresh morning air of the Earth plane.

Glara loved this recovery village, having made wonderful memories here with their daughter. "Thank you," she said, resting her head on Udar's shoulder.

A few Earth-plane moments later, the couple arrived at Glara's favorite café. Souls in human form filled the patio, many of them poking at smartphones and laptops, each of them thinking they were in some charming town on Earth.

Udar beamed at her, his eyes glittering. "Chocolate this time?" Glara nodded, and her happy companion all but bounced into the shop.

She scanned the patio, thoroughly enjoying the Earth-plane sun cycle, when her eyes landed on a man sitting at a table in the far corner. He was reading the *New York Times*, a black and white border collie at his feet. Glara's heart rejoiced at the sight of her dear friends, and without thinking, she rushed toward them. A few feet from the table, she caught herself and slowed her gate, pretending to study the bushes. It was too late anyway; they had already seen her.

Glara approached. "Love and—"

She stopped to ponder the appropriate twenty-first-century salutation. Ah, she had it. "Exceptional beginning to an Earth-plane sun cycle." She smiled, satisfied with the greeting, and then registered the human emotion of confusion on her friend's face. Oh, dear... I did not say that correctly.

"Uh, good morning?" the man said. "Isn't it a lovely day?"

That was it. *Good morning*, Glara thought, promising herself she would remember when the opportunity presented itself again.

She thought back to Udar's classes on communication filters. Don't get excited and try your hand at Earth slang, he'd told his students. Just speak naturally in whatever dialect you prefer, and let the filter do its job. If you work too hard, the words come out stilted, and you may shock the unawake soul you are trying to communicate with.

Okay, she just needed to relax.

Taking a deep breath, Glara decided on the language of light code. "Yes, truly it is so," she said in perfect Earth-plane English. It sounded musical in her 'ears,' and her smile broadened. "My name is Glara."

The soul laid his paper on the table. "David Carter. And this is Belle," he said, patting the dog's side.

"Exciting to meet you, David Carter."

Glara knelt to say hello to her other friend, who she knew was already awake. "Greetings and extremely well wishes of health and good tidings to you, Belle."

David Carter looked puzzled again, and Glara winced. She thought for a while, trying to remember what one would say to a dog on Earth. Belle gave her the answer telepathically. "Oh, thank you," Glara responded silently. Aloud she said, "Well, hello there, pretty girl," while scratching her fellow elder behind the ears. Feeling triumphant, she did a little dance in her mind, then she winked at Belle, and Belle winked back. Glara *always* remembered winking. It was one of her favorites, along with air quotes.

"Are you new to the area?" David Carter asked.

"Oh, no. My husband and I have lived here a long, long time." Okay, I've got Earth slang now, she noted, puffing her chest a bit. "What about you?"

"We've been here for about eight weeks, I think."

"And are you enjoying your new home?"

"We like it very much, don't we, Belle?" He tufted the dog's ears, and she responded by resting her head on his knee.

There were many animals in Morningside. But few were piloted by returning souls, and Glara thought her fellow elder was doing a smashing job of playing an Earth-plane dog.

Udar returned. "Here you go. Two scoops on a sugar cone, just the way you like it."

Glara accepted her treat with a smile, then licked the drips from the sides and said, "This is *David Carter*. He's been here for *eight weeks*."

"Uh, really nice to meet you. I'm Udar," he said, shaking the man's hand. Glara admired her mate's ability to drop right into Earth's speech patterns and customs. He even said things like, *uh*. It was beyond excellent.

146

"The pleasure is mine... Udar, that's a unique name. Is it European?"

"Something like that," Udar said, beaming at David Carter as he took another swipe at his ice cream. He placed a hand on Glara's elbow. "Well, honey, we'd better be going."

Glara adored it when they came to Morningside, and Udar called her that. "Goodbye, David Carter. It was lovely to make your acquaintance," she said.

"You as well."

Glara thought she saw a glimmer of recognition cross her dear friend's face and touched Udar's arm to stop him from leaving.

"Have we met before?" the elder who believed himself to be David Carter asked her.

Although Glara hated to do it, she said, "I do not think so. Why?" It wasn't a lie; she had never met David Carter before this moment. She knew the soul underneath.

"You two seem awfully familiar."

Glara smiled, her heart bursting with joy. "Perhaps a different lifetime."

The two souls left the café, holding hands and enjoying their Earth-plane treats as they strolled through the pretend town. Udar turned to her. "He looks joyful," he said, catching a drip with his tongue. Then he took a bite of the sugar cone and chewed thoughtfully.

Glara nodded. "I think so as well. Belle's awake. She cannot believe it is taking him this long. He usually springs right back."

Udar grinned. "Springs right back, huh? Your Earth slang is excellent, *honey*," he said, raising his brows. "Perhaps he simply desires to spend time in Morningside."

There was a moment of silence as each of them reflected on this, then Udar's expression shifted as if he'd just had an idea. "I know what might be nice," he said. "Would you like to see an Earth-plane film in the Earth-plane Cineplex? There are lots of new ones, or we could view one of your favorites."

Glara's hand flew to her face. "Yggdrasil!" she said, then looked at the ice cream, feeling confused. One could not shift objects into dark matter here; the village was bound by a different set of laws. "There," she said, pointing to a trash can.

Ice cream dealt with Earth-plane style, they headed for the woodlands path, laughing, and running like humans down Main Street. As they picked up speed, Glara found herself wishing she'd conjured track shoes instead of the chunky-soled boots. But she did her best, knowing her footwear would change once they reached the trees.

CHAPTER

~ 21 ~

Cabin Life

The Womb of Creation, Present Moment

My eyes fluttered open and landed on an unfamiliar quilt. Slowly, the reason I was looking at this fancily stitched patchwork in reds and blues came to me.

Groggy from one of my better night's sleep, I fumbled with the curtain surrounding the bed. The metal rings clacked as I slid the panel back, and I felt a little pride hearing it. You see, the trick to magic is in the details, and I'd applied a good deal of effort refining my surroundings. That sound had taken two days to perfect.

While obsessing over minutia was an okay distraction, what I *really* needed to do was get to the Summerlands and search the Akashic Records. But that wasn't an appealing option, and I wasn't about to head back to the Earth plane, so here I am, day sixty-two... roger that.

I reluctantly pushed myself up, slid my legs from the covers, and blinked at the bright light streaming through the window beside the bed. I smiled faintly at the tulips in the field just beyond the gurgling stream.

As any good farmer must, I rotated my crops…hourly—sunflowers, then poppies, then peonies. I'd even flashed up monster daisies with heads so big I had to fortify their stalks. The tulips were a holdover from several weeks ago when I'd last had the energy to care.

When magical farming no longer proved an adequate distraction, I conjured a doorway leading to my own version of Studio 54—complete with holograms boogying the hours away. Rock stars and actors from my current timeline partied with Galileo, Aristotle, Leonardo da Vinci, and William Shakespeare almost every night.

I'd put my new friends in funky disco clothes, of course: white polyester suits, sequins, platform shoes, afros, the works. (Joan of Arc and Isaac Newton could have won a dance competition the way they got down. And *Bertie*, my version of Einstein, didn't need any help from me in the afro department.)

I joined the groups they formed on occasion. Mostly I kept to myself, dancing alone, doing shots, and sulking in a private balcony perched above the undulating dance floor. But the noise, bacchanalia, and pulsing lights—while sufficient at numbing my senses—gave me pounding headaches…or that could have been the booze. In either case, I removed the door, choosing instead to wear a groove in the pine floor: bed, sofa, porch.

Sometimes I baked pies.

Okay, fine. I baked a truckload of pies.

Since manifesting this place, I'd crossed a few more trapped souls, packed on more than a few pounds, and changed the color of just about everything several times; the sky, the furniture, the logs in the fireplace, the cows. But no matter what I did during a pretend day, I felt the same as I do now—hollowed out and numb—like I was at the bottom of a deep dark hole with no way out.

I rubbed my face, then flashed myself showered and dressed, trailing my tongue over my teeth. Oops. Missed those. A minty-cool scrubbing sensation filled my mouth a moment later.

Basic hygiene complete (and I do mean basic because most days my hair looked like I'd stuck a fork in an outlet), mismatched sneakers caught my eye. One was black (the color I'd been going for), the other was hot pink with silver zebra stripes near the toe. But I honestly didn't care and left them that way.

Numbed by the insurmountable task of figuring out what to do next, I flashed a massive stack of pancakes onto my lap. Then I crammed a few into my mouth while staring at the wall. I didn't have enough energy to add syrup, which was just as well because had I spilled any on myself, it might stay there for a while.

After stuffing my face, I shuffled outside, flung the rest of those pancakes into the air with my mind, and shot them down with fireballs. I did this during most of my self-made mornings, this elemental pancake skeet.

Fresh out of confectionery targets, I stayed on the porch a while, watching my purple cows munch grass. Then I shuffled back inside, flopped down on the sofa, and buried my face in my hands.

The main reason I hadn't been ready to pop on into the Summerlands was one little troubling thought that invaded most of my waking hours. What if I do belong on DarkStar now? What if the moment I arrive home, Goddess sends me there? I rested my chin on a fist and contemplated the floor awhile. (It took a shocking amount of effort.)

Who was I kidding? Goddess could rip me out of any realm and toss me wherever she wanted. She knows where I am and what I'm doing, always.

While I still couldn't piece together my entire time in the Underworld or my reasons for going, little glimpses had come in fits and starts. Mostly, I saw Mortegol and I making love. And every non-X-rated memory I managed to pull looked like a scene out of a flipping rom-com. There was even a picnic by a waterfall, for Pete's sake. We had been happy—and dare I say—we were in love. But none of that made the slightest bit of sense. I'd gone over it so many times, I was on the verge of losing my mind.

"Oh, enough, Seraphina. Enough."

I stood and cast a wary eye around the room, saying a silent goodbye. "Yggdrasil, I'd like to go home, please."

CHAPTER

~ 22 ~

Homecoming

The Summerlands, Present Moment

In the time it takes to exhale a breath, I was standing in the Arrivals Meadow of the Summerlands. I closed my eyes and counted to ten. When I opened them again, I was still in the same spot, thank Goddess, and not inside the seedy train station on DarkStar.

Okay. So far, so good.

"Is that the latest fashion on the Earth plane?"

I turned toward the familiar voice, scrutinized my shoes, and smiled apologetically. "Not really? Hello, you," I said, hugging Udar to me.

Glara giggled and threw her arms around us both. Then she pointed to my head. "Should I make mine look like that?"

"Probably not, unless you're going for a throwing-in-the-towel look," I said, then flashed away my crazy snarls. I felt my hair slide over my shoulders, soft and straight again.

Although I missed my parents, I couldn't remember their faces, so let's just say that first glance was startling. The short answer, they look like me, same green eyes, same nose. Glara has my heart-shaped face. Udar's is more "square jaw" with a definite masculine quality but close enough. They even have my honey-blonde hair. Glara's is straight, falling past her shoulders like mine. Udar's is cropped close on the sides, longer on top, and swept-back like he just walked out of the salon. And here's a fun thing, both of them look to be my age.

"Have you just awoken?" Udar asked.

Between this and the comment about my shoes, I knew he was practicing. The Summerlands does a great job of filtering out third-dimensional concepts. There's no time here either, and while to me, it had been years between visits, they had just seen me leave and arrive at pretty much the same time.

Yeah, I know. Don't try to wrap your head around it. Even I don't fully understand time, and I've been here *since the beginning*—although that too is a figure of speech. There isn't a beginning to anything. Well, except for the third dimension, which kicked off the wild notion of time. Yep, try not to dwell. Just shake it off. It's easier that way.

Wait. It may help to know that souls do register events in chronological order. Otherwise, their experience of existence would be the equivalent of a smoothie inside a blender stuck on high.

"About six months," I told him.

Udar scratched his chin. "I think I remember how long that is. Less than an Earth-plane year?" Then he snapped his fingers and broke into a triumphant grin. "Half a year."

"That's right. Say, you're good at this game. Want to go for distance next?" Being with them was already doing my heart some good. I should have done this sooner, before Studio 54.

"Would you like for us to show you around, dearest one?" Glara bounced on her heels, reminding me they love playing tour guide when I arrive the first time in each incarnation.

I smiled at her. "I would like that more than anything."

I always remember them at some point during each awakening. This time while battling an epic case of depression inside my self-made log-cabin prison. But I don't recall much of anything else about my eternal home or my time here. *Meat brain*, as Helena would say, although I would never feed mine to a shark.

Glara clapped her hands. "Oh, that is truly wonderful. Come along, then. I have just the place."

We walked through the meadow like humans, which I just remembered they love, and a shadow crossed the ground in front of us. I shaded my eyes, squinting at the celestial beauty.

Above us, in all her radiance and light, was Hira, Dragon of the South Gate, her iridescent red and orange wings commanding the wind. She landed near us, and I rushed forward, threw my arms around her neck, and kissed the bridge of Hira's lovely muzzle. The skin of her SUV-sized body was warm and tickled my lips. Dragon energy is powerful stuff.

"Hello, beautiful lady."

"Love and light, Seraphina."

Hira lowered her head to the ground, inviting me to climb up. To her, I was always here, and she probably felt as if we'd just done this. For me, it had been a while, and I blinked at her, not sure what to do.

A saddle appeared over a hump between the dragon's shoulder blades. I ran a hand over the salamander crest embossed on the seat, grabbed the horn, stepped onto Hira's golden-red thigh, and swung my leg over. I slid my feet into the stirrups and wrapped my fingers around leather handles that fit my grip perfectly as if they were made for me. Then I remembered—they *were* made for me—*I* had made them.

The dragon took several long and graceful strides, then stretched her wings as we lifted off the ground. My stomach lurched as we did a steep climb, and I laughed as the sensation of weightlessness coursed through my body. But it didn't take long to get used to her movements, and a few minutes into our flight, I too felt as if we had done this only moments ago.

I pressed my thighs to guide Hira in the direction I wanted to go, and the dragon responded readily. We made several passes around the meadow, then Hira flew us over the crystalline lake and behind snow-capped mountains. I surveyed my eternal home, the wildflowers, the three waterfalls rushing over rocky cliffs, pooling into the farthest edges of the water below us.

We passed multi-tiered fountains and symmetrical gardens bursting with vibrant color. I saw the forest beyond and several enormous alabaster buildings in the far distance. Then I closed my eyes, savoring the warmth of the three suns and the wind in my hair as we soared through the pastel skies of the Summerlands.

After a few more laps, we came in for a landing near Glara and Udar. I climbed down and hugged Hira's neck, thinking this was much more cathartic than elemental pancake skeet *or* purple cows. Hira turned to meet my eyes. "In case you don't remember, just call my name whenever you need me, and I will come. It is good to see you, Fire Goddess. Love and light."

"Thank you, dear friend," I said, placing a hand over my heart. "I will."

The dragon bowed her head, then turned, sprang off her back haunches, and took to the air.

My parents and I continued to the edge of the same forest I'd just flown over. From this vantage point, the trees resembled the black oaks I'd seen in the book Dr. Chet loaned me, but unlike their counterparts on Earth, each one stood exactly thirty-three feet tall.

My eyes traced identical dark-gray trunks with grooves revealing smooth orange skin beneath. Above us, blue-green leaves joined so seamlessly it was hard to tell where one ended and the other began. There was a golden glow under the canopy, and sunlight dappled the ground almost as if the sun's rays could pass right through the dense foliage. However, I couldn't see the slightest gap between the leaves.

Glara and Udar crossed an arm over their chests, their hands resting over their hearts. "Love and light," they said in unison.

Each tree bent slightly, and the canopy rustled overhead, making a musical sound that flooded my heart with joy. I turned to my parents. "They're responding to you."

Glara laughed. "Trees are sentient beings, the wisest among us, even on Earth."

I inhaled, trying to identify the fragrance permeating the air.

Suddenly, I could distinguish each scent; oak, pine, jasmine, and honeysuckle, blending into a sweet aroma that tickled my nose. I touched one of the trunks feeling an overwhelming sense of peace as we connected telepathically. "Hello, Fire Goddess. It is good to see you. We have a gift we wish to bestow. Would you like to receive it?"

I happily agreed, and a new sensation rushed in. The forest offered me its strength, and I took it gratefully, allowing it to nourish my tired body. "Thank you. Love and light," I said, then started back to my parents, who stood patiently waiting.

As we walked beneath the dense canopy, Glara and Udar explained that soul trees made up the Interdimensional Travel Forest of the Summerlands. One could take this path to any dimension, except one, they said. Souls needed counseling before going to the Earth plane as it was the hardest of the seven planes of existence. That didn't need further explanation; it made perfect sense to me.

We arrived at a clearing, and I stopped cold, unable to grasp what I was seeing.

"This is your home," Glara said.

"But this *is* my house," I said, taking in the front porch, the swings, the ferns, and the big red door I know so well.

"It is the same," Udar said. "This dwelling changes with you, so you will always recognize home. Come. You have questions, and we will answer as many as we can."

I followed them along the brick walkway, taking the gray-painted wooden steps to the front porch. (To my amazement, the third step creaked, just like at home.) We crossed the threshold, stepping inside the exact replica of my foyer. It even had our round table with the same blue and white vase in the center and the same flowers as when I left, purple tulips. Ah, that's why the tulip field made me feel marginally better, I thought. It reminded me of home.

I walked through the house with my mouth hanging open, half expecting to see Julia and Braith around every corner. The living room, the library, the staircase, the furniture, everything was identical.

Once I'd finished my inspection, we took seats around the kitchen island, and I chose my favorite spot facing the backyard.

Silverware, napkins, and plates of steaming hot food appeared on the marble-topped surface: roast chicken, mashed potatoes, grilled corn on the cob, asparagus, and dinner rolls.

The selection was decidedly better than the pancakes, pie, and liquor that had been my steady diet for two months. I smiled, wondering why I hadn't thought to conjure this kind of comfort food while at the cabin. Depression is a cruel mistress, I decided but didn't say, reaching for something more cheerful instead. "These are my favorites."

Udar placed a napkin on his lap and grinned at me. "We know."

"Do you really eat here?" I asked.

Glara smiled. "Oh, yes. Eating is one of the great pleasures throughout all dimensions. Our nourishment has the same taste and texture as Earth food, but here it is Source Energy."

I took a bite of mashed potatoes; they were hot and creamy, and butter rolled over my tongue. I swallowed and took a sip of water. Nope, that was white wine in that goblet. "It sure tastes real," I said.

"Of course it does. Otherwise, what would be the point?" Udar said, his cheek bulging with Source Energy.

"Why don't I remember this place?"

Udar's smile widened. "Ah, this is a question we can answer. Memories of home are erased with each incarnation. Otherwise, everyone would want to come back to the Summerlands immediately, and that would be cruel. Earth is a brutal place, a dark lagoon of matter," he shuddered, "but we go there to gather experiences."

"So, both of you have been to Earth as humans?"

Udar took Glara's hand in his. "Oh, yes, countless times. We always plan that we will find each other. Do we not, dearest one?"

Glara stroked Udar's cheek and smiled into his eyes. "Yes, we do," she said to him, then turned to me. "Our mission in every incarnation is to give you life, Seraphina. We get to have many other experiences, of course, but the main reason we return is to bring the Fire Goddess to the Earth plane in human form."

"Every time?"

"Every time," Udar said, then grinned like he'd just taken first prize at the science fair.

"And how many times have you done that?"

Udar's green eyes gleamed, making me feel like I was looking in a mirror. "Let's just say the number would be a shock to the system."

I took a few more bites, then gathered myself to ask another question, one that had burned inside for as long as I could remember. "Why didn't you stay with me?"

There was a pause, but I could tell the two eternal beings knew precisely what I meant. Glara met my eyes. "That was not the mission, dearest one. It was your idea to be on your own this time. We did not plan your current life together as we usually do, either. You sent us a download with instructions."

"It was? I did?" I said, wondering why I would have done any of that.

Udar nodded. "Glara's right. Last time we did not interact with you. But I assure you, no one here carries out a task without a willingness to do so, not even elementals."

"Huh. And why can't I remember that?"

Glara placed a hand on my cheek. "Awakening is a delicate process. Soul memories must return slowly; otherwise, you would go mad. All will be revealed in due time. For now, try to enjoy the experience."

Although I couldn't remember Goddess fully, the comment pinged my radar as something she would say.

Glara's eyes widened. "Come with me. I have something for you." She took my hand and walked me to the living room, *my* living room. "Fire Goddess recall," Glara said to the air, then she turned to me. "You asked me to run this for you each time you come to us, and you always seem to feel better afterward." She kissed my forehead and left the room.

A hologram appeared as I was taking a seat. It was *me*, with a few minor exceptions; the hair was the same shade of blond, but it was wavy with crimson highlights. This version of me wore the red outfit from Braith's video game and had my elemental sword resting over a shoulder. I looked kind of saucy, and I liked it.

"Hey, kiddo. Nice to see you," my hologram said. "Can you do this yet?" She lit the blade with her fingertip, and the steel erupted in flames that fanned out wildly in all directions. Holographic me threw the blazing thing high into the air—no easy trick, that—and it disappeared through the ceiling, whirling end to end. A second later, it came back down, still on fire, and my hologram caught it behind her back. For the grand finale, she quenched the flames by inhaling them.

"Show off," I said, getting up to touch the shoulder of my doppelganger. It felt solid.

The hologram laughed. "A little freaky, right?"

"Yeah," I said. It was freaky, all right.

"Anyway—" She nodded at the sofa, and I dutifully returned to my seat. "The reason I made this little number is to get you up to speed on a few things. Right now, you're sitting there thinking all your elemental memories are back. They're not." She snorted and crossed her arms. "So annoying."

Wow. Holographic me was a snarky little thing.

"I'll bet you were just asking *the folks* to explain the Summerlands to you."

"I was not," I lied.

She arched a brow. "Uh-huh. So, look, I'm not going to tell you everything, just a few basics, lay of the land and all that, so you don't wander around clueless." She tossed her head over a shoulder toward the kitchen. "Those two lovely souls aren't your parents."

I felt a jolt. "What?"

"Nope. Only humans have a mom and dad, well, sort of. Goddess is both for us, I guess, because of that whole duality thing. Anyway, you are an eternal being created solely to be a commander in the Army of Light, cupcake."

"Okay," I said, needing a moment to let that sink in. I knew I was a soldier under Michael's command, kind of. He doesn't bark orders, more like he offers suggestions—quickly—when the heat is on. It was the "no parents" part that confused me. "But I love Glara and Udar, and I look exactly like them."

"Right on both counts, and they love you too. When they take human form, they do so as an amalgam of your features. It's so you'll recognize them. Get it?"

I nodded, although the surprise of it was still rippling through me.

"Archangels and elementals take orders from Source. Souls take orders from you." She placed air quotes around the *taking orders* part, and I asked why.

"Well, no one here gives or takes orders. We work together. Source lets you know what's needed, and you plan missions around that. You get to pick your team, though. Long ago, you chose Glara and Udar to be your parents on Earth, and you never switched. After a while, we were like a human family. It's sweet. I love it."

I'd spent the last two months hoping somebody forced me to do what I did. A fanciful notion, and no such luck it seemed. My mind ticked through several other possibilities. I had gladly given my life for humans many times, but I couldn't imagine that going to the Underworld had been part of a mission. Had I indeed turned dark? And if so, why didn't I feel it now? Why didn't I want to return to the Underworld to be with Mortegol? Why was I here and not on DarkStar?

"Your last life did a number on you, huh?"

I nodded.

Holographic me folded her arms again. "You made the right choice, you know. You'll understand...eventually."

I wasn't so sure of that. "Wait. You know what I did?" I asked her, um, me.

She smirked and cocked her head. "What do you think?"

"Then, why? *Why* did I do it." I felt the sting of tears, but they wouldn't come. I hadn't allowed myself a good cry since the memory hit, and I guess I was getting used to forcing down the pain.

Holographic me shirked off my discomfort with a shrug. "Sorry. Not time to know yet. You've still got too many lower-vibrational tendencies swirling around. Right now, you're wallowing in the human emotions of depression and self-pity. That's a nasty little cocktail."

"I am not," I said.

"Yep. Sure." She gave me an appraising look and tapped her head. "I'm not from your past, baby. I'm your present."

"Huh?" Then another thought hit me, and I licked my lips. "Oh, God. Are you—am I on DarkStar?"

Holographic Sera tossed her mane of red-streaked hair. "Don't worry about where I am. We're fine. Just pay attention." She touched the air in front of her, and a 3-D replica of Earth's solar system materialized around us. Twinkling stars filled the room, the sun and planets engaged in their orbital dance.

"So look," she said. "Earth has four main entrance portals, north, south, east, and west." She touched each quadrant with a fingertip, and as she did, swirling doorways appeared in red, green, blue, and yellow shimmering light. The red portal grew larger. "You are the guardian of this little baby here, the South Gate, three-hundred-thirty-three miles above Australia. You keep the bad guys out and let souls through when they jump to and from the Summerlands. You are responsible for opening it, closing it, and guarding dimensional space around it."

"What do you mean by jump?"

Holographic me ignored the question and snapped her fingers, making the portals disappear. Now Earth looked desolate—as if the life-giving sun had belched an enormous fireball at the little rock, burning it into a charcoal briquette. I gasped and pressed my back into the cushions.

"I know, but don't worry. The planet is fine. It's just cloaked." She gave me an empathetic smile and snapped her fingers again. In the next instant, Earth was beautiful once more, like a swirly blue marble hovering in a black velvet sky.

I shifted to the edge of my seat, listening to, well, me, explain how the universe works.

"If you don't know where the portals are or how to use them, you'll never get in," she said. "And you'll never see Earth as anything other than a dead hunk of rock."

I had always believed humans were not alone. This proved it. "Do aliens try to get in?" I asked.

"Oh, yes, and they're not all bad, of course. But otherworldly beings disrupt the natural order, and it's our job to keep them out. Most of them anyway, some are harmless and rather helpful...or

161

entertaining, a lot of famous people on Earth are aliens. Others are scientists, doctors, and engineers now that I think about it. Anyway, cloaking the planet is an extra layer of protection. Sort of a *move along, nothing to see here.*"

I must have looked puzzled.

"You've guarded the South Gate since the first Earth. We're on autopilot until an alien life-form tries to get in. Then it's showtime," holographic Sera said with a gleam in her eye. "Kricket, Andrea, and Helena guard the other gates. The four elementals, gatekeepers of the third dimension…has a nice ring to it, don't you think?"

I nodded as memories came flooding in. I saw every incarnation of Earth, all three hundred thirty-three of them. I saw myself and the three other elementals (as light code) standing watch over each one. I also saw the countless times Udar and Glara had helped me complete the missions I planned out.

Then I remembered something else. "Like humans, angels and elementals have free will," I said. The moment the words left my mouth, I realized it wasn't a comforting thought, given my circumstances.

"Yup. No one forces us to do anything."

"Right. I always have a choice," I muttered, wondering what in the world had gone so wrong to make me choose a life in the Underworld.

"So do Glara and Udar, but they stick with us, even though we've given them some bizarre assignments." Holographic Sera chuckled, then paused to study me. "You good now?"

I nodded, even though I wasn't so sure.

When I got back to the kitchen, Glara and Udar were wearing expectant faces. "Your mission in each lifetime is to bring me to Earth," I said. Even though they'd already told me that, I felt the need to reiterate, just trying to ease into the thing.

"Precisely," said Udar, and I noticed he seemed pleased with himself. "But we have many other experiences too. Last time, I worked on fear."

"Three months after you were born, we died in a car accident on an icy road in Kents Hill, Maine," Glara said. "Your guardian angel, Rachel, shielded you during the crash."

"Celeste told me an angel brought me to her."

Udar smiled. "We hovered between space and time long enough to see Rachel place you in Ms. Porter's arms. You didn't have a scratch on you, either."

I felt an overwhelming sense of love rushing through me. These two lovely beings were simply carrying out the missions I laid before them, and they did it with such passion and grace; it nearly broke my heart. "Thank you. You only ever do what I ask."

"We are honored to carry out your plans," Udar said. He placed a hand over his heart. "Love and light, Fire Goddess."

Glara did the same, and I returned the greeting choking back tears. The hologram I'd made explained everything. I was their commander, and they were soldiers in a never-ending battle between light and dark. I took them in my arms, and a moment later, the doorbell rang.

"I'll get it," Udar said, vanishing in a tiny pop of light.

Now I was hugging air on one side, and I lowered my arm. Okay. *That* will take some getting used to. "You have doorbells here?"

Glara raised an eyebrow and smiled knowingly. "Oh, yes. The Earth plane is like the Summerlands in many ways. It is so we will feel comfortable there—like we belong. Another gift from Goddess."

"Like soulmates," I said, my thoughts returning to Michael.

"You are thinking of your love?"

"Yes. How did you know? Can you read my mind?"

"No, we do not do that here. But a mother knows." She winked at me.

"Well, Michael sure can."

Glara laughed. "Oh, yes. That can be a problem. But it feels right, being with him?"

"It does," I said, my heart squeezing in my chest as I wondered if I could ever be with Michael again.

Udar appeared in the doorway. "There's someone here for Seraphina."

I tore the pain of deceiving Michael from my mind. I'd already given myself the universe's most elaborate pity party. Even that hadn't helped, and if Goddess were going to relegate me to DarkStar, she would have done it by now. I sighed and pasted on a happy face, deciding that was as good a place to start as any. "Me? Who knows I'm here?"

"Oh, *everyone* knows you are here," Glara said, making her green eyes huge. "You are the Fire Goddess." She swept her hands in front of her face, hamming it up like a magician pulling off the world's most remarkable magic trick. "It is a tremendous deal when you arrive."

She'd meant it tongue in cheek, an inside joke to amuse me. It worked. I laughed, and she did too.

Udar stepped to one side, allowing a young couple to pass into the kitchen. It was the soldier, a few years older than when I'd seen him in the Womb of Creation. I gathered him into my arms. "Sam," I said, thrilled at the sight of him looking so well. The embrace caused another memory. Here, his name is Ishan, and I recognized the soul standing next to him too.

"Love and light, Fire Goddess," he said.

"Love and light, Ishan. And this is Briggitte, who went to Earth with you as your sister, Peggy." I smiled into her lovely brown eyes, and she bowed her head.

Ishan sighed and gazed at his mate. "Yes, we planned it that way together. I wanted to experience remorse, and Briggitte agreed to go with me to help."

"The Vietnam War was his idea," Briggitte said, poking his ribs. "The council, his elder and I, all tried to talk him out of it, but he would not listen to any of us. They told him that letting his little sister drown while he was off doing something meaningless would do the trick, but he is stubborn."

Ishan blew out a long breath. "I am. And I sure felt remorse. It was my fault Peggy drowned, and it was also my fault those men died in the jungle. I gave the wrong coordinates to the air patrol, and it was friendly fire that killed us. I knew that as the bombs were falling.

That's why I got stuck in that loop, so I could throw myself a big old pity party."

"Oh, I know about those," I said under my breath.

A contemplative smile lit Briggitte's lovely face. "I do not think he will need to experience remorse again."

"You are right about that, dearest one," Ishan said. Then he turned to me. "I wanted to come here and thank you in person. You got through to me and sent me home to be with my love. I am eternally grateful." Then a smile formed on his lips, calling his dimples into action. "'I am an angel, and I'm here to take you home?'"

"You thought I was the devil," I said, smiling back at him.

Ishan's cheeks flushed. "I sure did." Then, switching to Sam Rodger's southern accent, he added, "I thought I was going to hell on a scholarship. But Seraphina here—Woo Wee—she kept on going till she got me moving to that light like a hound with its tail on fire."

Everyone laughed.

The five of us spent the next several hours—maybe, it was getting harder to tell—catching up and talking about our various missions throughout time. It felt good, and I found myself enjoying the moment and the company, something I had not done in a long while.

Once our guests had gone, Glara turned to me. "I want to show you one of my favorite places in the Summerlands. Yours too."

Before I had time to answer, we were standing at the edge of the Soul Tree Forest, and I rocked back on my heels. Unexpected flashing takes a little getting used to, I thought as I gulped down the acid that had crept its way up my throat. My vision floated in sideways and slammed to a stop, resting on the signpost in front of us. WELCOME TO MORNINGSIDE.

I stared at it as faint memories crashed around like tiny birds flying wildly inside a darkened cave. Glara was right, I had been here before, and I did love this place, but something about being here again left me swaying on my feet.

CHAPTER

~ 23 ~

Morningside

The Summerlands, Present Moment

Glara and Udar stepped from the forest path to the pavement. The moment they crossed some invisible line, their robes transformed into modern clothes, making them look like a pair of hip college students. I cleared my throat as my eyes focused on their new outfits, and for a moment, I found myself wishing they had lived long enough to raise me. But I slapped that thought away, deciding to spend no more time pining for absent parents on Earth—since that had been my doing, anyway.

"What is this place?" I asked, suddenly curious. "It looks a little like Leesburg."

"Morningside is a recovery village. When you are between lives, this is one of your favorites as well. We journey here together." Glara bounced on her heels, waiting for signs of recognition.

I had a look around and laughed. I hoped my parents would show me secrets of the ages, but we might as well have been on Earth.

"Oh, no, Daughter…dearest one…you are experiencing the human emotion of disappointment?" Glara's voice was warm and filled with concern.

"Not at all," I said, resting my hands on her shoulders. "And I like it when you call me *Daughter.*"

A smile brightened her face. "We hoped you would say that. You were the one who suggested it long ago."

"And you reiterate when you arrive the first time in every incarnation," Udar said, then met my eyes solidly. "We love it when you call us *Mom* and *Dad*, and we think of ourselves that way."

I smiled at them, warmth flooding my heart. "You *are* my parents, and I love you both very much." Their reaction was one of such pure joy, I will never forget it, no matter how many times I die. My own smile broadened until it felt as if it were taking up my entire face. "So, *Mom and Dad*, tell me about this place."

Glara put a finger to her mouth, and I smiled. Udar wasn't the only one who practiced being human. "Hmm. Explaining Morningside," she said thoughtfully. "Where to begin. Well, many new arrivals come with their most-recent mortal identity intact."

"And it takes time to readjust," Udar said.

Glara nodded. "That's right. Recovery villages like this one resemble Earth from various periods and locations. Morningside is where those who lived in the United States during the twenty-first century regain their eternal memories."

I thought about that a moment. "Why can't everyone recover in the Summerlands together?"

"The souls here still believe they are human," Glara said. "Can you imagine if one morning the people of Leesburg woke up to dragons flying, three suns in the sky, trees greeting them, and food and people popping out of thin air?" She placed a hand on her stomach and laughed. Glara has a beautiful laugh that sounds a little like wind chimes.

Udar scrunched his face. "And Goddess forbid a poor soul stepped onto a path that led to another dimension and could not figure out how to return."

"Good point," I said, feeling glad to be with them, in a third-dimensional construct village, on the moon, wherever. It no longer mattered.

"Recovery villages protect human ideas of reality for as long as each soul needs," Glara said.

I looked past my parents at a moving truck in one of the driveways. The side panel read:

MORNINGSIDE MOVERS

WE CARE FOR YOU LIKE FAMILY

BECAUSE YOU ARE

"There are movers here?" I asked.

Udar beamed. "Oh, yes. Morningside has hulking holograms carrying furniture in and out of houses and everything. Eventually, everyone wakes up and heads off. To those who remain, this looks like people moving in and out of any neighborhood on Earth."

I took in the quaint cottages then sniffed the air. "It smells like…coffee…orange juice…and freshly mown grass."

Glara jumped up and down and clapped her hands. "It is marvelous. Is it not?"

I had to admit. It was pretty terrific.

Glara jogged ahead of us then turned back. "Come along. Let us not stand around *speaking* of Morningside. We should experience it."

"She does love this place. Here, let's not keep your mother waiting." Udar took me by the hand, and we caught up to an excited Glara. Then the three of us sauntered down the street, probably looking like triplets out for a stroll.

We chatted with a few of the residents, and I realized my parents were right; everyone we spoke with believed they were still human. Although one couple confided that they couldn't remember the move to their lovely new home.

During the exchange, another memory came to me. Glara and Udar are what we call *elders*—experienced beings who counsel souls before and after each trip to the Earth plane. They are exceptionally good at it, I thought, as I watched them steer the two back on course.

When we left, the couple seemed comfortable and excited to get on with their pretend Earth-plane day.

A short while later, Udar led us to a cafe with outdoor dining. My gaze drifted across the large flagstone patio decorated with bright-blue canvas umbrellas and clay pots brimming with cheerful red and purple pansies. Servers ferried trays of food and drink, and most of the diners ignored their companions by staring at their smartphones. Yep, just like the Earth plane, I thought.

"This time, let's have coffee," Udar said, rubbing his hands together.

Glara's eyes widened. "Oh, and cherry tarts."

Udar nodded. "That will be delicious," he said, then happily headed off. He seemed eager to suffer the long lines, place an order by saying it out loud, and pay for his items with Earth money…all while human-looking souls texted one another.

"Your father and I were here *this morning*," Glara said, putting air quotes around the latter, reminding me of Michael; he likes those too. Then I remembered this was a habit of just about every eternal being I know, the other arcs included, and Goddess, I think. But memories of her were still a little fuzzy.

"Oh, here comes David Carter," Glara said, patting my arm. "He is not awake, so I shall attempt Earth slang. This will be highly enjoyable because I have been practicing."

The man approaching was tall and slim with short dark hair, an ebony complexion, and a radiant smile. A black and white border collie kept pace as he dashed across the patio, artfully dodging servers and fellow diners who wandered into his path. He stopped in front of Glara and met her eyes.

"It is a very *good morning* on Earth, David Carter," Glara said, glancing at me. I nodded, then noticed the village was already well into its afternoon sun cycle. Not a big deal, and although the whole thing was a bit clunky, she'd gotten the fundamentals right, so I just smiled at her.

"I was hoping you would come back. I waited for you…although I'm not sure for how long." He rubbed his chin, then placed a hand over his heart. "Love and light, Elder."

Glara returned the greeting with a broad smile. "Oh, you are awake."

Udar arrived with a tray of coffee and pastries. He set it down and stepped up to hug the man. "Elder Agan. I hope we did not startle you."

"Oh, no. I was beginning to have bleed-through before you two showed up *this morning*." (More air quotes.) "I was walking around my house, wondering how I got there, then I greeted a tree in my front yard and was surprised when it didn't respond. So, I tried several more trees, although I wasn't sure why." He shook his head. "My neighbor caught me and thought I was nuts. Then you two pretending not to know me; well, something just kicked over. Do you make a habit of studying bushes, Elder?"

Glara laughed. "I did not wish to confuse you with my presence, but I saw the two of you here in these lovely forms and couldn't help myself."

"Don't worry. You didn't. Well, I'll let you visit with Seraphina. We can catch up later." Then he placed a hand on my shoulder. "It's good to see you again, Fire Goddess."

I didn't fully remember him, but he seemed familiar, his four-legged friend too. "Do you mind if I ask you something?"

"Shoot," he said, hands on his hips.

I stifled a grin, thinking he was still well inside his Earth-plane persona. "What about your dog?"

"Belle is my soulmate." He smiled at his companion, who looked into his eyes and wagged her tail. "The transition for animals is much easier, so she woke up the moment we returned. She will transform once we're out of Morningside." He met my gaze and smiled warmly. "I'm not sure if you remember this yet, but magic isn't possible inside recovery villages."

He chuckled. "A good thing too. If any of these souls saw a dog turn into a woman, most of them would be on stretchers headed right back to the recovery center. And we elders would have a busy time of it…convincing them they hadn't gone insane."

Belle woofed her agreement.

"Do you mind if I ask how you got back here? From Earth, I mean?"

"Sure. We were sleeping when our house caught fire."

I winced as the image wormed its way into my brain. Not my idea of it, the event as it played out for them—that happens here—probably so other souls can live vicariously. Yikes. For a moment, I thought my lunch might hit the ejector button, but I cleared my throat and willed it to stay down. "What experience did you each want to have?" I asked, remembering this was the Summerlands' equivalent of *what are you doing this weekend?*

"Loneliness for me, and Belle just wanted to be a dog. I told the council I wished to go by myself, to feel completely alone and untethered, you know? But now I'm glad I listened when they suggested my soulmate come along. I think I would have blown my brains out without her."

Okay, wow. That's graphic, and I knew it was meant in the literal sense. The last download told me not much figure of speech goes on here, either.

"I feel complete with loneliness now," Agan said. "I won't need to repeat it. Next time, we're going to have a vacation."

"What's that?" I asked.

Merriment danced in Agan's brown eyes, and he gave me a winner-take-all grin. "Ah, I see you don't have that memory yet. That's when you go to the Earth plane with no experiential game plan. What makes it so enjoyable is that you don't carry your memories, so you just feel lucky. Humans call it a charmed life, but it's just souls on vacation." He ran a hand over his hair, possibly to feel it one last time before he became light code again. "Like that handsome actor with the salt and pepper hair."

I thought for a moment, trying to place who he meant.

"You know, the one in all those clever films about breaking into Vegas casinos?"

"*He's* on vacation?"

"Oh yes, that soul crafted a beautiful outline; rich, famous, charming, great love life, little drama. Many souls exclude the money and fame piece and take the rest. I think that's what we'll do next time too. Belle and I find it rewarding to bootstrap through human life. Don't we, dearest one?" The elder smiled down at his soulmate, and she responded by placing her paw on his shoe. "A pig for a pet, he had. Just marvelous," he said to her. "Probably his soulmate, too." He looked back at the three of us. "Well, we're off. Love and light."

We returned the greeting, then the two elders headed to the forest to slip out of their latest forms. I watched them go, then asked, "Why does food taste so good here? Oh, wait. A gift from God, right?"

They both nodded.

I sipped my coffee in silence, chewing on something they said earlier; we hadn't planned my current life together *as we usually do*. That meant they hadn't seen me between this life and the last.

Sweat stung my upper lip as I suddenly remembered. I'd been in hiding…here in Morningside. And that recovery villages like this one have veils that keep all-knowing beings from seeing inside. I'd been dodging Michael and the others, everyone, I guess, but there was a big hole in that plan. If my parents knew this was one of my favorite places in the Summerlands, Michael would know it too…he would have searched for me here.

"Daughter, when you came through the portal, you seemed distressed," Udar said, brushing pastry crumbs from his face. "Is there anything we can help with?"

I blinked back tears, wishing I could tell him everything, and then he'd fix it all in time to have a merry Christmas. At least that's what fathers do on the Feel-Good Channel, and I'd spent countless hours dreaming of having a family like the ones I'd seen in those joy-soaked movies. But I'm not fully human, and elementals don't lead lives with promised happy endings. "It's nothing," I said. "What do you want to show me next?"

Udar leaned back in his chair and gave me a studying gaze. Then his expression turned cocky as he rubbed a paper napkin between his hands. "I know something you cannot do on Earth."

I narrowed my eyes at him. "Oh, yeah? What's that?"

"See your past lives."

I sighed and studied my nails. "Did that."

"Not on a movie screen…like a cinematic film."

I brightened. "Well, okay, Mom and Dad, let's see some past lives."

Udar sprang out of his seat. "Excellent. I was hoping you would say that."

We left the café, retracing our steps, but instead of arriving at the edge of the forest, we came to a short alley. A large brick building stood at the end.

"Where are the trees?" I asked.

"Right in front of you," Udar said, smiling. He took my hand, and a moment later, we stepped through the brick wall and onto the woodlands path.

"Right," I said. "I guess you couldn't have a magical forest on the edge of town." I saw now that my parents were once again in robes and sandals. "Didn't you like what you were wearing?"

"Yes. Very much," Glara said. "But new arrivals expect to see us like this. So, when in Rome."

"Oh, perfect, dearest one." Udar did a little jig and planted a palm in the air. "If I didn't know better, I'd say you were a human lady."

Glara slapped his hand and grinned victoriously. "Like riding a bicycle," she said. Udar shot her a couple of finger pistols as a follow-up.

I smiled at their playfulness, thinking of every movie I'd ever seen about the afterlife. Glara was right. Most of the time, the inhabitants wore robes, and I wondered about the other recovery villages. Egypt, during King Tut's reign. England in the Dark Ages. The Ottoman Empire. The Summerlands was an elaborate costume party that never ended.

We followed the same path through the forest, emerging a short while later into a clearing. An enormous alabaster structure loomed in the far distance, and oddly, I remembered having seen it before. Wait. This is the Hall of Records. This is where I need to be.

"Records of every lifetime are stored in that construct," Udar said, jabbing a finger at it.

Yeah, including the one I needed to search.

It dawned on me that it wasn't a building before us. It was, in fact, pure light code, like everything else here. A *construct*, just as Udar said.

Real or not, I didn't think I'd have the guts to watch the movie of the life before this one. Besides, this wasn't the time for experimenting, especially if there was the slightest chance of going mad if I saw something too shocking. And who was I kidding? All of it was shocking. Nope, I needed to search the Akashic Records. Just read the information instead of watching it play out like a movie. At some point, I'd excuse myself and do some digging.

A knot formed in my stomach; this was happening much sooner than I'd hoped. Oh, boy.

CHAPTER
~ 24 ~
The Hall of Records

The Summerlands, Present Moment

"Isn't it marvelous?" Udar asked.

At that point, I could have turned and flashed myself right back into bed inside my cabin. And part of me wanted to do that, badly. But Udar tugged my sleeve and skipped sideways like a football player taking the field. "Come on," he said. Glara laughed, nodding for us to follow.

Before I had time to object, the three of us were racing across the grass. Those two were hauling buns like track stars in their flowing robes and sandals. I happened to be better dressed (for whatever this was) in jeans, a T-shirt, and mismatched trainers; one black, one pink. I still hadn't bothered to change them.

Several minutes—maybe twenty—of hard running later, we reached a glittering silver path that sparkled under each footfall. Udar and Glara didn't slow, and I wasn't about to suffer the indignity of begging for the rest I desperately wanted. So I silently asked my muscles and lungs to keep up, sparkling footsteps, sharp pain under my rib cage, and all.

We zipped by the reflection pool, speeding past souls strolling the serenity gardens I'd seen during my flight with Hira. The flowers and greenery didn't look so peaceful to me now, more like a blur of color as we raced by. Several light-filled beings cheered us on, amused by our enthusiasm.

When we reached the double glass doors, I was a little winded, my steady diet of carbs and alcohol taking their toll. No surprises there, I guess. I bent at the waist, wondering why we hadn't flashed ourselves to the entrance. The dream of being human, I decided as I huffed and puffed and wiped the sweat from my forehead.

Okay, wow. I was *really* winded.

"Now we are at Udar's favorite place," Glara said.

I nodded, eyes wide, hands on my hips. We'd run a little more than four miles and at a good clip. Going from couch potato to that, well, let's just say it's not pretty. Udar held the door, and I slumped into the cool marble interior as a hologram appeared. I jumped and grabbed my heaving chest.

"Love and light," the hologram said in a French accent. She wore a cream brocade gown, an enormous emerald-encrusted necklace, and a white powdered wig piled into a sky-high hairdo like Marie Antoinette. I watched the fabric sway, resisting the urge to towel off with her voluminous skirts.

Glara and Udar beamed at the light-filled courtier. They didn't seem to notice my flushed cheeks and the way I kept picking my T-shirt away from my skin. Both of them looked fresh and cool as if they had done nothing more than get out of an armchair inside an air-conditioned room.

"Welcome to the Hall of Records, where you can see your many lives," Marie Antoinette said. "Please take the escalator on the right to enter the Chamber of Memories. If you need assistance, simply think or say *guide*, and one of our many friendly attendants will join you. Have a joyful experience, and thank you for visiting the Hall of Records." She wiggled her fingers at us. "Please do try to keep your heads, and merci beaucoup," she added with a giggle, then vanished.

Glara waved at the empty space where the hologram had been. "Thank you."

Could Marie Antoinette still see us? I wondered.

"Here we go," Udar said, hustling us to the escalators that stretched so high, they disappeared into a cheerful cloud twelve stories up.

It was a shockingly long ride, and thankfully I'd caught my breath by the time we reached the top.

As we stepped off the mile-high escalator, another hologram appeared. This one was a tall thin man wearing a Homburg hat, a brown three-piece suit, and a pair of stiff wingtips. A delicate gold chain ran from a buttonhole to a timepiece poking out of a vest pocket. The ensemble made him look like a gangster from a 1940s film. All he needed to complete the effect was a Tommy Gun.

"Love and light," he said. "Welcome to the Chamber of Memories. You may follow the signs to the viewing rooms on your right." Gangster hologram extended a hand toward a hallway containing thousands of doors that stretched for miles and miles.

As we moved closer, three doors swung open, and I breathed a sigh of relief. I didn't think I would make it if Udar decided to run us to the end. Whether I stayed in the Summerlands, on the Earth plane, or even in the flipping Underworld, I *really* needed to get back into shape. First thing tomorrow, I promised myself.

"Will you come in with me?" I asked.

Glara smiled empathetically. "Of course we will, dearest one. Guide."

A third hologram popped out of nowhere. This one was in roller skates, a loud polyester shirt in a rainbow pattern, and terry cloth short shorts. He dropped the whistle out of his mouth, letting it dangle by the purple cord around his neck. "How may I be of assistance?" he said, stroking an eyebrow with his ring finger. He seemed annoyed we'd called him back to work.

Udar addressed him. "We'd like to go in with our daughter, please."

"Right this way," the guide said coolly. Then he turned to me, and his face brightened. "Oh...love and light, Fire Goddess," he said, flashing a grin of recognition. Then he pursed his lips, spun around a couple of times, and roller-skated backward through the open doorway, never taking his eyes from me.

"He's a little starstruck by your celebrity," Glara whispered.

Huh. An out-of-shape, depressed celebrity. Sounds about right. All I needed to add to this fun little mix were drugs and a few more questionable choices. Maybe shave my head and have a full-blown meltdown in a public place.

The room we entered was round with silver glass-beaded walls that extended twenty feet, exactly, into a domed ceiling made of the same material.

The ability to judge speed, trajectory, and distance is built into my brain, overlaying dotted lines and right angles. The information is immediate when I choose to engage it. Probably so I can dodge broadswords careening toward my neck at top speed. Useless measurements complete, I let my curiosity take the wheel.

"This is like an Imax Theater," I said to Udar.

He studied the ceiling with his hands on his hips, like a contractor sizing up a job. "Yes, this is where humans got the idea. Well, except for the wraparound images. They missed the best part in the twentieth century." He shrugged. "They remember it…eventually."

The attendant cleared his throat, and we turned around.

At some point, while I was busy gawking at the ceiling, I guess, he'd transformed his outfit into a dark suit. He'd accessorized with mirrored shades, a whisper-thin, black scarf, and silver sequined sneakers. There was an off-white angel-wing stencil barely visible on his white T-shirt, and his slim-cut pants were short enough to expose bare ankles. It looked good on him.

The guide touched a finger to the air on either side of the white chaise lounge, and two more appeared, forming a neat row of three. "Please take a seat," he said, then handed me what looked like a smart tablet.

The three of us got comfortable.

"Well then, Fire Goddess," the guide said, then he giggled and placed a hand over his mouth. Just as quickly, he dropped his hands to his sides, shook them out, and rolled his head. "Okay. Okay. Get it together, sister."

He pulled another tablet from thin air, holding it near his face and pointing like a flight attendant doing a safety demonstration.

I realized I hadn't been on an airplane since 1965, and I hadn't been to my current timeline for several incarnations. I'll bet a lot has changed, reality shifting and all. I smiled, thinking of Braith's same comment the day I'd met him; witches do know just about everything.

"So, you simply select icons to bring up your desired gender category…like I do daily," the guide said, then winked at me. I smiled.

"Here's where you choose your ethnicity, and right here is where you pick all the lovely little sprinkles; happy, sad, mundane, pleasant, vacation, tragic." He took a deep breath and rolled his eyes. "Violent, heroic, ups and downs, poverty, wealth, and so on. Next, under the Life Expectancy category, you have short, medium, long, painfully long, or dear-God-sister-how-long-can-this-possibly-go-on? long."

He laughed at that, and we did too.

"And finally, if you find there are too many choices, you may *spin the wheel*, and Source will select all categories for you." He waved his hand with a flourish. "Enjoy. Love and light," he said. His clothes transformed back into the first outfit, then he put his thumb and pinky to his face like a telephone. "Call me, girl. I know where all the hot-spots are." He blew an air kiss and vanished.

Udar looked at me. "So, what will you choose?"

I thought for a moment, deciding *spin the wheel* was out of the question. I punched up *Male, Heroic* as my *lovely little sprinkle*, and *Medium* for life expectancy as those seemed the safest choices. "You'll just have to wait and see what you see," I said, smiling at him as knights on horseback filled the screen.

Glara clapped her hands as she settled in to watch.

The riders wore white tunics with red crosses emblazoned on the fronts. Huh. I'd been a Knights Templar—that's cool, I decided as I studied the ceiling. It was a stormy day with streaks of lightning in the distance—I could even smell the coming rain—it was so real. I pressed *sound*, and a moment later, we heard thunder, horses snorting, the muck of hooves in the mud, and voices. My eyes landed on the man I was in that life. I had expected to see myself as a hulking brute, but I was much smaller than the others.

One of the riders raced up and trotted alongside me. Now, *this* was a straight-up storybook knight, broad shoulders, muscular build, tall in the saddle with a regal air. I couldn't see his face or mine; we were all wearing helmets that covered our heads: welded metal with cross cutouts.

I tapped *fast-forward*, and in the next scene, the knights were walking into a magnificent stone castle. The knight who had ridden alongside me grabbed my hand, led me up the stairs, and through a massive wooden door into a bedroom. He shut the door behind us with his foot, took off his helmet, and pulled me to him.

I gasped. It was Michael—maybe in his late forties, although he was as handsome as ever. My stomach clenched at the sight of him, and I toyed with the idea of turning this awful movie off. I couldn't believe I hadn't thought of this before now; Michael has been with me in every life I've had. I blinked at the screen, thinking this might be the only way to see him again. So I kept going, even though my guts were churning.

The knight who was me in that life removed his helmet too. Wait. It was *me*, in my current form, also older. Michael drew me into a kiss, and I watched us on that screen, longing for him until I couldn't take it anymore. Tears welled in my eyes, making the tablet challenging to see, but I found the *death* icon and pressed it, wanting to torment myself for what I'd done to us.

The scene flashed forward. Several of us were strapped to stakes with kindling at our feet and twig bundles leaning against our bodies. Our heads were shorn, and I looked like a scared little boy in my bare-headed crew cut as I struggled against my bindings. Michael was tied to the stake next to mine, and each of us had men tethered behind us.

The executioner (decked out in the uniform one might expect for such a job: brown tunic, rope belt, a lifetime of eschewing salad) stepped forward, torch at the ready. Go ahead and kill me, I thought angrily as I watched myself about to be charbroiled over an open flame.

I didn't have long to wait because our one-person death squad got down to the business of setting us aglow. He paused when he got to Michael and retracted the torch.

"We are not guilty of the financial crimes against us, and we are not the heretics you believe us to be, good sir," Michael said to him. "And once you realize that, please know that we forgive you."

The executioner lingered, and I realized it wasn't Michael's words; it was the archangel's love for him that was casting doubts. He could feel it, just like all humans could. He shook his head as if regaining his senses and lit the kindling at Michael's feet.

The flames started slowly at first, then grew higher as a *whoosh* of air hit. I could see Michael talking to me, but I couldn't hear him. I found *Zoom* and pressed it. "Sera," he said. "This realm will lose its power over you if you just relax into death. Surrender, and the flames will not hurt you, my love."

"I'm scared!" I said as this version of me remembered why. Usually, I died during a battle, a few times of disease, sometimes even of old age. I *am* fire, so it was confusing to die in this way—like your own people turning on you in a moment of insanity-fueled rage.

"Don't be afraid, my darling," Michael said as the flames licked higher. "Just breathe, relax into it."

I saw myself cough and struggle with the bindings a few moments more, then I slumped. Destroyed by fire. How fitting.

I watched as a soft glow radiated from within the other knights and me, and all of us but Michael left our bodies.

Why hadn't he gone?

I held my breath as Michael's beautiful face contorted, his skin blistered, erupting in red welts. Then something unexpected happened. Michael split himself in two; one of him stepped down from the pyre. The other remained there to burn.

The scene faded, and the lights came up.

CHAPTER

~ 25 ~

New Arrivals

The Summerlands, Present Moment

I gripped the sides of the chair, struggling to understand what I'd just seen and thinking maybe I shouldn't have pushed the *death* icon after all.

"Sera," Udar said. "Are you all right?"

"I think so."

Glara put a hand on my arm. "Daughter?"

"I saw Michael step off the pyre, but also stay on it," I said.

"He is an archangel, dearest one. They cannot die."

I knew the arcs couldn't be killed inside the third dimension, but I didn't remember if they felt pain, and now I had a desperate need for the answer. "Did Michael feel the flames?"

"No. Earth fire doesn't burn him just as Earth's steel won't penetrate his skin," Udar said. "What you saw remaining was a hologram to look as if his body burned with all the rest."

I breathed a sigh of relief. "Oh. Thank Goddess. Did I feel the flames?"

Glara nodded somberly. "You did. But just as Michael said, the moment you relax into death, you are gone."

Part of me wanted to go to Michael, but I knew I couldn't. Not yet. Not while I was still in the dark about so much, and maybe not ever. I swallowed hard, thinking of the way I looked in the castle and on the pyre. "Do I look the same in each lifetime? To Michael, I mean?"

"Yes. Your eternal forms remain," Glara said. "Archangels and elementals use overlays when needed; centuries with photographs, the Internet, and instant-recognition nanobots make them necessary. Or when you present as a male."

Of course. I knew about the overlays, Michael had told me. As Elizabeth McKenna, I had another body entirely thanks to one. And had I given it more than a passing thought, I would have known Michael has always been with me, whether I presented to the rest of the world as male or female. Eager for more distraction, I had walked right into that dung heap in the Hall of Records, thinking that choosing a male lifetime would keep me from seeing Michael. I silently chastised myself for being so reckless.

Then, another thought hit me, and I patted myself down like a cop searching for a weapon. "Do I have an overlay in this lifetime?"

"You do not," Glara said. "None of you do. They were not needed this time."

I got up from the lounger and rubbed my temples, fighting off the first twinge of a stabbing headache. The Akashic Records would have to wait. "Could we go back to the house?" I asked.

We were in the living room before I'd even completed the request.

My parents took seats on the couch, and I curled up in the armchair opposite them. There was a sick feeling in my stomach, not from the flashing this time. "Michael always sees me as I am now?" I asked.

"He does," Udar said.

Glara poured tea from a service that had just appeared on the coffee table and handed it to me. I shook my head. "He does not see your overlay, just as you do not see his." She glanced at me and placed the cup and saucer back on the tray.

"I never change, and Michael doesn't lose his memory. How can he still be in love with someone who stays the same for eternity?"

"The arcs do not register the passing of time as you do," Udar said. "Even I don't understand it entirely. But I think Michael experiences a sequence of events that can be stopped, started, or interchanged at will. That ability also allows him to adjust the Earth-plane clock as needed. Don't ask me how that works," he said more to himself than to me.

A new question sprang to mind. One that filled me with sudden fear and made me feel like an idiot because I still couldn't remember. "Can Michael see his future? Or mine?" I said, licking my lips. If he could and decided to take a peek, I was in big trouble.

"No. Archangels cannot see their futures," Udar said. "And they can't search the Akashic Records for details about their lives or the lives of elementals."

Oh, thank Goddess, I thought, placing a hand on my stomach as blessed relief washed through me. I'm not sure what I looked like at that moment, but Glara caught my face, and her expression changed. She was beginning to click some puzzle pieces into place.

"They cannot see an elemental's present, either," she said, studying me. "It is designed that way so you may discover the wonders of life together. It's—"

"Another gift from Source," I said, rubbing my eyes.

"You are missing him?" Glara asked.

Not exactly what I was thinking, but I managed a nod.

My bedroom here is identical to my room on Earth, a bit confusing when you're not fully awake…from sleep, I mean. I rolled over, thinking Michael would be lying beside me. He wasn't there, of course, and suddenly remembering the reason for that, I groaned and threw an arm over my eyes.

I'd set up a twenty-four-hour sun-moon cycle outside the house. Otherwise, a thousand years could slip by without me giving it much thought. I ticked off the days in my mind and swallowed hard, shocked to realize I'd been here almost six months. I know how absurd that sounds, but in a place where time does not exist, an Earth-plane year feels like a handful of days.

I'd resumed my training and thankfully dropped the *ten pounds* I'd packed on while at the cabin. Now I could outrun Glara and Udar whenever they chose to sightsee at top speed.

I spent my days engaged in mindless tasks, planting flowers around the house, sipping coffee in the Morningside Café. I visited recovery villages from various periods on Earth, playing dress-up there and dropping into different languages to communicate with the inhabitants. Anything and everything to continue avoiding my feelings, but sometimes they crept in on me like they were doing now.

I still hadn't perused the Akashic Records. I just hadn't found the courage.

Today was the day I decided. "Just do it," I said to the ceiling. But I said the same at the beginning of each new sun-cycle and was still no closer to acting on it. I buried my face in the pillow then heard a muffled knock at the door.

"Sera?" It was Glara.

"Come in."

"Good morning, Daughter." I caught the irony in her voice. There is no morning here. "Come with me. There is something I would like to share with you, and you will not want to miss it."

A short while later, I was standing in the foyer, showered and dressed. My parents were in white linen ankle-length tunics. Looking down, I saw that I was too; that was Glara's work. I'd whipped up jeans, sneakers, and my NASA T-shirt, which was now so threadbare it deserved a Viking funeral.

Udar shot me a lightning-quick grin and rubbed his palms together. "Okay, here we go."

He flashed us to the Arrivals Meadow, and I popped in like an old pro. I was used to them flashing me around now. It didn't bother me in the slightest anymore. One minute I was in a garden smelling a flower from another dimension. Then poof... I was on a rocky cliff with the wind blowing my hair, and Glara and Udar excited to show me something new. I'd gotten good at rolling with their *flashing* punches. I liked it, just another distraction.

A dark shadow swallowed a significant portion of the meadow, and I looked up to see hundreds of dragons coming in for a landing. They settled in, forming a perfect circle around us.

My breath caught when I saw Michael land at Hira's feet, a radiant light glowing from his body as he bowed his head and stretched his wings. He was taking his position in the south quadrant of the circle...our quadrant.

My first reaction was one of slight discomfort, bordering on mild displeasure. I'm sure I reached for something more substantial, but my lower-energy human emotions were muted by the Summerlands Effect. Anger, pain, fear, depression, and more were beginning to get fuzzy around the edges.

Meanwhile, the higher vibrations of joy and pleasure were amped up, like sky-high. If I thought something was lovely, it quickly became the most beautiful I'd ever seen. If I was a little happy, I was euphoric a split second later. Now, for example, I was reaching for *hurt* and *betrayal*. How could Glara have done this to me? I dug deep, focused on reclaiming those feelings, but couldn't quite make the connection.

Wait. There's no way she could know I was avoiding Michael, although she might have suspected. Michael had no reason to believe I was avoiding him either. He could no longer read my mind, whether I was here or on the Earth plane. To him, I had just stepped through Yggdrasil's portal from Helena's shop. He'd arrived a moment later, here in this field, where the sight of him was tormenting me. Well, more like mildly annoying me.

The other archangels were here too. Raphael stood with Kricket's dragon, Heron, in the east quadrant of the circle. Gabriel was next to Helena's dragon, Hita, in the west. Uriel with Andrea's dragon, Halbom, in the north.

The air was thick with the fragrance of fresh grass and wildflowers, and silence swallowed every sound in the meadow. The three suns brightened then softened their rays, casting a golden glow over us—beautiful and eerie—like the still and quiet moments before a storm.

The dragons bowed their heads as Gabriel raised a horn and blew a note sounding like a choir of a hundred voices hitting the same key at once. When the sound died down, Glara walked to the center of the circle, and Hira, Hita, Heron, and Halbom stamped a foot three times in unison.

I felt a jolt, and it took a moment to realize they had just engaged the cosmic doorbell of the four elementals. I remembered that if I were still on the Earth plane, I wouldn't even know I was getting tapped to do my job. My soul would answer the call automatically.

Since I was here, I did feel it and thankfully knew what to do. I focused my mind and opened the South Gate over Australia. The really odd thing was I could feel it expanding, tickling my insides as it grew larger. The portal came to a thudding stop I could hear in my head and feel in my chest. My gate was fully open now, my attention split between two realms—my soul standing guard in deep space, my body here in this meadow. And although they were still on the Earth plane, I felt the other elementals open their gates too.

A tower of light forced its way through the ground near where Glara stood. It grew brighter, the wind whipping a circle faster and faster until it transformed into a golden box slightly larger than a phone booth. A laser beam shot from the top, piercing the heavens and lighting the meadow in a brilliant white blaze. The dragons became translucent, and energy streamed from their magnificent bodies joining with energetic waves pulsing from the golden box.

A selenite wand appeared in Glara's right hand. She turned clockwise, her arms outstretched, pausing briefly in each of the four directions as she called upon the elementals. "Goddesses of Earth, Air, Water, and Fire, clear and protect the path of our journeying brothers and sisters." She bowed her head. "Michael, Uriel, Gabriel, Raphael, receive these souls into your arms to comfort them." She turned her face skyward. "God, Goddess, Source; we welcome your children home." As she spoke these final words, four doorways materialized in the magical phone booth, undulating with a golden liquid.

My heart pounded in my ears as the energy around us intensified, playing on my skin like electricity, and a good feeling came over me.

Then *good* quickly shifted into *mind-blowing* as the Summerlands Effect had its way.

Gabriel blew a second note, more beautiful than the first, and Glara stepped back as hundreds of humans streamed from the four doorways. There were men, women, and children. Some walking, some in wheelchairs, some carried on stretchers. Beings I immediately recognized as guardian angels came through cradling infants.

"Welcome home," Glara said, reaching out to take the hand of a startled-looking young woman who had just emerged from the golden liquid. The words WELCOME HOME also appeared in the sky above us, written in puffy white clouds. It was so cheerful and comforting I almost wept.

A crowd of light-filled souls stepped into the circle from behind the dragons. Some were shaped like women, others like men. All of them glowed as they moved toward the new arrivals in a way that told me they had come to welcome their loved ones home.

Glara spoke again. "You are safe here, and the confusion will pass shortly. Please follow your greeters to the recovery center where refreshment awaits you."

An older man standing near me burst into tears and touched the face of his greeter, a light-filled being in the shape of a male. "Mama?" he said.

The soul transformed into a young woman wearing a gray wool jacket and pencil skirt; her clothes and hairstyle suggesting she belonged in the 1950s. "Yes, my darling son, I am here," she said. The man slumped into her as she stroked his hair and spoke to him in soothing tones. Then the two of them turned and walked away from me, and I cried tears of joy for them both.

The rest of the light beings had shifted into human form as well, filling the meadow with what appeared to be hundreds of people. All races, shapes, sizes, and ages, hugging, laughing, and crying.

A stooped woman who seemed more than a hundred years old straightened, threw her walker away, and did several handsprings ending in a roundhouse flip. The moment her feet touched the ground, she was young again. Her short gray hair now long, red, and luxuriant. The woman clapped her hands. "I'm home! Blessed be the Goddess!"

The four elemental dragons stamped their feet again, and I closed the South Gate as the golden box descended into the ground. The dragons took flight, creating a warm breeze that felt good on my skin. I shut my eyes, telepathically scanning the skies over Australia for signs of trouble.

"Hey, Valentine. You coming home anytime soon?"

I nearly gasped at the sound of Michael's voice. I opened my eyes and smiled up at him. "What do you mean? You just saw me."

"I got a read on it when I arrived. You've been here a while. Something I said?" He gave me a love-struck smile and wrapped his arms around my waist.

I tensed.

Michael released me and took a step back. "Oh. I'm sorry. Are you okay, Sera?"

"I can't do this now," I said more tersely than intended. I wasn't mad at Michael, of course. I was furious with myself...and with *She* who created all. I knew Goddess had something to do with my memory loss. I could feel it with my super strength intuition.

The arc's brow furrowed. "You can talk to me. I can help."

"Not with this... I need to figure some things out, that's all. I'm sorry."

"All right," he said. "I've got work to do...in the recovery center. Find me when you're ready, okay?"

I agreed, not sure that time would ever come.

Michael turned away slowly, probably hoping I would say something else. I didn't, and he jogged ahead to catch up with the other archangels.

Tears welled as I watched him go.

No matter how afraid I was to learn the truth, the time had come for answers. And whoever erased my memories better hope they were in a dimension where I couldn't get my hands on them—and yes—that included *Her, Him, It*.

I flashed myself to the Hall of Records, arriving in a burst of anger-fueled red light, and flung the doors open.

A hologram appeared. "Welcome to the Hall—"

"Save it," I said, rushing past him and his ridiculous gladiator outfit. His armor clanked as our shoulders brushed.

"I hope you have a pleasant experience," he called after me. I didn't respond; I just hurled myself onto the escalator and took the stairs two at a time.

"No," I said to the greeter at the top who came at me like a department store clerk with a spritz of cologne. Then a few paces up, I realized I couldn't remember where to go. Red-faced, I spun around, stomped back to the hologram, and spoke to her through gritted teeth. "Where will I find the Akashic Records."

She told me, and I took off at a run, not even bothering to thank her. Not exactly a public meltdown but close.

I reached the doors and flung myself inside only to be met with an infinite number of leather-bound books on endless shelves that stretched as far as the eye could see. I turned slowly, not knowing where to start.

Another hologram appeared at my side—she wore a matching sweater set with glasses suspended from a chain. "Welcome to the Universal Library," she said, hands folded at her waist. "How may I help, Fire Goddess?"

I stood motionless for a moment, not sure how to ask for what I needed. "I want to see the full account of my life before this one."

The hologram licked her lips. It took me by surprise, and I relaxed my shoulders. "I'm sorry. Will you please help me?"

"Of course, right this way."

We walked for a while, her heels clicking on the hardwood floor. The sound—while soft and maybe comforting to some—drummed into my head like a jackhammer. She stopped, and the bookshelves to our immediate left parted to reveal a cozy reading room—wood and leather, and green shaded lamps.

"This is the Angels and Elementals section," the librarian said. "As a reminder, you will only be able to search your own records, and they will exclude information about the other warriors of light. And they will not contain events from your future timelines."

I grunted my understanding as I walked toward an oak table and chairs in the center of the room. The librarian invited me to have a seat, but I shook my head, preferring to stand.

"Very well," she said as a large leather-bound book appeared on the table. "I am Vandalia, and I am the head librarian here. Should you need anything else, just say or think my name." Her expression softened, and a look of sorrow washed over her. "Love and light, Fire Goddess."

Vandalia slipped from the room, leaving me alone with the truth I wasn't sure I wanted to know.

The book was divided into sections. I flipped through them until I got to the part that mattered, then began ticking off the number of Universal Bylaws I'd broken with my little venture into the dark realm. I had taken Yggdrasil to the Underworld in 1967; there's broken law number one. Living as Mortegol's mate for thirty years took care of laws two through fifteen. I rifled past all the fornication (pages and pages). I'd already seen plenty of that in shocking detail at the cabin and felt no desire to walk further down that memory lane.

Actions were next on the list, and I was relieved to see I didn't participate in Mortegol's dark business on the Earth plane. But that brief respite was quickly followed by a realization there was still a fair bit missing from the records. Nothing too glaring, just small skips in the data, little pockets of time that left me wondering. The entry concluded with the dagger poking from my chest (something I was eager to forget) and my arrival in the Summerlands one hour and thirty-two minutes later.

Wait. That was too long. The whole journey is over in minutes.

I flipped to the *Motivations & Conclusions* section. While these pages should have outlined my reason for going and the outcome of that lifetime—lessons learned and how my actions affected the Earth timeline—they were blank.

I hurled the book across the room and pounded a fist on the table. "Where is the rest of it?" I screamed at the ceiling, but I was not addressing Vandalia, so she did not appear. "Tell me why I went there! And tell me who erased my memories! Was it you?" I didn't need to shout. I knew she could hear my thoughts before I could think them. But I was furious, and the yelling felt good.

Without warning, I was inside an empty space—white floor, white ceiling, white walls. (If there were any of those things. Probably not.) My heart raced at the sudden change in scenery—or lack of it—but I gathered myself and squared my shoulders. Good. I had questions, and she was going to answer every last one of them. Then she would fix this. I wouldn't accept anything else, and I would not leave until she'd made things right.

CHAPTER

~ 26 ~

The Goddess Appears

Seventh Plane, Present Moment

"Seraphina, why do you speak to me in this harsh manner?"

I couldn't see her, but she sounded pissed, and her tone nearly swept my resolve right under the carpet. Although it was in the middle of a desperate escape, I managed to take hold of my indignance. "I want you to tell me why. Why did you allow this?"

Nothing happened for a few moments, so I stood there seething into the void, fists balled at my sides, wondering if the Creator would attend the impromptu showdown. My mouth went dry when she finally materialized—not because she had shown herself—because of the way she looked. Goddess had selected a vessel resembling my Celeste; her brown hair spilled over a shoulder, her mahogany skin shimmering with eternal light. Still, the package was close enough to sober me right up.

Suddenly overcome with emotion, mental exhaustion, and being in the presence of the Eternal Mother (who looked like my mother on Earth), I began to cry. Before I knew it, Goddess was holding me in her arms. "That's it, dearest one. Let it all out," she said quietly, stroking my hair. I didn't need a second invitation and let the floodgates open. I cried until my throat burned, my face hurt, and I had wrung every ounce of energy from my half-mortal body.

When I'd finished, Goddess drew back and wiped the last of my tears away. I noticed now that she even smelled like Celeste, a floral and fresh linen scent. It was Celeste's favorite perfume—one I'd bought for her on special occasions. The thought surprised me. Then I realized Goddess flipped that snapshot to make me think of my human mother. To remind me of all eternal beings who went to the Earth plane to gather experiences there. *She* never does anything by chance.

"That's it, my child. It's good to cry, and you have not allowed yourself to do it. Not over this."

"How do you know?" I said through one final sob.

Goddess raised her eyebrows, her golden-flecked-brown eyes filled with knowing.

"Oh, right," I said, conjuring a handkerchief and blowing my nose. I threw it away from me, and it vanished into thin air.

"I am always with you, Seraphina, even when you were there."

Although she meant them to be comforting, her words stung me, and I covered my face as hurt and shame took turns walloping me in the gut.

"There is no reason to be ashamed, dearest one," Goddess said, plucking the thought from my mind as easily as one might pick a piece of fruit from a basket.

"I lived in the Underworld among the demons, with Mortegol... as his mate."

Goddess looked at me with love in her eyes. "Think of the first Persephone. Did she not sacrifice herself to end the blight upon the lands and bring prosperity to her people?"

"It was a mission?"

She nodded. "It was."

"But I loved Mortegol. How could I—?"

"Is it not within your heart to do so? He is my creation, and I love him as much as I do you and Michael and every soul."

"But I love Michael, and Mortegol is evil incarnate," I said, then closed my eyes as shame bulldozed me again. While at the cabin, I remembered lovingly tracing the scars on Mortegol's back where his angelic wings used to be. The many times I eagerly awaited his return after he carried out some loathsome mission on the Earth plane. I remembered too that I couldn't stand the thought of being without him, and now I couldn't understand any of it.

"Your feelings for Mortegol did not replace your love for Michael. And he is not evil, Seraphina. He simply has a job to do. One that was given by me...and his role is just as important as yours. Mortegol is my son, and he rules the Underworld to help preserve balance. Otherwise, the Earth plane would be just like the Summerlands, and what good would that do?"

She placed her sparkling brown hands on my shoulders and met my eyes. "And I might have given you a little nudge in that direction, to ease the pain of it."

I couldn't believe what I was hearing. "A little nudge?" I said through gritted teeth. "You made me flat-out love him. Passionately. Against my will. I pined for him when he was away from me. Oh, my God—dess," I stuttered, trying to catch the blaspheme, wishing I could stuff it right back inside my mouth.

Her eyebrows raised, but she didn't say a word.

I squared my shoulders, my anger boiling. "I even pined for Mortegol when he was by my side. How is that a *little* nudge?"

"Okay. Perhaps I overdid it a bit. So shoot me," Goddess said, raising her hands in a sign of surrender.

I scoffed at her. "Oh, you *think*?"

Yes. I was that angry.

"You had already agreed to go. What good would it have done for you to be miserable? Why would I allow you to suffer in that way, and for so long?"

I glared at her, feeling sick to my stomach. She had betrayed me. I turned away, afraid of what I might say next if I didn't.

"If everything were as black and white as you say, the Earth plane would be an even harsher place," Goddess said to my back. "Would you like to remember why I asked you to do this?"

I spun around and looked her squarely in the eyes—Celeste's eyes—anger still ripping through me. I was about to say something smart but decided against that and nodded instead.

"All right, but it might be easier if I show you."

I pursed my lips and glared at the Almighty as she placed a warm palm on my forehead. A second later, I was drifting through a wormhole. This time, I had my arms tightly folded as I moved through, feeling no joy in the journey. But I began to relax as the years ticked by.

I arrived seated at a desk, and a room formed around me, an office on a high floor overlooking the city. "I remember this place," I said, taking in the Danish-modern interior. This was San Francisco in 1967, where I was a junior partner at a law firm. We were an anomaly, a pro-bono outfit funded by a rather large family fortune. The court didn't assign our clients; we chose our own. I exhaled a long breath, realizing the trip had worn away a lot of my anger.

"This is where I came to you. The place where you agreed to this mission." Goddess's voice sounded just as clear as if she were in the room with me.

"What do you mean, I agreed? I would never—"

"But you did, Seraphina. I asked for your help, and you gave it willingly."

I ran a hand over the desk, my eyes drifting to the window; the Golden Gate Bridge was cloaked in a heavy fog. My hurt drained away as I remembered how much I loved this place, this period, defending those who had no one else. Wait. I had selected San Francisco to be near my children from a previous life. I smiled as those memories came to the forefront of my mind—all the creative ways I visited them.

I was a volunteer who helped Mary with a few charity auctions. I lunched at the same spot Ruby and her life partner Margaret frequented. I also popped into the cafeteria at Stanford to see George. He let me share his table and even gave me a cookie from his tray. Alden and I had a friendly chat near the vending machines at St. Francis. It was a rare afternoon when he'd finished his rounds early. We'd sipped horrible coffee from horrible Styrofoam cups, talking for nearly an hour before he was called away for an emergency.

All of them had grown into such lovely adults.

In their minds, I was just a nice young lady who took the trouble to make conversation, and I'm sure none of them gave me another thought afterward. But I was also there at the end of each of their lives. Just as I have been for all my children through the ages. Being an elemental does have its perks.

"Hello?"

The child's voice broke the lovely spell of being here again, and I turned around. A little girl wearing a pink jumper and canvas sneakers stood in the doorway. She rubbed the tip of her shoe over her shin and looked at me with pooling eyes.

"Well, hello there," I said.

"I have something to tell you."

Thinking she might be lost, I decided to park her in my office. "Okay, why don't you come here and have a seat?" I rested my hands on the back of a chair as the girl crossed the room in mincing steps. She reached me and climbed into the seat, her feet dangling a few inches off the floor. "May I?" I asked, pointing at her sneakers. The girl nodded and rubbed her eye as I tied her laces. That taken care of, I moved around my desk to ring my assistant. "Hey, Kat, there's a young lady in my office who has misplaced her parents. Are they in with Bill?"

I smiled at the girl and opened a drawer, rummaging around until I'd found a stick of gum. I offered it to her, but she shook her head. So I undid the wrapper and popped the gum into my mouth, studying her delicate features as I listened to Katherine query our colleagues. The child was five or six, but the look in her eyes was unnerving, like she was ancient, a little spooky. I was twenty-nine at the time, had been awake for seven years.

Then a light blinked.

This was not a child. It was a messenger. No. Wait. It was Goddess herself. Cripes. "Never mind. I found them." I fumbled the receiver back into its cradle.

"I need to tell you. The world is going to end."

I almost spat the gum from my mouth. "What?"

"Mortegol will set the world on fire, and you are the only one who can stop him." She waved her hand above her, and a replica of Earth hung in midair.

Explosions fired off all over the planet, followed by billowing mushroom clouds. A moment later, Earth was a lifeless rock wobbling through outer space with asteroids smashing into it because it had been knocked from its orbit.

"This is the last incarnation of Earth, and Mortegol will destroy it unless you go to him. He has just changed the course of these events, so I am afraid you must go now."

Whirling light, color, and sound filled the room as the scene moved forward in time. I seemed to be hovering near the ceiling now, looking down on myself, and watched as that version of me stepped through Yggdrasil's portal, headed to the realm of demons. I was wearing the same clothes, and the light streaming into my office windows hadn't changed, so I must have gone only a few minutes after Goddess's visit. I already knew I hadn't told the others before leaving.

I drifted back through the wormhole and found myself once again standing before the Goddess. "I remember it now," I said, sobbing into my hands. I had willingly gone to the Underworld— had voluntarily given myself to Mortegol to save the Earth plane. Even so, Michael would never feel the same about me. Not after he learned what I'd done, no matter the reason.

"But he will, Seraphina," Goddess said, reading my thoughts.

She sat down on nothing, the air supporting her as if it were a wooden chair. "And you know better than anyone Michael would do the same. He loves humans, my lovely daughter. He would never allow harm to come to them."

"Then why couldn't he be the one to stop this? Why did it have to be me? And in that way?"

"Mortegol has always longed for you, and he is jealous of Michael for having you," she said. "Even as my beautiful Archangel Lucifer, he could not understand the permanence of your bond. He believes the Fire Goddess should be his, and his alone." Goddess paused, and I could tell she was choosing her next words carefully.

"He was angry with me for not promising you to him. It was Lucifer's reason for the rebellion. You know that, too, when you are between lives."

I sucked in a breath. Goddess was right about one thing; I had forgotten that war was my fault. The rebellion nearly split the Summerlands in two. Lucifer and three-hundred thirty-two fellow angels had been cast out for defying her. She had stripped him of his wings, his holy name, and afterward made him King of the Underworld, I thought as punishment. But hearing her words, I wasn't so sure of that anymore.

"Your time with Michael is not through," Goddess said. "I know his heart. Michael will understand. He will accept this. You know as well as I do, Seraphina, that if presented with this choice, he would have done the same." She rose from her air seat and took my hand in hers. "But you must not tell him. The events have not yet fully taken shape. You must wait until it is too late to change them. Do you understand?"

I shook my head. "What do you mean? Did I fail?"

"No. All is as it should be, but this is a mission spanning two lifetimes."

"Then what sense did it make for you to erase my memories?" I spat; my words fueled with enough anger to light her hair on fire.

"Seraphina, you did not arrive in the meadow as you remember. You came to the seventh dimension and begged me to erase your time in the Underworld. You couldn't bear the pain of knowing you had deceived Michael…and that you would have to again. I only did as you asked because I could not stand to see you suffer."

I rocked back on my heels; her confession more sobering than if she'd doused me with a bucket of ice water.

"When you came to me, we went through every part of this mission. To complete it as we planned together, you must return to Michael and put your house in order. Spend no more time in that cabin with your pancake skeet and purple cows. Although I did rather enjoy seeing you shoot them down with those spectacular fireballs. The pancakes, I mean. Not the lovely cows."

A bittersweet smiled curved the edges of her lips, and she placed a hand on my cheek. "I know all seems lost, but you must have faith." She held my gaze. "I'm afraid your mission has one final step, and it will be hard, harder than anything you have ever faced."

I wiped my eyes and looked at her intently, tasting the salt in my tears as they ran over my lips.

"You must go to the Underworld again, but this time, you must take Michael with you. He is the key."

My mind reeled—she couldn't mean it—the Underworld is the only place an archangel can suffer everlasting death. I backed away from her as horror clawed at every part of my being. "No! I would have never agreed to that."

"It is the only way, Seraphina…that is why you asked me to remove those memories. You couldn't stand knowing what you had yet to do, and you were afraid you would back out if given too much time to think. I am sorry to remind you of this now, Daughter, but if you do not return to the Underworld with Michael, the world will end. And this time, it will not regenerate. The current incarnation of the Earth plane is the last."

I cried harder than before, slumping to the floor of the void. "Michael will die there. I won't do it," I said, choking on the words.

Goddess knelt beside me and wrapped her arms around my shaking body. "Dearest one, you always have a choice. If you decline to finish this mission, the world will end, but you and Michael and all souls will spend eternity in the Summerlands. Or in the dimension of your choosing, anywhere you like." She rubbed my back for several minutes as I cried. Then she stood, leaving me to work through the pain on my own.

I sat with my head buried between my knees, breathing hard, letting her words sink in. Then I looked up at her, fear and pain coursing through me. "Does Michael have to die?"

"He will have a choice. And if he chooses everlasting death, I cannot stop him, nor can you."

Despair crashed into me, hitting with such force that I doubled over and cried even harder. I thought of the countless souls who found joy in the harsh realities of their lifetimes on Earth. They loved the experiences they collected there, and I and the other elementals and archangels had always protected their ability to have them. It was the sole reason for our being.

I could not be the one to end it for them now, and I knew Michael would not want me to make this choice for him. He would do anything for the Earth plane, no matter the cost. Michael would gladly give up everlasting life to save a single human being, and I knew it.

After what seemed like an eternity in itself, I stood up, dried my face, and met Goddess's eyes. "How will I know when the time is right, and how will I know what to do once we get there?"

"The opportunities will present themselves, dearest one, and you will feel them with your overinflated intuition. You know, the one you set to the highest level against your friend's better judgment?"

I didn't know what she meant by that, but my intuition is so keen, I figured I must have done something to it. It had never been this spot-on.

Goddess smiled at me, resting a hand on my cheek. I closed my swollen eyes, allowing her love-fueled touch to heal me. A moment later, I could feel all physical evidence of my crying jag had been erased.

"I've never been prouder of you than I am right now. Love and light, Fire Goddess." She kissed my forehead, and I felt her leave.

When I opened my eyes, I was back in the meadow, with an even bigger secret wedged in my heart, and deep-seated anguish over knowing I might lose Michael…forever this time.

I made a vow to love him for as long as I could. Whether we had a day or a week, or an entire lifetime left, I would cherish every moment.

CHAPTER

~ 27 ~

Soul Contracts

The Summerlands, Present Moment

I called Michael's name in my mind, and the air shifted as he appeared before me. I studied his face as the light of the three suns backlit his blond hair. Suddenly, I understood how a human might mistake that for a halo.

"I'm sorry about before," I said, smiling up at him, pushing the mission from my mind as best I could. "Where did you go?" He'd told me, but I'd forgotten. Anyway, I just wanted to hear his voice.

Michael hooked a thumb behind him. "The other arcs and I were at the recovery center, helping ease the shock of dropping the body."

"That's right. Does that take a while?" I said, trying to sound like I hadn't a care in the world.

"For some. The elders get back into the swing quickly. Most of them jump up and start pitching in within a few minutes."

Michael was back in his leather jacket, T-shirt, and jeans. He stuck his hands in his pockets and scrunched his shoulders. "You stayed away for a long time, is everything okay?"

"I had some thinking to do. Just needed some perspective."

"But you're all right?"

I nodded.

"And there is nothing I can do to help?"

I shook my head. "I'm fine." I took his hand and held it to my face.

"Are you sure, Sera? What's wrong, babe?"

"I love you," I said. "With every fiber of my being and every beat of my heart. Promise to remember that always?" I looked into his blue eyes, and he leaned down and kissed me tenderly as if it were the last kiss we would ever share. Then he drew back and met my gaze. Although he could no longer read my mind, Michael knows me better than anyone, better than I know myself.

"I love you, Sera. There is nothing you could say or do that would ever change the way I feel about you. I hope you understand that."

I nodded, encircling him in my arms. "I'm just a bit pensive, I guess."

"Then why don't you come with me? I can show you something that will brush that pensiveness right off. Something cool."

"Cooler than souls springing out of a space-age box into a field of dragons and archangels?" I asked.

"Yep, cooler than that."

"Well, I'm in, mister. Lead the way."

Michael flashed us to the base of a mountain and placed his palm on a rock outcropping. A moment later, a door appeared. It creaked open on its own, and we walked into a crisp, dimly lit cave with two mine-shaft style elevators on either side. There were signs above each, LAUNCH SITE and PLANNING CENTER.

A hologram materialized. "How may I help you?" she asked. Then her expression changed to one of surprised delight. "Oh, love and light Archangel Michael, Fire Goddess."

"We're here to visit the planning center, please," Michael said.

"Of course." The hologram smiled at us, then vanished as the elevator doors on the right slid open. I took Michael's hand as we stepped inside, relieved to be near him again.

"You need special clearance to gain access here. Archangels and elementals are the exceptions," Michael said with a wink.

"Why can't anyone come here whenever they want?"

"Oof," he said. "This place is an all-you-can-eat buffet of experience. Souls need one-on-one counseling first, or they get excited and load too many horrific items onto their plates. The elders advise sprinkling the harder stuff throughout several incarnations, so the poor human doesn't become overwhelmed. All that levelheaded advice gets reiterated here, but it usually goes right out the window. Free will," Michael added with a sigh.

It seemed fitting he would bring me here moments after I'd made the gut-wrenching decision to put both of us on a course to protect this experience. Me knowingly, Michael unwittingly. God, I felt like Mata Hari…lookout for that firing squad, my internal voice added nastily.

The elevator stopped on LL, and the doors slid open. Michael sprang into the hallway and spun to face me; his arms spread wide. "Humans are wonderful, magical, incredible beings. Oh, how I love them, every single one. And all that glorious humanness starts inside these walls."

My heart squeezed in my chest, knowing Michael would gladly sacrifice himself for even one human being, no questions asked.

"Even murderers?" I asked as we walked down the long corridor.

"Especially murderers."

My head snapped toward him. "What? Why would you especially love *murderers*?" That seemed a little too unconditional, even for him.

"When souls plan experiences, that means all of them, not just the happy ones," he said. "A human who kills another is working through a contract signed right here before souls go to the Earth plane together. A *murderer*"—he placed air quotes around the word—"is simply holding up their end of the bargain. Even in the most ruthless individuals, there's a tiny voice that tries to prevent harm to another. Human complexity. Just marvelous."

He stopped at a set of double doors. "We're here." I looked beyond him to see we were standing outside an enormous auditorium.

"Elder Varun is giving a lecture to a group about to go into planning," Michael said. "He's nearly finished, but want to listen in?"

"Sure," I said, thinking seeing other souls signing up for horrific experiences might help ease my mind. I flashed myself back into my NASA T-shirt, jeans, and a pair of runners, matching this time. Michael smiled at me as he opened the door. We stepped through, and the door popped shut behind us, causing everyone to turn our way. I winced. It didn't have to do that. It was a magically created door on a plane of existence where mass doesn't exist.

The elder looked up, and I groaned.

"Ah…we have special guests," he said. "Welcome."

There was a collective gasp. Michael waved, and so did I like we were the Royal Couple taking our seats at Wimbledon.

Since we'd arrived mid-thought, I didn't pay much attention to the words being spoken from the podium. Instead, I focused on the room—all impressively done up in Earth plane matter. The venue had high ceilings and rows of cushy folding chairs sloping down toward the front. A blackboard spanned the wall behind a large oak desk with books and papers stacked on top, and souls in young human-looking bodies filled most of the available seats.

The soul dispensing sage advice was Elder Varun, and he had shaped himself into a professorial-looking mortal, right down to the glasses and disheveled graying hair. I marveled at the combined effect; if you didn't know you were in the fifth dimension, you'd think you were inside a lecture hall at some Ivy League school.

The elder cleared his throat then paused for a sip of water, and it caught me off guard. He didn't have an actual throat to clear or any need of something to drink, but it was an effective attention grabber…which may have been the point.

"Many of you will go to the third dimension to gather experiences, individually and as a group," he said. "Some of you will stay behind as spirit guides. Others still will remain to pilot extras as needed. And there is a give-and-take to that, isn't there?"

Several nodded.

"So, let's say you turn to the soul sitting next to you and say, 'I want to learn about remorse.' Well, there's no way to study negative emotions in the Summerlands. They do not exist here. Your friend, who loves you dearly, says he can assist. That when you go to Earth, you can do something to him that will help you *feel* remorse."

He looked into the crowd and shrugged. "Simple, right?" he said, then ran a hand through his hair, causing it to stick up on one side. "Not so fast. Each of you has a personal plan in mind right now. While you will work on your own experiences in your next human life, you must also find ways to move collective goals forward. Let me hear some emotions you wish to experience. Come on, just blurt them out."

I realized he was speaking in Earth slang, probably part of the overall experience they were so eager to have.

"Loss," someone shouted.

The elder swooped a fist through the air. "Excellent, what's another?"

"Frustration."

"Perfect. Those two go together well. Anything else?"

"Sorrow."

"Now you're getting somewhere."

"Joy."

"And that's what I was waiting for." Elder Varun shielded his eyes against the overhead light as he searched the room. "Who said that? Don't be shy."

A wave of nervous laughter rippled through the audience.

"I did," said a soul now standing.

"Ailsa, wonderful to have you back with us, dearest one," he said, nodding in her direction. "Now, how does Ailsa experience joy when so many in her group wish to have unhappy human lives?"

"Black sheep."

"Oh, that's good. Please expound, Cairbre."

"Ailsa could be in a dysfunctional family," the soul said. "Then, when she's old enough, she disassociates and creates a life filled with joy."

"That is an attractive option," the elder said. He raised a finger. "And it also has layers, doesn't it? Ailsa will endure the pain caused by such a family for perhaps the first eighteen years or so. Then, she will create a life of joy for herself. But," he added, "would that life be joyful start to finish? Sadly, no. One might carry the scars of those early interactions to the grave. Most do, you know. It's a gamble."

He shrugged. "If Ailsa chooses to study the dichotomy between joy and pain, it's an excellent suggestion. But perhaps another path to consider is a vacation life. Those are wonderful. I have just returned from my own, and I highly recommend it."

He paced the room, addressing his shoes. "Now, do you wish to have layers, or would you rather focus on one emotion? These are the questions I want you to ask yourself before adjourning to your planning room. It can get tricky for those of you looking to experience the harder side of human life."

He turned back to his audience of souls. "As we know, energy cannot be created or destroyed. It can only change from one form to another. You *are* energy, pure light code. You know you can never die, so the temptation is to cook up an elaborate plan to capture many experiences at once.

"Let's say you want your human self to be destitute and living on the streets. Perhaps you'll layer in a horrible childhood and construct the most unthinkable abuses one could imagine. And the big finish?" He paused for dramatic effect. "Is that one of you will murder the other, hoping the one left behind will feel loss, grief, sorrow, or remorse.

"But you must remember…the *human you* is the beneficiary of your plans. That part of you will most likely believe that one life is all there is, and in that form, you might even think death is everlasting.

"You may compare yourself to others and wonder why your life is so hard when everyone else has it so *easy*." He chuckled. "Even though that is never the case…you will believe it is so when you're there. Now, with that in mind, who can tell me the problems associated with baking all those negative experiences into one earthly life?"

Some in the audience began to laugh.

"It's too complicated," came the joyful reply.

"Exactly. The difficulties leading to the desired experience are too great. Now, if you took an idea like that to Metatron, what might they say?"

One soul raised her hand.

"Yes?"

"Let's tone this down a bit."

The professorial-looking elder smiled. "Precisely. I would venture a guess this has been said to you, dearest one."

The comment got another laugh from the room.

"The council explains that heaping all that negativity into one lifetime might cause you to go mad or to abandon the mission before it's complete. So a more neutral path might be suggested. And here's something else to consider; scripting too many tragic events into one mortal life is cruel. Does everyone remember what *cruelty* is? Come on now. You just studied this one-on-one with your respective elders."

Another soul stood. "It's when you willfully inflict pain on another."

"That's right. I see you are doing well in your studies, dearest one." The elder pressed his brows together in a look of concern. "I want you to think carefully about *cruelty* as you plan your human lives. If something terrible is to happen to your mortal self, keep it to that one thing and make the rest of your time there pleasant if not joyful."

He placed his palms up. "But, as you know, we elders only offer suggestions; the choice is yours alone. Now, as you go forth, please remember what we have discussed." Elder Varun raised his hand and swished it in the air before him in an elegant figure eight. "Let your next life softly ebb and flow and gently lead to the experience you wish to have. We are complete. Love and light," he said, packing papers and books into his satchel.

The audience got up and began filing out of the auditorium with souls excitedly talking and hugging one another. I overheard a conversation going on behind us.

"I want to be beheaded."

I raised my eyebrows at Michael. He shrugged.

"Oh, that's good," said her companion. "I'd like to be a drug lord. We can help each other."

All right. That was bizarre. A small part of me understood, though. While an eternity of peace and joy sounds like an excellent idea on the surface, I knew it wasn't what they wanted. I also knew they used their journeys into humanness to break up all that eternal bliss.

Forever is an exceptionally long time, no matter how you experience it.

I squeezed Michael's hand, thinking of the terrible price we might have to pay to protect this way of life for them. Goddess said he would have a choice and that I had to have faith in her. I hoped Michael would choose life, although I wasn't sure what kind of choice he would have to make. Maybe one that destroyed Earth if he didn't sacrifice himself.

I pushed the thought from my mind. I'd made my decision, and now I had to trust Michael to make his, whatever that might be.

As the room emptied, the elder walked over. "Love and light, Archangel Mick-Eye-Elle, Fire Goddess," he said, formally addressing us. "It is wonderful to have you at one of my lectures…that no soul pays attention to anyway." He waved his hand and sighed. "But what can one do? Free will, you know. It's lovely to see you again," he said to me.

I paused, trying to place him.

"You don't remember me yet. It's all right. I know this is your first visit after awakening this time." He nudged the light-code strap of his light-code bag higher onto his shoulder. The movement was convincing—the whole package was. "How are you finding the Summerlands?" he asked.

I couldn't say what I was thinking, so I snatched the first alternate thing that came to mind. "It's fascinating. But I do wish I remembered more. It's as if I'm learning all of this for the first time."

"As it should be. All will unfold as Goddess intends. It is a gift, you know, getting to rediscover this place each time you wake. And it is *such* a joy when you visit us. What's next for you *today*?" He was practicing too.

Michael turned to me. "We can go with this group to planning if you want?"

"Sure. That would be great."

"That's a fine idea," the elder said. "I'm headed that way. You can follow me."

Elder Varun led us back down the hallway to a door marked PLANNING THEATER. "Ah, this is where I leave you. I have another lecture about to begin. Love and light." He placed a hand over his heart.

I returned the gesture. "Thank you, Elder."

"You are welcome, dearest one," he said, then blinked out of sight.

Michael and I climbed several steps and took seats in the dimly lit auditorium. My eyes wandered over the room as we waited for everyone else to settle in. Black movie-theater-style chairs on stepped risers encircled a sizable stage below us. Black velvet curtains hung floor-to-ceiling on curved walls, with drop-down canister spots lighting the floor. It had a thespian vibe, and I found myself wondering if an aristocratic theater critic might pop out from behind a column.

I turned to my left and noticed a group of souls whispering and pointing at us. It felt a little like high school, only more loving. Two of them smiled and waved. Oh, yes. *Far more* loving. I smiled and waved back. I'd just made some new friends, I think. Michael kissed my hand as the elder stepped to the center of the stage.

"Love and light, dearest ones. I am Elder Bai," she said, pushing her gold-framed glasses higher on her nose. This elder had raven-black hair arranged in a tidy bun at the nape of her neck and wore a sensible navy-blue pantsuit. She looked more like a prosecutor than an afterlife advisor, but she broke into a smile so radiant it lit the room.

Books and covers, I told myself.

"I welcome you with my whole heart," she said, beaming up at the crowd. "Soul Clan Dunn, please join me on the floor."

"You know the two souls who waved to you," Michael said. "You just don't remember, and they don't approach when you're visiting from the Earth plane."

"Why not?"

"Because they know you have limited memory in your elemental half-life and don't want to embarrass you."

"That's really sweet."

Michael's blue eyes sparkled knowingly. "I thought you'd like to see this particular session."

I realized that every planning session that had ever been was going on now, sort of. Events happen in chronological order in the Summerlands. However, you can take a little spin over to the Universal Library, look one up, and pop right in. Kinda cool, right? I remembered that little nugget while Elder Varun was talking.

A group of souls headed down the stairs. There were at least a hundred of them gathering below, and just as many remained seated. The elder spread her arms as if herding a flock. "First, I'd like to separate you into main groups, Spirit Guides, Extras, Ups and Downs, Tragedy, Sorrow, Grief, Pain, Love, Hate, Joy, and Mundane." White glowing letters appeared in the air above each section as she spoke. "Please find your places."

Only a few souls elected to stand under the milder headers, my new friends included. Most crammed into the grueling life-experience sections, standing shoulder to shoulder there. Meanwhile, the Joy and Love groups could shoot a cannon through their open space without hitting a thing. I shook my head, remembering Elder Varun's speech on cruelty.

Elder Bai walked to the Grief section. "Now, let's see how each of you experienced this emotion in past incarnations. Herapho, Luciana, let's start with you." Two souls stepped forward as curtains at the front parted to reveal a glass-beaded screen identical to the one I'd seen in the Chamber of Memories. A large leather-bound book flickered into view.

"That's the Akashic Records," Michael whispered. "It's the universal compilation of every thought, deed, action, and idea."

Oh, I knew what it was, all right. I nodded, thinking of the librarian. I'd been rude to her, to all the attendants. I made a promise to apologize the moment I could. Holograms have feelings here. I know how bizarre that sounds, but they do, and now I felt ashamed of myself for the way I'd acted. Oddly enough, my shame wasn't muted by the Summerlands Effect. Not in the slightest. The Goddess at work, I decided.

The elder flicked her finger in the air, and the pages of the book turned with the motion. "Let's watch this shared experience in 1977."

The leather book on the screen vanished, replaced by a video of a little boy playing with a golden retriever. The boy threw a stick that landed in the driveway, and the dog ran to fetch it. At nearly the same instant, a car barreled into the drive, hitting the beautiful animal, hurling it several feet forward. My hand flew to my mouth as the poor dog landed on the pavement in a motionless heap.

"That's me. I'm the one driving the car," Luciana said.

"That's right, and as Herapho's father in that lifetime, did you experience grief over killing your son's dog?" said Elder Bai.

"I did, but only for a few days. I had a lot on my mind and decided it was only an animal, after all. I was glad to be rid of it because it shed all over the house." The confession pulled a startled gasp from the audience. Luciana looked down at the floor, seeming ashamed of the uncomfortable truth she'd just shared.

The elder patted her arm. "It's all right. You did not know that was your friend in canine form." She turned to the male soul. "And Herapho, you grieved the loss of your dog?"

"Yes," he said. "But eventually, my grief faded. I got into drugs at college, and they numbed my senses. I would like to live with grief for an entire lifetime this time, decades and decades."

"And you, Luciana? Would you like this as well?"

Luciana nodded. "I would because in that lifetime with Herapho," she said, pointing at the screen. "I left earlier than originally planned."

"You suffered a fatal heart attack when you were forty-eight." Elder Bai flicked the air again, bringing up a new piece of information. "I see here that you had the choice to stay or go, and you chose to go. Do you know why?"

"Yes," Luciana said, casting her eyes to the floor once more. "My son's drug addiction was hurting the family."

"And you experienced grief over your son's choices?"

"Yes. But there were other reasons too. My marriage was not going well, and I had just lost my job."

"I see here, Luciana, you used exit three of your five exits to leave. Had you stayed until exit five, you would have overcome these challenges and learned to live with your grief."

"Exits?" I asked Michael.

A heart-melting smile crossed the archangel's lips as he met my curious gaze. I could see the intense love he felt for me in his eyes, and I almost wept. I swallowed hard and gathered myself. I had to focus on staying present. That was the only way I'd get through this.

"Every soul goes to the Earth plane with up to five choices to return home," Michael said. "They can choose any one of the first four or remain to carry out the experience. During each exit, the soul asks the human's subconscious to make a split-second decision, and it does. The fifth exit is the last stop on the bus. One can't override it."

I thought about that a moment. My body stopped aging when I set foot in the demonic realm, and I left the Underworld when I was fifty-nine at Morgana's hand. That had probably been my last stop on the bus, I decided. My Goddess-driven love for Mortegol had been strong, and now I was sure it kept me tethered to him. I probably brushed off the first invitations because of it.

However, I age on Earth, and Michael's body clock syncs with mine once I'm awake. I studied his thick hair, bright blue eyes, and smooth skin, knowing that would begin to change. Michael matures with me. (At least he *looks* like he does.) And he and I had spent a handful of lifetimes together well into my eighties. It's beautiful, sharing a family and growing old with the one you love.

Michael sat in rapt attention, watching the souls on stage. He was so trusting, and I had betrayed him, was continuing to keep secrets from him. But how could I ever tell him the terrible truth? The elder raised her voice, drawing my attention back to the floor.

"Herapho, in that lifetime, you left on your twenty-sixth birthday, two years after your father's death." She motioned with her hand, and the scene changed to paramedics rushing an unconscious young man into the emergency room.

"Heroin overdose," the paramedic said. He thrust a clipboard at a waiting ER nurse, who wheeled the gurney at high speed down the hallway and out of sight. The screens faded to black.

"Didn't you also experience grief over the loss of your father?"

"My drug addiction kept me from feeling much of anything," Herapho said.

"All right, I have a suggestion…and I will go with you to assist."

Herapho's human-looking forehead creased with concern. "That is a great sacrifice, Elder. We cannot ask you to do it."

Elder Bai put a hand in the air, a delighted smile on her lips. "I have decided, and I am happy to do this." She paused to address the others. "What I am about to propose will be an excellent study in grief for Herapho and Luciana. And, rest assured, that before we leave this room, I will work with every one of you to help find ways to experience the emotions you want to feel in human form."

She turned back to the couple. "For you, what I suggest is an experience so painful," she took Luciana's hand, "that if you live with it into your eighties, you should not feel the need to study grief again. But you must also agree to make the rest of your mortal lives easy. We will not be able to layer this lifetime if you wish to have any chance of completing the mission successfully."

"Yes, please," Herapho said. "We would like to hear your plan."

The elder looked at them somberly. "The death of your child."

I gasped and dug my nails into Michael's arm, then immediately loosened my grip. "I'm sorry," I said, looking into his smiling eyes. "But she can't mean that. Why would Goddess allow innocent children to die?"

"Goddess does not *allow* terrible things to happen, Sera," Michael said, taking my hand in his. "These are her children, using their free will to learn. To them," he pointed at the souls on the stage below, "it will be like going to sleep and having a bad dream. When they wake, they will have learned valuable lessons."

I nodded, thinking of my own crummy dream of living in the demonic realm, glad to be awake and here with Michael. I found myself wondering why souls put themselves through so much trauma, then realized I'd been doing exactly that. I had tormented myself by reliving each moment of my time in the Underworld. Well, the parts I could remember.

I shuddered, wondering what else could be inside the little blank spaces still lurking, waiting to spring out and say, "got you." I turned my attention back to the floor. Wringing my hands in worry and wallowing in grief were luxuries I could no longer afford. "Put your house in order," Goddess told me, and that's what I had to do.

"I want you to keep this in mind," the elder said. "The one who signs up for the loss of a child will experience grief in earth-shattering ways. If you live with it well into your eighties, you will suffer, but that one experience might be all that's needed."

She turned to address the rest of the group. "It is the bravest souls who sign up for the most extreme forms of any experience." She laughed and shook her head. "Please don't take that as a challenge."

"Yes, please," Luciana said. "We would like to have this experience exactly as you have laid it out before us."

Herapho nodded his agreement, and Elder Bai walked to the Tragedy group. "Do any of you wish to be the child?"

One soul stepped forward immediately. "I would like to go," he said. "I have yet to experience death as a young human."

"Thank you, Aodhan. Please join Herapho and Luciana to work through the details."

The planning continued until every member of the Soul Clan Dunn had received suggestions and advice. Table and chair groupings appeared on the stage, and the souls took seats, excitedly talking and laughing. Some pulled parchments from the air and wrote on them before passing the paper to others.

"Bear this in mind," Elder Bai said. "Each of you will be at the center of your own life experience, and you will also aid the other members of your group. Please work together on these details and feel free to ask questions."

Michael leaned in. "They're signing their soul contracts with one another. The souls over there," he said, pointing to one small group, "are working through details of the darkest experiences. They will agree on actions and outcomes around rape, murder, incest, child abuse, brutality in general. It's how you get perpetrators and victims, and it's up to each soul. They sign up for the experience, quite happily."

He was right. They did seem glad to be locking themselves into painful, even violent experiences. At least this explained the tragedies that occur all too often on Earth. Even so, it didn't make them any easier to swallow.

"And that's where forgiveness comes in."

I met his gaze, unsure of his meaning.

"The human on the receiving end arrives at *a dark night of the soul*—a spiritual crossroads where they have a decision to make. They can choose to remain angry, blaming God, themselves, another person, or the entire world. Or they can forgive and learn to deal with the pain in positive ways. It's nearly impossible to do, and it's the ones who navigate to the place of forgiveness who become elders."

I nodded slowly, wondering what terrible challenges Glara and Udar had overcome. I closed my eyes and told them where I was and that I loved them. Telepathy is the Summerlands' version of cellular service.

"Those two groups," Michael said, pointing to the part of the stage marked EXTRAS and SPIRIT GUIDES, "have most recently returned. They stay behind to guide other members through their elected human challenges, just as those going this time did for them.

"Extras show up after the event to help pick up the pieces. They could be a counselor, a kind stranger, a wise neighbor. Or even a kid in the grocery store tossing out random comments that make sense on a deeply personal level. Spirit Guides whisper words of encouragement from here. Everyone works together. It's quite lovely."

We watched for a while longer. Then souls began filing from the room. "Would you like to follow them to the council chamber?" Michael asked.

I nodded. I was so caught up in the dramas playing out before me I'd almost forgotten my own.

CHAPTER
~ 28 ~
The Council of Metatron

The Summerlands, Present Moment

"All planning rooms lead here," Michael said. He put his hands on his hips as he glanced around the enormous room, a grin of expectation lighting his face.

Where the planning theater had been all black and dimly lit, this room was bright, and everything gleamed. Gloss-white crescent-shaped bleachers formed a horseshoe pattern around a glossy white floor below. Frosted glass walls had a soft glow of light emanating from them. There was a white, crescent-shaped judge's bench with nine, white high-back chairs centered on the floor, and the ceiling was a lovely sky blue with cheerful puffy white clouds painted onto it.

No, wait. Those are real clouds moving across an actual blue sky.

Michael and I took our seats as souls in human form filled the bleachers around us in mere minutes. Or it could have taken an Earth-plane year. At this point, I'd lost all sense of time. The concept had slipped away from me like feathers on the wind.

Souls were crammed together, packed in so tightly, you couldn't fit a slip of paper between them. Whatever was about to go down in this room was the hottest ticket in town.

A moment (or a hundred years) later, Archangel Gabriel appeared in front of the bench. His wings unfurled behind him as he pulled a scroll from the air. "Please rise for the Council of Metatron," he said.

Like the other arcs, Gabriel's wings are white, and they extend a good seven feet on either side when fully extended. But unlike his brothers, Gabe's wings have silver tips for added punch. It's quite impressive when any of them unfurl, even when you've seen it a million times as I have.

I got to my feet with the rest of the crowd as nine light-filled beings flashed behind the bench. I couldn't tell if they were male or female. They looked like aliens, stark white and glowing with light from within. Their heads were large and oblong. Their eyes were huge and dark. At least they matched the room, all bright light and very mysterious.

"In the here and now, we are reviewing the life plans of the Soul Clan Dunn," Gabriel said. "With the blessing of Source, the Council of Metatron will now advise. You may be seated." He rolled up the scroll and vanished then re-appeared in the seat beside me, which wasn't there, um…before.

"Hi, Sera," he whispered.

I smiled at him. "Hey, Gabe. Thanks for your help with Sam and the others."

The archangel flashed a movie-star grin. "Yeah, that bunch was a little panicked at first. But now they're at the feast having the time of their lives."

Michael punched his brother in the arm. "You and your fancy-pants job."

Gabe shot him a look of mock exasperation, then smiled at me. I studied them both as they turned their attention to the floor, thinking it felt like old times, us together like this.

The four arcs are brothers. They communicate telepathically, have been together since *the birth of time*, and have knock-down-drag-out brawls on occasion. (Ones that include resetting entire cities, towns, and villages back to their original states.) And let's just say more than a few memories need wiping after one of their squabbles.

I'm never privy to the aftermath, and I've never pressed Michael about it. But I'm sure they each get the archangel equivalent of a good bawling out. Goddess is one parent you don't want to see glaring at you with her arms crossed and foot tapping. I laughed at the thought.

Michael looked over, and I shot him a smile.

Elder Bai stepped up to the bench. "Love and light, Metatron," she said, placing a hand over her heart. "These are the souls in my charge."

One of the middle beings spoke, his large dark eyes slowly blinking as he addressed the group.

"Are these aliens?" I asked Michael.

"Not exactly," he said, offering me popcorn from the red and white-striped bag he had just pulled from thin air. "They are Metatron, the Scribe of God," he added as if that explained everything.

I smiled at him. "No, thank you."

"I love this next part," he said, passing the magic bag to our neighbors. Everyone else took handfuls of popcorn, including Gabriel, so I did too when it came back my way. Why not?

"Elder Bai," said the being. "Have you discussed life paths and missions with these souls?"

"Yes, Councilor Metatron, and we have reviewed past-life experiences from the Akashic Records."

"Wonderful. Please continue," he-she-it said.

I couldn't make out their gender or species, and it seemed they were all named Metatron. So I decided to number them and make them all males to keep them straight. Bad form, I know, but what else was there to do? Stand up and demand they identify themselves? I don't think so.

The elder explained the personal missions of each soul and the interconnected plans of the entire soul clan.

Nine raised a slender finger. "All of you have willingly volunteered to play these roles?" he asked, reading from a parchment that had just appeared in his translucent hands.

All agreed that they had.

"Elder Bai, going to the Earth plane with your students is a great sacrifice," Three said. "Do you do so with a gladdened heart?"

The elder squared her shoulders. "I do."

"You will need to rely on the heavily veiled memories of your previous experiences as a human being to guide you while on Earth," Two added.

The elder nodded. "I accept this condition."

Six extended a glowing finger into the air.

"Yes, Councilor?" said Seven.

All nine aliens closed their eyes to speak to one another telepathically. When they'd finished their silent conversation, One said, "We advise each of you to have at least ten moments of soul clarity. If you agree, your intuition will help keep you on course. Is this acceptable?"

Elder Bai conferred with each soul. Murmuring and head-nodding followed. When they finished, she addressed the council. "Aodhan wishes to have no moments of soul clarity and only one exit as he wants to be on Earth for just a short while."

The nine beings closed their eyes and quickly reopened them. "We have noted these wishes in the Akashic Records," said Four.

Eight leaned forward. "Aodhan," he said. "Am I reading this correctly? You do not wish to have the ability to override your one exit through free will?"

"That is correct, Metatron," the soul said. "I wish to give up my right to free will for this one lifetime."

The crowd gasped, and I heard a thud that sounded like a body hitting the floor. Michael chewed quickly and took an audible gulp to let his mouth hang open. I looked over at Gabe; he'd gone ghostly white.

"We do not recommend this," One said. "Free will is a gift given to all creation by Source."

"I adore being human," Aodhan said. "I always dismiss my first four exits, and I am afraid that if I keep my free will, I will choose to stay in this lifetime too. That would defeat the purpose of this mission for Luciana and Herapho, and I do not wish to let them down."

When Aodhan finished speaking, there wasn't a dry eye in the house, including the two blubbering arcs at my side.

Nine leaned forward. "Is this your true desire?"

"It is," Aodhan said. "I want it with all my heart."

"This, too, is recorded," Seven said with an uneasy sigh.

Michael swiped a tear with his knuckle. "He just gave up his right to free will. I can't believe it."

"They are going to let him do it anyway?" I asked in surprise.

"Well, sure," Gabriel said. "That's why they are the *Council* of Metatron and not the *my-way-or-the-highway* Metatron." I knew he was going for humor, but he choked on the words a bit. Sitting beside me were two of the fiercest warriors in the universe, crying like little girls. I flashed a tissue box into my lap and handed one to each of them.

Gabriel blew his nose. "I'm fine. Thank you."

Michael shook his head. "The greatest gift to humankind and he gave it up, just like that. Aodhan is so brave." The archangel sniffed and wiped his upper lip with my magical tissue. I smiled at my tenderhearted warrior and looked into his teary blue eyes. Michael chuckled, his nose red. "What?"

"Nothing," I said, patting his leg.

The session went on until the Council of Metatron had addressed every life plan, giving the two arcs at my side time to compose themselves. Michael had his arms folded over his chest like a superhero. Gabe was leaning forward with a forearm on his knee. He looked more like a model hawking men's slacks.

"To those standing before us, I wish to say that Source, and we, are eternally grateful," Three said. "For some of you, these experiences will be brutal, and before I send you to the launch site, I need to know that it is still within your hearts to carry out this mission."

Every soul agreed that it was.

Four studied them all carefully, then a proud-papa smile crossed his otherwise nondescript face. "To use my favorite human expression, *last chance dance*."

The room erupted in laughter.

As the crowd began to settle, Four spoke again. "You have chosen your lifetimes well, and we send you forth in love and light."

The elder stepped forward, waving a hand. "One moment, please."

"Yes, Elder Bai?" Nine said. The alien leaned down to confer with the elder, each of them glancing at my two new friends.

Michael raised an eyebrow and gave me a sizzling smile as Nine addressed the crowd. "I am so sorry. We have two more life plans to review. My sincere apologies to you both." He paused to read the scroll that had just appeared in his hand. "You each wish to have a life filled with ups and downs, I see." He chuckled. "Oh, this part is wonderful. I'd like this for myself."

Then he rubbed his chin and looked down at the two souls fidgeting before the bench. "I'm afraid I don't understand this next part." He looked so baffled; it came across clearly in his almost featureless face. "You wish to be...heartbreakers?"

A light finally blinked in my half-mortal brain. That's why Michael brought me to *this* planning session. I slapped my forehead, feeling silly I hadn't recognized the pair of them before now. Michael's smile widened as he watched the memory return to me.

"Musicians, Metatron," said the soul who sings my travel song. The same eternal being who sees me off before every trip to Earth. The very one about to spend sixty-six years as a human named Thomas Earl Petty.

CHAPTER
~ 29 ~
Launch Site

The Summerlands, Present Moment

"Could we follow them to the launch site?" I said, feeling excited for the journeying souls.

Michael grinned and gathered me to him. "Sure. Come on, Valentine. Let's go see tiny balls of light launching to the third rock from the sun."

We said goodbye to Gabriel, and the next moment, Michael and I were standing inside a bright control room with glass on all sides. I looked out the window and saw we were on top of the mountain. "We didn't have to use the elevators?" I asked.

Michael's smile widened. "Archangel, baby."

I laughed as souls filed into the room, excitedly talking and hugging one another. "This feels good," I said.

"It is good, Sera. They are happy to be returning to the Earth plane together. Here, let's join the group. This part is fun," Michael said, leading me forward.

Attendants bustled around the control room; they wore jumpers of red, blue, green, and yellow—the colors of the four elementals.

The one in blue addressed the crowd. "If I could have the *Ups and Downs*, we'll get your coordinates locked in first. For the rest of you, please help yourself to refreshments at the back of the room. Oh, and the strange sensations are human-emotional bleed-through; this place is rife with the stuff. And it's perfectly normal. Just think of it as a preview of what's to come."

Once he'd finished speaking, he sauntered over—a cocky grin on his handsome face. "Love and light, *Fire Goddess*," he said, placing a hand over his heart. But where others here had greeted me with respect, I noticed he did it all tongue-in-cheek, punching the words *fire goddess* sarcastically.

I inspected his piercing gray eyes. "Love and light. Your name is…" I paused, trying to remember. "Alden. Is that right?"

He raised his eyebrows and waved a hand in my face. "You're in there somewhere."

I shot him a puzzled look, then had a thought. "Oh, my goodness. Michael and I had a son named Alden."

He laughed. "Only one?"

"More than one?" I said, trying to remember.

"Oh, I do so love it when you're like this. All bright-eyed and not a bone in your body that wants to torment me or get my head bitten off on some faraway planet. I know your boy, well." He clapped Michael on the shoulder, a calculated Earth-plane male gesture. "Hey, Pops. Oh, will you both excuse me?" he asked before returning to his station.

I studied the soul as he went, remembering he *really* liked male energy.

Michael beamed at me. "Um, that *is* our son."

Tears welled as I remembered my boy's sweet face that day in the rose garden, realizing it was the soul I'd just met behind those kind little eyes.

A smirk made its way to the edge of Michael's mouth. "Three thousand six hundred twenty-four."

"Huh?"

"That's how many times Alden's been our son on the Earth plane." Michael shook his head. "And the two of you have pulled more stunts in the fifth dimension than I care to remember just now."

I focused my attention on the soul. Then memories of our wild adventures came roaring in, and my mouth flew open. I'd just treated my best friend like an acquaintance whose face you can't nail down. Then I remembered my last launch to the Earth plane and snorted a laugh. I'd cut the boom filter on him.

Alden flicked a glance over his shoulder. "Uh-huh, I'm too quick for you, Seraphina." He gave me a heartwarming smile then turned to help one of the excited souls onto the lounger.

Michael was right. I had gotten us into quite a lot of trouble. The Gila Monster of Mandaroon sprang to mind. Alden and I were nearly tasty snacks on the garden planet inside the fifth dimension, a place filled with creatures the size of city buses.

Mandaroon is stunning, with its crystalline lakes, idyllic waterfalls, and golden Earth-style sunsets. The sun is eternally setting there, which is how I'd convinced Alden to take physical form and come along. You know, for a sunset picnic. The trip started out pleasant enough, then it all went south...quickly, and we wound up fighting for our lives. It had been my idea to go, of course, and Alden protested at first, then finally gave in. The usual with us. He didn't talk to me for the equivalent of four Earth-plane months afterward.

"Memory Erase Code?" Alden said.

The attendant in yellow gave a series of numbers, and Alden entered them into his handheld. The two of them systematically went through the rest of the coordinates, then Alden asked the soul if she were sure she wanted to go. She nodded. "Love and light, Clara Elizabeth Price," he said, placing her hands on the sub-generator.

I sighed as I watched my friend.

Another attendant gave longitude, latitude, birthdate, birth time, sun sign, moon sign, and finally, the soul's elected elemental sign. It was fire: strength, will, determination, and action. I choked back tears. "I will watch over you," I whispered.

Michael pulled me close. "She'll be entering through your gate."

I nodded, feeling an overwhelming sense of joy as the soul who would be Clara Price transformed into a tiny ball of red light, the interdimensional color of fire. It flickered once, then flew through the window.

"Do you remember this?" Michael asked, pointing to the screens circling the room. "These show everything about the mission."

All monitors came to life at once. Some of them ticked through Earth-plane coordinates—longitude, latitude, date, and time. Others showed a pregnant woman inside the delivery room, her husband speaking words of encouragement at her side. Another gave information about the couple getting ready to welcome their daughter into the world. He was a deacon at the church, his wife was the church secretary.

I felt a tickle in my chest and knew it was the South Gate opening, but I was on autopilot this time. Still, it felt a bit odd—like pollen in your throat that makes you want to cough, but you can't.

"The parents receiving these souls are all part of the Soul Clan Dunn as well," Michael said. "They come and go in waves."

One of the monitors showed the birth of Clara Price. I watched it with a hand over my mouth, remembering souls could change their minds last minute, and the suspense was killing me. The baby wasn't responding, and now I was holding my breath. Then I saw the red ball of light enter the sweet human's third eye.

"She's in!" cried one of the attendants sitting at the console, and the room erupted in cheering applause. The moment Clara took her first breath, the memory-erase countdown started.

Michael and I stood with our arms around each other, watching as each soul took their turn. Some were entering the womb, and some chose to enter moments after birth, sending my emotions on a wild roller coaster ride. Most of the souls went as humans, but some were dogs. Others were cats. There were birds, tigers, hamsters, horses, and more. All but one elected to stay on the Earth plane. His name was Ganesh.

We watched him transform into a tiny ball of blue light. He shot through the window and reappeared a few seconds later, sprawled over the lounger, limbs outstretched, skin glistening with sweat.

"Once I took my first breath," Ganesh said through chattering teeth. "I remembered how brutal that place is. It came crashing in on me. I couldn't stay. I just didn't have the strength to do it."

Alden wrapped a shiny blanket around Ganesh's shoulders. "It's all right. You never have to go back if you don't want to," he said quietly, then caught the eye of an attendant at the control board and passed a finger over his throat. A moment later, the monitors showing the infant who suddenly died on Earth blinked off.

Ganesh pulled the fabric tight around his trembling light body as concerned souls huddled around him. I choked back tears, feeling sorry for Ganesh and the parents who had just lost their child. I glanced at Michael; his eyes glistened as he bit his bottom lip.

"Volunteers?" an attendant in green shouted to the crowd.

A soul rushed forward. I recognized her as one of the extras. "I'll do it," she said.

Ganesh threw the shock blanket off his shoulders and hugged her. "Thank you, dearest one. I will watch over you."

The volunteer patted his shoulder sympathetically. "I love you, Ganesh, and I'm happy to do this. Besides, I was busy feeling the human emotion of disappointment I didn't get to go this time."

"Really?" Ganesh said, breaking into a grin as big as Texas.

"Cross my heart."

A few moments later, Alden helped the volunteer onto the lounger and held her hand. "I love you so much right now, I could just kiss you," he said, smiling at her. Then he *did* kiss her. It was a surprisingly long kiss, and one the volunteer kept going until a look of delight crossed Alden's face. He straightened and smoothed his hair, seeming a little punch drunk.

"I'll see you when I get back," the volunteer said, looking up at Alden dreamily.

My friend cleared his throat, nodded enthusiastically, then entered the coordinates. The next moment, the lounger vibrated, and she was off. The monitors came back on, and everyone in the control room remained silent as we watched the tiny green ball of light enter the infant's third eye. The baby boy's lips were blue, but he finally took a breath, and color returned to his sweet face. The room erupted in a roar of applause.

I sighed, knowing I had just witnessed a miracle on Earth *and* a budding romance for my best friend. I leaned my head on Michael's shoulder.

"Are you tired, darling?"

"A little. Tired but happy. I think I might be ready to go back through Yggdrasil."

"We'll say goodbye to your parents, and then we'll return. How's that?"

"Well, perhaps just one more night here?" I said.

Michael kissed me, filling me to the brim with unconditional love. I hoped the feeling would last. I needed every ounce of strength I could get, and I needed it for both of us.

CHAPTER
~ 30 ~
King of the Underworld

Earth Plane 2021

Michael and I stepped from Yggdrasil's portal to find Kricket, Andrea, and Helena still drinking tea inside Helena's English-garden mirage. Interestingly enough, Michael was in his seat, too, and turned to smile at me.

"Pretty neat trick, isn't it?" the version of Michael beside me said.

"Right. You haven't stepped through the portal in this timeline yet. If you touch yourself, will you explode or something?"

Michael laughed. "Hardly. But the premise makes for good TV."

For me, it had been almost a year since I'd seen them, and I was about to hug everyone when both Michaels vanished.

Helena cocked her head. "He's here," she said, looking as though she were gathering information from the air.

"Who's here?" I asked. My lower-vibration human emotions were back in full force—and more keen than usual—if the rapid pace of my heartbeat was anything to go by.

"Come with me," Helena said, turning me around by the shoulders. Then she herded the three of us down the path leading to Yggdrasil and shoved us all through the portal. But we emerged right back where we started. The water elemental met my startled gaze. "We're in the mirror image of my shop. We're safe in here."

Helena sprang across the bridge like an antelope and ran back down the path, the three of us hot on her heels. We knew not to ask too many questions when one of us tuned into some clear and present danger. We just blindly follow and take orders, as not doing so had gotten each of us killed on several occasions.

Helena swept an arm across the table—sending china, beautiful cakes, and hot tea smashing to the floor. Andrea's eyebrows shot up, and she gave me a wide-eyed look as she cleared the heaping mess— magically—with a snap of her fingers. Something Helena would have thought to do had she not been so thoroughly freaked out.

I did a double take. Helena wasn't kidding; we were in the mirror image of her shop, all right. The titles of the books were backward, and everything in the room was flipped around. It was a little disorienting. "What's going on?" I said, tearing my eyes away from the crazy-looking book spines.

Helena didn't answer. Instead, she flung the doors of a cabinet open, pulled out a massive iron stand with a hole in the middle, and shoved it at Kricket. "Here, set this on the table."

Kricket did as she was told—under that self-preservation umbrella instilled by time and experience—and Helena wrestled a large crystal ball into the holder.

"Hirahcryst." Helena's pupils were huge as she said it.

"That's who is here?"

"No. This is Hirahcryst." Helena nodded at the massive orb and wrapped her hands around it as she squeezed her eyes shut. "Show me," she said.

Purple smoke rolled inside, and once it cleared, the rest of us got closer to have a look. My heart sank as I saw Mortegol in the alley behind the diner, looking smug in a bespoke suit and white dress shirt. I took in his dark, good-looks, short blue-black hair, the unlined, handsome face of a twenty-five-year-old human male, slim hips, and broad shoulders. I also knew what was beneath his fine clothes; having been an archangel, Mortegol enjoys an eternally fit and muscled body.

The sky darkened, and a shadow fell over the four archangels as they advanced, their swords trained on the demon king. But Mortegol didn't seem concerned. Instead of running, he smoothed his jacket and crossed one foot over the other to lean in the doorway. Then he turned his head, looking straight at me. *I see you,* he mouthed.

A flash of lightning streaked across the sky. Then it zipped through the crystal ball and shot out one of the overhead lights. I sprang backward as a bead of sweat forced its way to my upper lip.

"How did he do that?" Helena barked.

"How does he do anything? He breaks the flipping rules," Andrea said, her topaz eyes lit with worry and tinged with green. It was a sign she was considering shifting into her elemental form.

"Sound," Helena shouted as the four of us cautiously leaned back in. Now we could hear as well as see.

Michael gritted his teeth. "What are you doing here?"

"Well, hello, Michael," Mortegol said. "Is this any way to greet family?" The demon pushed Michael's sword out of his face with a finger.

Hearing him again startled me more than seeing him. His British accent was only one of many, but I knew he used that one to charm human women. Unlike the rest of us, Mortegol could lie with humans or witches. Morgana was one such witch and my disgruntled executioner during the last go-round.

"You're not supposed to engage us, Mortegol," Raphael said. "Light is to reign the Earth plane for another century."

"Oh, don't get your tunic in a rumple," Mortegol spat at the arc, who was not wearing a tunic. Raphe was in a pair of faded jeans and a button-down shirt with the arms rolled. "I'm not here to call war early. I find our battles tedious, and I'm looking forward to a hundred years of not having to see your smug faces."

"Why *are* you here, then?" Uriel scoffed. "Not that we'll believe anything you say. So, maybe just save your dragon breath."

"I'm glad you asked…so rudely," Mortegol shot back. "I've come to collect Sera. Just completing the plans she and I made long ago. Sera wants to be with me. Did she not tell you?"

Gabriel trained his sword on Mortegol's throat. "What do you mean, demon?" Mortegol winced, then glared at Gabriel with hatred in his eyes, and I knew the reason. Being called a *demon* was a slap in the face to the former archangel. Gabriel knew it. They all did.

Mortegol composed himself, then tilted his head back slightly, probably looking down his nose at them. "Why, if it isn't girly man Gabriel. You're looking buff, old sport. Trying to make up for all those images of you as a female angel? Why don't you just do as an aging human male and get yourself a candy-apple red Corvette? Oh, wait. A Maserati is a flashier choice for those with tiny…brains." He grinned and slid his hands into his pants pockets.

"How is that little wife of yours, Gabe?" Mortegol said. "I see you're aging with her. Although not as well as one might hope. Have you tried eye cream? It can do wonders."

Uriel stepped forward. "Get back to the Underworld, demon. Or I will beat you into the ground myself."

Mortegol ignored the threat and sniffed the air. "What's this? I smell human. Oh, wait. Witch."

The four arcs turned to see Braith standing behind them, a bag from the diner in his hand. "Braith, get back into the building," Michael said.

The demon king vanished in a puff of black smoke.

"Whoa…who's the scary dude?" Braith asked.

It was Michael who responded as the four angels continued to search the alley. "Mortegol, King of the Underworld. Braith, get back to the diner."

"I guess I scared him off, huh? Take that, Underworld scum bag," Braith said, thrusting his lunch bag into the air.

Mortegol re-appeared and curled an arm around Braith's throat. "This one seems to be a pet," he said.

Michael narrowed his eyes. "Mortegol, we have a contract."

"Oh, you know, brother, contracts have loopholes. You should get a better attorney. I tell you what, though, let's make a trade. Your pet witch for Sera." Mortegol tightened his grip, and Braith dropped the bag in surprise, his face growing red as he struggled for air.

I swallowed hard as I watched them, knowing the time to return to the Underworld had come. My overinflated intuition told me so, just as Goddess said it would. I ran back down the path, took the bridge in one giant leap, and threw myself through the portal. "Yggdrasil, take me to Mortegol," I said, and a moment later, I was at his side. "I'll come with you. Let Braith go."

Mortegol pushed Braith away to slide an arm around my waist. "Oh, here you are," he said smoothly. "Hello, my love. Did you miss me?"

Braith held his throat, gasping for air, then ran toward the arcs. Uriel placed himself in front of my friend, and Raphael joined him. Now Braith stood behind a concrete wall of archangel.

Michael's eyes went wide. "Sera? What's going on?"

"I can explain, Michael," I said, staring into Mortegol's dark eyes. He had a demon lock on me, making his gaze mesmerizing, and I found myself remembering how I once loved the attention he lavished on me. Mortegol's doing. He was planting his thoughts.

He drew me closer still. "Looks like you're caught with a hand in the Underworld cookie jar, darling." He turned his head toward Michael. "She belongs to me now. Sera gave herself to me willingly. Isn't that the rule set forth by *your* Goddess?" Mortegol met my eyes again. "You know, time is linear for me, Sera, and I've missed you." He kissed me, but I remained rigid, and he drew back in surprise. "What's wrong?"

"I—"

"Don't tell me your love for me has grown cold?"

"Sera. What does he mean?" Michael said.

I forced my mind to relax and willed myself into the Underworld. Mortegol felt the shift and flicked his eyes at me approvingly. "Think about it a while longer, Michael," he said. "We'll just leave you to sort through your feelings."

A moment later, Mortegol and I vanished in a puff of black smoke.

CHAPTER
~ 31 ~
Love Lost

The Underworld 2021

We arrived inside a chamber filled with centuries-old paintings. Then I remembered. The world's most valuable art is in the Underworld. The works tourists clamor to see in Earth's famous galleries are masterful forgeries created by the one who stood before me now.

Mortegol offered me a glass of wine, probably something rare and expensive. I shook my head, feeling a tickle on my skin. My clothes shifted, and a red-velvet strapless gown formed over me, one I had worn here all those years ago. I looked down at myself, the slit in the fabric that reached my upper thigh, the gold high-heeled sandals on my feet. I felt naked and shivered, running my palms over my bare arms.

"This one is my favorite," Mortegol said, giving me an appraising look. He held the goblet up to me again, and I glared at him.

"Oh, come now. This is a celebration. Have a drink with me, Sera. I know you've only just awakened. It will take time for you to love me again. But I know you will, and I am a patient man. I won't rush you."

Mortegol set his glass on the table, slid a hand around the back of my neck, and looked at me tenderly, trying to rekindle the intimacy we once shared.

"No," I said, turning my face away from him. "And I thought you said your patience was growing thin."

He removed his hand and moved around me like a panther stalking its prey. "Oh, so you did recognize me when I told your fortune? How did you like my green skin and long crooked nose? Quite fantastic, wasn't it? I felt rather pleased with myself. I do love witches as I know you do."

"You strangled my friend. Is he one of the witches you love so much?" I said hotly.

"I swear. I meant no harm," Mortegol said, his eyes filled with longing as he stroked my hair. "I just needed you to come to me. I wouldn't have hurt him. I love you, Sera. Please come back to me. You're breaking my heart."

I softened my expression, torn between the memories of loving him and the way I felt nothing for him now. I met the demon king's tormented eyes. "I did love you," I said. "But there is something you should know. Goddess—"

I heard footsteps on the stone floor and looked up to see Michael standing in the doorway.

Mortegol straightened and turned around. "Oh, Michael. You're just in time," he said, swiping a knuckle over his nose and clearing his throat. "Sera was just telling me how much she loves me. I'm sorry you had to hear it that way, but there it is. We should probably just all move along now. Isn't that what you said to me as the four of you frog-marched me out of the Summerlands?"

Mortegol left my side, strode to the table, and picked up his wine. He swirled the dark liquid, then took a long, leisurely sip, glaring at the archangel over the rim of his glass. "Did you have any trouble crossing the river, by the way?"

"No," Michael said. "It was a little too easy. Where are the fallen and your giant demonic goons?"

Mortegol waved his hand and sniffed. "I gave them the day off. Today is a special day, and I did not want them hovering around upsetting Sera."

The other archangels and elementals entered the chamber.

I couldn't bring myself to look at them, so I turned away, my heart sinking. Now all of them were in danger, the arcs especially. When elementals die in the Underworld, we reincarnate. But if an archangel died here, it meant everlasting death. I shuddered. I couldn't think about that now. I had to figure out a way to get them out. All but Michael, I suppose. I nearly cried at the painful thought but managed to push the emotion back down before it took hold. I couldn't let it. I had to be strong for Michael. For all of them.

"I see you've rounded up a posse," Mortegol said, swiping the wine bottle from the table. "Come to take me in, sheriff?" He took a seat in one of the Barcelona armchairs, crossed his legs, and studied the label. "This is delicious. May I offer you some? It's not a battle year, so we could sit and talk this through over a lovely pinot."

He paused, turning the bottle in his hands. "Hmm...this is a wonderful vintage, and when's the last time we sat and talked, like civilized adults. Oh, yes, before the rebellion, I think. Right, darling?" he said to me.

Raphael took several steps toward us. "What is it you want, demon?"

Mortegol slammed the bottle on the table, uncrossed his legs, and sprang out of the chair with surreal quickness. "You mean other than Sera? Not much," he said, leveling his gaze at Raphael. "I suppose my holy name, my wings, my angelic title, and restoring my place in the Summerlands would be an excellent start."

"We don't have the power to do that," Michael said coolly. "Only Goddess can restore you, and I seriously doubt she would even consider it after your failed rebellion."

Mortegol gritted his teeth, his eyes flashing with rage. "Don't talk to me about the Goddess. She's the one who imprisoned me here. Now I'm just her cosmic garbageman, handling the stinking rubbish of the world."

"Can you blame her?" Kricket spat. She held the weight of her sword with a forearm, pointing the tip toward Mortegol as she made her way across the room. "Sera, I don't know what's going on, but you need to come with us," she said, looking as if she were struggling between the scene playing out before her and the bond we shared.

Kricket understood she couldn't kill Mortegol here, but knowing my friend, she'd make an impressive go of it, nonetheless. I kept my eyes pinned on her. The Goddess of Air, keeper of knowledge, mother of creative thought, was trying hard to disguise the fear only I could read on her face. I knew she wasn't concerned about losing her own life; her worry was for Raphael and the other arcs.

"I can't, Kricket," I said, my lip quivering. "I have to stay. Please leave and take the others with you. Before it's too late."

"That is an excellent idea, darling," Mortegol said to me. He wheeled around to address the group, the tip of his nose nearly brushing the end of Kricket's blade. With breathtaking speed, he disarmed her, wrenched an arm behind her back, and tossed Kricket like a rag doll toward Michael and the others. It happened so fast that if you blinked, you would have missed it. Mortegol smoothed a hand over his jacket. "You heard the lady, please leave us. Seraphina and I have a lot of catching up to do."

Michael handed his sword to Uriel and walked over to me, placing his palms on my bare shoulders. His hands were warm and felt good on my skin. I wanted to grab him and run, but I fought the urge and lowered my eyes instead.

"Please, Sera. I don't understand. Explain this to me," Michael said, his voice filled with so much hurt and confusion it broke my heart to listen.

"Enough!" Mortegol's voice rang through the room, booming so loud, it shook the massive iron chandelier suspended above us.

Mortegol adjusted his lapels and ran a hand through his thick, black hair. Sudden rage swallowed his handsome features, making him look like the devil humans believed him to be. "Step away from her, brother. She doesn't love you anymore. Can't you see that?"

I took Michael's hand in mine. "Michael, I—"

Mortegol pounded the table with his fist, causing the wine glass and bottle to fly. They shattered on the stone floor, and wine fanned out along the edges of the Persian tribal rug under my feet.

The other arcs and elementals drew closer still, ready to give the demon king a run for his money if he lashed out against Michael or me.

"I said to step away from her, archangel, or I will kill you where you stand. This is my domain, given to me by *your* Goddess. You don't have your powers here, boy. Don't tempt me." The veins in Mortegol's neck protruded. "Guards!" he shouted at the ceiling.

The guards in question were even scarier than the seven-foot demons in Mortegol's charge. I knew he was calling for the fallen angels who sided with him during the rebellion. Three hundred thirty-two of them to be exact, and I feverishly hoped all of them wouldn't come at the sound of their master's voice. Unlike your giant slobbering-variety demon, these guys were smart, having been angelic warriors. Even worse, they knew all our tricks.

Two such exiled menaces appeared in the doorway—Moloch and Belial—the nastiest demons in Mortegol's army of darkness.

The look on Helena's face told me she recognized them too. "Well, well, if it isn't Frick and Frack," she said, sneering at the two former celestial beings who did most of Mortegol's bidding. "So, not everyone got the day off, I guess? Hope you boys are getting overtime pay."

Moloch smirked at her, then he and Belial clanked over, looking hateful in their red and black armor, and dragged Michael away from me. To prove they still harbored a few hard feelings, they flung Michael into Raphael and Uriel. Gabriel caught his brothers, helping them stay on their feet.

The fallen are just as strong as archangels, and Mortegol had given them Underworld powers by turning them into hybrids. Now they were half-angel, half-demon. He'd also restored their wings, big black troubling ones. But the King of the Underworld had never been able to regain his own wings, and I knew it filled him with shame and even more hatred for the Goddess.

Speaking of the Goddess, she hadn't told me what to do once I got Michael here, so I was on my own. I knew I had to play Mortegol like a Stradivarius if Michael and the other arcs had any chance of survival, and I wavered between two choices. I could pretend to have regained my senses and throw myself into Mortegol's arms in a fit of passion, in which case he might let them all go so we could be alone. Or I could go with plan B...which might get all of us killed on the spot. Something in my blasted gut told me to go with Plan B. So that's what I did. Goddess help us.

"I will agree to stay with you if you let Michael go," I said to Mortegol, my tone intentionally defiant.

As I figured might happen, Mortegol erased the distance between us in a few angry strides. He took my chin in his hand and glared at me, rage filling his dark eyes until they looked as desolate and implosive as two black holes. "Oh, you will, will you? You would sully yourself and suffer the hardship of being with me if I let *him* leave, Fire Goddess?" He jabbed a finger at Michael, his aim incredibly accurate for not looking in Michael's direction.

Mortegol's eyes remained fixed on mine, the full thrust of his demon energy directed at me. His rage was hot and forceful enough to blast a hole through my soul. He dropped my chin and ran his hands through his hair in agitation.

"Do I repulse you now, Seraphina? If memory serves, I did not force you into the Underworld. You came to me. You asked *me* to take you in, and you gave yourself to me willingly." He spun on his heel to throw his next hateful words at Michael. "Several times a day." Then he turned back to me. "I think you need some time to warm up. Remember what we had. What do you think?"

I jutted my chin in defiance.

"Take them to the dungeon," Mortegol said, nodding toward Michael and the others.

More guards flooded the room. Two of them grabbed Michael and pushed him out the door first. Then, one by one, my companions disappeared, leaving me alone in the room with Mortegol, Moloch, and Belial.

Mortegol put his hands on his hips and looked down at the floor. "Will you change your mind, Sera?" He raised his head slowly, and I could see the anguish etched on his face.

I looked into his dark eyes, no longer cold and cruel but filled with love. Although I could remember cherishing his affection, the memory was distant, hazy, like some bizarre dream you soon want to forget.

"Come back to me," Mortegol said, his voice breaking.

I took his hand in mine, suddenly ashamed of my part in his deception. "No, Mortegol. I tried to tell you earlier. None of it was real. Goddess made me love you, and I wouldn't have without her influence. She sent me here to be with you...so you wouldn't destroy the Earth. It was a mission."

Mortegol squeezed my hand, and the room grew so quiet I could hear my heart beating in my ears. When I winced, he dropped his grip and backed away, staring at me in disbelief. He stood still for a long time, processing my words. Finally, he flashed up a second glass of wine and drained it in one gulp. Then he wiped his mouth with a hand and made his way back to stand before me.

"Well, then you've failed your little mission, haven't you? You may not love me, Seraphina, but you love this rotting planet and the warring people on it, all of them consumed by hate." He drew closer, his dark eyes fixed on mine, his voice threatening. "When the dying are at your feet pleading to *your* Goddess for mercy, I want your archangel to know all of it was your fault. His beloved humans destroyed because of you." He turned his back to me. "Take her."

The two dark angels didn't waste any time getting to the task.

"Moloch," Mortegol said quietly.

"Yes, Milord?"

"If either of you lay a hand on her, you'll find yourselves a foot taller with a very different set of wings."

Moloch bowed and scraped as he gently took me by the arm. "Milord."

The earthen and rock-lined tunnels Frick and Frack half-dragged, half-pushed me through, smelled of centuries-old dust and mold. Torches lined the jagged walls on either side, casting dim light across the arched ceiling only two feet from the top of Belial's perfect head of golden hair. He was six-four, but it still felt too claustrophobic for my liking.

We arrived at the same cell the others were in. Moloch dropped his grip on me to open the door, and Belial threw me inside with such force I went like a battering ram into Kricket and Andrea. The two elementals helped me stabilize then quietly walked back to their mates. The looks they gave me were heartbreaking. It wasn't contempt or distrust. They were simply struggling to understand.

The cell was dark. The only light that reached inside came from the flickering torches in the hall. You could see, but it took a while for your eyes to adjust. Adding to the overall charm of the place was a bone-chilling draft. I shivered against it, rubbing my arms to help warm them as my high heels sank into the dirt floor.

After several minutes of unnerving stillness, Uriel pulled Andrea to him. "I'm not sure what's going on, my love, but this feels like a betrayal. Like we walked into a trap."

"Uri, you know Sera," Andrea said, looking into her mate's eyes. "There's a solid explanation for all of this. You know there is, just like I do. You're upset, that's all."

Uriel let out a deep sigh and nodded. Then he looked at me. "Sera, I love you. I would do anything for you, any of us would. But I just don't know what to make of this."

Andrea walked over and took my hand, her eyes pleading. "This is where you were all that time…with him?"

I nodded and swiped a tear from my cheek.

Kricket and Helena joined Andrea at my side as the three other arcs huddled around me, worry and confusion on each of their faces.

Helena glanced back at Michael, who had not moved from his spot. Then she looked into my eyes. "Honey," she said soberly, "You need to tell us what's going on."

Kricket put her hands on my shoulders and squeezed gently. "Helena's right. We always confide in one another, and no matter what you say, we *will* understand." She paused, then her eyes widened as a sudden realization took hold. "This had to be a mission. I just know it. You don't have to carry this burden alone. We can help."

"Yes, we can, and we will," Andrea said. "This isn't the end of us. We're not going to die in this stinking dungeon. We've gotten out of tougher spots than this."

Uriel, Raphael, and Gabriel parted, allowing Michael to step between them.

"Sera...help me understand this," Michael said. "If this *was* a mission, I need you to tell me that."

Goddess said I couldn't tell Michael my secret until the time was right, and my intuition told me this still wasn't it. I gritted my teeth. If not now, then when? I thought angrily, knowing she could hear me. But no response came. I looked down at the floor, trying to choose my words carefully. "I came here to be with Mortegol, but it's not what you think—"

"You didn't finish, Sera. You didn't say it." Michael's eyes narrowed. "Do you love him?"

"Michael, I want to tell you, but I can't. I need you to trust me."

"Do you love him, Sera?"

"I did...while I was here. But it's not that simple."

Michael turned away from me and walked to the farthest corner of the cell. He placed his palms on the rock wall and leaned his head against it. A moment later, Moloch and Belial appeared outside the iron door. Belial unlocked it and stepped inside.

"Well, well, if it isn't the diabolical duo," Helena said.

Moloch snorted at her then thrust his chin at Michael. "He's first."

Belial stepped forward, pushing the other archangels out of his way as he went.

"First, for what?" I demanded.

"Execution," Moloch said coolly. "The rest of you better not get too comfortable. It will be your turn soon enough."

My heart nearly shot out of my chest. I knew Mortegol was angry with me, but I never imagined he would go so far as to blatantly defy the Goddess in this way. "Mortegol," I screamed. "You can't do this. Universal Bylaw demands that you let us go."

Michael stepped forward, his hands up in a sign of surrender. The other archangels bowed their heads and turned away. I was so shocked at the sight of it, my knees nearly gave out. Usually, the four arcs would have charged the two dark angels by now. I'd never seen any of them go down without a fight.

Andrea threw herself in front of my mate. "No, you're not taking him. Take me."

"And me," Kricket said, joining hands with the Earth Goddess.

"Me too," Helena said as the three locked arms, creating an elemental body shield around Michael.

I stepped in front of them all. "Take me to Mortegol."

Belial glared at me, then craned his neck to have a look down my dress. "You had your chance, Fire Goddess. The master is angry with you now. But don't be so eager to get your pretty head on the chopping block. You may get out of this yet...if you have the sense to smarten up."

"Gabriel, do something," Helena said. "Why aren't you helping him?"

"We can't, darling," Gabriel turned to look into my eyes. "Michael told us...he wants to die."

Helena sucked in a breath. "I didn't hear him say that. Michael, is that true?"

Michael didn't answer.

"No, Helena. He didn't say it out loud," Uriel said. "Although we don't have our powers here, we are still telepathically linked."

"But if he's killed in the Underworld..." Helena said with tears in her eyes. "He'll be gone...forever."

Raphael rubbed his neck with both hands. He was trying hard to keep it together. "Michael's spirit is broken. He can't live with this. He has chosen everlasting death, and the four of us have said our goodbyes."

Gabriel turned to me, his violet eyes brimming with tears. "If you have something to say, Seraphina, I suggest you say it now."

I heard Helena gasp, then she collapsed in violent sobs.

"Stop delaying my orders, or I'll drop you into the lava pit," Belial growled. He pushed all of us aside with his broad shoulders, then took Michael by the arms, hoisting him out of the cell.

Moloch locked the door behind them and tapped his temple, a taunting smile spreading over his lips. "I heard him think it too. Everlasting death is what he wants. Everlasting death is what he shall have." He clapped Michael on the back. "Good decision Mick-Eye-Elle. You always were the smart one."

"Please look at me," I said to Michael through choking tears.

My beautiful arc raised his head and met my eyes. "I love you, Valentine."

I read the soul-crushing despair on Michael's face, and my heart shattered. Goddess told me he would be presented with a choice to live or die, and he had chosen everlasting death. I slid down the wall of the cell as pain and fear shredded me to ribbons. Dear God. I had made the wrong decision, and now I would surely lose my mind, knowing I had been the one who had condemned him. I buried my face in my hands and wept.

Moloch laughed at me, a taunting wicked laugh. Belial joined in, all too eager to find joy in my pain. "Any last words for your mighty angelic warrior, Fire Goddess?" Moloch snorted. He was deliberately dragging this out, enjoying every moment.

Wait. What did the arcs say—and Moloch too—they *heard* Michael's thoughts. Goddess said I couldn't *tell* Michael my secret until the time was right. I didn't understand at the time, but now the answer pinged my internal radar so hard, it nearly blew a hole through my stomach.

The time would never be right to tell him. That left only one choice, and it would take all the courage I had. If I did this, Michael would see everything—every sorted detail I remembered of my time in the Underworld—every intimate moment shared with Mortegol. There would be no softening the edges, no fade-to-black moments like in the movies. Every grain of truth would be exposed in the harshest light possible. But when Goddess asked me to have faith, she didn't mean in her. She was telling me to have some honest-to-god human-style faith in my man.

I found my conviction and stood up, staring into Moloch's hateful face. "I do have something to tell him," I spat.

I met Michael's eyes and softened my voice. "I have faith in you," I said. "Unwavering faith in you, Mick-Eye-Elle. You are the defender of humankind. You can't abandon the ones you cherish so deeply. No matter what happens with us after this, they need you. And I need you to be in the universe, my love. Even if I must live without you until the end of time."

I cried as I took down the barrier in my mind, baring my soul to the one I have loved for so long.

Michael winced as the ugly truth hit him full-on; every one of my memories rushing into him in lurid detail.

For one horrifying moment, I felt sure I had only driven him closer to the desire for everlasting death. Then a miracle happened.

My beautiful mate straightened his shoulders and looked deeply into my eyes. "Mortegol," he said. "I call war."

CHAPTER

~ 32 ~

No One Expects the Dark Ages

Earth Plane 2021

When Michael called for war, the eight of us were immediately flashed back to the Earth plane, arriving in a heap near the Potomac River. There is a rock outcropping near the water's edge beyond the town, a portal to the Underworld. While we could exit there, only a demon could use it to get in, which is fine by me; I saw no need to go back.

It had been nearly three months since our return. The air had grown warmer, the sun higher in the sky, and the first buds of spring were showing themselves around Leesburg. Helena had roped us all into celebrating the Vernal Equinox to let our collective hair down, and my 'hair' had been a bit foggy this morning as a result. I'd had to flash away a budding spring hangover. Magic can be quite practical.

"Hey, guys," Trevor said in his ever-cheerful tone. "The usual?"

I nodded as I peeled off my jacket and had a seat. "Yes, please."

The *usual* was a skim mocha latte for me, a cup of Earl Grey for Michael, and we were about to enjoy them in our favorite coffee shop in town. The door jingled, and I looked up to see the only other patron had left. Now Michael and I were alone in the little twenty-by-twenty room decorated with yellow curtains and blue tablecloths. It was a happy little place.

At my direction, the eight of us had ventured from home often over the last several months, trying to draw Mortegol out. But we never strayed too far from one another. Most days, Michael was at the diner with me. Raphael and Uriel were at the doctor's office with Kricket and Andrea. Gabriel stayed with Helena at her shop, all within a two-block radius of the other.

But today was Monday, and many businesses in town were closed. Including the ones that employ the four elementals—gatekeepers of the third dimension since the beginning of time.

Once Michael called for war, I hoped we would return topside and have the battle then and there. After all, Mortegol had to agree. When the Army of Light's general declares war, a battle year or not, we must go to war. That part is a strict code in our Universal Bylaws. That's why Goddess told me Michael was the key. *He* is our general.

Mortegol had agreed, but only if he got to choose the time and place. That part was a loophole, and Mortegol has never met one of those he didn't like.

I had reconstructed my entire time in the Underworld since our return, recalling many things about Mortegol's personality and how he rules his kingdom. As Sun Tzu said, "If you know the enemy and know yourself, you need not fear the result of a hundred battles." He also said a bunch of other stuff about war, had written a book on it, in fact, and I knew Mortegol was a fan of the Chinese general *and* the book.

The point is, I knew his tactics, and the eight of us had gone over them in exacting detail since our return.

While I had regained my eternal memories in their entirety, Goddess had been tight-lipped on the plan to successfully conclude our current mission. Namely...how to keep the King of the Underworld from destroying the planet. I knew Michael calling for war a hundred years early was a large part of it. We all did. But I couldn't imagine Mortegol collecting his toys and heading home if we won. He's not really known for being a good sport.

You'd think having direct access to Source would give you all the answers. Not my experience. Most of the time, Goddess forces you to work things through on your own…like any good parent, I guess. "Let the battle play out as it will," she'd said, and I couldn't help but wonder what she was cooking up in that universal stove of hers. But my problem-solving skills had been our salvation that day in the Underworld, so maybe she does know a thing or two.

For instance, she knew giving Michael access to my memories was the only way to save us. Perhaps when I arrived in the seventh dimension, pleading with her to erase my memories, I did too. I shuddered involuntarily. Good thing I didn't know that part going in.

Once I dropped the mental blockade, Michael understood everything. He'd also realized Goddess had made me love Mortegol to ease the pain of the mission—a love I would have never felt without her *little nudge* as she'd called it. I think that was the part that eased his mind the most.

He also assured me that if presented with the choice, he would have done the same, just as Goddess said he would. "You saved the beings and realm I love so dearly. I will be eternally grateful," he'd told me. His loving words washed through me like a cleansing river, and I cried in his arms at the incredible relief I felt afterward.

The moment I'd let Michael into my thoughts, the other arcs told Kricket, Helena, and Andrea. It felt good to have my horrible secret out in the open. And their combined gratitude and unwavering love for me worked like a salve on my frazzled mind.

Michael and I were even closer than before. A few days after our harrowing time in the Underworld, he'd confided he knew I'd gone to Morningside after my previous life ended. He had also withheld the information from his brothers, something he rarely does, and he'd not come back once he felt sure I was safe. That's my archangel, ever the gentleman, ever the caring soulmate.

I looked over at him; he was fully engrossed in a magazine article while we waited for Trevor to finish whirring my latte.

Michael likes to read, although I'm not sure why. He could simply pull whatever he wanted from the aethers. He has access to every thought ever put to paper. Well, every thought, period. The dream of being human, I decided, glancing at his lovely eyelashes as they flicked across the page. He loves it as much as I do, and if I survived this next battle, it would be a dream come true.

Archangels can't be killed on the Earth plane. Not by a demon, one of the fallen, or even by the King of the Underworld himself. But elementals sure could. Be killed, that is.

Mortegol must kill all four elementals with a nasty blade called the Demon Dagger to win in battle. I chewed my lip, contemplating what would happen if he managed to do that; Earth would be ruled in darkness for a thousand years. Plagues, death, destruction, and mayhem reign during a dark time. Thankfully, the good people of Earth had not had the misfortune of living through such bleakness for a long while.

In fact, that's only happened one time during this version of Earth, an unsavory period known as the Dark Ages, and I still believe Mortegol cheated somehow. Although I could never prove it, I'm sure he used doppelgangers. Otherwise, there's no way he could have covered so much ground so quickly. The entire battle was over in twenty minutes—the final ruling stuck—and poof! Dark Ages. (Historians confine the period to Europe, but the rest of the planet suffered just fine, thank you.)

On the other hand, if the Army of Light won this battle, light would reign. Sure, there's still darkness during light-reigning years; this is the third dimension, after all. But the balance leans toward goodness, love, and humans working together for the betterment of all. And let me tell you, no matter how angry you get with the state of affairs during light-reigning years, it's nothing compared to the alternative. Better the devil you know, as they say.

The Army of Light wins battles by slaying all three hundred thirty-two of the fallen before Mortegol kills the four of us. And I had my sights set on running two of them through myself; Frick and Frack.

I assure you I'm not some heartless monster. I value all life. Our wars are not as gruesome as I make it sound, either. The moment angels die in battle—light or dark—they immediately show up in the Underworld or the Summerlands good as new. The only difference is if they 'die' in battle, they're no longer allowed to play for the championship title.

The wars between light and dark are no more than an elaborate game of keep-away...with blood and swords. The fallen are forbidden to kill elementals. Their job is to wear us out and distract the arcs, giving Mortegol the chance to pick us off one by one. The Army of Light is there to help make sure that doesn't happen, and we elementals just have to stay alive to the end. Rules I have always found incredibly odd, but there you have it.

Kricket, Andrea, Helena, and I do our best to live through each battle. But if it doesn't work out, we just pop back to the Summerlands like every other soul, ready to do it all again; lather, rinse, repeat.

Don't get me wrong, dying stinks when you're just getting started in a newish body. And I'm looking forward to a handful of quiet decades, living with Michael as husband and wife, having a family, and battling the occasional cosmic bad guy. Plenty of those lurking around—trying to get through our protected gates—eager to inflict a bunch of terrifying weirdness on Earth.

Nope, the frightening part of our battles isn't potential death; that's just a tollbooth on the universal highway for all of us. It's the whole *humankind ruled by darkness* thing, and I wasn't about to let it happen again. I'd often thought if humans knew we played for such high stakes, there would be anarchy in the streets. Better they didn't know.

Trevor arrived at our table. "Okay," he said cheerily. "Skim mocha latte for Sera. Earl Grey for Michael." He spun on his heel, then turned back to us. "Hey, Michael. Don't you ever want to try anything else?"

"I've tried," I said, hooking a thumb at my mate. "This one's set in his ways." I turned to my archangel love, who cannot tell a lie. "How long have you been a tea drinker again, Michael?" I blew on my latte to add an extra dose of innocence to the question.

Michael finished his sip and smiled up at the boy. "Oh, a long, long time. This is good. Thanks, Trevor."

Ooh. An artful dodge. Michael wiggled his eyebrows, letting me know I hadn't won that round.

"Okay. Just thought I'd check." Trevor shrugged and walked away.

Michael watched him go. "Hard to believe he was once the most feared knight in all of Great Britain."

"I know," I said, studying the boy's scrawny frame, wishing we could employ his former self for the battle ahead. I opened my mouth to say something meaningless, I'm sure. I can't remember what, precisely because it was that moment the door to the coffee shop ripped off its hinges and flew into the hood of a parked car. I heard it rather than saw it because Michael had already hauled Trevor and me out the back door.

CHAPTER
~ 33 ~
Battle for the Earth Plane

Earth Plane 2021

Several car alarms went berserk, their piercing squeals ricocheting off the buildings that lined the narrow streets. Somehow, that has always been more jarring to me than the sound of cannon fire.

"Run," I said to Trevor.

The boy shot away from us, his arms and legs forming pinwheels of motion fueled by sudden fear. The sight would have been funny on any other day. In a previous lifetime, the soul now occupying the body of an awkward teenager took care of most of the killing, deserved or not.

"Time to go to work, Valentine. You feelin' it?" Michael said. The silver and blue armor of the Army of Light formed over him, and his wings unfurled.

"Oh, yeah," I said as my clothes shifted—red outfit, low-heeled red boots—my elemental sword materializing in my hand. "I'll take action over waiting any day."

"Come out, come out wherever you are." The demon king's voice was getting closer with every word. Michael flew us to the roof just as Mortegol stepped through the back door into the alley. "Oh, there you are," he purred, shooting a fireball up at us. It whizzed by my head, narrowly missing as Michael and I ran hard for the other side and jumped down onto the pavement.

The others were already there in battle attire—the arcs in silver and blue armor, the elementals in blue, green, and yellow—the six of them with their swords at the ready. We formed a tight circle, standing with our backs to one another to get eyes on all sides.

Mortegol stepped around the corner into my view. "Hello, my love. Well, this doesn't seem fair. Eight of you against me?"

"Get off the streets," I shouted to the gathering crowd as I sent a fireball ripping through the air at Mortegol. I wasn't trying to kill him. I just wanted to keep him at a healthy distance. Good thing, I guess, because my missile hit the car behind him, blowing it sky-high. That did the trick for the onlookers. Now there wasn't a soul on the street except for Mortegol and the eight of us.

Andrea waved a hand, and I heard a soft pop. She'd just cleared the area, sending the innocent humans to another place. Probably to their homes where they would arrive feeling pretty confused, I'm guessing.

"Let's see if we can even this out a bit," Mortegol said, glowering at Michael.

The Underworld army appeared in a haze of black smoke, and now a wall of the fallen stood shoulder-to-shoulder. They covered the entire width of the pavement and sidewalks beyond, stretching back for blocks. More perched on building ledges and others hovered above us, their black wings unfurled, keeping them aloft. I didn't need to count them; the Underworld army—including Mortegol—is the sacred number, three hundred thirty-three.

There was a moment of stillness, then Gabriel blew his horn.

Light-warrior angels appeared behind us in silver and blue armor, making our number the same. Now here we were in our entirety; Archangel Michael and his Army of Light, ready to battle for the Earth plane.

None of us moved, not our side, not theirs. We couldn't until Gabe blew a second note. At least Mortegol was still playing by the rules, but I found myself wondering how long that would last.

I studied our enemy, all holding still as we were, looking like an oil on canvas—dark angels on a modern street. Their red and black chest guards were emblazoned with Mortegol's crest, a snake slithering through flames, a little too fitting. Their glossy black wings loomed over them like dark towers rising behind their broad shoulders. Their swords, shields, and armor gleamed in the midday sun, and their general, Mortegol, King of The Underworld, front and center, striking a regal pose.

The stakes were high, and I probably should have been scared, nervous at least, I usually was at this point. But I was angry and ready to take a pound of flesh from Mortegol for threatening to kill Michael, and that seemed to be doing a bang-up job of blocking my fear.

The other elementals and I took our positions in the middle of the ranks, and I could feel Mortegol's eyes fastened on the four of us as we went. I saw Gabriel lift his horn again, and I grabbed my sword from the scabbard on my back. I ran a thumb over the salamander on the hilt, a good luck tick I've had for a long time. I didn't know what would happen next. What I *did* know is that I would not be going down today.

The second horn sounded, and the street and the skies above us became a blur of flashing steel as the fallen and the Army of Light engaged.

A ring of angels remained around us, a wall of muscle and white-feathered wings. They backed us further from the mayhem, swords drawn, ready to defy anyone who tried to attack the elementals. Two at our back fell, and our remaining protectors closed ranks, moving us in a sidestep toward the coffee shop as the fighting raged on.

I caught a glimpse of Mortegol, not an ounce of love in his eyes now as he moved through the warring angels. I knew his red and black battle gear was enchanted, and I watched swords glance off him as he marched through the crowds in our direction.

"Close in," one of our protectors said. He had noticed Mortegol too.

I looked at Kricket, who did not seem the least bit happy being a damsel inside an angelic cage. I knew she wanted to break ranks and get down to the business of kicking demonic butt, but I shot her a warning look I hoped said *hold steady.* Our time for fighting would come soon enough. Before the thought had time to thoroughly bake, the angels surrounding us went down in a heap, run through by the fallen. But Goddess help those demons; we came out swords blazing.

Kricket flashed a take-no-prisoners smile and sprang forward, dispatching our immediate opponents with several swift jabs of her blade. Then she spun on her heel and ran into the swarm.

Andrea and I stood back-to-back, slowly turning, our swords pointed outward, getting our eyes and weapons in all directions. A brood of the fallen came running. They weren't allowed to kill us. But tiring us out was a different story, and now it was six hulking angels against the two of us, steel crashing against steel. A flash of white light streaked our way, mowing the enemy down in its path. I knew it was Michael, and a moment later, he was fighting by our side.

The other arcs battled their way toward us. "Where's Kricket?" Raphael said through gritted teeth as he ran one of the dark angels through with his broad sword.

"I—don't—know," I said between clashes of my own blade.

The next instant, Raphael had taken to the skies, probably in search of his mate. Kricket was always wandering off in battle, getting into the most terrible trouble she could find. I almost laughed, knowing she could take care of herself, but one of the fallen kicked me squarely in the rib cage. I doubled over as breath wheezed from my lungs, then straightened and ran him through with my sword.

He smiled a terrible smile as he bled out at my feet, knowing he'd delivered a punishing blow. A few minutes from now, this guy would be back in the Underworld telling the story, probably with a mug of frothy ale in his hand. I held my aching side as I twisted my blade deeper into his gut and locked eyes with him. I couldn't tell if my ribs were broken, but close enough, I decided as I gasped for breath.

He held my gaze then vanished once the job was all the way done. Good riddance, I thought as I magically patched my ribs. They *were* broken, and now I could feel them snapping back into place. The pain of it almost made me blackout, and for a split second, I thought I might vomit, but I gathered my strength as anger took hold.

I sent my sword to the aethers to free both hands and shot a steady stream of fire at the demons who'd stepped in to fill the temporary void surrounding us. But they blocked it with their shields and advanced, weapons drawn.

Okay, now I was a little scared.

Kricket appeared at my side and blasted energy from her palms. "This is gonna get a lot worse before it gets better," she said as the wind whipped up and began to howl. It gathered force until it was a dark tornado that hurled dozens of the fallen into the sky where their heads met with the wrong end of holy swords.

While Mortegol was busy watching the carnage overhead, Michael charged him. But Mortegol vanished at the exact moment the steel should have made contact, and Michael's blade ripped through the pavement, shooting sparks. My mate whipped around, searching for the demon king, and then turned on his heel to address the enemy at his back.

I steadied my weapon as Michael and the other arcs battled furiously against the fallen closing in all around us. Helena and Andrea were back alongside Kricket and me, and I studied our opponents, searching the crowd. "Mortegol, where are you?" I said under my breath.

Careful what you wish for, I thought as Mortegol flashed in behind Michael. He sent several fireballs rocketing our way. Not enough to kill us, just enough to barbeque us into submission so he could finish the job.

"Shield the elementals!" Michael shouted as he ran toward us.

The three archangels turned at once and held their shields over Helena, Kricket, Andrea, and me. Just in time to catch the wall of fire and hold it back. Although demon fire can't kill archangels, it can burn them, and now the arcs were smoldering, their armor blackened, their skin charred and bubbling.

Michael took the brunt of the flames across his back. He waved a hand in anger and healed himself, a look of intent fixed in his blue eyes. The three other elementals and I didn't have a mark on us, and I breathed a sigh of relief.

Michael reached us and wheeled around just as Mortegol disappeared again. The other arcs healed themselves, and they and Michael remained in a tight formation. I took out three of the fallen advancing from the rear, then kicked another away from Uriel's back.

The squeal of tires on pavement caught my attention, and I whipped around to see Cormac behind the wheel of his sixty-five Lincoln, driving like the hammers of the devil. He fishtailed to a stop, connecting with a gaggle of fallen angels, sending them flying in all directions. He kicked the door open and sprang out, broadsword first. "Battle!" he said, then went to work on any left standing.

Like Kricket, Cormac likes fighting.

Andrea backed an angel onto the hood of Cormac's car, finishing him and the paint with a gouging jab of her sword. "Sorry, Cormac!" she shouted as she turned to cut down several more of the fallen coming at her hard.

"That's okay, lass," he said, glaring at one of the dark angels stumbling to his feet. "You dented my car, demon scum." Cormac ran him through, then turned his attention to the hoard storming across the roof. "Jesus wept. Get off the car. I'm right here." He took down an impressive number, his steel ablaze as the ancient warrior kicked into high gear, but more demons swarmed him, and in the next moment, he was trapped with no way out.

I ran to help, then stopped as I saw Kricket in her elemental form, clearing a path toward him, trampling warring angels under her massive hooves. She approached at a hard gallop, and Cormac swung himself onto her back, mowing the enemy down with his broadsword as they made a U-turn and rode back toward us. A dark angel swooped down from the sky, his blade connecting with Cormac's side, and I watched in horror as my friend doubled over, grabbing the horse's mane with his free hand.

While the arcs kept the opposition at bay, Helena raised water through the pavement. "Show yourself, demon. Cuz now you're just making me angry." She flung her hands in the direction we'd last seen Mortegol, and a thick fog covered the street.

Cormac slid off the horse's back to land beside us. Although he was hurt badly, he too was peering into the mist, his weapon drawn. I studied him as he staggered around a bit, wishing I could heal him. But our magic doesn't work on immortals for some reason. What I could do was flash bandages and sterile gauze onto my friend, and I did just that.

"Thanks, Sera," he said, looking down at my magical patch job.

Cormac's face had gone pale from blood loss, and I hooked an arm around him to help steady his six-foot frame, wobbling like a building ready to topple over. I cursed under my breath. We couldn't shift time, or flash ourselves or anyone else around during battle, or I would have sent him to Dr. Chet. Immortals heal, but they do it slowly and painfully with a wound this severe. Thankfully, my ageless friend wouldn't die, at least there was that.

Kricket was back in her human form. "There he is!" she shouted, pointing to a barely visible outline moving through the mist before us. I launched several fireballs in its direction and heard Mortegol scream as one of them connected. He flashed back into focus, howling in agony and holding his leg where my fireball had burned his flesh to the bone.

Michael put Mortegol in a headlock and seemed singularly focused on killing him with his bare hands. Mortegol managed to remain on his feet and was fighting back. But he was no match for the warrior of light, and Michael, his face red and filled with anger, kicked the demon through the plate glass window of the coffee shop.

A crowd of the fallen charged Uriel, Raphael, and Gabriel, trying to break through them to get to the four elementals. But Andrea shot vines from her wrists, binding the dark angels together, and the three arcs smote them, hastening their return to the Underworld.

Cormac was doing a great job fighting through his pain, and I watched him advance on our opponents, driving them further away. Then I caught something I wished I hadn't seen. It was Braith running through the warring crowd toward me. Curiously, the dark angels surrounding us didn't notice him.

"What are you doing here?" I said, realizing it was hard to hear my voice over the increasing noise.

"I came to help!" he shouted.

I turned on my heel to run through the enemy at my back. "These warriors are too strong for you, Braith. Go home," I said, kicking another dark angel away from me. Andrea caught the pass and lopped his head off with an elegant swing of her battle sword. That ability to judge speed and trajectory is inside all eight of us, factory installed.

"They can't see me," Braith said. "I am invisible to my enemy."

I could tell now that he was right. None of Mortegol's warriors were paying the slightest attention to him. I turned to clash swords with one of them, but I was tiring, my movements jerky and mechanical. The dark angel took advantage of my fatigue and ran the edge of his blade across the meat of my shoulder, leaving a big bloody gash in its wake.

The burst of pain went off like a bomb in my head, but I fought through it and was just about to heal myself when Frick and Frack appeared. Moloch wrenched my arms behind my back while Belial punched me in the stomach repeatedly, knocking the breath from my lungs.

Braith placed his palms out, thumbs together, his eyes locked on my punishers. "Deditionem."

Belial stopped throttling me and froze in place, a look of bewilderment on his loathsome face. Moloch released his grip, and both demons dropped to their knees on the pavement in unison. Okay, that was impressive, I thought, breathing heavily as I looked at Braith in astonishment.

I raised my sword to deal with Frick and Frack but couldn't get my mangled shoulder to cooperate. No matter, because Cormac raced in like a comet and relieved them of their heads before collapsing at my feet. I knelt beside the immortal, placing a hand on his forehead. He was burning up, and his lips had gone blue. "Hang in there, my friend." I looked up at Braith.

The young, impressive witch extended his hands to his sides, and a beam of white light encircled the three of us. He'd created a protection bubble. I took the opportunity to heal myself, wincing through the pain as tissue rebuilt itself around my rotator cuff. Then a couple of things happened, almost at the same time. I watched several dark angels (and Andrea) bounce off the invisible shield surrounding us. And the four parts that used to be Moloch and Belial vanished—back to the Underworld where they belong.

"You've got to get Cormac out of here," I said to Braith.

He met my eyes solidly, a look of brave determination on his face. "I can help you, Sera."

I shook my head. "No, this is our fight. The biggest help is getting Cormac to safety. I appreciate your willingness…and bravery…and mad witchcraft skills. But I've got it from here."

Braith nodded and helped Cormac to his feet. "Come on, man. Let's get you to my grandpa."

"Thank you," Cormac wheezed.

"The thanks you can give me is asking Julia on a date," Braith said as Cormac slumped into him. "Uh, once your guts are all back in place. But hold on a minute." Braith locked eyes with the immortal and muttered an enchantment. "Okay, dude. Now you're invisible too." Then he looked back at me. "Are you sure?"

"I'm fine, but you've got to get him to Dr. Chet."

Braith nodded and took his shield down. Then he helped Cormac lumber through the chaos, unnoticed by the enemy.

I sent my sword to the aethers, ready to launch a few fireballs at the dark angels who had just noticed my position. Then I realized Braith's protection bubble had made the three of us invisible while inside it too. That's not allowed in battle, but I didn't do it, so I shrugged it off.

Before I had time to take another breath, a massive chain thunked down over my shoulders and jerked tight under my arms. The rough metal bit into my neck, and I heard a *clicking* sound between my shoulder blades.

"Hello, Fire Goddess. We got you some jewelry," said the all-too-familiar voice. I swung around to see Moloch and Belial glowering at me, their lips curled into sardonic smiles. I struggled to break free, but the harder I pulled, the tighter the harness became.

"Phoenix," I shouted, thinking I could transform to slip the chains. Nothing happened. "Phoenix," I said again.

Moloch sneered at me. "Your magic doesn't work anymore, babe. Underworld steel. Good luck with that."

"Yeah, good luck," Belial said. Then the two of them vanished.

I searched the streets for the other elementals, and my heart sank when I saw all three of them struggling against their own harnesses. I whipped around, casting my eyes over the warring angels, looking for the arcs. I found them all right, heavily engaged in their own battles, oblivious to this fun new twist. Great.

I was without my sword, my power was locked up, and several fallen had turned their sights on me. They wore the wicked grin of unrepentant sinners on their devilish faces, and they took their time, almost approaching at a stroll. There was no way to get the chains off before they reached me, and I wasn't about to run; I wouldn't give them the satisfaction.

My mind raced through possibilities. Okay, they're not allowed to kill us, I thought. But Mortegol sure could, and that's precisely where they would take me, Helena, Kricket, and Andrea, to the tip of the demon king's blade.

My stomach wrenched as the enemy grew closer still. We were about to lose, and the Earth plane would be ruled in darkness for a thousand years. Goddess help us all.

CHAPTER
~ 34 ~
Fire in the Belly

Earth Plane 2021

I allowed this gruesome thought to stew until it made my stomach sick.

Wait a minute. I am the Goddess of Fire; I don't give in…and I most certainly *do not* go down without a fight. These clowns might take me to Mortegol, but they were going to look a lot worse than I did when we got there. I scanned my surroundings for a weapon—something, anything—to hold them off. Then I remembered.

Call my name.

I had no idea if this would work between dimensions, but I didn't have anything to lose by trying.

I looked to the sky and focused my mind, feeling a tingle on my skin when I linked up to Universal Energy. "Hira," I shouted, my voice ringing through the streets. Before the echo had time to die down, a sonic boom ripped through the heavens. A heartbeat later, my familiar charged through the swirling red portal that had just appeared in the sky above us. The dragon descended, hitting the street at a run. I judged her speed, latched on, and swung myself up at the exact moment she raced by. We were airborne a second later.

Hira and I flew a search pattern as the fighting raged on, the remaining dark angels clashing swords with what was left of our Army of Light. At least the battle was contained in the streets now, leaving us alone in the sky. I counted fifty-two of the fallen below. Having just finished off their opponents, the four archangels ran toward Kricket, Andrea, and Helena.

"Get back!" I screamed.

The sound of my voice sent the Army of Light scattering for cover—as far away from what remained of Mortegol's troops as they could get. They knew what was coming next.

The dragon was breathing hard, and I could feel the heat in her belly rise into the back of her throat. "Hold steady," I said, waiting for the arcs to get the other elementals to safety. The moment they were out of striking distance, Hira unleashed a stream of fire over the remaining dark angels, sweeping that beautiful, terrifying head of hers from side to side. Now what remained of Mortegol's army were cinders that drifted away on the wind.

We landed just as Michael and the other arcs finished breaking the elementals free of their chains. I slid off Hira's back, and Michael, using his bare hands, ripped the Underworld steel from my body. I rubbed a shoulder where the metal had broken the skin, then healed myself, relieved that my power was back.

I wrapped my arms around the dragon's neck as tears sprang to my eyes. "Thank you, my beautiful friend. You saved us."

Hira's body was warm, and she pressed herself into the embrace. When I finally let go, she took several steps forward, then turned back to me. "I will always come when you call, Seraphina." Hira bowed her head, then took to the skies. The portal opened, and she was gone.

I looked around me. Our warriors were gone too, and that only happens if...the realization sent a jolt down my spine. We had done it. We had just won the battle for the Earth plane, and now light would reign for a thousand years.

The eight of us were alone, peering out into the street as fire ripped through the centuries-old buildings around us. Car alarms and the sounds of shattering glass filled the air but not a fallen angel in sight. I called my sword from the aethers, ready to hold it over my head in victory.

"Where's Mortegol?" Michael said. While I was eager to take the win, he was still on high alert.

Gabriel nodded at the burning coffee shop. "Last we saw, you kicked him through that window over there." We turned in time to see the building collapse in a fiery heap.

While we were distracted, twenty fallen angels appeared. In a few surprisingly quick moves, they relieved us of our weapons and pinned our arms. Four of them lifted Andrea, Kricket, Helena, and me into the sky. They flew us at lightning speed, descending on the street where Mortegol stood waiting. He had healed himself of my fireball shot.

The archangels broke free of their captors and were on us in an instant. But twelve more of the fallen flashed in, two of them restraining each arc while a third clamped Underworld steel around their necks. Raphael coughed as he tried to pry his away, but it was no use. The demon-forged metal not only removed their magic, but it also seemed to take their strength as well.

I gasped as one of the fallen ripped Michael's chest guard away to smash a fist into his stomach. My fearless warrior doubled over on impact, then straightened and smiled into the dark angel's face. "Is that all you've got, Astaroth?"

"Enough," Mortegol said and turned on his heel to face the four of us, his guards holding us in place as he paced back and forth like a lion settling in on dinner. "Well, well," he said, pointing the Demon Dagger at Andrea's throat. "Who wants to go first? Should it be you, Earth? Or should we do it in the order you come to this wretched planet?" He walked down the line and stopped at Helena. "That puts your head on the trident first."

Gabriel struggled against the dark angel holding him, his face filled with rage. "I will kill you with my bare hands."

Mortegol looked unimpressed by the threat. "Well, as you can see, I am terrified."

"We killed the fallen," Michael said. "These guys came back from the Underworld to take us. That means you forfeit, demon, and we win by default. Even though we won in the first place."

"Oh, yes? Who's to say? These *guys*, as you so eloquently state, could have been hiding out while Sera's beast gave their brethren that spectacular fire bath. I'd have to check the rulebook, but I don't believe celestial dragons are allowed in battle."

"Your soldiers came back from the Underworld before Sera called her familiar. In fact, that was the reason she had to do it." Uriel said. "Turn them loose, or Goddess will be so far up your demonic backside, you'll taste her shampoo."

Mortegol walked over to stand before me. "I should start with you, lover. What do you think? You're the one who got them all into this mess. Perhaps you should be the first to go. Then Michael gets to watch you die, and I have the pleasure of killing you for deceiving me. Win, win…for me, anyway."

The angel restraining me threw me forward. I stumbled, and Mortegol caught me, crossing an arm over my body, holding his blade to my throat. I struggled to break free of his grasp as Helena leveled a slew of curses at the demon king.

Mortegol raised his eyebrows in surprise. "My, my, Water Goddess. For a light being, you have an interesting vocabulary. Do you kiss your archangel mate with that saucy mouth?"

"Let Sera go," Raphael growled, his gray eyes filled with anger, his skin glistening with sweat. "We defeated your army, and now you must concede. That is our law, demon."

"Oh, I don't think so, brother," Mortegol said. "Instead, I'm going to kill this traitor in front of you. The other elementals are next," he told me, "so you won't feel singled out, my love."

Michael broke free, but Frick and Frack popped in to restrain him.

"Oh, you're kidding me," I said in disgust. "Dear Goddess, will the two of you just stay gone? Cormac killed these two in front of me. I watched them die at my feet, and then they came back to lock the four of us into Underworld steel. You've broken every battle law we have, Mortegol. You lost, and now you must surrender."

"And where is this Cormac now?" Mortegol said. "He's not here, but my soldiers are."

Michael lunged again, but Moloch and Belial had a tight enough hold to keep him from breaking free. Astaroth took that opportunity to punch Michael in the stomach a second time. "So, let's see. I've got that," he said. His lips curled into a menacing grin. "Want to see what else I've got, Michael?"

Mortegol glowered at Michael warningly, pressing the blade deeper into my throat. "I would stay put if I were you, brother. We've got you beat. Best to just get it over with. Better luck next time."

I felt a trickle of blood roll down my neck, and Mortegol bent to lick it before returning his dark gaze to Michael. "I'm doing you a favor, angel. Giving you a decades-long break. Isn't that how that works? You process linear time while you wait for Sera to wake. I'm not sure how you can stand to be with the same mate for all eternity. Grueling monogamy isn't natural. Mix it up a bit, boy. Where's your sense of adventure?"

Mortegol moved closer, and I felt the heat of his breath on my cheek, his voice a low, resonant growl. "Say goodnight, Seraphina," he said. "I'll see you in the next life, and maybe we can try this again once I've made the rivers run with blood. I'm not sure how humans came up with that, but it would be stunning." He opened his mouth to say something else, but the ground shook beneath our feet, causing Mortegol to stagger backward, me with him.

A giant sinkhole opened in the middle of King Street, and from its depths, a booming voice rang out. "Father! Let her go."

A figure rose from the crater, and my gaze followed it a little stupidly. Now a six-foot-three demon in red and black armor hovered in midair, his black wings extended, keeping him aloft. At first, I thought my mind was playing tricks on me as I watched his honey-blond hair move slightly in the breeze. He descended, landing near me, his bright green eyes fixed on mine.

New memories unlocked themselves and rushed into my third eye. A quick glance at Michael told me he had arrived at the truth the same moment I had.

"Well, this is unexpected," Helena said, breaking the silence.

Mortegol glared at the newcomer as I struggled with a range of emotions. All I wanted was to break free and throw my arms around him...my son... Luc. How had I forgotten? He was everything to me. Tears streamed down my cheeks as I watched him; his steely gaze trained on Mortegol, his eyes flicking to the dagger now positioned over my heart.

"Lucius, you are one for flashy entrances," Mortegol said. "Aren't you supposed to be in Paris with that little Satan worshiper of yours?"

"I won't let you kill her, father. Not this time."

"I didn't kill your mother, boy. You know that."

"You may not have been the one holding the blade, but you brought the one who did."

Astaroth pushed through the crowd. "I let Morgana in. You were laying our realm to waste as you doted over the Fire Goddess like a lovesick human," he said to Mortegol. "I had to put an end to it. I wasn't about to let you ruin everything we stand for over a warrior of light. I would have killed you, too," he said to Lucius. "But mama bear hovered over you day and night, protecting her little mutt prince. You're a cosmic joke, and oh, do we laugh. A half-breed will never rule the Underworld."

Mortegol's eyes lit with fire, his lips quivering in anger as he stared at the dark angel. I think he was confused by Astaroth's confession, and I realized at that moment, he didn't know who let Morgana in to kill me all those years ago. "It doesn't matter anymore," he said. "It was all a lie designed by the Almighty meddler." His body grew rigid, and he pressed the tip of the dagger into my flesh, ready to drive it all the way in.

Lucius lunged at us, and I took the small window to slip Mortegol's grasp, but the knife came down hard in the scuttle finding its way into my stomach. My eyes and mouth flew open wide, and I stumbled backward. Without thinking, I grabbed the dagger and pulled it from me, throwing it to the ground. Blood splashed onto my boots as I doubled over.

With breathtaking speed, Lucius snatched the blade from the pavement and plunged it into Mortegol's heart.

I heard Michael shouting as I fell to my knees, but I couldn't make out what he was saying. I was busy trying to heal myself, but it was no use; the Demon Dagger had done its job. I collapsed, gasping for breath as the eternal cord tethering me to the other elementals gave way.

"I have defeated my father in battle," Lucius said, holding the blade over his head. "I am the keeper of the Demon Dagger. I am your new king."

"The king is dead. Long live the king," the dark angels shouted in unison.

Astaroth's wings sprouted, knocking down several fallen angels around him as he took to the skies. Suddenly beholden to my son, and probably hoping to gain favor, six dark angels pursued him. Within seconds, all of them were out of sight.

Droves of the fallen appeared, crowding around us, a shadow creeping over them that cooled my skin. At first, I thought a cloud might be passing, but I looked up to see more of the Underworld army floating above, their black wings blotting out the sun. I heard a trumpet blast far away, then hundreds of dark angels chanted, "The king is dead. Long live the king!"

Belial brought a tusk to his lips and blew a note that rang out like thunder across the heavens, silencing the fallen. "King Lucius, long may he reign the Underworld!" he shouted. "The Earth plane shall be his dominion, and all shall bend the knee."

The pronouncement sent the Underworld army into another uproar, but Lucius thrust a fist in the air. "Silence," he said, dropping to my side.

The shouting stopped, and I could hear Michael again. "Get away from her, demon."

Lucius snapped his fingers at the guards. "Let Michael come to her."

The dark angels holding the arc turned him loose, and he rushed forward, falling to his knees beside me. He gently rested my head in his lap, and I looked into his teary-blue eyes as he took my hand and kissed my fingers. "Oh, Sera. No," he said, pressing a palm to my wound. I knew Michael couldn't heal me from this, Underworld steel or not, and so did he. I could see it on his face.

"I love you, Michael."

Lucius came closer. "Mother, don't leave me again." He was crying too.

I reached up to touch Luc's cheek, remembering the joy I felt while carrying him, teaching him the ways of the Summerlands, loving him for all those years. "Luc, my lovely boy of dark and light," I said through my tears.

Then I turned my attention to Michael. The light around him receded until it seemed as if I were peering down a long tunnel with the walls closing in. "See you soon," I said to my beautiful weeping angel. It was the goodbye we'd used for thousands of years. But no matter how many times we did this, it never got easier for either of us.

"See you soon," Michael said, his voice choking as he wiped tears from his face.

As I lay dying, Lucius looked deeply into my eyes. I held his gaze for as long as I could, then everything went dark.

CHAPTER
~ 35 ~
Gabriel Blows His Horn

Other Side of the Veil, Present Moment

The funny thing about leaving the Earth plane as an elemental is a little tidbit I hadn't fully remembered until now. We hover between realms when we die, for a handful of minutes, anyway, probably to help ease the shock. Then we get sucked through Gabe's portal, riding our own energy home without much fanfare. So I knew I had only a few moments before the cosmic vacuum fired up. Luc and Michael were slumped over my lifeless body, and I must have stepped out quickly because I was in time to see my hand slip from my son's cheek.

"Mother, please come back to me," Lucius said.

It's not that I could hear him, I couldn't hear anything, but I could sense him, all of them. What they were feeling and thinking. Now I understood why Luc let Michael come to me. From this side of the veil, it was all so clear. My son had an odd fascination with the arc.

Although I loved Mortegol while in the Underworld, a part of me missed Michael, and I'd told my little boy countless stories of the mighty archangel. Now I realized Michael was somewhat of a superhero to Luc.

I gazed at the two immortal beings I love with all my heart, one light, one dark, not understanding why I hadn't remembered Luc until a few moments ago.

"Because, Daughter, he is the reason the world does not end."

I turned my head slowly to gaze into the loving eyes of the Goddess. She still looked like Celeste, her way of mothering me, I suppose.

"Why would it make any difference if I remembered him?" It was a question borne of mild curiosity, not burning desire. I'd forgotten how peaceful death is. Dropping the body has the same effect as chugging an opioid cocktail. You know that whatever happened is rife with emotion. You just don't care.

"Seraphina," she said, giving me one of her all-knowing looks. "If you knew of him before that moment, you would have gone in search of him, and that series of events would not have brought you to this moment. You and I weighed all possibilities before choosing this one, and there were plenty," she said, raising her eyebrows. "This was the only path that led us here. Right where we need to be," she added, patting my hand. "You chose to die in the struggle so your son would claim the throne. Now Mortegol will not have the opportunity to destroy the Earth."

She was right. I would have gone to Luc, and I realized I'd asked her to wipe his memory from my mind for just that reason. It would have changed everything. I wanted to stroke his hair now, tell him I loved him, that I was sorry for leaving him in the Underworld with Mortegol.

Suddenly, I felt Michael's overwhelming pain as each one of my human deaths rushed in on him at once. He was sinking into the depths of despair, and it didn't make sense at first. So fearless in battle, my beautiful angel, so loving, so willing to do anything for humans, felt defeated and alone in the universe. Then I remembered what he'd said—that he feared losing me might end him. Now I understood his anguish. This never-ending loop of death and rebirth, the waiting, the longing for me to return had worn away at his heart.

"I hate to see Mick-Eye-Elle suffer," Goddess said, then she turned to me. "Would you like to return to him, Seraphina? In this lifetime?"

I looked at her, feeling a bit zoned out, but hopeful too. "That's allowed?"

She smiled a smile so filled with unconditional love I almost wept. "Goddess, baby."

I nodded, my heart flooding with enough joy to break through the haze of death. "I would like that more than anything."

Her lovely golden-brown eyes flared with delight. Then she giggled, a sound that could light the darkest corners of the galaxy. "So mote it be, dearest one, but stay with me a moment. You'll like this next part. It will be very dramatic."

I watched as the guard holding Raphael turned him loose. The archangel walked purposefully toward my lifeless body, and without a word, he pushed Michael and Lucius away from me.

Goddess snapped her fingers, and voices rushed into my ears.

"She's gone, Raphael," Kricket said with tears in her eyes, trying to break free from the dark angel that held her. "You aren't allowed to bring her back."

Andrea and Helena were crying too, and I knew how hard my death was on them. They felt my life force drain away. We elementals are energetically tethered, and when one of us dies, it's like losing a part of yourself. You feel it in your soul as if you were the one who was dying.

"Raphael," Kricket pleaded. "You can't."

The archangel knelt beside me and closed his eyes. He placed his hands over my wound as a swirl of light emanated from his body, washing me in the green, healing energy of the universe. His beautiful white wings unfurled from his back, and he enveloped me inside them. However, when he retreated, I was still lying motionless.

"That should have worked, shouldn't it?" I asked Goddess. Not that I cared. I was pretty numb at this point.

"Yes, but I need one more event to unfold," she said, nodding her head toward Michael and Lucius. "Just another moment, and you shall return."

"It didn't work," Michael said, his voice trembling. "Raphael, please try again. Please bring her back."

Raphael remained silent.

Michael lunged at Lucius, and both of them sprang to their feet. Then he threw a haymaker, catching my son square on the jaw. "You killed her!"

Luc's eyes bugged out on impact. He stumbled backward, bounced off a light pole, and came back swinging. He caught Michael in the stomach, then kicked the archangel's legs from underneath him. Now the angel and demon were rolling on the pavement landing hard blows.

Several of the fallen rushed forward to help my son, but Luc told them to get back (in a muffled voice because Michael was grinding a hand into his face). To everyone's amazement, they obeyed the command, and the fisticuffs continued as hulking dark angels looked on in confusion.

I understood their bewilderment. The Prince of Angels and the Underworld king could be fighting in the sky, leveling thunderbolts, dropping buildings, and shooting atomic fire. Instead, the two of them were scrapping on the ground in a human-style street brawl—their respective wounds healing almost as fast as their fists were flying.

"Why did you want them to fight?" I said, feeling a little sleepy. What I wanted more than anything was to curl up in a ball and smell the grass of the Arrival's Meadow. The drug of death had taken a firm hold. There wasn't an ounce of emotion or adrenaline to be had.

"I needed them to take their rage out on each other," Goddess said, placing a hand on my shoulder. "It will make sense in time. Now, are you ready to go back?"

I yawned, nodding while I did so, and a moment later, I felt myself slip back into my body, every breath ripping through me like hot sparks. Okay, now I was wide awake. Thankfully, the fire ebbed from my lungs enough to speak. "Michael?" I said, blinking into the sky. Then I looked down at my stomach; the gaping wound had vanished.

Michael stopped throttling Lucius and rushed to my side. "Sera? Oh, thank you, Goddess. Thank you," he said, his face turned toward the heavens.

With Michael's help, I got to my feet. "Raphael, that angel light is good stuff," I said to the arc, who had just pulled me back from the realm of the dead. I felt surprisingly good.

Lucius stepped forward. "Mother," he said, looking into my eyes.

"Careful, demon," Michael growled. But oddly enough, he didn't move a muscle as I took in the details of my son's face.

"Luc. I'd forgotten you look so much like me."

Although he had an angelic father and elemental mother, being born in the Underworld makes Lucius a demon. They stop aging when they reach twenty-five, so my son, parents, and I could pass for quadruplets.

"Uh, does she understand she has literally spawned demon seed?" Helena said.

"Shh!" Andrea shot back, biting her lip.

Lucius snapped his fingers, and his entire army vanished in a cloud of black smoke, leaving the nine of us standing together in the empty street. Destruction, chaos, and fires raged around us, with Mortegol's lifeless body sprawled on the pavement at our feet.

Uriel, Raphael, and Gabriel stepped in front of the three other elementals. "He may look like you, Sera," Uriel said. "But he is also Mortegol's son, and he still has a job to do."

"Can't we call a truce?" I asked Luc. "Just for a few moments?"

My lovely boy nodded and wrapped his arms around me. I could feel the hilt of the bloody Demon Dagger, still in his hand, pressing into my rib cage as we embraced. Michael lurched forward at the sudden movement.

"It's all right," I said before kissing my son on his smooth cheek.

Lucius rested his forehead on mine and looked into my eyes. The exchange only works between light beings, and he knew that, but he also knew what it would mean to me.

We stayed that way for a while, then Luc squeezed my hand and drew back. "Michael, you are correct," he said, sliding the dagger into his side belt. "My father called the fallen back from the Underworld. That's a forfeit, and I will honor the contract." He narrowed his eyes. "With one minor adjustment."

Michael glared at the newly crowned demon king. Then he pointed to the steel band clamped to his throat. "I will not bargain with you, son of Mortegol." In the next instant, the bands disappeared from all four arcs. "Good," Michael said, but I noticed he looked a little confused as he rubbed his neck.

The archangel thrust his right arm over his head, and a scroll appeared in his hand. "You will sign our contract as is. That is the only deal we are making today." He unfurled the parchment over one of the remaining car hoods, then pulled a short blade from his belt, sliced his palm, and passed the knife to Lucius.

My son squared his shoulders, solidly meeting Michael's eyes. "As I said, I will honor this agreement on one condition."

A growl escaped Michael's lips. "That's *not* the way this works."

Lucius stared him down. "I am the new King of the Underworld, and I inherited my throne during a battle unfairly won."

"That's because your father is the one who cheated," Michael said hotly. "It has nothing to do with this. Your side lost, and now you sign."

"Universal Bylaw states that battles won by deceit must be repeated unless the two parties reach an agreement," Luc said, looking hard into the archangel's eyes. "And not to put too fine a point on it, but my mother called her familiar to assist. I'm not as vague about the rules as my father. Celestial dragons are not allowed, no matter who fired the first deceptive shot."

I must admit. I felt a little motherly pride at that moment. I'd taught my son our laws, and he knew them well. He wasn't even flinching as the angelic warrior of light bellowed and stared him down.

Michael's reputation as the mightiest opponent in the universe is there for a good reason. And most of his challengers would have given in by now, not wanting to put that title to the test. Not my boy, though; he was holding his ground. I could tell by Michael's body language; he was the one giving in. That doesn't happen often, and now I think about it, I honestly can't remember it ever happening.

Michael's jaw tensed, and he narrowed his eyes at the new king before speaking. "What do you want?"

"I want to see my mother...whenever I please."

"Absolutely not," Michael said, his arms crossed over his chest. Believe it or not, that's his relaxed stance, even though it can look scary to those opposing him, so I knew we were headed in the right direction. No more flying fists, at least. I tore my eyes away from the two of them long enough to see gathering crowds gaping at the burning buildings and the massive sinkhole in the middle of King Street. A little boy stepped forward to peer down into the smoking crater.

"Get back from there! Are you trying to get yourself killed?" a woman barked, jerking the boy by the collar.

"Oh, this is bad," Andrea said as people crowded around us, listening to the bizarre negotiation. "I didn't send them far enough away."

I touched Michael's arm. "Weren't you the one who told me that without the dark, there can be no light?"

"This is different, Sera. Lucius is setting a trap. If he takes you to the Underworld, he'll kill you. We have no powers there."

"Michael, you just saw him try to save my life."

"I saw him help Mortegol jam a dagger into your stomach then murder his own father in a power play to become the new king."

"That's not what happened, and you know it. We don't want to repeat this battle, and if we do this, light will reign the Earth plane for a thousand years. Isn't that a victory worth having, especially when all we must do is grant this one small request?"

Michael looked into my eyes, and I could see the decision weighing on his heart. "Sera. If we do this, he can take you to the Underworld whenever he pleases, and there's nothing I can do to stop him. You would be signing over your consent."

"Please agree, Michael," I said gently. "He is my son... I love him, and I want this."

Michael held my gaze a moment longer, then he turned to Lucius and stepped forward until their faces were only inches apart. "If you hurt her in any way, I will bring heaven and earth crashing down on you. I don't care if I destroy us all."

"I understand," Luc said.

The three of us sliced our palms, letting our mingled blood drip onto the page. Once our signatures materialized on the contract, the deal was finalized, and the parchment vanished.

My son kissed my forehead. "See you soon," he said.

When Lucius was a boy, I told him bedtime stories of the warriors of light; the eight protectors preserving balance on the Earth plane. He had just heard Michael and I use the *goodbye* I'd shared with him in those stories. He knew the phrase meant a lot to me, and it touched my heart that he said it.

"See you soon," I said.

Lucius strode toward the crater in the street, took a running leap, and disappeared into the Underworld.

"Awesome," said the little boy who was back at the edge, peering into the sinkhole with a delighted smile. The woman, his mother, maybe, was still holding him by the jacket.

The wind picked up and began to howl. I turned to Kricket. "Are you doing that?" She shook her head and shrugged.

A moment later, the Goddess appeared next to Mortegol's body. "Arise, dearest one," she said, extending her hand to him.

Mortegol stood up. Not his spirit, his physical body, and I felt my anger stirring. If he were alive, everything I'd sacrificed would have been for nothing. *Breathe, Sera, breathe*, I told myself.

Goddess took Mortegol's chin in her hand. "Tell me, child. Tell me what you desire...above all else." Mortegol was as docile as a schoolboy in her presence, and I saw tears in his eyes as he looked into her beautiful face.

After a long stretch of silence, Goddess nodded and touched her forehead to his. Then she placed her palms on Mortegol's shoulder blades, and black wings sprouted from his back. The former archangel, overcome by emotion, wrapped his wings around his body, covering his face as he wept. His mother, whom he had grown to despise, had given him what he longed for more than anything else, and I could almost feel his gratitude washing through me as he cried tears of joy.

"You must be the one to restore the purity of light to your wings," Goddess said. "And if you succeed, you may reclaim your holy title as the Archangel Lucifer. But I warn you, my son. It will be hard to win my trust again."

Mortegol tucked his wings and threw himself into her arms. They stayed that way for several moments, then Goddess drew back and spoke to us. "I will take Mortegol to DarkStar, where he may begin anew. There, he will not get the chance to carry out his darkest deed." She turned back to Mortegol, took his hands in hers, and the two of them vanished.

We stood looking at one another for a long while. I don't think any of us had ever seen Mortegol stunned into silence.

"Okay, so that just happened," Andrea finally said, pinching the bridge of her nose. "Gabe, you should probably fix that up," she added, fluttering her hand at the onlookers who had grown to startling numbers.

Gabriel nodded, then spread his wings and floated above us. "I am the mighty Archangel Gabriel," he said in his commanding angelic voice.

Helena rolled her eyes. "Oh, boy, he's *really* milking it."

People in the crowd pointed and gasped, and a stunned-looking group of men and women threw themselves to the ground. "We worship you, Archangel Gabriel!" one of them cried.

"Oh, no. Please don't do that," Gabriel said. "I am your equal." A look of discomfort washed over his face as he reached up and pulled his horn from thin air.

"Sweet Jesus, it's the end of days!" a man said, grabbing the woman and child standing next to him. "Sweet, merciful Jesus, take us with you." The man dropped to his knees and thrust his hands toward the archangel. His strong reaction sparked a herd response, and now others were screaming and crying and running in circles.

"Please, sir. I am not Jesus," Gabriel said. "Uh, but he is a wonderful soul, and he loves you," he added quickly.

Helena crossed her arms and looked up at her mate. "Oh, just blow the dang horn already."

"Keep your sword on, honey," Gabriel said. "I'm getting to it."

Helena scowled. "When? After several of these poor folks have full-blown heart attacks?"

Gabriel gave his wife a loving look then snapped his fingers. The onlookers froze in place, and the raging fires and billowing smoke hung in midair. Like pausing a video, everything went still and quiet. "There," he said to Helena. "Now, you won't have to worry about the lovely humans and their lovely hearts."

Suddenly, the four arcs glowed with light from within. It receded almost as quickly as it appeared, and I realized they had just received a communication from the Goddess. It was Uriel who spoke. "Sera's son taking the seat on the Underworld throne is the sole reason the world does not end," he said to the three other elementals.

Andrea gasped, and Kricket cupped a hand over her mouth as fresh tears sprang to her eyes. Helena gave me a blank stare. She was speechless, and that's unusual for the water elemental, no matter the situation.

"We are eternally grateful to you," Raphael said.

The archangels and elementals placed their palms over their hearts. "Love and light, Fire Goddess," Michael said as the seven of them bowed their heads. I returned the sentiment, feeling their love rippling through me, then I looked up at my dear friend Gabe. He *was* milking it a little, just as Helena said. He didn't get to do this very often.

There's a big misconception about Gabriel's horn. It doesn't signal the end of days or bring Armageddon upon the earth…no rivers running with blood or plagues of locusts. All souls come here agreeing to have their memories of each Earth-plane battle wiped out. It's in the boilerplate language of every soul contract. Always has been and always will be.

When Gabriel blows his horn this time—if he ever gets around to it—a supersonic frequency will ring out. The sound vibrates at tremendous velocity, reshaping atoms, working like a cosmic reset button. Just another mechanism designed by Goddess to keep the dream of being human alive.

Helena, Kricket, and Andrea huddled around, and I gathered them to me, knowing any of them would have done the same. We cried together, with our energies entwining, reconnecting our eternal bond.

"We are the four elementals," Andrea said with tears streaming down her cheeks. "Gatekeepers of the Earth plane since time immemorial, and I love you, Sera. I love all of you."

When we parted, Michael gathered me in his arms and kissed me tenderly. Stars exploded in my vision as I felt his intense love wash through my body. Somehow it was deeper, even stronger than before.

Gabriel broke into a face-splitting smile. "Let's get this baby fired up," he said, placing the horn to his lips.

Michael took my hand in his just as the thunderous blast rang out. Any glass remaining in the cars and buildings shattered as light shot from Gabriel's body, spreading out like a mushroom cloud.

When the light receded, everything was in its proper place, with people moving about as if nothing had happened. The eight of us, healed of our battle wounds and back in twenty-first-century clothes, gave one another knowing glances as we blended into the foot traffic on King Street.

We walked a few paces, then Michael stepped to one side, allowing the others to pass. He smiled and took my hand, gently tugging me toward him. I came to a stop against his chest, and he brushed a thumb over my cheek.

"Even after all this time, the universe continues to surprise me," Michael said. "Who knew when I woke up this morning, I'd have the King of the Underworld as a stepson by nightfall?" He chuckled. "The boy's got pluck, I'll give him that. He gets that from you, you know."

My archangel looked deeply into my eyes. "Now, what about a cup of coffee you get to finish, Valentine? I know a little place that's recently been renovated, run by a kid who's not much of a warrior these days, but he whips up a mean latte."

I stood on my toes and kissed him. "Anything. As long as I am with you."

And just like that, we were simply a couple enjoying a beautiful spring afternoon in a charming little town on the Earth plane. A town called Leesburg, Virginia.

CHAPTER

~ 36 ~

The Endowment

Earth plane 1995

Nearly three thousand miles away (and at the same moment we left the arcs and elementals in 2021), Robert Harrison looked out the window in the year 1995. In Robert's forty-seven years as a practicing attorney, he'd never run across this kind of madness, and it was coming from a man he admired. "I'm sorry. You want me to do what?"

"You heard me. Give Don and Holly the house, and I want everything else to go to that," Mac said, poking the folder with the tip of his cane.

Mac's Irish accent had softened a bit over the years; time had creased his fair skin, slackened his jawline, and turned his reddish-blond hair white. The years had also snatched a few inches from his height, but his mind was still sharp, and his now six-foot-one frame continued to command attention in every room. Even though these days, his ventures from home consisted mainly of lunching with fellow retirees.

He carried the cane for sentimental reasons, not out of need. Vera, his beautiful wife of more than six decades, had given him the walking stick as a joke just before she passed last spring.

"Yeah. I heard you," Robert said. "But...we're talking about *a lot* of money here."

"I might be ninety-three years old, Bobby. But I've still got all my marbles. You don't think I know how much money I have?"

"It's not that," the lawyer said, looking out at the sea of headlights on the Golden Gate. He rubbed his forehead and returned to his seat. "Look, I've been your attorney for more than forty years." He softened his voice and leaned in. "More importantly, as your friend, I'd be remiss if I didn't tell you I think you're making a big mistake."

Mac sat stone-faced.

Robert sighed and donned his reading glasses. He'd long since learned there was no use arguing with the tough-as-nails former surgeon. The man was used to getting his way. Not because of his money, but because he could be as stubborn as an old mule. He glanced at his friend then pointed at the line items with his pen as he read down the absurd list. "I mean, no budget caps; all expenses approved. These living quarters are a palace."

The old man smiled. "Good, I never want her to leave."

"How do you know it will be a woman? Anyway, it will take at least three years to do all these renovations," Robert added over the rim of his glasses.

"Here's the name of your director," Mac said, retrieving an index card from his jacket pocket. He slid it across the desk. "Put that name down, and they have two."

"Two what?"

"Two years to complete the renovations."

"All of this in two years? I'm not sure that's possible."

"That's what money's for, Bobby. Hire extra crews and get it done."

The lawyer flicked the pages as he read on. "For the main building and grounds, let's see, eight-hundred thousand dollars for landscaping. Four million for a gut-job remodel." He raised his eyebrows. "A million in furniture? And the balance in an interest-bearing account that's a bottomless pit of money for a place you've never been to and have no connection with that I can see."

Robert removed his glasses, rubbed his eyes, then looked squarely at the man who'd been more of a father to him than his own father had been. "You could do this for so much less and leave the rest to your kids." He let a smile escape his lips. Mac's 'kids' were in their sixties; it was a running joke between the two men.

Mac waved his hand, dismissing the thought. "They have plenty. Besides, just one of their trust funds would take care of them both until their grandkids are in the grave and long after. Look, I've never done anything to leave my mark on this world. But this...*this* is my mark," he said, leaning forward.

"Oh, come on. You helped open the burn ward at St. Francis for God's sake, and you made it possible for countless people to return to normal life for decades after. Lives that would have been ruined if not for your ground-breaking work in the field. I'm fairly certain that counts as a *mark*."

"And now I want to help those kids get a better foothold in life. That's the kind of difference I'm talking about. This is my parents' money, Bobby. They left it to me to steward, and this is what they would want."

Robert didn't need to be told how his friend came into his incredible fortune; the family holdings were vast, including mines, banks, transportation companies, and more. In addition to managing trust funds for Mac's grown children, grandchildren, nieces, and nephews, Robert's firm wrote checks to distant family members worldwide. Had done for years, and maybe would do forever. As unbelievable as it was to him, the amount they were discussing didn't even scratch the surface.

"Now, don't look at me like I'm some crazy old coot who doesn't know his own mind," Mac said. "I know what I'm doing. My brother and sisters are gone, but I know they would agree, and I want to do *this*," he added, jabbing at the folder again.

The lawyer licked his lips and looked down at the pages in his hand. "We're talking about an endowment of thirty-eight *billion* dollars."

"Yep," Mac said, crossing his arms. "And I want it to go to that place and make those improvements, every single one. And if you don't, I'll come back from the grave and haunt you. It needs to look like a castle when you're done with it, Bobby. I want those kids to have everything. You know, to feel like they've all died and gone to heaven whenever they get out of their comfortable four-poster beds to eat their five-star breakfasts."

"This place is across the United States," Robert said, scratching his head. "How did you even find it?"

"Well, it's not like I'm gonna commute. And it doesn't matter a tinker's hoorah how I found it. Do it pronto, kid," Mac said, leaning forward to stare down the seventy-three-year-old man sitting across from him.

Mac wasn't about to tell his friend about the angel who'd paid him a visit in the wee hours of this morning. While he had good reason to believe in such, most of the world did not, and he didn't need Robert sending men in white coats to chase him around with a giant butterfly net. He couldn't run anymore. His knees had given up the ghost long ago.

"I'll sign whatever you want, but I've got to do it before I leave tonight," Mac said. "That's where I want my money to go, and that's that. Oh, and I want the endowment to be in my parent's name. Not mine."

The lawyer blew out a breath. "Okay. If this is what you want, I'll draw it up." Robert Harrison shook his head as he wrote the directive for his paralegal.

'Land, buildings, and thirty-eight billion dollars bequeathed to Sherman Hill Orphanage, Kents Hill, Maine, in the name of Elizabeth and William T. McKenna. Celeste Corrine Porter of 54 Lovelace Road, Augusta, Maine, named by will-maker as director. (See *Exhibit A,* attached, for hire-package details.) Robert Harrison, Executor. Sherman Hill Board of Directors named as The McKenna Trust.'

"Now, let's have a drink while Sandra gets the documents ready, you crazy old coot."

Thirty minutes later, Mac inspected the papers, ensuring his wishes had been recorded as he'd directed. He ran a finger over the names of his beloved mother and father and chuckled. If people only knew. He came to his signature line and paused. He'd been called *Mac* since med school and hadn't needed to sign many things after retiring.

His mother named him after her best friend, and she'd told him of their wild adventures together. Mac suspected more to that story and poked around the edges of it often when his parents were alive. His father was always silent during those interrogations. He knew the *man* was incapable of lying, so it forever left him smelling a rat.

When he turned twenty-one, Mac's parents offered a choice of magical abilities along with an explanation of his unique lineage. His brother, George, and his sweet sisters, Ruby and Mary, had received similar gifts.

For George, it was knowledge of the human anatomy. He had become a biologist and led his team to countless breakthroughs in the medical field. Mary asked for command of water, and she and her husband traveled the world, creating magical wells from nothing but sand and rock. For Ruby, who doubtless knew her romantic leanings at a young age, it was protection. She and her partner ended up in many war-torn countries where sweet Ruby used her magic to save women from horrendous conditions.

Mac had asked for the gift of healing. That was the only reason he'd become a well-known surgeon, the reason he could perform actual miracles, and that was fine by him. His only desire was to be of service to his fellow human beings. Well, that and to lead mission control at NASA. It was a fantasy he'd never quite shaken, along with the deep-seated feeling he'd be remarkably good at that job too.

He picked up the pen and signed *Alden Michael McKenna, M.D.*

The will witnessed and notarized; Robert's three staffers left the room. "I'll get your umbrella," the attorney said, rapping his knuckles on the door frame. "I still think you're nuts, by the way."

"Noted," Mac said, smiling at his friend.

Alone in the room, the old man looked out at the drizzle and twinkling lights of San Francisco. The city was pretty this time of day, rain or not, he thought.

A dull ache began to thrum in Mac's left arm. As the pain increased, he noticed a shimmering ball of red light hovering a few feet away. He'd never read about patients having visions in the throes of cardiac arrest. Still, he didn't need to rely on his medical training to know that's what it was; he'd felt this coming for weeks. Death had settled in his bones, curled up next to his fire, sipped from his cup like an old friend.

The light changed form, stretching oddly this way and that until his mother stood before him. She was young and beautiful in her blue linen dress, looking just as she did on so many summer days working in her rose garden.

Suddenly, it all clicked into place, and he threw his head back and laughed. Of course. Now the NASA dream made perfect sense. That was his job at home, sending souls to the Earth-plane…and he *was* remarkably good at it.

Alden got up, ready to take his mother's hand but feeling different energy in the room, he turned. Robert was attempting to revive the body left behind. Sensing the pain in his friend's heart, he walked over. "So long, Bobby. You were a good friend to me. I'll see you soon, lad."

He turned back—his spirit body growing younger as each second passed—his features transforming into the eternal form he'd adopted long ago. But instead of seeing his mother there, he smiled into the loving eyes of the Fire Goddess. Alden chuckled and pushed the tortoiseshell glasses higher on his nose, knowing he was about to catch an elemental wave bound for home. He also knew he'd never let Sera talk him into stepping foot on Mandaroon ever again.

A Note from the Author

Thank you for reading *The Summerlands*, book one of the Angels & Elementals series. I hope you enjoyed the story as much as I enjoyed bringing these lovely characters and the town I adore to the page. If so, please leave a review on Amazon. Reviews not only show your support, but they also help other readers find the book.

For previews of upcoming books and more information about the series, visit www.susanbutlercolwell.com.

The adventure continues in *The Demon Dagger*, following the fully awake Sera, the incredibly hunky and loving Archangel Michael, and their eternal friends. We'll also learn more about the Underworld's newly crowned king, Sera's lovely boy of dark and light. There's no telling what Lucius will do with the unusual bargain he struck with Michael.

Stay *tuned*.

 SUSAN BUTLER COLWELL

Acknowledgments

Many helped me through the process of bringing my first novel into the world. Thank you, lovely souls.

Cerphe, the love of my life, my husband of twenty-one years, and my real-world Archangel Michael. Thank you for being mine and agreeing to be a *novel bachelor* on nights and weekends over the last three years. With you, all things are possible. I love you so very much.

I give thanks daily for my incredible friends Caroline and Mike, who are real-world angels and support me in everything I do. I cherish your friendship, savvy, humor, and warmth. The two of you are loved more than you could know, and thanks, too, for my favorite nephews, Jasper and Ziggy (two of the cutest Westies on the planet). I'm sure they will show up in future books, or they might need books of their own.

Thanks to my beautiful, otherworldly friends Reverend Andrea and the sword-wielding Kricket, who allowed me to use their first names as my characters (and perhaps a smattering of their personalities) in this book. You two are goddesses, indeed. I'm awed by your grasp of spirituality, spot-on advice, cleverness, (sometimes deliciously dark) humor, and your deftness as fearless warrior-mothers.

This book could not have been written without another goddess's cheerleading, my dear friend, Helen, who is lovely in too many ways to count. Helen allowed me to stick an "a" on the end of her name and use a dash of her bubbly, bossy, wonderful personality for Helena. You are a bright light in my life—a cherished member of my soul clan—and the one who kept me marching toward the finish line with words of encouragement (okay, by bossing me). You are also the one who *finally* got me to turn the manuscript over for publishing (with a dash of tough love). It's hard to send one's baby out into the world. Thank you for keeping me on track, Helen(a). And thank you, too, for that beautiful logo.

And to my other steadfast cheerleader, my lovely talented friend and world-class singer-songwriter Pamela. Along with Helen,

Pamela read this manuscript countless times, asking questions that made me realize some concepts needed more fine-tuning. You two are power women. Your love, friendship, humor, and encouragement were indeed a divine gift throughout the writing process and in my daily life.

Thank you to Polly Jones and Patty Johnson Cooper, who provided me with excellent advice and direction. The two of you are literary rock stars.

Charles David Young, a friend, extremely talented writer, and lovely soul, gave me words of encouragement and shared his expertise in writing, publishing, and agents.

I would also like to thank my elected hometown of Leesburg, Virginia, lovely Loudoun County, and all my friends here. You surround me with beauty and love every day.

And I especially thank you, Archangel Michael. I am so grateful for the soul-nourishing truths you share, for your unconditional love of humankind, and for this book idea. I will always grab a pen when you wake me in the wee hours with a story to tell.

About the Setting

Kents Hill, Maine: I've spent years looking at a placard from the prep school my husband attended in Kents Hill, Maine. Having been married to this wonderful man for two decades, I know a lot about the New England town by now, and in Cerphe's stories, it just seems like a magical place. So, poof...in it went.

Leesburg, Virginia: I created a fictional version of Leesburg, of course. We don't have demonic battles on King Street (that I remember, anyway). And archangels and elementals don't live inside our charming homes or work in our downtown businesses (or do they?). Regardless, this book is also a love letter to this beautiful town and the amazing people who call it home.

If you, dear reader, have not been, come for a visit, and you'll see what I mean. The people, places, and sense of community here are lovely beyond words. We have many talented people here: authors, award-winning graphic artists, singers, songwriters, chefs, and artists who work in every medium. We also have a cornucopia of wineries, breweries, distilleries, restaurants, wine bars, art galleries, and lots more.

Here are a few of my favorites, including website information:

Eyetopia, Inc., mentioned in chapter two, is an enchanting boutique and prescription eyewear center in historic downtown that deserves your attention. I would never consider going anywhere else for glasses and delightful gifts. Eyetopia's owner, my dear friend Paige Buscema, will take excellent care of you should you stop by for a visit. *eyetopiainc.com*

Fabbioli Cellars, run by dear friends Doug Fabbioli and Colleen Burg, has lovely wines and an adorable kitty who roams the grounds and poses for photos and wine labels. A great way to spend a Saturday

or Sunday afternoon…tasting delicious wine at Fabbioli Cellars while taking in their glorious vineyard.
fabbioliwines.com

Mom's Apple Pie, Co. shows up in the book as a fictional diner owned by the fictional Bob Nash. Here in the real world, Mom's is the world's *best* pie shop owned by a lovely person named Avis Renshaw. I'm convinced Avis came to Earth to make the world's best cherry pie (my favorite). Mission accomplished.
momsapplepieco.com

The Barns at Hamilton Station Vineyards run by dear friends Andrew and Maryann Fialdini. They offer fantastic wine, tours of their beautiful vineyard, and a magical setting for weddings, special events, and concerts inside their lovely barn and on their gorgeous grounds.
thebarnsathamiltonstation.com

Lightfoot Restaurant is owned by the powerhouse-sister team of Ingrid Gustavson and Carrie Gustavson. It's the perfect place to host a special event or indulge in a delicious brunch, lunch, or dinner inside the beautiful restaurant or outside on the patio.
lightfootrestaurant.com

DIG Records & Vintage is Leesburg's ultra-cool vintage vinyl shop run by the ultra-cool Kevin Longendyke.
facebook.com/digrecordsvintage

The Tally Ho Theater is owned and operated by Don Devine and Jack Devine, Leesburg's dynamic father-and-son team. The Bodeans, The Outlaws, Pat McGee Band, The Gin Blossoms, 80s hair band Kix, and many more have played their 1932 Art Deco theater and concert hall. The Tally Ho is also home to Leesburg's annual holiday show, Jingle Jam.
tallyhotheater.com

Leesburg and Loudoun County have excellent original music and concert series, too:

Songs Stories and Gas Money is spearheaded by dear friends Stilson Greene and Don Chapman (world-class musicians themselves). It's a lovely evening of just what the billing says. Check it out at The Barns at Hamilton Station Vineyards during the fall.
thebarnsathamiltonstation.com

Acoustic on the Green is the brainchild of Stilson Greene and lovingly tended by him for more than a decade. His popular outdoor concert series, now run by the town, is a great summertime Saturday night out.
leesburgva.gov

Jingle Jam, also the creation of Stilson Greene, is Leesburg's annual holiday Rock n' Roll Concert. Loudoun County residents get in line as early as 11 pm the night before tickets go on sale to snag a seat at this special event. Hats off to the Jingle Jam Band: Todd Wright, Gary Smallwood, Jon Carroll, Michael Sheppard, Kim Pittinger, Mark Williams, Cal Everett, Tobias Smith, Prescott Engle, Stilson Greene, and special guests. Their eleven years of jingle-jamming has resulted in more than $150,000 raised for the Juvenile Diabetes Research Fund.
leesburgva.gov

You should look us up. Then come on out. The people of Leesburg and Loudoun County will welcome you with open arms.
visitloudoun.org & *leesburgva.gov*

A Little on That Diner Menu

Cerphe's Up Veggie Sub is, of course, named after my amazing hubby, who is the voice of Mortegol in the audiobook version of The Summerlands. He wrote an excellent book with co-author Stephen Moore, called *Cerphe's Up*, which I hope you'll look up on Amazon. It's an eclectic memoir of his life among rock stars. Cerphe has worked for all the great radio stations in Washington, D.C., and now spearheads our online radio station, Music Planet Radio. Check it out when you have a minute and hear my guy's super-sexy voice. The music he plays is ultra-cool too.
musicplanetradio.com

Todders Boxed Lunch Special is named after our dear friend and incredible singer/songwriter/performer/recording artist, Todd Wright. This charming music man writes scores for TV and film and runs a production company called Half King. He's got a string of hits you should check out on your favorite music source too. Todd wrote (and sings) the Visit Loudoun theme song *Coming Home*, which I adore.
halfking.net

Tammy Loves Bacon is a literary embrace to my incredibly smart, beautiful, kind, and dear friend, Tammy—who loves bacon more than anyone I know. She is married to our other dear friend Stilson, an award-winning graphic artist. Stilson is also a super talented singer/songwriter/performer/recording artist. You might remember his name as one of Sera's birthday party guests who raises his bottle of iced tea to toast her. He, Todd (Todders), and Cerphe really do all love a specific brand of tea, and I really do panic whenever I run low. And I'm sure if Bob Nash were a real person, they would convince him to drink it.
StilsonGreene.com (Stilson Greene Graphic Design & Illustration.)

Big Red's Bawdy BLT is named after my dear friend and Music Planet Radio show host, Tim Burch, Jr. Tim has strawberry blond hair and stands above six feet, thus the nickname, which he's had since high school. It also works well for the rock show he does on Cerphe's station. It's full of fun and heavy-metal hair bands—Big Red's Rock Show—Saturday nights at eight p.m. EST. *MusicPlanetRadio.com*

Juliana's Julienned Green Beans pays homage to our lovely friend and unbelievably warm and caring soul, Juliana MacDowell. She is a singer/songwriter/performer/recording artist who is talented beyond words. Juliana's new album *Leaving Home*, is about realizing the love and recognition sought elsewhere can all be found *at home*. It's a fantastic addition to an already stellar catalog. *julianamacdowell.com*

Mayor Burk's Breakfast Bonanza is a tribute to Leesburg's wonderful mayor and dear friend Kelly Burk. Kelly got a fictional menu item because she is such a charming and lovely soul. She's also a great mayor and deserves a namesake menu item in every restaurant. *kellyburkformayor.com*

Roger Hates Brussels Sprouts is named after Loudoun County Treasurer Roger Zurn. I don't think I'm going out on a limb when I say Roger really does hate brussels sprouts, as evidenced by his social media posts on the subject. So, of course, I had to include *Roger Hates Brussels Sprouts* on that diner menu.

Umstattd Omelet is named after Kristen Umstattd, Leesburg's District Supervisor, our former mayor, and dear friend. I love omelets, and I love this amazing powerhouse woman, so it's a perfect fit.

References

Petty, Tom. "Runnin' Down A Dream." *Full Moon Fever.* MCA Records, 1998. Song.

Tzu, Sun. "On the Art of War. Translated by Giles, Lionel. London: Luzac and Company, 1910. Book.

About the Author

Susan Butler Colwell is a writer, the wife of rock-radio legend, Cerphe, mother to the world's cutest gray cat, an entrepreneur, passable baker, and lover of magical things. She lives in Loudoun County, Virginia. *The Summerlands* is Susan's debut novel.

Connect with Susan Butler Colwell online at:
www.susanbutlercolwell.com
Facebook, Instagram, or Twitter